A Winter Morning's Sun

A Winter Morning's Sun

Robert Goble

WAKING LION PRESS

Dedicated to the grandparents of this generation

ISBN 978-1-4341-0241-6

Published by Waking Lion Press, an imprint of The Editorium

The Editorium, LLC
West Valley City, UT 84128-3917
wakinglionpress.com
wakinglion@editorium.com

Acknowledgments

A special thanks to Betsy for your patience and willingness to read each version of each chapter as it came line by line; also to Colin Douglas for all your work and helping me to see the things I wouldn't have otherwise. The cover photo is by Rebecca Tesch. The author photo is by Doug Lind.

Part I

1

There was only one place where Broadie Bennett felt truly at peace. Forgotten and walled off from the rest of the world, it was a place of green purity: an archipelago of grass, fruit trees, large bushes, and a thick, mysterious grove of chestnut trees that hid a sanctuary of secret shade. In the center of the lot stood an ancient box elder whose branches reached out freely in all directions, blessing this obscure paradise with majesty: a symbol of a time left behind. It was once part of a larger tract of land owned by a church when houses were few and farms and orchards were plenty. Generations of farmers had worked it, gathering fruit for their personal stores. It had fed hungry mouths during the Great Depression. A president once passed by it on a tour of the church's welfare program, but little by little the city came and swallowed it away until only a small sliver was left behind to tend itself.

Neighborhoods now lay siege on three sides with their cinderblock walls and tight wooden fences; on the fourth grew a natural barrier of old yellow rose bushes. They lined an irrigation ditch that still received its cloudy water from the Jordan River that ran through the Salt Lake Valley. Grapevines covered the walls and fences, distracting the curious with their sweet, abundant offerings. Many a casual passer-by followed the trail along the ditch that runs the length of the neighborhood, never discovering the secret treasures that awaited beyond the rosebushes.

But Broadie Bennett found them.

It was a dry, early summer day when his feet crunched along the gravel ditch bottom. He followed it, lazily swinging a stick like a sword against the helpless grass, until he arrived at the rose bushes. Instead of climbing back onto the trail that eventually led to the vine-covered fence at the road, he knelt down to see what was hidden in the shadows beyond the cascade of new, yellow bloom. He found a dark tunnel created by years of unchecked growth. With tenacity unknown to most beyond the age of eleven, he gently pushed aside the fresh green runners that blocked the entrance, hunched, and scooted his way into the darkness like a spelunker.

He traveled a few yards, discovering a bright opening on the opposite side of the ditch, and climbed up through it, careful to keep the scrapes at a minimum. As he explored his new place of refuge (the sun warm in his hair; the breeze tousling it like a friendly uncle), he saw that his sanctuary wouldn't be complete without a clubhouse; and, like an old diviner, he searched, studied, then chose the place where he would build the greatest clubhouse ever built.

His thoughts pulsed with freedom and creativity as he circled the giant tree. He wasn't surprised to find old lumber scattered around the base. Nailed into the trunk were several graying boards once used as footholds. He was inheriting someone else's great work, and he felt exalted that he could add upon it a new, hopeful vision.

He began his work promptly that evening. Without saying much to his grandpa, Broadie borrowed his tools with a promise that he would return them undamaged. He gathered the usable lumber. On the back of an old school assignment he planned a two-level fortress with a clubhouse on the bottom and a tree house on the top for a lookout. Then he felt himself moved as if by divine guidance until he stood back, hammer in a sweaty, dirty hand, and admired the solid, straight frame of the lower clubhouse. In the heavy dusk he followed its perfection. Night creatures stirred in the cooling air around him. For the first time in his life, he felt what it was like to have something that no one else in the world had and the loneliness of wanting to share it, but not being able to see how anyone could treasure it as he would.

2

A few days later, as the summer morning quietly approached noon, Broadie sat on the roof of his clubhouse, now completed, and contemplated how he was going to build the tree house. The hushed breeze moved gentle, liquid patterns of light. He imagined the tree house's masterful structure within the awesome weight of the great branches. Outside his imagination, distant voices carried over the moving air, echoing in a hollow quality from the brick walls. He lay still letting them go by along the ditch trail. He was now used to hearing people cut through behind the houses. Sometimes they would come quite close, but he was confident in his secret, and watching people had become something of a game.

Several people had already passed by today, and he was getting tired of making the effort to sneak down to the rose bushes just to spy on them. Only once had he really had any fun, and that was when a teenage couple had stopped to make out. He kept throwing small rocks to annoy them until they left. He wished he had some cool binoculars or a pellet gun or—

—Familiar voices.

They broke over him like a falling pane of glass. He inched himself up one of the great branches and looked out beyond his green shield. John Hamel and Joey Wolff, two of the worst bullies he had ever known, trudged gaily along the ditch bank, talking about the Utah Jazz, stupid neighborhood girls, then back to the Jazz. Broadie formed a tube with his hands and watched them through it as if it were a telescope. They walked on until they reached the opening in the fence that led to the street. He puffed his cheeks with a breath of relief and climbed slowly back down to the roof. He wondered how dangerous it would be to build a tree house. Maybe it would stand out like the bruise on his eye, advertising its location. He absently probed the swelling above his right cheek, an angry reminder of his place in the order of life. He lowered himself by a rope that he had tied for a swing, walked on a few feet, and crawled into the tall grass to examine his work from a different angle.

He lay on the ground motionless, looking up. The white clouds were a vivid contrast against the deep blue glow of the sky. Sunshine shattered and spilled through the trees onto the ground in crazy moving shapes. He squinted as he watched the sun work in and out of the tall branches above him. Its beauty paralyzed him. The world was perfect here. He was accepted. Nature loved him and made him its master. The trees never jeered at the clothes he wore. The grass never shoved him away. The soil would always bear his weight. Here he was free. This was his. No one would take it away.

A twig snapped, echoing into the background of his thoughts. He held his breath and listened. Another snapping noise and a rustle through the grass close by. His stomach churned and turned cold. "God, don't let them find this place," he silently prayed.

Footsteps.

He slowly sat up peeking through the grass. A girl had approached and stopped at his clubhouse. He was relieved that it wasn't John and Joey, but there she stood with her hands on her hips admiring his work, *his* work. She walked closer and studied the door. He waited until she reached out to push it open.

"Hey!" he yelled.

She jumped and screamed.

Broadie popped out of his hiding place, marching toward her to chase her off. She had no right to be here. This was *his* secret. How had she found it? And had John and Joey seen her? Worst of all, was she with *them?*

She stood wide-eyed but didn't run from his advance. Instead, she reached down and picked up a large stick, holding it like a baseball bat. The closer he got, the more her eyes squinted.

"What are you doing here?" Broadie shouted.

She opened her mouth to speak, closed it, then set her jaw in determination.

He slowed his advance, realizing that she wasn't going to run. She took a step back but held firmly to the stick.

"You can't be here," he said, stopping a few feet short of her swing radius.

"Why not?" She still held her defensive posture.

"This is *my* clubhouse and *my* property, and no one can be here but me!" he said—though he really didn't have any idea whose property it was.

"I didn't see a 'No Trespassing' sign."

"How did you get here?"

"I walked."

Broadie was quickly running out of authority. She should have run away scared, but here she still stood. He had never seen this girl before. She must not live in the neighborhood. She must have been passing by and by some fluke had found the secret entrance. "Who are you?" he asked.

"Who are *you?*"

"That doesn't matter; you're not supposed to be here."

"Well, *excuse me*, but I didn't know!" She began to back away.

He suddenly felt guilty. He had bullied her. He wanted to tell her to get going, but she looked ready to cry. Her eyes were innocent. She hadn't done anything different than he had a few weeks before. Her arm began to tire. She slowly lowered her stick, but didn't let go.

"Where do you live?" Broadie asked.

"That's none of your business!"

He stood quietly as she turned to leave. The guilt continued to pinch in his stomach. "I'm sorry," he blurted out.

She stopped and looked back at him again with innocent eyes. They were bright. The fear in them had turned to anger.

"I'm sorry," he repeated.

"You're not going to hurt me are you?" she asked.

"No, I—"

She turned to walk away again.

"Wait, please. . . ."

"What?" she said, still heading the other direction.

"Please don't tell anyone this is here—I mean the whole place."

"I wouldn't know anyone to tell." She stopped, turning to face him. She was still holding the stick. They faced each other in the open area where the sun steadily beat against drying grass. She took a small step back to avoid a passing yellowjacket.

His guilt overflowed. He had treated someone exactly how he didn't want to be treated. He desperately wanted to make it better. "You can see it if you want. You can stay and play. I just got done building it."

She looked at him cautiously.

"What's your name?" he asked.

She paused uncomfortably, then spoke: "January."

"I'm Broadie Bennett. I live a few houses down that way." He pointed north of where the ditch ran. "What's your last name?"

"My last name is Larson, but I like to use my middle name, Wind, because I like January Wind better.

"That's a cool name."

"Thank you."

Another uncomfortable pause.

"Well?"

"Well what?"

"Do you want to come and see it?"

"See what?"

"My club house."

"Not if you're going to be mean."

"I'm not. I thought you were probably with *them*." He cocked his head in the direction that John and Joey had gone.

"Who?"

"Those guys that just went past."

"I don't know who they are. I saw them go past my back yard, so I followed them."

"Did they see you?"

"Why?"

"Did they *see* you?"

"No, I was too far back. Why?"

He took a deep breath, ready to indict them for all of their crimes against him. His mind flew to the worst things he could think of to try and shock her and force her preemptively onto his side. He wanted her to hate them as much as he did, and he didn't even know her. He started to speak, and the words stopped short in his throat. Everything he had to say made him look like a wimp. She would probably laugh at him, like everyone else.

"It doesn't matter. So, do you want to see it?"

"Yes," she said cautiously. She followed him into the shady area. He pushed branches from smaller trees out of the way, holding them to let her pass. When they entered the clubhouse, they sat down together on a small bench that he had made from an old railroad tie that he had found on the property.

"This is so cool," she said, looking around. "What's that hole in the roof for?"

"That's where I'm going to put my ladder for the tree house. I don't have any more wood left to build it, though. I have to find it somewhere else."

She nodded. "So, is this like . . . a fort?"

"I guess you could say that."

"What grade are you in?"

"Fifth—I mean going into sixth."

"Me, too."

She stood and looked up through the hole in the roof. He had replaced the old boards that had been nailed like a ladder and extended them up past the roof. She took hold of one and tested its integrity. Satisfied, she began to climb. He noticed that her shoes were new and expensive looking. His own shoes had been bought at a discount store somewhere and were now dirty and full of holes. She continued beyond the ladder, shimmying past the massive crotch, then out onto the largest branch. Her fearlessness was impressive. She climbed until she sat on a natural plateau where other branches formed a protective cage.

"I can see all the way to my new house. We're waiting for the moving truck to arrive this afternoon. I've actually been here since the day before yesterday. Maybe we're going to be neighbors," she said.

He was quiet but remembered that his Grandma had said something about getting new neighbors. He'd been so caught up with his construction project that he hadn't paid attention to the activity next door.

"This could be a perfect place for the coolest tree house." She smiled down at him.

Broadie felt a small rattle of unease and mistrust. She was already speaking as if she had her own plans for a tree house. This was still his, not hers. If she was moving in close by, that meant that it wouldn't be long until she met the other kids. How would she keep it a secret then?

She inched her way back down slowly and gracefully. She reached the third rung from the bottom and jumped the remaining distance.

"I love this place," she said, brushing off her pants.

"*Janni?*" A woman's voice carried from a few houses away. She turned in response to the voice.

"*Janni?*"

"I better go. That's my mom," she said.

As she walked out into the sunlight she turned and asked: "How did you get such a big black eye?"

He had completely forgotten about his purple shiner. She waited for a response but he didn't have much to say.

"I fell," he lied.

"Oh, ouch."

"*Janni?*"

"Wait!" he said.

She turned impatiently.

"Please promise me not to tell anyone about this place."

"What?" She looked surprised.

"Do you promise not to tell anyone about this place?"

"Why?"

"Because it's a special secret that only I know about, and now you do. If anyone else knew, it would be ruined. Now, promise me?"

"Okay," she said dismissively.

She ran through the grass disappearing into the rose bushes. He watched her with a troubled mind. He couldn't seem to hold on to good things for very long. She would either be his friend and keep the secret, or she would join the other kids in their constant campaign of torment.

3

Watching the new neighbors move in was exciting for Davie, Broadie's little brother. He ran back and forth across the yard, hiding behind the lilac bushes and playing soldier. He ran up to Broadie, who sat relaxing on the porch. "We're on a reconnaissance mission," he said, probably not knowing the meaning of the word. He ran back hunched over, then crawled up behind one of the bushes. A careful eye from the neighbor's perspective would have discovered a dirty face among the leaves and purple flowers. They shuddered as he shifted for a better view.

January disappeared, then reappeared in the space between the truck and the house, carrying small boxes.

Davie ran back to Broadie. "We have to spy on the enemy, and then bring back their secret code to the base. The base is on the back porch."

"Okay," Broadie said, trying to sound as grave as Davie.

Davie aimed a stick at a man carrying a bookcase. "Bam! Bam! Bam!"

Another person jogged up the ramp, returned carrying something delicate, and teetered slightly on the descent. A woman, probably January's mother, stepped forward and reached out nervously.

"We're search and destroy!" Davie yelled. "I need backup! Cover me!"

Broadie scampered low and joined Davie at the bush. "We were separated from our platoon and were stranded deep in enemy territory. They're unloading their weapons, and we have to destroy them before they destroy us. If we shoot the truck, we can take out the other soldiers."

"Yeah!" Davie said.

Broadie broke off a withered twig and aimed it like a gun at the truck. "Take aim!"

"Yeah, take aim!"

Someone ascended into the truck.

"Duck! We might be spotted!" Broadie whispered. They ducked quickly.

The sound of feet clambered over the metal ramp and echoed from the side of the house.

"Now!" Broadie said.

Davie shot.

"It's a nuclear bomb! Watch out for the shockwave!" Broadie said, and threw himself backwards. Davie did the same, keeping a close eye on his brother. "Quick, press your personal forcefield button so you'll pop out of phase with the universe." Broadie pressed his wrist and made a beeping noise. Davie did the same.

They lay motionless, out of phase with the universe, as another stack of boxes descended from the truck. The metal ramp clinked and pounded as January followed her dad with a box of clothes. Soon she rounded the corner and walked to where Broadie and Davie were still experiencing the effects of nuclear fission. She stood by the lilac bush and examined the purple flowers with the severity of a botanist.

"My grandma planted those," Davie said proudly.

She ignored him and continued her examination. Broadie smiled and propped himself onto one elbow.

"My grandma said that she got the roots from her mother a long time ago," Davie added.

She reached up and began to tug on a bunch, then let it go and selected one lower.

"Hey, you can't pick those! They're not yours!" Davie was horrified. He turned to Broadie: "Don't let her do it!"

"They're on our side," she said smugly.

The purple flowers snapped off with another tug. She turned with a coquettish about-face and walked away holding them to her nose.

"How come you didn't do anything?"

Broadie shrugged.

"I'm telling my grandma!" Davie yelled to January. He walked back to the house on a serious mission to expose the flower thief and probably the brother who didn't do anything about it.

"I don't think grandma's home," Broadie said.

The evening drew down into a purple dusk. The dark western mountains were outlined in a diminishing orange. Mexican salsa music echoed faintly through the sleepy Salt Lake City neighborhood. Broadie still sat with Davie as he watched intently the neighbor across the street wrestle a Frisbee from a large golden retriever. The dog planted its feet firmly and shook its head from side to side. The tug-of-war continued until the dog's mistress had complete possession of the Frisbee. She held it high, and the dog leapt playfully. She feigned a launch, and the dog charged halfway across the yard before realizing that the Frisbee wasn't in the air. She let it go, and the dog chased it eagerly into the neighbor's yard.

Davie laughed and looked down into a small white box that contained a fresh collection of potato bugs that he'd picked out of Grandma's garden. Grandpa always called them pill bugs, but the kids called them potato bugs. He picked one up, and it immediately curled into a round ball.

"Look," Davie said. He rolled it with a flick of his finger, and it disappeared over the edge of the porch into the bushes. He crawled to the edge and looked into the shadowy undersides of the bushes. He leaned over.

"Watch out, there's stickers," Broadie said.

"Can you help me get it?" Davie asked solemnly.

Broadie sighed. He was tired and felt he'd spent enough time with Davie for the day. That thought brought a spark of guilt. Davie didn't have many friends to play with, except for Alan Peterson down the street. Dad ignored them, and Mom was too busy fighting with Dad. So he was either with Grandma or alone. He usually tried to follow Broadie around, but Broadie would chase him away or give a disappointing excuse. The one place Davie wouldn't go was the back ditch area, because, for some reason, he would always get scared, so Broadie wasn't worried about Davie exposing the clubhouse.

"I can't see," Davie said.

Broadie reached around inside the door and turned on the porch light. Down below, runoff from the roof had exposed a long line of pebbles and old paint chips. The paint on the porch was a dull gray, but the chips below were green and white, evincing a paint job from the distant past. Broadie and Davie both leaned out further.

"I can't see it, Davie." Broadie was about to pull back when he spied a small black coin among the pebbles.

"I can't just let it die down there," Davie said worriedly.

"I think it can take care of itself." Broadie reached out further, brushing his head against a dry, orange branch that hung low. He felt stickers catch his hair. He stretched out as far as he could reach. A spider web tickled the soft hairs of his arm. His fingers came within inches. He shimmied back in frustration.

"What is it? Is it my potato bug?" Davie asked.

"It's nothing." He quickly picked a thin, dry twig, and repeated the process, holding it out as an extension to his hand. He retrieved the coin, spat on it, and rubbed the dirt off onto his shirt. It was a penny. On the back were the sprigs of wheat. He felt a thrill of excitement. Davie leaned over his shoulder and he nudged him back.

"Let me see," Davie said.

Broadie flipped the coin over. Next to Lincoln the date said 1949. Another thrill. He stood, brushed the dust and stickers from his shirt, and walked away with his new treasure.

"Let me see, let me see!" Davie hopped up and down behind him.

"See!" He said a little too harshly. He held it out. "It's a stupid penny."

"Oh." Davie followed behind him, his curiosity quenched.

The television droned in a cluttered living room. He could have shown his dad the penny, but he had learned well lately that when Dad was sitting in the big chair with the stuffing coming out of the arms, holding a bottle of beer, it was best not to approach him. He might get in the way of the football game or something.

They slipped past quietly, walking into the kitchen.

"Mom?" Broadie looked around. Davie went off somewhere, probably forgetting all about his "potato bug."

He wandered to the back bedroom. Mom was busy changing the diaper of his younger sister, Alisha. A smoldering cigarette hung crookedly from the side of her mouth.

"Mom?"

She pulled the cigarette away with two fingers and snapped: "What do *you* want?"

Broadie recoiled a little. "I found something pretty interesting out—"

"Can't you see I'm busy?"

"I just—"

"Go take a bath, you're filthy. And make sure Davie takes one, too."

He pocketed the coin and walked away. Grandma and Grandpa weren't home yet, so there was no use looking for them. Grandpa liked coins, but it might be too late by the time they got back to show him.

The downstairs bathroom was an insult to his nose. He switched on the light that dangled from a broken fixture and walked across a sticky floor to the toilet. He lifted the lid and was repulsed by the drying offal around the bowl. The bathtub was grimy. He would rather use the bathroom upstairs, but Mom insisted they stay downstairs as much as possible. He reached into the tank to flush the toilet, then started the bath water running. He didn't miss his old apartment in Kearns; it was a lot worse. Dad was a mechanic but seemed to be between jobs most of the time. Things had gotten tough, so they had moved in with Grandpa and Grandma, and things were sometimes crowded and difficult. The house was split into two apartments. Broadie felt lucky to have his room upstairs where he could breathe.

A commotion behind the door.

"Brian!" Mom yelled.

The door burst open. His father regarded him with glassy, bloodshot eyes. A muscular hand darted forward and grabbed Broadie by the upper arm, lifting him off the ground. His other arm swung back and slammed his elbow into the edge of the sink. His fingers tingled.

"Where's my half inch socket?" Dad roared.

Broadie was stunned and couldn't speak.

"You used it on your bike; now, where is it?" Dull, greasy hair fell into Dad's face. He shook Broadie violently.

"That was three days ago. I put it back when—"

"Don't lie to me!"

"I'm not lying! I put it back!"

"It's not there now! where is it?"

"Brian!" Mom hollered from the hall.

"Stay out of this!" He pointed at her threateningly.

"I saw him put it back," she said.

"Then, where is it?"

Broadie started to cry from shock and the pain in his arms.

"Let him go!" Mom screamed.

"Don't tell me what to do!" Dad let go of Broadie and slapped him on the side of his head.

"Brian!" Mom screamed again, pulling at Dad. "You didn't have to hit him!"

Broadie fell against the steaming tub, ducked, and crawled between it and the wall. He tried to take a breath against the pain in his ribs.

The screaming match between his parents marched down the hall away from the door. He crawled back out, face stinging, and quickly locked the door. The tub had filled too much and was threatening to spill over. He turned off the water and pulled the plug to let it drain a little. His sore eye throbbed. He glanced into the mirror, then looked away, not wanting to see his bitter, tear-stained face.

* * *

Broadie's window was open. He tried to concentrate on the peaceful outside noises, but his mother's sobbing danced on his nerves. It carried loudly through the heater vent. He turned and pulled the pillow over his head. Dad had left earlier, slamming the door. He was probably out drinking by now.

The familiar wheel-crunch of Grandpa's car in the driveway.

Broadie felt heartened and lifted himself to look out the window. The dull ache in his ribs rose to an angry stab. He gasped and straightened himself. The headlights panned the backyard as Grandpa maneuvered into the garage. He couldn't see them from that angle, but he wanted to look anyway. The cool air felt sweet over his bare shoulders and back. He suddenly wanted to dive out into the darkness as if he could swim in it. He leaned out, pulling himself completely into the windowsill. The air sent goosebumps up and down his legs. He felt small slivers of wood poking into his underwear.

A stray cat exposed in the headlights hunched, then ran down the alley to escape the car. Broadie made a hissing noise, and it ran faster over the mossy soil. He laughed quietly.

"That was mean." A voice spoke from the darkened window directly across from him.

He threw himself back into his room, startled and embarrassed, for the voice was January's, and he was only in his underwear. He banged his ear against the hard plaster edge of the window. He growled, vigorously rubbing it. She leaned out her window, the moonlight turning her blond hair to silver. She tittered mischievously.

"That's not funny," Broadie grumbled.

"Ssh, be quiet," she said.

"Why?"

"Because I'm supposed to be in bed asleep. I'll get in trouble if there's too much noise."

"So?" Broadie said louder.

"Ssh!"

Broadie laughed.

"You're going to get me in trouble," she said nervously.

"Go to bed, then."

"I don't want to."

Broadie scooted himself to the window on his knees, feeling self-conscious. She probably couldn't see him, but he stayed hunched down.

"Our windows are in the same place," she said.

"Are you related to old lady Larson?"

"You mean my *grandmother?*" She sounded annoyed.

"No, the cat."

"Shut up!" January reached up to tug on her window.

"I'm just kidding," Broadie said, laughing.

"Don't be mean," She said, sliding the window down a few inches.

"I'm kidding. Don't go."

"Then don't be mean."

"Fine, I won't. Your grandma and mine are—were friends."

"Hmm." She sounded angry but didn't shut the window.

"Where are you from?" he asked.

"Idaho."

"Where in Idaho?" he asked.

"Idaho Falls. Have you ever been there?"

"I've been through there to go fishing with my uncle and my grandpa."

"We lived down the street from the Mormon temple," she said. "I used to could walk right down to the river and sit by the falls and feed the ducks."

"So how come you moved here?"

"Grandma died, and we inherited the place, and my dad wanted a job transfer."

"What does he do?" he asked.

"Computer networks. What does your dad do?"

Broadie paused, not wanting to tell her that his dad was out of work. "Mechanic," he finally said. He changed the subject. "What's Idaho like?"

"We were all friends in my neighborhood back home. People didn't seem to pick on each other as much. My best friend's name was Candice. She was nice. Do you want to see her picture?"

Broadie nodded.

She left her window, then came back with a binder that she had pulled from under her bed. "This is my scrapbook." She passed it over, pointing to a page that she had opened it to. "That's my house—I mean my old house." She stopped him on one of the pages. It was a small house with white aluminum siding and a large, fat pine tree in front. Though it was in color, the darkness made it look like an old black and white picture. All of her photographs were carefully bordered in colored paper and happy, cartoonish stickers of small animals and flowers. She reached out and motioned for him to turn the page. "That's Candice." She pointed to a picture of a dark-haired girl in a soft pink sweatshirt. "We write each other every week. Do you like sports?"

Another touchy subject. "I guess."

"I collect cards," she said. "I have a lot of Utah Jazz. I also have a lot of Forty-niners. My dad gave me some Steve Young cards from before Steve retired."

Broadie had heard of Steve Young but didn't know exactly what he did, and he didn't want to ask and feel stupid.

"I collect coins," he said.

She nodded. "Do you want to see my cards?"

"Sure," he said, passing the scrapbook back over. There wouldn't be any harm in looking. He could see who Steve Young was, anyway.

She disappeared into the darkness of her room, then reappeared with a long, gray box. "I had to try hard to keep them from getting mixed up with all the other boxes." She reached out.

"Hold on," Broadie said. He retrieved a pair of pants.

While he was busy dressing himself, she had climbed into her windowsill and sat sideways on the brick ledge. She had her back against one side and her feet against the other. She looked perilously close to falling, and as comfortable as a cat. He thought that was neat, so he also lifted himself out and joined her opposite so could face each other. His sore ribs hummed softly and constantly.

"Here," she said.

Grunting in pain, he reached as far out as he could. They were short six inches.

"Wait," he said. The ground was far enough down that he could break an arm. He'd had enough pain for one day.

"I can reach," she said. She grabbed an old, iron bar that might have once been a window shade and leaned out further. It looked loose. Broadie reached back out, took the cards, and returned to his place.

"Cool," he said, opening the lid. They were all neatly stacked together, each in its own plastic cover. He lifted a few to examine them closer in the washed, gray light.

"That's Thurl Bailey," she said, pointing.

Broadie nodded.

"That's Steve Young."

He held the card closer, trying to discern Steve Young's features. "I've seen him on TV," he said. "Do you want to see my coins?"

"Sure."

Broadie came back with a small box. He lifted the lid. The newest addition was a blank, dark circle over lighter grays. He replaced the lid and carefully eased out. She met him, and he felt a soft scratch from her fingernail.

"I can't see much detail," she said, squinting into the box.

"Turn on your light."

"I know if I did, someone would just happen to be awake, and I'd get in trouble." She stirred the coins with her finger and lifted one.

"I can tell that's my buffalo nickel," he said.

"It has an Indian head. I heard pennies used to have Indians on them."

"I have one in there, if you could see it."

"Really? Nuh-uh."

"Uh-huh. I could show you in the morning."

"Maybe." She replaced the lid, then tossed the box to Broadie without a second thought. He caught it with an accidentally smooth swipe of his arm. A small jingle. He wished that he could be that lucky with a football. He wondered what his new friend would think if she knew how clumsy he was about sports.

"Did you know my grandma?" she asked.

"I used to bring her paper to her."

"I wish I could have gotten to know her better," she said. "We've always lived so far away."

"She used to invite me and my little brother over for cookies and stuff. I always liked the pictures of the national parks that she had for place mats on her table."

"She used to travel a lot when my grandpa was still alive," she said. "I saw her more often when they would pass through Idaho on the way to Canada."

"Did you ever see her china closet?"

"Yeah, the one with all the souvenirs from Yellowstone Park and places like that."

"Did you see the picture of the jackalope that your grandpa took?" he asked

"What's a jackalope?"

"It's a half jackrabbit, half deer or antelope, or something like that. She said they were an endangered species and you could only find them in Wyoming. Seriously."

He found himself working hard to maintain his look of sincerity. Mrs. Larson had shown him an old postcard when he first came over and had him fooled for weeks.

"There's no such thing," she said.

"Yes, there is. The picture might still be in your house."

"You're full of it."

"Okay," he said, "if you don't want to believe me."

"Fine, I won't. What else did she show you?"

"Do you really want to know, or will you not believe me?" he asked.

"I'll believe you as long as you don't make it up."

Her tone of voice took the practical joker out of his mood. She really wanted to know more about her grandma, and she listened intently. Their conversation flourished in the changing moonlight. Shadows drifted too slowly to be detected. Crickets droned unnoticed behind their words. Little by little they gave in to the need for sleep until by early morning the windowsills were vacant but remained open.

4

A cool morning breeze tickled the curtains that hung near Broadie's bed. Bright, clean morning sun shone through them. It rose peeking and twinkling through the pear trees that lined the back yard. The air was sweet and damp with dew. Spider webs glistened in the bushes like Christmas ornaments. He rubbed the sting of sleep from his eyes, stretched, and his ribs shouted a loud memory of yesterday evening.

Bacon was cooking.

He wandered sleepily from his room scratching the mosquito bites he had received in the windowsill. Soft, warm carpet molded itself around his feet (such a large contrast to the grime downstairs), and he wandered into the comforting sounds of Sunday morning. Grandpa sat at the table reading a book as Grandma piled bacon onto a plate.

"Well, hello there." Grandpa said. He threw a wink from behind his reading glasses.

Broadie smiled shyly and noticed a reflection of his "chicken feather" hair (as Grandma called it) in the toaster.

"Are your clothes ready?" Grandma asked, setting breakfast on the table.

"Yes," Broadie said. He reached for some hashbrowns.

"Let me see that eye," Grandma said. She gently cocked Broadie's head back and looked him over. "No fights lately?"

Broadie shook his head.

"Good."

"Have some bacon," Grandpa said. "That's from the Haywards in Tooele. Got it on a discount right from the slaughter house."

Broadie thought of squealing pigs being led to their death. "That's the smell of death," Grandpa had said once when they were driving past. A shiver tingled down his back.

Grandpa chewed with relish. Broadie took a bite to be polite.

"Want some cottage cheese and peaches?" Grandma asked.

"Sure." Broadie said.

Grandpa looked up at the bacon, then back to his book, and chuckled.

Broadie squeezed ketchup liberally over his hashbrowns and ate faster as his stomach decided it was hungry. He liked eating upstairs better than downstairs. Mom would get annoyed and ask him why when her food was just as good. He would do it anyway and not say anything. Davie always came up, too, when he smelled food cooking.

Grandma and Grandpa were Mom's parents. The differences between them were so extreme that even Davie noticed. Mom and Dad smoked and drank; Grandma and Grandpa never had. Upstairs was spotless and new, rich for Broadie's standards; downstairs smelled of beer, garbage, and dirty diapers. Sunday was a point of friction in the house. One of the conditions of moving in with Grandma and Grandpa was that the kids went to church every Sunday. Grandpa had baptized Broadie when he was eight. Dad protested, but Mom reluctantly gave in. Dad must have had his way before, because Broadie couldn't remember having gone to church until they moved in.

He finished his food and went back to his room to change. The window was still open and the breeze was getting warmer. Today would be hot. He dreaded putting on the tie that hung in the closet. January's window was also still open; her curtains were closed. They were pink with white ballerinas frozen in uncomfortable poses. They breathed in and out, revealing a strip of darkened room. He wondered if she went to church like his grandparents did.

* * *

Before they entered the chapel, Grandma took Broadie aside and combed his hair. He winced as she pulled at snarls with brisk, fussy, little movements. He could get away from her if he wanted, but his awareness of her recent sacrifices was beginning to grow. He felt more inclined to tolerate her comb. She looked him over, brow loosening, indicating that he passed her inspection. She moved onto Davie.

Soft organ music played. People milled back and forth, shaking hands and scouting for vacant seats. Broadie scanned the congregation, hoping to see January. Grandma tugged on his elbow, and he followed her to their seats. John and Joey sat in the back with Tim Burton and Steve Bartlett. Their attention was focused on something Steve had been playing with.

The meeting passed slowly. During the sacrament Steve Bartlett came down his row carrying the trays of bread and water. He passed to Broadie's family. Broadie wondered how Steve could stand there so piously when just a week before he had tried to rub dog poop in his face. Steve looked away when Broadie tried to look him in the eyes. He moved to the next row, then the next.

Near the conclusion, Davie restlessly lay on his back, taunting Broadie with kicks until Broadie finally swatted him on the leg. Davie whined; Broadie received a tug on the ear for not ignoring his brother as he was expected to. There wasn't any use complaining, so he brooded in silence. The meeting finally ended, and the congregation split up for the various classes that followed. Broadie took Davie into Primary. Davie sat happily by Allen Peterson. Broadie slid into a vacant seat, unnoticed by John and Joey, who were looking over some trading cards from a game that was popular lately.

A teacher stopped at Broadie's nearly empty row. "You have to move to the back one."

He sulked, not wanting to move.

"Let's go," she said, impatiently motioning with her fingers for him to follow her. She pointed to a chair right by the bullies. He slowly rose to his feet. When he walked into the back row far enough, she was satisfied and quickly moved on to other things.

John saw him coming and slid into the vacant seat. "Broadie Grodie can't come past," he said, blocking him with his legs. "He's contagious."

"Eww, gross," Vanessa Dean said from behind.

January walked shyly through the door. Broadie's stomach froze. She was their same age and would get sucked right into Vanessa's group. The Primary president led her right to the back row.

"Everyone, this is January. She's new in the ward. Please make her feel welcome."

Vanessa smiled sweetly and moved over a seat.

"I'll let your teacher know you're here." The Primary president walked away.

Broadie sat down.

John leaned away: "Oh, sick, get away."

Broadie shook his head, stood, and moved a few seats down.

"He's still contaminating the row," Joey said.

"He has to sit with the girls," John said.

"Eww, he's not coming over here," Vanessa said. Some of the girls moved over a seat to close any spaces.

Broadie moved down another seat. John and Tim Burton followed him. He leaned back and pushed Broadie on the leg with his foot. "Get off our row," he said.

Broadie stood feeling anger burning hot in his chest. It leapt and twisted like arching electricity. January sat, quietly witnessing the whole thing. It wouldn't be long before she joined them, he thought.

John pushed again with his foot. Broadie slapped it away violently.

"Don't touch me." John's voice turned darkly hostile. He used words under his breath not meant for church, or anywhere else for that matter. His eyes glanced to the teachers whose backs were turned.

"Ooh, Grodie thinks he's tough," Joey said, his face stupid and petulant. He reached out and flipped Broadie's ear. Broadie slapped back and Joey fell down into his chair, acting like he had just been touched by toxic waste. He held his hands up to his throat like he was choking.

All the girls laughed except January. She looked down shamefully.

Broadie felt a flush of rage and jammed his knee into John's thigh. John jumped up with the promise of violence. Broadie drove a fist into John's eye before he could gain his balance, and he fell back onto Joey.

"He hit him!" Vanessa cried.

A teacher, Tim Burton's mother, sailed over and indignantly grabbed Broadie by the arm, pulling him jerkily out into the hall.

"I can't believe I just saw that!" Her voice shook.

"He started it," Broadie sobbed. His rage finally broke through into tears.

"You don't hit people in church!"

"He was going to hit me."

"You hit *him*. I saw it happen."

"But they were making fun of me."

"You don't hit people just because they make fun of you."

She gripped his arm so tight that it began to tingle. His ribs ached again. He tried to pull away, but she grabbed both of his arms and faced him directly. People passed and stared. The embarrassment was unbearable. "I want my grandpa," he sobbed. He could see through the door that another teacher was over by John, her arm around him, consoling him. He was overacting, with both hands pressed against his eye, rocking from front to back.

"I think we need to have a talk with the bishop." Her eyes glared.

Broadie yanked himself back as hard as he could, breaking her grip. She took a swipe for his shoulder. He dodged her, colliding with a brick wall. Running through a haze of stars, he nearly missed an old lady being pushed in a wheelchair. His cheek stung badly as he made his escape out the doors, into the parking lot. He stopped between a truck and a minivan and turned to look. Some people had followed him. He wandered in and out of the cars toward the ball field. The gates were locked, but that wouldn't keep him from climbing.

"He ran out this way," Mrs. Burton yelled.

Broadie didn't look back. He bounded the fence like a gymnast and disappeared over the small hill.

The noon sun blazed brilliantly into the warm, moist grass. He lay trance-like, watching seagulls glide in a circular updraft. He was safe and alone in this secret section of the church grounds. The tears had long since dried, but his eyes still burned from crying. The anger that had shook in his chest like an earthquake had died into small aftershocks. John and Joey would be liars right there in church. Most would stick up for them.

Grodie Broadie: the Villain.

Poor Johnny didn't move quickly enough out of the way, so Broadie hit him. That's what they would say.

John *was* going to hit him.

He had seen the look in John's eye as he stood. *They* were the real bullies. "It's always someone else; never you," Mrs. Burton would say. Angry teachers never saw what happened around lonely corners, on lonely streets when neighbors weren't around. He couldn't ever go to the park by himself, because John-and-friends were always there. Grandma and Grandpa always wondered why he stayed close by and never had any friends.

You don't hit people in church!

A sliver of guilt stung him, then disappeared with the gusty, warm air. Hitting someone wasn't right, but bullying wasn't right either. John had started the name "Broadie Grodie," and it had infected every kid in church and school. Even the younger kids called him that now. No one ever stepped in to stop *them*. No one was there to tell *them* to not push, hit, or flick him in the back of the neck during a prayer. *They* never got in trouble. All hell would break loose the moment that he broke. It never broke loose for them.

Voices drifted from the parking lot, car doors opened and shut. Engines cranked. He waited, knowing John-and-friends would be out there, somewhere, waiting to take revenge where no one would see. He couldn't risk the walk home. Grandma and Grandpa would be angry, having the full story by now. It was probably the gospel lesson of the week. He wanted to disintegrate into the soil, disappear from life. It would be *their* fault if he did.

He waited until most of the cars had left, then he walked along the fence line where he could easily hide if he had to. Grandma and Davie stood waiting by the car. Grandpa must have gone back in to look for him. People mingled by the doors, but there was no sign of John-and-friends. Davie saw him first, pointing him out before he climbed back over the fence. Grandma lifted her hand into a salute to shield her eyes from the sun. She saw him, dropped her hands to her hips the way she always did when she was really upset. He walked slowly, scraping his heels against the pavement.

"Get in there and let your grandfather know you're here so he won't have to look for you anymore." Her voice warbled with a fury he seldom heard.

His face burned with sour embarrassment. His head hung low, tears pushed their way up again. There wasn't any use trying to explain. He didn't want to go back in where everyone would see Grodie Broadie, the troublemaker. The faster he walked, the sooner it would be over.

They completed his humiliation by making him apologize to John in front of his family and Mrs. Burton. The same John that had tormented him in school, had beaten him up numerous occasions, and had stolen his backpack to throw it into the creek that ran through the park by the school. John's eye didn't reveal any darker purple than what was there naturally under the eye. His mother acted like he needed life-saving medical help.

Of course there was that look again from John (when no one else noticed), the telepathy that burned across the room to Broadie, saying that it wasn't over, no apology accepted. He would have to watch his back as long as he lived. He was a dead man walking.

Later that night, Grandpa finally listened, but it was too late to make a difference. He told Broadie to stay away from them and not to speak them. The same adult sermon: just ignore them, turn the other cheek, and pretend their constant harassment was just the quacking of ducks.

He went to bed early and lay boiling in bitter fantasies of beating John and Joey to a pulp. He spent an unknown period of time that night somewhere between dreams and semiconsciousness suffering alone.

5

Broadie didn't know when he had finally fallen asleep. It hadn't been long before Mom and Dad's fighting had crept into the rhythm of his dreams. There was a crashing noise. A peculiar awareness settled over him like a cold blanket. His mother's voice cried out, begging his father to stop hitting her. The sound carried from downstairs, muffled through the heater vent.

Grandpa's bedroom door opened, and footsteps shuffled quickly past his room.

More violence, more violence, a struggle; Grandpa's voice, Alisha crying. . . .

The cursing and hollering between Grandpa and Dad drifted outside. He tossed his covers aside and threw himself in the direction of the light switch, pounding it upward with the palm of his hand. The room snapped to brilliance. He yanked his door open in terror and ran into the hall. He slipped, banging his knee against the heater vent. His ribs and knee sang a dissonant chorus.

Grandma stood in her bathrobe at the top of the stairwell that led to the basement apartment. She turned her head in response to the sudden clatter behind her, her face sullen and haunted.

"Broadie, stay there!" she commanded.

He cried out, stumbling to his feet: "Grandma!" He ran and wrapped his arms around her waist, almost tumbling them both over the edge. She gripped the railing in a sudden need for support. She pulled at his panic-tightened arms and winced in pain from arthritis.

"What in the world's the matter with you?"

Grandma, visibly disturbed by the strangeness around her, walked him away from the stairs.

"No, wait—" Broadie tried to run for the stairs.

"This is not the time to make trouble. You go back to your room!"

"No Grandma, I . . . My mom!"

"They were having a bad argument, there's no—"

Eight cylinders of his dad's old Chevy Nova roared to life in the garage. A loose belt in the engine chirped, and tires squealed out of the driveway into the street. Grandpa's heavy footsteps pounded back up the stairs.

Grandma broke away. Broadie sat down on the couch with shaky legs.

"I'm gonna kill that—" Grandpa roared. His eyes bulged with emotion. "If I were thirty years younger. . . ." He stopped and regarded Broadie. Blood dripped from his nose. He looked tousled, battered.

"Ray! What did he do? Did he hit you?" Grandma followed him into the kitchen.

Davie, in his Spiderman pajamas, crept slowly up the stairs. His tallowy face glistened with tears. He saw Broadie and ran to hide behind the big chair in the corner.

"She needs to go to the hospital." Grandpa's voice drifted from the kitchen.

—*She needs to go to the hospital.*

He ran down the stairs into the TV room, where Mom rocked his crying sister with one hand and held a bloody towel to the side of her own head with the other. Her face was badly bruised and swollen. She shuddered with each sob. Tears mingled with blood.

"Pick up that glass before Davie steps on it," she blubbered.

He found the broom and jerked with a start as Grandma appeared from around the corner.

"Watch out Broadie-bear," she said, scooting past. "Let me take her, Michelle." She took Alisha into her arms.

The kitchen was destroyed. The new microwave oven that they had gotten with Christmas money lay on the floor, its door twisted like a loose tongue. A large hole had been punched through the wall where a picture had hung. Glass from the microwave oven and broken dishes was scattered across the floor. Broadie began to pick up the bigger pieces. A loud knock sounded from the upstairs door. An authoritative voice reverberated from above, sending an avalanche of cold tingles down his nerves: the police were already at the door.

He dragged the sticky garbage can away from the wall and threw the glass into it, listening to the clinks and plinks. Heavy footsteps thundered down the stairs. Grandpa was leading them downstairs. Tears were pushing their way up. He fought them back and knew that it was bad for the police to be there. His mother once told him that, if things got real bad, the state would take them away and give them to other families. He was never to tell anyone at school or church that Dad drank beer, that they didn't have any money, and never to mention to a soul that Dad hit them. He suddenly wanted to grab Davie and Alisha and take them to the clubhouse until the police were gone. He could take them to their other grandparents in Riverton. He knew the way by bus.

The air shifted in the room as Grandpa entered, followed by two large men in uniform. One of them, a huge, bald, black man, smiled and moved past him; the other spoke to Grandpa. A blond crewcut glistened above a pink, sunburnt scalp. Broadie stepped aside to let them pass. Heavy musk cologne filled the shattered kitchen.

"No, Momma!" Mom cried out.

"Honey, you need to talk to them and tell them what happened," Grandma spoke above her weeping. Alisha joined in crying.

Broadie stood paralyzed, looking at the guns (real guns) that sat in holsters on their hips. Handcuffs glinted from a leather pouch. A large baton dangled at the hip of the man with a crewcut. He slipped on some rubber gloves and squatted to examine Mom. They asked questions, but Grandpa did most of the talking. Radios on their shoulders sputtered. The officer stepped away to answer. He tilted his head to speak into the radio on his shoulder and looked directly at Broadie. Broadie glowed with guilt and embarrassment. He was in his underwear. He ran out of the kitchen and back upstairs. Another officer stood at the open door, swatting at bugs that swarmed the porch light. Some came in and buzzed around Grandma's small chandelier in the entrance. An ambulance arrived, adding to the blue and red disco lights that danced across the curtains.

He ran into the living room. Davie's little foot poked out from behind the big chair, giving away his hiding place. He peeked out.

saw Broadie, then his head popped back like a mouse retreating into its hole.

Broadie needed clothes. He wondered again about the clubhouse and its possible safety. There was food in the cupboard if he needed it. He walked into the inviting light of his room. If he couldn't get away to the clubhouse, he could always hide his little brother and sister in one of the closets. There was a good place to hide behind the boxes in Grandma and Grandpa's room.

A stretcher banged against the front doorway. Radios hissed and garbled behind more and more footsteps.

He looked into his closet for his backpack. He needed matches and a flashlight. As he pawed through his things, he caught movement in the corner of his eye. January sat in her window staring at him. She waved at him eagerly. Again embarrassment poured into his face. He ran to his chest of drawers and pulled on a pair of pants, then a shirt. He paused, realizing he didn't have to face her. He could pretend that he hadn't seen her there. He pulled out his bottom drawer, found his allowance and stuffed it into his pocket. Five dollars would cover bus fare and more, should he need it.

Grandma's consoling voice drifted from the living room. She had both Davie and Alisha with her. Maybe the fear of being taken away was irrational. Grandma and Grandpa wouldn't ever let that happen. He sat on his bed.

A tap on his window.

He sighed. His emotions were beginning to stir again. He dreaded crying in front of a girl.

More tapping.

He got up, moved slowly to the window, and lifted the old heavy wood and glass. She was still sitting there, comfortable in her pajamas. Police lights reflected off of the peeling paint on the old bricks.

"Who got hurt?" January asked.

Broadie paused and felt like wanted to cry. He took a deep breath, cleared his throat, then answered slowly, "My mom."

"What happened to her?"

Broadie didn't speak. He stared out between the two houses. A young woman in a shortsleeved uniform stood outside the ambulance, waiting for the stretcher.

"I heard screaming," January said. She lifted one foot higher and broke off pieces of crumbling paint with her toes. Broadie noticed her bony ankles and thought of bird feet.

They sat in silence as his mother was lifted into the back of the ambulance. Neighbors gathered in their driveways. The ambulance drove away to the hospital and Grandpa's car followed behind it. The police hadn't left yet and he wondered if they would try to speak to him. He crawled out into the sill and breathed deeply the night air.

"I saw your dad fighting with your grandpa out front," January spoke again.

Broadie was still silent and noticed that January was becoming uncomfortable. He didn't know what to say. After the fight in church and then this, she was probably thinking about how weird he was. So far, he'd been able to keep most of his family's problems a secret. If word got out that his dad was an alcoholic, people would just pester him worse. He saw all the neighbors standing around in their nightgowns and realized that the whole neighborhood knew about their problems by now. He looked back at January and felt angry. It was a hopeless anger, because he knew that it wouldn't be very long before she wouldn't be talking to him anymore. Vanessa Davis would probably have her wrapped up in her little net of followers.

"That's my dad talking to the cops," she said with a gasp.

Sunburnt crewcut walked along with January's dad. He was probably pointing out all the details of the fight in the front yard. Soon they were out of sight behind the lilac bushes.

"I have to go now," Broadie said. He began to pull himself back into his room.

"Wait," January said. There wasn't any meanness in her eyes.

Broadie trusted her even less.

"Is your mom okay?" she asked sincerely.

Broadie shook his head and looked down into the mossy rain-gravel.

"I'm sorry," she said.

He started to pull himself back again.

"Wait," she said again. She looked as though she were fishing hard for the next thing to say.

"What?" Broadie sounded more annoyed than he meant to. He ducked and began to swing his legs around.

"I have an idea for the clubhouse," she said quickly.

He bumped his head with surprise. "Ow!" He rubbed it vigorously. "What's that?"

"There's wood behind the shed in my back yard, and my dad said that I could have it if I don't get stuck with a rusty nail. It would be perfect for the treehouse." She smiled. Her eyes sparkled like she really meant it.

His stomach leaped at the idea. If only he could trust her. His hope began to grow. He nodded thoughtfully, then smiled. "Okay."

January looked relieved. "When can we start?"

"Tomorrow." Broadie smiled wider. He had something to look forward to. He grabbed onto it inside like a lifeline for a drowning man.

"I can go after I do my jobs."

"See you there tomorrow."

He left January sitting in her window. There were new voices in the living room, and he couldn't tell for sure if the police were still there. He walked into the kitchen, looked into the fridge, then closed the door, not feeling hungry.

"Broadie?" Grandma called. Alisha was squealing and laughing now like she did when she was being played with.

"Oh, Mom, don't be silly!" Broadie heard Aunt Cheryl speak from the living room. A small thrill tickled through him. Aunt Cheryl and Uncle Will were always a treat. How had they gotten there so fast? He walked slowly into the living room, hands in his pockets. A mild perfume took the place of the heavy cologne left behind by the police officers.

"And there isn't any word yet?" Will asked.

"I won't know for sure until your dad calls." Grandma said. "They've taken her to LDS Hospital."

"Why won't she divorce that bum?" Aunt Cheryl nipped.

"Little ears." Grandma said.

Broadie leaned against the doorway.

"Broadie-Bear," Aunt Cheryl said. He was too old for that name, but she always won a smile with it.

"Hey, Broadie! Come here and give me five!" Uncle Will said. Davie sat on his knee playing with a toy.

He walked up, and they slapped hands.

"Do you want to come and stay with us for a few days?" Aunt Cheryl asked.

He loved playing with his cousins. "Yes . . . I mean I'd like to, but I'm working on something. I better stay here."

"Tommy and Jared are waiting for you to come over. They have some awesome computer games. We'll have some fun."

"I don't think so. I'm tired. I just want to go to bed." Broadie turned to leave.

"We really need you to come. Things are a little rough here, and it would be nice for your mom if you came and stayed for a while," Aunt Cheryl said, losing some of the happy flavor in her voice. She seemed nervous and kept looking toward the door.

"You need someone to help clean up around here," Broadie said to Grandma.

Uncle Will looked down at the floor and sighed impatiently. He rubbed his eyes for lack of sleep. "It's not safe for you to be here. Your dad's still out there, and he left very drunk and angry. We'll bring you back when things are safer. Maybe in just a couple of days."

"I can take care of myself," Broadie argued. His voice wavered, and his eyes moistened.

"Come on, buddy." Uncle Will put Davie aside and invited Broadie into the kitchen. He put a strong hand on his shoulder. Broadie felt strange. He wanted to yank himself away, but he recognized the masculine affection and all at once became desperate for more. Will slid his arm around his shoulder, and Broadie started to cry. He buried his face into Uncle Will's chest and shuddered with grief and also relief. At least tonight he wouldn't have to face his father's rage. Broadie finally let go. He grabbed a napkin to wipe his nose. Uncle Will poured him a glass of water.

"Your dad could be back any minute," Uncle Will said.

"I want to stay and work on my clubhouse. I could camp out there if I had to." Broadie took a drink.

"Clubhouse? Aren't you a little old for a clubhouse?"

"It's the biggest one ever built."

"Where is it?"

"That's a secret."

"It doesn't happen to be down the irrigation ditch a little way, in an old vacant lot filled with trees, does it?"

Broadie stiffened, then sat silently looking down at the old floor tiles.

Uncle Will nodded his head knowingly, and smiled. He leaned back and rested against the counter. "I know that place pretty well."

Broadie remained silent, but noticed Uncle Will glancing up at the clock on the wall. Broadie followed his eyes. The clock said it was almost four thirty A.M.

"I had a secret club back there once."

Broadie surrendered his full attention to Uncle Will. His story was too fascinating to ignore.

"Let's see." Uncle Will paused. "There was this one big tree surrounded with smaller ones, and along the side were some fruit trees. Grapes had grown over some of them, killing them off until they were nothing but big green domes. Oh, and the big rose bushes, they always kept it a secret. Sound familiar?"

Broadie rolled his eyes then nodded.

"Well, you're one of a select few."

"I guess those old boards back there were yours?"

"Every one of them."

"You had a tree house?"

"We had the biggest tree house ever. In fact, there were these old—" Uncle Will stopped talking and looked up at the door. Aunt Cheryl was standing there.

"How's it going, guys?" she asked.

"Great!" Uncle Will said.

There was a heavy pause. Broadie felt himself in the path of an unseen communication between the two. He looked down to the floor tiles.

"Davie and the baby are all ready for a sleepover." She smiled her winning smile, but behind it was a shadow that made Broadie want to go hide until they were gone.

"We'll be there." Uncle Will winked and nodded at her. She smiled again and left the doorway.

"Let's go to my place, and we'll talk more about the secret club-house. I think Davie needs you there with him."

"Okay." Broadie still looked at the floor tiles.

"Let's go get you ready, then."

He gathered what he needed into a small suitcase that Grandma lent him, then wrote a note to January and taped it onto his window. Uncle Will made sure Broadie didn't say exactly where he went or who he was with. Braodie hoped she would see it in the morning.

6

"I'm going to blow it up," Davie said. He pushed a little green tank along a dirt path that he had smoothed with his hands. Little sticks were stacked into log cabins. He stepped carefully to avoid crushing part of his miniature town.

"No! No!" Tommy screeched, manipulating his voice to mimic a cartoon character. "We have to stop him!" He dug a foxhole for his action figures with a little blue garden tool.

Davie pushed his tank, making growling noises in his throat. His pants were matted with mud at the knees. "We will not retreat!"

Tommy screeched. He threw small plastic missiles at the advancing tank.

Davie tapped sticks that he had positioned as catapults that flipped dust like small explosions. "Boom! Boom! Boom!" he said.

Broadie sat alone in a large cherry tree, watching his little brother play with his cousin in the garden. Uncle Will and Aunt Cheryl's yard was bigger than his grandparents' yard and more manicured. Every blade of grass had its own place. A large wooden swing and a slide set, nicer than the one at the park, adorned a corner. They had a mower you could ride on, and every child had his own bicycle. The house was new and always smelled like clean clothes. In the family room was a digital entertainment center that was like being at the movies. The oldest kids had their own rooms. Each was furnished with a computer. Their cars were new, with full tanks of gas. He had accepted long ago that only other people lived like this. He picked a bunch of late cherries that the birds hadn't eaten. He put one in his mouth, divided the fruit from the pit, and spit it out to see how far it would go. It landed inches short of the fence.

Three days had passed since his mother had gone to the hospital. He hadn't received much word about her except that she was doing all right and that she'd be home soon. Finally, tonight, they would be able to see her.

He was insanely bored. Jared used to be fun. At thirteen he was closest to Broadie's age. They used to pal around embarking on adventures through the fields and neighborhoods around his house, but now he had his own set of friends and had quietly dubbed Broadie a nuisance. Kristen was a few months younger than Broadie but hated boys and spent her time doing what girls did with their girlfriends. Kelsi and Kassidy were in high school and fought over bathrooms and boyfriends. He spit another cherry pit, and this time it connected with the fence and bounced into the grass. He rejoiced at his little accomplishment and eased himself down until he was hanging, then let go. Happily, his ribs no longer ached as bad.

The sounds of battle disappeared behind him as he walked into the house. Aunt Cheryl had gone to the store and left Kelsi to babysit. She had Alisha playing with some toys on the floor as she lay on the couch gabbing on the phone. She didn't notice Broadie as he wandered like a ghost downstairs into the family room. He thought about his clubhouse like a hungry man thinking of food. He closed his eyes and felt the sweet solitude where the trees whispered to him and the wind softly blew away the things that caused him pain. Spots of sunlight danced for him in disorderly patterns. Sweet smells of life and decay carried him on rose-petal cushions. He wondered if January had gone back to the tree house by herself. Would she keep it a secret? The question constantly vibrated like a violin string below his conscious thoughts, occasionally surfacing to leave him swimming in a pool of anxiety.

In the family room was what Uncle Will called the "love me" wall. It was covered with plaques and trophies honoring the family's accomplishments. Each person had his own section: Uncle Will's was the biggest, with shelves full of sports trophies dating back to the seventies; Aunt Cheryl danced and played the piano when she was younger. Her high school and college diplomas sat next to Uncle Will's; Kelsi followed in her mother's footsteps; Kassidy was the rebel but didn't lack in her share of glory; Jared excelled in everything from baseball to youth golf tournaments. The centerpiece in his arrangement was a sheepskin covered from top to bottom with every award a Cub Scout could achieve: the Bobcat, Wolf, Bear, and Webelos patches fit into a perfect diamond surrounded by gold and silver arrows, beads, camp patches, and the coveted Arrow of Light.

Broadie had been involved with the Cub Scouts off and on, and used to love it but he never knew what it was like to have a father's support in it. He had his own Bobcat patch and some beads from when he was younger, but he should have had everything Jared had by now. He used to love the pack meetings, day camps, and pinewood derbies and longed to move to the Boy Scouts when he turned twelve. There he hoped for fraternity and accomplishment, but it was harder to go without any friends there. His den leader used to pick him up for each meeting, but after being excluded and picked on (some of the adults had labeled him the troublemaker) he stopped going.

He caught his reflection in a shiny plaque and noticed that his eye was almost healed. He probed the orbit and found a tender spot on the edge of his eyebrow. He had lost count of his war wounds, but this one had come from his dad. It had been more than a week, and that stupid theme song from the TV show M.A.S.H. played in his head every time he thought about it. Dad was back in his chair sleeping the sleep of beer (or at least so he thought) when he let the door slam. Dad didn't seem to notice, and he tiptoed past the TV when the blow came as sudden as an explosion. When the stars cleared he saw Dad standing over him, fists clenched, and trembling like a wild animal.

Broadie blinked away the memory and looked up at the antique shotgun over the fireplace mantel. He carefully lifted it from its brace and looked down the barrel. It felt heavy and alive in his hands. He pointed it at one of the trophies and pulled the trigger: a smooth click. He thumbed the hammers back, aimed at the sheepskin: click. Click. He aimed at the entertainment center. John's face reflected back at him: click.

7

From Mom's hospital room, he could see the black western mountains against the monotone leftovers from sunset. Their shape reminded him of a roller coaster. City lights twinkled and wobbled from the day's heat rising into the night air.

"They had to take her spleen."

The nurse's words echoed into the room from the hall where the adults gathered in conference. Mom sat in her bed, sipping broth through a straw. Her jaw was cracked, and her face shone with bitter, purple bruises. Davie sat in a soft chair next to the bed, playing with a rubber glove that uncle Will had blown into a balloon.

"Have you guys had fun?" Mom mumbled through her bandages.

"We played army men," Davie said.

Broadie turned around from the window but didn't speak.

"I'm coming home soon," Mom said through clenched teeth. Her eyes were solemn, but she forced a small smile.

"Did the doctor give you a shot?" Davie asked.

"Yes," she said. She reached out to caress his head.

"Did you cry?" Davie asked seriously.

"No," she whispered.

"Then you're a big mommy."

She cracked another smile and looked at Broadie. "I'm sorry, it's all my fault. I'm sorry he hit you." A tear trickled from the corner of her eye.

Broadie folded his hands behind his back and scuffed his heel against the baseboard. He looked down at the floor tiles. Grandma and Grandpa had come just before dinner with the news that the police had found his father and arrested him. He had never pictured his father as a criminal. He imagined his dad sitting behind bars. Emotions twisted and merged in strange patterns. There was guilt that it was partly his fault. There was also relief blended with a strange flavor of pain and longing. He was also ashamed because he couldn't look at his mother. He had seen her nursing bloody noses and bruises so often that it was unusual for her not to, but he had never seen her come close to death. Emergency surgery was a strange new tragedy. He wanted to give her a hug, and also for her to comfort him. She continued to look at him with tear-filled eyes. He left the window and sauntered to the side of her bed. He stared at the tubes that protruded from her hands. He didn't know if some of the bruises on her arms were from needle pricks or from his father. She caressed his arm. He stiffened, wanting to pull away, but held his place.

"Broadie, honey, I—" Mom started to speak again. The nurse entered. She was an older woman with a stern demeanor. She looked at both boys with a smile, but her eyes said she was there because she had to be. "Hi, Michelle," she said, setting her clipboard on the counter. "Are these your boys?"

Mom smiled and nodded the best she could.

"You guys come to see how good your mommy's getting better?" She opened a drawer and took out a small bottle and a syringe.

"She's coming home soon," Davie said.

"Well, that's good! Is that your balloon?"

"It's my hand balloon." Davie held it up proudly, making sure she looked at it well.

Broadie stepped away form the bed, leaned against the window again, and looked out. The afterglow had disappeared completely, leaving glittering patterns of city grid that stretched across the black valley.

"Now, I'm going to put some medicine in this IV to help your mommy get better faster."

Davie watched in intense fascination as the nurse filled the syringe from the bottle and stuck it into a connector on the plastic tube that was stuck in Mom's hand.

"So what grade are you in?" the nurse asked Broadie.

"Sixth." He looked away from her eyes. The nurse must have known how his mother had gottten there.

"Do you play any sports?" She paused for an answer.

Broadie fumbled. The idea of sports was a miserable thing that only brought to mind his self-consciousness and the taunting voices of the kids at school. He finally shook his head and looked at the floor.

"I've never known a boy who didn't play sports." She tossed the open syringe into an orange bag that said "Biohazard," made some quick marks on her clipboard, then regarded Broadie as he remained silent. She turned to Mom. "Is there anything I can get you?"

"No," Mom whispered.

"Well, just buzz me if you need anything." She left the room as the rest of the family filed in.

Aunt Cheryl approached Mom holding Alisha. Alisha reached out happily but then fussed when she wasn't allowed to crawl into bed with her mother.

"We're going to give you a blessing before we go," Grandpa said to Mom. He pulled a small flask of olive oil from his pocket. "I hope you don't mind, but we have enough priesthood here to give you a proper anointing this time."

"Okay," Mom said

Uncle Will and Grandpa stood on each side of the bed, and the room became reverently silent. They placed their hands on her head. Grandpa spoke with a tone he reserved for prayers. He promised healing and protection and wellbeing for her children, then admonished repentance. Broadie knew peeking was bad manners, but he couldn't help but watch this event that was considered sacred to most of his family. This was something reserved for times of need and comfort. Grandpa had once put his hands on Broadie's head when he was real sick; it was something in which Dad never took part.

The blessing concluded. Everyone said "amen" in agreement with what had been said and as a way of adding their own faith to the process. Grandpa leaned forward, kissed her, then stepped away from the bed. Mom had tears in her eyes.

The mood in the room settled back to normal. Family gossip spilled into place. Grandpa put his arm around Broadie and gave him a wink.

"I say we better get the little ones back to bed," Uncle Will spoke up.

"Can I come back home now?" Broadie looked eagerly to Grandpa.

"I think so." Grandpa pulled him tighter, then let go.

"I haven't washed any of their clothes yet," Aunt Cheryl said. She gave Alisha a bounce and adjusted her weight on her hip.

"Can't I go home tonight with Grandpa and get the clothes later?" Broadie asked.

"Don't you want to stay one more night?" Uncle Will asked.

"I don't think you can keep a boy from his clubhouse for very long," Grandpa said, with a smile and a wink.

"I don't want to go." Davie began to cry, revealing how tired he was.

"It's okay, honey, you can stay until tomorrow," Aunt Cheryl said, bumping him playfully with her hip.

"You sure you don't want us to take the kids tonight?" Grandma asked.

"Oh, don't worry about it. They can go back tomorrow," Cheryl said.

Mom reached over and caressed Davie's head again. She looked up at Cheryl gratefully.

"We'll take Broadie tonight, then come back for the younger kids tomorrow," Grandma said.

When all were in agreement, Broadie no longer looked at the floor, but vibrated with anticipation of working on the tree house.

* * *

The note to January was still on the window where he had left it. He pulled it off, opened the window for some night air, and wondered if she was awake. He was desperate to know what she'd done to the clubhouse. Her light was off, and her curtains were drawn. He waited indecisively, feeling the tiredness in his legs, and his eyes burned with sleepiness. Finally, he crawled to the ledge, moving carefully, not wanting to be discovered by her parents. He eased himself to her window and tapped lightly.

No response.

He waited, then tapped again.

There was movement behind the curtains; they parted slightly. She peeked hesitantly, then parted them completely. Her hair was ratty, and her sleepy face looked mousy, making Broadie want to laugh. He helped her lift the window.

"You scared me!" Her whisper was strained.

"I'm back." He hoped for a happy response.

She blinked, slightly disoriented. "What's going on?" She walked back to her bed. As she sat, her nightgown pulled up, exposing a skinny thigh. She pushed it back modestly to her knees. Broadie looked away bashfully, surprised at the funny feeling that arose in his stomach. She waited groggily for him to speak.

"I . . . uh, have you been back to the clubhouse?"

She nodded and lay back onto her bed. "I've started it. It's going to be cool." She shifted back into a comfortable position, then became silent.

"How much have you done?"

She didn't answer.

He watched her sleep in the glow of the street light. He knew he should go, but cracking through his tiredness was a new feeling that he didn't understand. It was a needy glow, a wanting to be near her. He watched her shoulder rise and fall as she breathed in the shadows. The glow splashed through him into a maddening heat. His heart beat faster. He eased himself into her room, imagining himself kissing her. The room was clean but still carried the "old people" smell that he associated with her grandmother. He tiptoed closer until he saw the soft skin of her cheek. Sleeping Beauty came to mind. Any minute, someone could walk in to check on her. He was crazy to be standing there in her room in the darkness. He took a step closer and touched her soft blankets. Maybe if he kissed her once the madness would be satisfied. He leaned closer, trying not to lose his balance or jar the bed. He rested one hand on the bedpost, then leaned even closer. He was so close he could smell her hair. His heart pounded, and he realized he was shaking. Her breath was warm, and he lingered, feeling it on his face. He was terrified of waking her up. What if she screamed? What if she hated him and told everyone what he had done? He had to leave, but the strange spell carried him until his lips brushed her cheek. He stepped back slowly.

She was still asleep.

He found the edge of her blanket and gently laid it over her. She stirred. He lifted himself into the night air, across the black chasm, and into his own room.

If he had looked back, he would have seen her raise her head to watch him leave.

He undressed, fumbling at his shirt with shaky hands. He was exultant; he had never kissed a girl before. If he could have gotten away with it, he would have gone back to do it again. The burn in his chest rose to a rapturous longing for her to like him back. He tossed his pants into the laundry basket and crawled into bed. The smell of her breath still tickled his nose. Her warm skin tingled on his lips. He wondered if he would sleep now. He calmed himself by tracing invisible shapes in the spots of glow-in-the-dark paint that Uncle Will had put on the ceiling back in the early eighties. His mind drifted to the day that he had met January, the way she had smiled down at him from the tree.

8

The workmanship was exquisite. Every nail was in its perfect place. The treehouse was like a tiny Victorian mansion. Broadie touched the brilliant, white boards of the windowsill. Outside, there was no neighborhood, only meadows and trees that stretched west to the Oquirrh Mountains. He wanted to cross the verdant valley and climb the mountains. January called up to him. He wanted her to see the valley. The dream disintegrated with a flood of pure morning light.

"Broadie, wake up!" January sat in his window.

He fought sleep away with heavy blinks. White sun gave her a halo. Her ponytail glowed.

"Good morning, sunshine." Her smile was bright and eager.

He stretched and twisted and wiped a numb hand across his sweaty forehead.

"Let's go finish the tree house!" Her chipper voice poked annoyingly at his nerves, but he was happy to see her, anyway.

"Give—ee—a—minah—ooh—ih—up." He yawned widely as he spoke.

"I don't understand Chinese," she said.

"Give me a minute to get up."

She hopped down and walked to his bed. "I worked on it hard while you were gone."

"You didn't tell anyone, did you?"

Her smile faded. "No!"

"Sorry, I just didn't know for sure."

"I promised, didn't I?

Broadie looked down uncomfortably.

"I nailed footholds all the way to the top and started a floor."

"Cool!" He motioned with his hand that she had to turn around.

"Oh." She bashfully climbed back into the window and sat facing out. He put on a clean pair of pants and a shirt.

She turned her head slightly to talk. "Like I said, I got most of the floor done, but I couldn't get the boards up for the walls."

"You can look now."

She turned again to enter the room, favoring a leg. "Ow!" She said. She bent her knee up slowly and picked at a mean-looking scratch. "So where did you go?"

"I went to stay with my cousins."

"Did you know you have a Mohawk?"

He flushed with self-consciousness, scrambled for a comb, and left the room. "I'll be right back." While he stood in front of the bathroom mirror, he wondered for the first time what a girl might think of how he looked. He soaked his head under the faucet, then combed it, taking care to make it look good. When he returned, she was sitting on his bed looking through his coins.

"Sorry, I was just curious. I didn't get a good look at them the other night."

He sat by her, and together they looked into the box. She pulled out the Indian head penny. She turned it this way, then that. "I've never seen one of these before."

"That big one there is an Eisenhower dollar. And that little dime is a silver Mercury dime."

"Wow, I never knew that the money was so different back then."

"A lot of things were different back then. My grandpa tells me a lot of stuff."

She nodded thoughtfully, still looking at the coins. "We better get going." She handed them back and watched him put them into his drawer.

On the way to the clubhouse, they passed the opening in the back fence, followed the trail until they had to drop into the ditch, then skirted the gravel because water had been there the day before. He stopped at a small puddle. "Cool!"

She leaned close to see what he was looking at. "What is it?"

He liked the fruity smell of her hair. "Leeches." He pointed to a large greenish worm lazing on the muddy bottom.

"Eww, gross!" She pulled back.

He grabbed a stick and tried to lift it out of the water.

"Don't touch it!" She backed away further.

He couldn't catch it on the end of the stick, so he stuck the stick into the mud and brought out a small clump. He swung it over to January. "I got it. Watch out, it bites!"

She screamed and ran a few steps back.

Broadie laughed.

"Don't be a jerk!" she fumed, checking herself for splashes of mud.

"I'm just kidding." He dropped the stick and walked on.

"Don't be so mean."

"Sorry." He hissed and meowed like a cat.

She rolled her eyes and pushed ahead of him.

They reached the opening to the rosebushes. He picked up a rock and threw it at the puddle, making a large muddy splash. He picked up another and threw it harder. It glanced off of the muddy water and landed in the grass.

"Don't kill it!" She stopped him from throwing a third rock.

"Why?"

"I think even a leech wants to live."

"It doesn't know it wants to live."

"How do you know?"

"It can't talk, so why do you care?"

"It's alive, and it wants to live."

"It's a stupid worm."

"Everything alive knows in its own way that it's alive." She walked up the embankment, then paused to nurse her knee.

He looked at the rock in his hand. This new idea about life shook him, and guilt rose up in a bitter little squirt. He tossed the rock aside and wondered if he had also inadvertently killed some insect by that action.

The treehouse was a magnificent crown above the clubhouse. She had built it close to what he had in mind, so he put aside any temptation to complain.

"Do you like it?" She put her hands on her hips and looked it over with pride.

He smiled and slipped the hammer that he was carrying into his belt loop. His sweaty hand was making the paper bag of nails damp.

"The boards for the walls are too heavy," she said. "I got a good idea, though, of lifting the boards by rope."

He inspected it like a pleased supervisor. He stepped through the door and loved the smell of dry wood. She leaned into the window. He turned to look at her and was assaulted by a thousand tingles up and down his neck. He shuddered, still feeling the aftermath of his dream. "We could use the rope for my swing," he said.

"That was *just* what I was thinking."

They climbed together to the platform and looked out over the rooftops. He sat the hammer and nails aside. She leaned tiredly against a large branch and brought her knee up to inspect it again.

"What did you do to your knee?" he asked.

"I scraped it a couple of days ago, but it doesn't seem to be getting better." She pulled a Band-Aid away and probed it gently. The skin glowed red hot around the scrape. "It hurts worse today."

He watched her closely until she replaced the Band-Aid. They sat quietly in the shade, feeling the wind's gentle push on the tree. The boards creaked and shifted slightly.

"You know," he said, "I bet if I tied the rope right here and you tied the boards on down there, I could lift them and put them up easy."

"Ok." She closed her eyes and leaned her head back.

"Hold on," he said. He climbed out onto one of the branches, retrieved the rope, then fought off a wave of acrophobia on his way back. He wondered how January could seem so lithe and confident up on the higher branches.

"Okay, we're ready," he said, tying the rope to a strong two-by-four.

"A-huh." She continued to sit with her head back, eyes closed.

"You know," he said. "I've been thinking, I bet if we can see the trail this good from up here, someone down there could easily see up here."

"A-huh."

"Do you think we should camouflage it?"

"A-huh."

He picked up a dry twig that had fallen onto the platform, broke it into small pieces, and flicked them out over the edge. "We could cut branches and hang them over the walls when we get done."

No response.

"Janni?" He shook her shoulder.

"Don't make me move," she said.

"Don't you think we should get started?" he asked.

"I want to take a nap. It's so nice up here."

"Shouldn't we finish the walls before your mom calls you in to eat or something? Once you get back home, she doesn't let you back out."

"Fine." She stood, favoring her knee, and brushed off her shorts. "I hope we have enough nails."

"A-huh." She climbed back down slowly. When she arrived at the bottom, she put her hands on her hips, then took her time selecting the first board.

"Send me up the two-by-four," he said, pointing.

She tied it on, and he pulled the rope, feeling its rough bite with welcome excitement.

"Do you have any brothers and sisters?" he asked, selecting some good nails.

"No, I'm an only child, but I have a lot of cousins close to my age."

"Why didn't your parents have more kids?"

"My mom had some miscarriages and got too scared to try again."

His mother had one between him and Davie. He didn't understand at the time but later overheard a conversation between Aunt Cheryl and Grandma that his mother had taken lots of drugs and got real sick and lost the baby. Aunt Cheryl seemed to think his dad also had something to do with it. He almost wanted to mention it but thought better and kept quiet.

"How many brothers and sisters do you have?" she asked.

"There's three of us. Davie's seven years old, and Alisha is one and a half." Alisha was another touchy subject. Both he and Davie had dark hair and dark eyes, but Alisha had blond hair and blue eyes. He'd also overheard things about that and had noticed that things got worse between his parents after she was born. That was also something he didn't mention.

"I always wished I had a little brother." She tied the rope to another board. Broadie lifted it, then began to nail it into place.

"If we was brother and sister," he said. "I'd be the older brother."

"I bet my birthday is before yours."

"I don't know about that. If you were any older than me, you'd be in the seventh grade this year and not the sixth."

"Oh, yeah?" she said. "When's your birthday?"

"November twenty-eighth. When's yours?"

"September thirtieth."

"Hey, no fair," he said. "What did they do, hold you back?"

"No, I just missed their silly deadline. It's better though. I like being the oldest out of all the kids in the class."

By the afternoon, they had completed four solid walls and part of the roof. He drove in the last nail on a roof board, feeling fatigue in his arm. She sat on the ground, also looking tired. He climbed down, then sat by her. They both looked up, admiring their work. She sat back, exhausted.

"I don't think I could tie another board," she said.

"I think we're done for today."

She lay down looking pale and curled up in the grass.

"Are you okay?" he asked. He lay back, putting his hands under his head. The wind had picked up and the sky was graying from dust that was blowing in from the west.

"I'm tired," she mumbled.

They were silent. Wind roared through the trees, and the large branches swayed gracefully. As he watched her rest, he felt himself falling asleep. He closed his eyes and let himself relax. He couldn't remember ever having had so much fun in the past. His new friendship brought sweetness to his thoughts. He felt now for sure that he could trust her. Having worked together on the tree house proved it to him. For the first time he could remember in a long time, he was aware that he was happy.

The sun was well past its zenith when she shook him to wake him up. Shadows had shifted a little, and the sky was beginning to cloud a little more. He awoke with a burning thirst. He stretched and scratched the itch from the grass on his arms and legs.

"Do you want to have a picnic?" she asked.

He rubbed his eyes. "I thought you were done for the day."

"I feel better now that I got some rest," she said. "I just need to get something to eat."

"Yeah, I think that would be fun. I need a drink. Hey, you know what would be better? Let's go to 7-Eleven and get some nachos."

"Ewe, sick," she said.

"They're not sick. Have you ever tried them?"

"No, but they look all greasy and sticky."

"Come on," he said. "We could get some and bring them back here."

"If we went there, I'd rather get a hot dog and an ice cream bar. I don't have any money anyway. My mom went shopping and got some sandwich stuff. She bought some pop too."

Her mention of "pop" increased his desire for a nice big Coke. "If you go with me, I'll pay." Now he was wondering if he had enough money.

"Okay, as long as you're paying."

He felt the weight of commitment. If he wanted to have his coke and nachos and have her along, too, he would have to fulfill. He thought about his meager savings and weighed it against the Pioneer Day celebration at the park that he wanted to go to tomorrow. What if he invited January along to that? She probably hadn't heard about Pioneer Day, since she hadn't grown up in Utah. "I hope I have enough for the carnival in the park tomorrow. Hey, are you going to the Pioneer Day celebrations?"

"My dad said he might take me, but my mom said that she didn't want to go because she hates crowds and the people around here are too crazy."

He stood and brushed off his clothes. "You can go with us if you want. My grandpa said that he might take me and Davie."

"That would be cool. I just hope my mom lets me go."

The clubhouse disappeared in the trees behind them as they walked back to their homes. He was the first to crawl out from under the rose bushes. He stayed hunched down like soldier and looked around in case anyone (especially John-and-friends) might be coming their way. He satisfied himself that no one was coming and relaxed.

"Would you go, already?" she snapped.

He felt embarrassed and moved quickly, hoping that he hadn't annoyed her. She stepped into the sunlight and stopped for a moment.

"I thought you were in a hurry," he said, sounding angrier than he had meant to.

"I'm just feeling tired again." She started to walk and gave him a tug on the arm. "Let's go before my mom decides that it's time for me to come in for the day or something."

"Why doesn't your mom ever let you do anything?"

"She lets me do stuff. She just thinks that everything around here is dangerous because it's a big city. She's never lived anywhere bigger than back home, and dad says it scares her."

They reached the shed, then stopped by the opening in the fence.

"Wait here while I go get my money," he said.

"No, I need to tell my mom where I'm going."

"What if she says no?"

"She won't say no if I'm just going to the store."

They parted and he went in.

9

The house was empty. Grandma and Grandpa had probably left to get Davie and Alisha. He went into his room and pulled his money from the bottom drawer, then thought about the Pioneer Day festival at the park tomorrow. There would be rides, popcorn, drinks, pizza: everything good he could think of. Best of all were the fireworks when it got dark. Grandma and Grandpa always made them stay home to watch them, but it would still be exciting. He knew he didn't have enough money for everything, and if Mom were home she probably would have given him a few dollars.

There was another alternative. He left his room and walked downstairs. Dad kept change in a big jar for cigarettes and beer. He didn't need it anymore. No one would notice if any turned up missing.

—Where's my quarter-inch socket?

Broadie winced at a shadow of pain in his ribs. He felt an irrational fear that his dad had just been let out and was coming up the walk right now. He would want cigarettes; would come looking for the money; would know some was missing. . . .

His fear turned to anger. Let him find it gone, he thought. Anger solidified into determination, and he convinced himself that Dad owed him something.

He was surprised to find the basement clean. All that was left of the destruction was a hole in the wall, and Grandpa had stripped the wallpaper to prepare it for a patch. The garbage and cigarette odor was almost gone. The grime was out of the kitchen. The sink sparkled. His parents' bedroom was still a mess but not as bad as usual. The blood-soaked towel still rested in the dirty clothes' basket. He lifted it, then tossed it back in revulsion. It had dried stiff.

The jar was hidden behind the closet door. He carried it over to the bed, feeling its heavy bounce as he sat it down. It tipped over, spilling some of the change. He filled his pockets with quarters, losing count at eight dollars—that was more money then he usually had at one time. He expected an extravaganza at the park. He refilled the bottle, then replaced it, covering it with dirty clothes.

He ran back out and saw that January wasn't outside yet like he had hoped. The thought of her not being able to go crept into his mind, and he started to worry. He knocked on the back door, and she opened it, looking disappointed.

"I can't go."

"What? Why?" The need for food and the fatigue from the day's work made his voice sound sharper than he meant.

"She just told you she can't go," Mrs. Larson said from the kitchen.

He sank inside.

"I'm sorry," January said. "We have things to do for the rest of the day, and she was going to call me in anyway."

"Did you ask about tomorrow?"

"Not yet, but I will."

He left her porch feeling more let down than he should have. He went back into his house, got a needed drink of water, and wandered around feeling like he'd lost the desire to go now that she couldn't. He looked in the refrigerator and didn't see anything that would cure his appetite. He went back downstairs and looked at the changes again: everything felt so strange and empty with everyone gone. He realized that this was the first time he had ever been home completely alone.

His parents' room was dark and moody. He sat on the bed wondering if he should put the money back. The coins shifted heavily in his pockets, and he looked around at all of the things that he normally wasn't allowed to see. As Grandpa had books upstairs, so his dad had a library of heavy-metal rock albums. CDs were scattered all over the house, of Metallica, Godsmack, and Ozzy Osbourne. He began to explore through the drawers and the closet until he found a box stuffed under a pile of old, dirty clothes. He unfolded the cardboard flaps, discovering some strange magazines, and wondered if his mother knew about them. At first he thought that they were like the busty swimsuit magazines that he had found lying around their old apartment at times, but he took a closer look and was mildly shocked to see that they weren't wearing any swimsuits. He jumped up, flipped on the light and ran back to study them closer. He knew that these were things that he really shouldn't be looking at, but he spread the magazine out flat onto the floor anyway and studied its centerfold. The woman in the picture looked younger than his mother and a lot prettier. His face flushed and he compared what he was seeing to January: would she grow up someday to look like this?

The wind was starting to blow outside, and it caused creaking noises somewhere upstairs. Thinking that someone might be home, he gathered the magazines up, stuffed them into the box, and hid them back in the closet. After he was done, he poked his head out of the door to the bedroom to listen. The house was still deserted, and he was becoming more unpleasantly aware of his solitude. He also noticed his growing hunger and wished for nachos again. He looked back at the places that he had snooped in, contemplated stealing his dad's bone-handled knife, then thought better of it—Dad might not be in jail very long. As an afterthought, he grabbed a box of cigarettes. He had done it before with the notion lately that he would look older and tougher if he had a cigarette. He wondered what would happen if he smoked one on the way to 7-Eleven. He picked up a lighter from the coffee table.

He stopped in the kitchen to look at the dent in the linoleum where the microwave oven had crashed. The wind blew harder outside. He could feel its movement through the house. The upstairs bathroom door slammed shut as it always did on windy days, but it still startled him and caused him to move quicker. The late afternoon light gave the shadowy environment of the basement a brownish quality. He didn't like to be down there, especially when no one was home. He climbed back upstairs, his desire to explore not yet satisfied, and wandered into his grandparents' bedroom. They had a large closet full of boxes. His grandparents had to move things around to fit everybody in when his family moved in. He climbed to the top shelf and pulled down Grandpa's coin collection. He wasn't supposed to look at it without permission, but what Grandpa didn't know wouldn't hurt him.

He quickly lost interest in the coins and sat back against the dusty clothes in the corner that were worn only during winter. A plastic cover crinkled from one of Grandma's "dry clean only" dresses. He sighed. Above him was one thing that did catch his interest: Grandpa's gun box on the top shelf. He replaced the coins, then brought down the metal box that contained Grandpa's Thirty-eight Special. He knew where the key was hidden. He stepped out of the dusty, stuffy closet and took a deep breath of the fresh air that blew between Grandma's white lace curtains. He opened the top drawer where he had seen Grandpa hide the key when he wasn't looking. It was in an antique case for bifocals. He searched carefully, trying not to displace Grandpa's "special things." He finally found it under an ancient Book of Mormon that had belonged to his great-grandmother. He took another look out the window to make sure they weren't coming back, then he re-entered the closet.

Grandpa had taught him how to shoot in the desert west of the Stansbury Mountains. He remembered being there together with Uncle Will's family, shooting at bottles and an old rusty car door that Jared had pulled out of the sagebrush. Grandpa had put the gun in his hands, unloaded at first, teaching him about the safety catch, then taught him to aim, saying, "Never, ever point it at a person. Never assume that it's unloaded, and never, never, never touch it if I'm not there."

His hands shook with guilt as he sat remembering in the closet, but he was fascinated with the dead-metal weight and the sleek craftsmanship. He liked the oily smell and the sense of dangerous adventure that he got from holding it in secret. Grandpa never kept it loaded, but he turned the cylinder just to make sure.

Grandpa had let him "dry fire" it until he was used to the pull of the trigger. Then came the ammunition. The first BANG had caused him to drop the revolver in fright. He missed the target by a few feet, hitting a far-off boulder.

"Everyone duck!" Uncle Will had said.

A couple of more tries and he had the hang of it. He remembered the kick in the palm of his hand like a hammer slap. He thought about John, and his hands started to shake again. He approached the window. Down at the corner he could see a stop sign. He raised the gun and pointed at it. He depressed the trigger, but it didn't click, because it was on safety. He pointed at a chimney across the street, the neighbor's license plate on the back of their truck, then at a cat that sat lazily in someone's windowsill.

"Pow!" he whispered.

His worry that Grandpa would be back soon finally overcame him. He went back to the closet and put the gun away.

Outside, the air still blew as if a storm were coming. The sky was mostly clear, but heavy clouds gathered in the west. A sky like that would bring a spectacular sunset. Broadie had several hiding places under the eaves of the old shed in his back yard. He took a cigarette from the package that he had stolen from his dad and put it behind his ear; the rest, he put into a hiding place. He then put most of the change in an old dusty jar that he used to keep seashells in. He kept enough in his pockets for nachos.

The neighborhood wasn't very active, except for a man who was watering his flowers. Broadie kept a constant eye out for John-and-friends. If they happened to come his way, he could duck into someone's back yard. The neighbor who watered his flowers stood shirtless in the sun. On his back was a dark brown tan, spray-painted with sunburn. He must have been out all day. Broadie hid his cigarette in a cupped hand, afraid that the man would recognize him and tell his grandfather—worse, January might see him. He reached the end of the street; satisfied that the man had turned away, he put the cigarette into his mouth and lit it. He sucked the smoke into his mouth only (not daring to breathe it), then blew it out slowly, feeling mature. He let it smolder between his fingers, breathing fresh air, and looked around hoping to be seen, but not by someone who knew him.

At the end of the street, he peered out from behind a tall row of bushes. It was empty, except for a man fighting dusty gusts of wind on his bicycle. He turned the corner feeling safe. A tiny dog connected to a large chain sprinted yapping across someone's yard. The chain stopped fully extended before the sidewalk. The "yap-dog" flipped off its feet, then scrambled up to bark again. Broadie thought it was funny, so he did a small dance, provoking the dog into hysterics. It ran back and forth, only inches from his pant legs. He stomped his foot. The dog charged even more violently, flipping off its feet again and letting out a yelp.

"Hey! Get away from my dog!" A tough, leathery woman with a gravelly voice appeared from behind a cinderblock wall. A Harley Davidson bandanna was tied tightly over her head. Broadie sprinted across the street, laughing. "Yeah, you just run, you little shit!" the woman yelled. "Don't let me see you come by here again!"

Broadie showed her his middle finger and won himself a long string of obscenities. He laughed so hard that his side seized with a stitch. He finally stopped and bent over to catch his breath. He still held the smoldering cigarette.

At the 7-Eleven, a dangerous-looking Mexican with a shaven head and tattooed arms stood at the pay phone. Broadie wanted to stare curiously at the designs on his arms but thought better of it. The only other person around was at the checkout counter talking to a lady at the register. He put out his cigarette and tucked it behind his ear. The man left the counter, passing him at the door. Broadie thought that he looked directly at the cigarette and shook his head. Broadie felt powerfully self-conscious. He went to the nacho bar, emptied a bag of chips into a tray, and filled it deeply with cheese and chili. His mouth watered. He filled a Big Gulp cup with ice and Coke and approached the counter. As the lady counted out his change, his worst fears came walking through the parking lot: John, Joey, Steve, and Tim were almost to the door. The lady was nightmarishly slow at counting the change. He looked for an aisle to hide in, but four people were too many to hide from.

The restroom!

"Ma'am, do you have a restroom?" He danced distressfully. She pointed around the corner. He swiped his food off of the counter. As he made it out of sight, the door opened. Steve's boisterous voice carried to the back of the store. Broadie reached for the doorknob to the restroom door. It was locked. Steve's voice was coming closer.

The next door over was a dark utility closet. He pushed it open and slipped out of sight just as Steve found the Slurpee machine. He watched through the crack in the hinges as John joined Steve. Joey wandered through the candy aisle with Tim. Broadie breathed a sigh of relief as they filled their Slurpees and walked to the front. He leaned against the scuffed wall, relaxed, and started eating his nachos. He hoped he didn't have to wait too long for them to leave. He was somewhere that he shouldn't be, but getting caught there would be better than getting caught by John-and-friends. He set his drink on a storage rack and dug in.

The door swung against him, almost knocking the nachos out of his hands. He stiffened as the lady from the counter looked around the door to discover what she had hit. Broadie stared into her face in horror.

"What the . . . what are *you* doing back here?" Her voice was slightly amused, her eyes suspicious.

"I—" Broadie tried to speak with a mouth full of nachos.

"Go on! Git!" She pointed the way out.

He grabbed his drink and shimmied past her. He could still hear Steve's voice somewhere in the store. He had to think quickly. "I was looking to see if there was another bathroom because that one was closed."

She gave him a funny look, turned her suspicious eyes to the area where he had been standing. She did a quick inspection of the rest of the storage room, then turned back to Broadie. "I guess someone left it locked when it was cleaned." She flipped through her keys then opened the restroom door. "Hurry up, then get out."

"Thanks." He closed the restroom door behind him and fought back a wave of panic. He ate a few more nachos, and when he felt he'd waited enough he flushed the toilet. She was still standing there when he came out. She pointed to the door. He walked past her, face glowing red, then slowed down. The guys were still there playing video games.

"Well, go on!"

He hesitated, put his head down, and started walking fast. He held up his drink hoping to conceal his face. His eyes met Steve's. Was there a flash of recognition? He pushed his way through the glass doors into the windy heat. He leaped off the curb and ran as fast as his legs could take him until he cleared the corner. He stopped behind a brick wall and peeked back. No one had followed him. The parking lot was still empty. Dust lifted and curled around him with every gust of wind. Bright orange clouds sailed low overhead. Sunlight cut past an angry thunderstorm that was rising in the southwest. Seagulls would glide in place, then break away, giving in to the force of the wind.

He felt overexposed, that things weren't over yet. He began to jog, taking quick glances over his shoulder. He made it carefully past the "yap-dog" house, staying across the street, hoping the dog wouldn't come barking and give him away. Maybe Steve really hadn't seen him, that it was all his imagination. Maybe he was worrying for nothing. He kept an eye out for any bushes or walls that he could hide behind. He slowed down to eat some more. A garbage can rattled down the street, startling him. No one was coming, and it gave him an eerie sense of desertion. His street was less than a block away.

He took a sip of coke. The "yap-dog" sounded an alarm. He glanced back. John and friends had rounded the corner and were closing in on him at a full run. He became weak in the legs and almost stopped in horror.

Steve, the biggest boy, who had finished the sixth grade late, was ahead of them all. His eyes were bright and bloodthirsty. He was the most enthusiastic about the chase. His large basketball shoes slapped the pavement.

Broadie pushed his legs as hard as they would go. His chest burned. The stitch quickly came back to his side turning into a wicked cramp. He wanted to pass out. It didn't occur to him that he could gain more speed by simply throwing his food aside. Instead, in shock, he held it tighter trying to keep it from spilling. He ran through an opening between the tall bushes on the end of the street. He cut through the corner yard on a diagonal, not knowing if there was a dog or not. In front of him was a chainlink fence with a gate. He lifted the latch in time to see Steve enter the yard. He swung it open, ran through, closing it behind him, hoping it would make an obstacle. He was slowing down, shaking with adrenaline and wanting to throw up. Grandpa's house was only four houses away now. He could make it. They wouldn't follow him into his own house. Steve burst through the gate. Broadie couldn't look back for fear he would slow down. The boys were gaining on him quicker than he'd hoped.

Only three houses to go.

A hard blow between his shoulders.

He sailed forward, grating his elbows mercilessly against the pavement. Cold Coke splashed him in the face. His elbows were instant blowtorches of agony. The nachos survived the tumble, rolling into the yard where the shirtless man earlier had stood watering the flowers. The man was nowhere in sight.

"Oh, no! Did widdo Bowodie Gowodie get hoct?" Steve panted.

Knowing what was coming, Broadie curled into a ball to shield his bleeding elbows

John arrived also panting. "I've got a bone to pick with you, punk!" He kicked Broadie in the ear.

The blow was a white shock. His cheek slid across the pavement.

"That's for hitting me in church!" John kicked him again.

"Get those nachos." Joey said.

Steve picked him up: "What a wuss."

"Hey guys, that's enough." Tim sounded scared.

Broadie tried to stand up and received another kick where his ribs had been sore before. He gasped convulsively for air. He closed his eyes and curled up again. Someone coughed up a sour glob of spit and let it go right into his ear. He reached down and smeared it into Broadie's face.

"Gimme the nachos," John said.

"Dude, do it," Steve taunted.

Broadie looked up in time to see his nachos coming for his face. He ducked. John laughed sadistically as he smeared the cheese into Broadie's hair. Someone poured the rest of his Coke down his pants. He felt the ice cubes slip into his underwear. John stuck the paper nacho dish onto Broadie's back and gave it a little pat. The sticky cheese held it tight. The boys laughed hysterically. He looked up and saw, bathed in dusty red glow of the sunset, the pleasure that pulsated across John's face. John would kill him if he could get away with it.

"Think you're tough now?" John grinned.

"He's got a cigarette." Steve said.

"Make him eat it," Joey urged.

"When will they quit?" Broadie thought through his pain. He couldn't fight. He couldn't run. He was paralyzed with humiliation.

John tried to force the cigarette into his mouth. Instinctively he turned away. Someone grabbed his head to hold it still. Sharp fingernails pulled his lip up, tearing at his gums. John's hand viciously rubbed the grainy tobacco over his teeth. Like a trapped animal, Broadie relaxed his jaw and John's fingers slipped between his teeth. He bit down violently. In a hard panic, John pounded Broadie's face with his other fist. Broadie didn't let go. He bit until he could feel skin break, then ground harder.

John screamed.

Salty, coppery liquid filled his mouth and dripped down his chin—his blood mixing with John's. In gleeful horror he thought he might bite them off.

A blast of stars.

Someone kicked his head like a soccer ball. Stunned, he loosened his grip on John's fingers and floated in a sea of stars.

"Get off him!" A man's voice commanded.

A scuffle.

"I said, get off him!"

"My hand!" John cried out. "My hand!" He cupped his injured fingers and ran away crying.

Tim stared at Broadie in horror, then ran with the other boys. They fled like hyenas.

"Unbelievable!" It was the shirtless gardener. "Margaret, I need some help!" he called to his wife, who was coming down the steps. He helped Broadie to his feet. Tiny rivulets of blood ran down Broadie's arms and dripped from his hands onto the ground like a leaky faucet. He shook with heavy sobs.

10

"Why don't you come down and see what they did to him!" Grandpa bellowed into the phone.

Pause.

"That's no excuse for four against one! He didn't have a chance!"

Pause.

"To hell with his fingers! How do you think they got there in the first place!"

Another pause, then Grandpa's voice was muffled as he walked into the other room and slammed the door.

"Ow!" Broadie screamed as Grandma rinsed cheese sauce out of his hair. She had him leaning over the bathtub awkwardly, trying not to bump his raw elbows. Davie stood at the door, entranced by the injuries.

A door came open, and Grandpa's voice boomed down the hall again. "Don't give me that bull!"

Grandma grimaced at the language but stayed quiet as she swabbed sticky coke and blood from Broadie's arms.

"Oh yeah? I'll have a lawyer by tomorrow!" Grandpa passed the bathroom door.

"Does Broadie need stitches?" Davie asked.

"Davie, get out!" Broadie's voice sounded hollow from the bath-tub. He started to sob again.

"No, Davie, honey," Grandma said with strained patience.

"I think not! The only charges will be against *your* boy. I have a neighbor who witnessed it. They ran him down like a pack of wolves!"

Pause.

"No, I'll tell you where *you* can go!" Grandpa slammed the phone into the receiver.

The pain in Broadie's elbows was maddening. He knelt over the edge of the tub, trying to support his weight with his waist while his ribs sang the Star Spangled Banner. Grandma had stripped him to his Coca-Cola stained underwear.

Grandpa stood in the door. "The nerve of some people! Those dirty—" Grandma stopped Grandpa's cursing with a quick look over her shoulder.

"Grandpa'll help you get changed, then we'll put some gauze on those scrapes," Grandma said, vigorously rubbing his head with a towel.

He looked at his battered face in the mirror. An image of his dad in a drunken tirade flashed through his mind. He winced, trying to blink swollen eyes. He looked like an alien with a purple shiner blooming on his left eye and swollen lips for a mouth. He felt like he had to talk out of the side of his mouth.

"Let's go to the kitchen now, Davie, and help me get the Band-Aids," Grandma said.

Broadie put on clean underwear and some shorts. He hurt too much to put on a shirt. Grandpa was still watching him silently. Thunder rumbled outside; the storm had finally arrived.

"I want you to talk to the sheriff," Grandpa said. He had calmed down a lot since the phone call with John's parents.

Broadie felt weak and tired. He wanted to sleep. The room swam in light and colors mixed together as tears pushed their way up. To talk to the police would only make things worse. School wasn't far away, and he would have to spend every day under their ridicule and every afternoon running for his life just to get home, just like last year, only worse.

Grandpa left the doorway. The dial phone clicked and echoed down the hall like the tickle of rat's feet.

11

The Twenty-Fourth of July Pioneer Day parade babbled from the television in the living room. Broadie awoke late. He hadn't slept well until the early morning, when he finally gave in to exhaustion and slept a hard sleep. His arms were stiff, and he could tell that the gauze bandages had stuck to the scrapes. They would probably have to be soaked off. His left eye barely opened. He rolled over, being careful to not put any pressure on his elbow, and slid out of bed on his stomach.

The night before was a jumbled memory mixed with dreams. A police officer had stopped by briefly, asking questions and taking notes while Grandpa coached Broadie with his answers. He felt anxious about where things would go now. The officer had probably talked to the sunburned neighbor and then to John-and-friends.

Grandma stood at the stove stirring soup while Davie kept Alisha entertained in the living room.

"Good morning." Grandma smiled and left the simmering pan to check him over. "Let's see your eye."

He stood still, allowing her to push his eyelid open. She grimaced. "Did you keep the ice pack on it?"

Broadie nodded. "I can see okay."

Grandma smiled. "Grandpa's gone to get your mother. She's being released this morning."

He smiled and sat groggily at the table. He thought about his clubhouse and January. Her curtains had been closed, and the room looked dark. He still wanted to go to the park and hoped that she had gotten permission. Whether or not *he* would feel up to it was a whole other question that he hadn't quite contemplated yet.

"Come and eat," Grandma called into the living room from the kitchen.

Davie led Alisha over to her highchair. Grandma helped her in. Davie looked Broadie over cautiously. "How come those mean boys beat you up?" He was momentarily distracted as Grandma placed a bowl of soup in front of him.

"They're just that way," Broadie mumbled. He felt floaty and disoriented. He wouldn't normally eat lunch just after waking up.

"Did it hurt?" Davie asked more boldly.

Broadie nodded. He blinked away a hint of dizziness. He hadn't eaten much yesterday, except for a few nachos. His stomach growled violently.

Grandma placed a plate in front of him, then folded her arms. "Who wants to say the prayer over the food?"

"I will," Davie answered eagerly. He bowed his head reverently and folded his arms like Grandma. "Dear Father in Heaven, please bless this food, and bless Broadie to get better. Amen." He smiled bashfully and began to eat.

The smell of hot chicken noodle soup was overwhelming as Broadie dug in, slowly at first, then with gusto. Davie's prayer stirred his emotions. He was a sweet little boy, and Broadie felt guilty for not spending time with him like a big brother should. He also didn't feel worthy to be prayed for. He had stolen his dad's money and had smoked half a cigarette. He knew both things were bad and wondered distantly if maybe God had punished him by letting John-and-friends get to him. Yesterday's chase rolled repeatedly through his mind like a broken record. Everything that possibly could have gone wrong had gone wrong. He should have ducked away somewhere until he was sure he was safe. He could have ran to someone's porch and pounded on their door. Bullies always cower when adults are around. He also could have run down to the other corner where there was an opening in the fence that led to the clubhouse.

When Mom came home and saw Broadie, she became distraught, thinking that his dad had been let out of jail and had gotten to him. Grandma calmed her down and explained the situation. She hugged him, then sat back in the big chair with a hollow, defeated look. She moved around carefully in a neck brace and still sported a bandage that held her jaw shut. For the next few weeks she would only be able to eat liquids, like soups and shakes or whatever she could get through a straw. Sometimes when she spoke, drops of spit popped out from between her clenched teeth.

Later that day, Mom and Alisha went downstairs for a nap. Davie stayed upstairs and watched Disney videos. Broadie was told to stay home and watch Davie, not just for Davie's sake, but for his own safety. He was terribly disappointed and tried to argue, but Grandma wouldn't have it and threatened to ground him if she had to.

It was stuffy inside. The air conditioning wasn't working again, and he could smell the barbecues and feel the excitement of the holiday around him. He felt surprisingly better after getting something to eat. He had looked forward to the Twenty-fourth of July and now felt like it was ruined. Someone burned a string of firecrackers close by. He went to his room and carefully fought a shirt over his soreness. Injuries or not, he couldn't take being cooped up. He picked up his small savings, then slipped out the door. Summer heat closed tightly around him as he looked back, hoping not to get caught. He walked into the back yard and saw Mrs. Larson watering her garden. He was about to ask if January had gone to the clubhouse, but he felt uncomfortable because she had acted like he wasn't fit to play with her daughter. He moved quietly past her and down the hot, dusty trail behind the houses.

The sky overhead was the high and dark blue of late afternoon. Grasshoppers escaped his advance in crazy parabolic scatters as his legs swished through dry knee-high grass. A bumblebee buzzed indolently among the thistles lining a wooden fence. The thin fragrance of a distant field fire carried lightly in the breeze. Being alone wasn't as fun anymore. He liked January's company and had hoped they could go together to the park, where all the fun was. He would have been safer in the large crowd. He had to at least find her and tell her he couldn't go.

The clubhouse stood as they had left it the day before, and, to his surprise, the tools they had left remained where they were dropped. He figured Grandpa would say something if he missed his hammer. He would have to bring them back soon, though.

"Hi." January waved from up in the tree house.

He would have waved back, but it hurt too much to raise his hands. He stopped wondering with what horror she might interpret his appearance. His neck ached as he watched her climb wordlessly down the trunk of the tree. She reached the ground and stared at him until he spoke.

"I'm sorry" was all he could say. He hadn't expected to start crying. He turned to walk away, terribly ashamed at how awful he looked.

"Wait," she said, trying to catch up.

It was a mistake coming out, and now he was embarrassed more than he could endure, but he couldn't bring up the energy to run.

"Wait," she said again, cutting off his path.

"No," he sobbed, and pushed his way forward.

"Please, don't go away!" Fear was in her voice—or something close to it.

"What . . . what happened?"

He stared at the ground still unable to talk.

"Did your dad get out and—"

"No!" He cut her off quickly. He didn't mean to snap at her. "No, it was John and his friends; it was four against one." He could have embellished his story to come out a conquering hero, but the pathetic truth had already been whispered all over the neighborhood. January would find out anyway.

"You mean that red-headed loud-mouth at church?"

Broadie nodded, then looked away, trying to hide his shame.

"Why did they do that to you?"

Broadie shrugged then shook his head. "They've always been like that, since I moved in. It's been worse lately."

Her face darkened. She looked pensively at the ground. A string of firecrackers crackled in the neighborhood close by. "I don't like the kids around here very much."

They sat silently in the warm shade of the particle board roof. The railroad-tie bench was weathered smooth but still threatened a sliver in some places. He sat carefully, looking up at the tree house. His neck flashed a pain, and he straightened out with a grimace. His elbows hurt too bad to climb.

Pops, whistles, and tatters, some distant, some close, continued to echo around the neighborhoods. His dad had taken him once to Evanston, Wyoming, to get the good illegal fireworks. They had smuggled them, along with alcohol and some videos that he wouldn't let him see, across the state line like moonshiners, wrapping them in sleeping bags, and burying them in coolers in case they got pulled over. Those were the fun times, when Dad didn't drink so much. Davie was too young to go then, so it was just the two of them together, driving through the Uinta Mountains. He wanted to tell her about these things, but it was still hard for him to talk without crying.

A mosquito whined annoyingly past his ear, and he absent-mindedly slapped at it, winning himself a tearing pain in his elbow. He cried out and babied it until the pain died down to a quiet throb.

She jumped when he yelled. "Are you okay?" She reached down and picked at her sore knee, like she did yesterday.

"I'm fine. How's your knee?"

"It's worse. It's hurting to walk now sometimes." She stared at it for a moment longer, then changed the subject. "I'm so bored I can't stand it. I've never been to a big carnival before."

"Let's go," he said, feeling rebellious.

"I can't do that. I'll get in trouble."

"Why?"

"My dad won't be back until late, and my mom told me to stick around here."

"I'm too sore to climb, but I feel like some cotton candy." He was suddenly furious inside and wanted to cry again.

"How far away is the park?" she asked.

"Only a couple of blocks. We could go and come back before anyone ever noticed." He paused, slowly turned his sore neck to look at her. "I'm going."

"Have fun," she said, looking disappointed.

He felt bad leaving her behind, but anticipation tickled his stomach. Maybe he could play one of those games where you knock over the bottles and win her something special. What if she got all excited and hugged him the way women did when men brought them roses? He felt funny thinking of her that way. He crept to the shed, watching the quiet house, until he was able to find his criminal stash, then followed the trail back past the rosebushes to the opening in the fence that led to the road. He hunched down, trying not to scrape his sore elbows, and started to push himself through.

"Wait!" January called from the ditch.

He pulled himself back and turned stiffly around to look.

"Wait for me. I'm going."

The gray-green pines of Liberty Park appeared fearless over the swarming masses of people. Cars lined the streets tightly, and he felt himself become more and more anonymous the closer they got. Police stood at each intersection trying to weave order out of the chaos of those who fancied finding a parking space close to the park, and those who discovered the impossibility of such and were trying to wind their way back out and into the neighborhoods. A shiny, purple low rider filled with tough looking Latinos with shaven heads boomed its rap music past the conservative families that traveled along the sidewalk.

The park was a patchwork of blankets and coolers. Music from a rock band reverberated over the crowd. Seagulls scavenged on the edge of the large pond, competing with the resident ducks for popcorn and breadcrumbs. The water was green and cloudy, and, where they walked, a small navy of beer cans drifted against the cement shore. A teenage girl wearing tight shorts and a bikini top danced inside a circle of drum-beating hippies. He watched her with deepening interest as she moved dazedly, entranced by the pulsating rhythms. Her stringy hair swung limply from side to side. His gaze panned the colorful crowd, then spring back to the bikini top. The way she moved brought his attention to the curve of her breasts. His face flushed, and his heart beat quickly. January also seemed to be interested in the strange group of people.

He broke away, feeling weak in the knees, and felt an insane need to go back and drink more of the view. Her long slender legs moved lithely in his mind. Her hips swayed maddeningly until he had to fight to catch his breath. An image of the magazine picture he had found yesterday flickered through his thoughts. He was surprised and guiltily frustrated at such a powerful reaction. It lingered in his head like pungent perfume. He was embarrassed and self-conscious, wondering irrationally if January could read his thoughts.

"Look, they have a Ferris wheel!" she said, pointing excitedly.

He was glad that she had distracted him at that moment. "Check this out," he said, pulling a hand full of quarters from his pocket.

Her eyes widened. "Where did you get all the money?"

"Let's play some games first," he said with confidence.

They wandered until he found the game booths. They passed through noisy throngs until they found the game where you could pop balloons with darts.

"One dollar gets you three darts. Hit three in a row and you get the stuffed animal." The pitchman hollered.

Broadie waited until it was his turn. He counted a dollar from his bulging pocket.

"Just one dollar!" the pitchman schmoozed, holding darts between the fingers of one hand and a wad of bills in the other. He handed Broadie three darts in exchange for four sweaty quarters.

January pointed out a massive giraffe that hung like an executed criminal from an aluminum pipe that supported the overhead tarp. On the sides were progressively smaller gorillas, elephants, and tigers. Purple monkeys hung in abundance along the back wall by Velcro hands. Their eyes and tongues hung lustily at the crowd. Broadie raised his arm to throw. He winced in pain but let the dart go. It hit its mark, and a piece of orange balloon flipped limply out of sight.

"A hit by the boy who was hit by a Mac truck!" the pitchman hollered. "Two more to go and you get the stuffed animal. Add another dollar and double your chances."

Broadie looked up at the lonely giraffe, then sent another carefully aimed dart into a doomed balloon. There was a twinge of pain in his neck and he felt a swim of dizziness.

"Another hit!"

The last balloon disintegrated, revealing a slab of heavily pock-marked particleboard. The pitchman gracefully plucked a small purple monkey off of the pipe and tossed it to Broadie. He tried to catch it but it fell into the trampled grass.

"But I wanted the giraffe." Broadie said picking it up, both elbows burning fiercely. He set it on the counter.

"That's four in a row." The pitchman motioned to someone else in the line.

"But I just got three. All I need is one more."

"That's four threes in a row, son. One more dollar gets ya the parrot. Keep your luck streak going?"

"No, thanks."

"I think it's cute, she said, taking it from his hands and playfully wiggling its face. They walked away, letting the pitchman scam some other poor fool.

His elbows screamed as he scuffed his feet against the ruined turf where thousands of feet had walked it bare of grass. A purple snowcone lay spilled and melting into the cracked dirt. January, for some reason, didn't seem to be doing so good, either.

"Should we go on the ride?" he asked.

She nodded, smiling tiredly, and was beginning to limp.

The Ferris wheel line was long, but they both knew that they had to ride it at least once this summer. A gaggle of girls, not much older than January, heckled and gossiped in front of them. Broadie found himself studying their smooth, summer-tanned legs and tight shirts, then looked down at January, who had just sat down and was picking at her knee. She was starting to look a little like them but was much thinner. He tried to imagine again what she would look like in a year or two. It again occurred to him how strange it was to be thinking like this.

The one directly in front of him, in a thin tank top, turned to glance around. Her gaze fell upon Broadie. He noticed the small swells of her chest, then met her eyes. She looked him up and down with a horrified fascination that she tried to conceal, then dismissed him like a bad painting. He felt sad being reminded again of how he looked. For awhile he had forgotten his troubles.

Their turn finally came, and they stepped onto the white line as an empty seat rolled into position. A tattooed bald man, pierced in every place possible, swung the guard bar out. They sat together and were lifted a few feet into the air. They moved up one place. Broadie looked back as a couple of high school kids holding hands sat back into their chair. The tattooed man swung their gate, and he thought of the "Illustrated Man" in *"Something Wicked This Way Comes,"* by Ray Bradbury. He shivered in the heat, picking at the gauze on his elbows.

They were finally moving. As they were lifted above the trees, he saw the shadows of late afternoon stretch out beneath him. The girls that had been in front of them were now behind them. He heard them cackle, and he turned to look at them, feeling an urge to spit.

"Oh my gosh! That's Tommy Land!" The oldest looking girl squawked out like an exotic bird, pointed, and waved at an older boy wearing stylish clothes. He had a feminine look to his eyes—like a model.

"I see him!" The girl who had looked at Broadie pointed excitedly.

"Eww, its Tommy!" they bawled out in unison, ending their chorus in giggles.

"They sound so stupid," January said, annoyed. "I hope I never act like that."

He hadn't realized how quiet she had been until she spoke. The wheel began to turn the other way, this time not stopping for passengers. They reached the top again. He was still watching the girls as they rocked their chair and screamed dramatically as it overcorrected. They were trying to draw attention to themselves. He spat, missing them by inches. By the third time around he felt nauseous and just wanted the ride to end. The girls' screams jabbed his nerves, and his head and neck ached from turning around. January moaned and leaned over the side. She didn't seem to be feeling very good, either.

The ride finally stopped. They walked away, both of their heads pounding in the sun. He lost another dollar at the knock-our-bottles booth, then bought two puffs of cotton candy. January nibbled at hers a little, then held it loosely at her side as if she had lost interest in it. The hemp-vested drum-beaters and their bikini dancer had moved on somewhere else. A police officer on horseback with a shiny white helmet stood in their place.

"Let's sit down," she said, as they reached a vacant spot under a big tree.

"Fine with me." It was cooler there, and he needed to sit down just as bad.

She immediately curled up in the moist grass and closed her eyes. She couldn't have fallen asleep that fast, could she? He locked at her knee, which was swollen and glowed a mean red around the Band-Aids. He didn't feel right about the way she was acting. He gave her some time and watched the crowds of people walk by. Slowly he settled against the trunk of the tree until he was comfortable. Somewhere the drum-beaters started up again.

"Hey!" He shook her.

She moaned weakly.

"Let's go back now."

No answer.

He stood, scratching his ribs, and gave her a soft shove with his foot. She grunted and swiped a sluggish hand back at him.

"Hey!" He bent down and shook her harder. She was terribly hot and wasn't acting right. She waved him on, and her hand fell weakly onto the ground.

"Hey, are you okay?" He rested a light hand on her shoulder. She pushed it away and moaned, "Don't."

A gust of wind made the trees above them sway. His uneasiness increased and he looked around at the crowds again. He felt slight relief as he spied the policeman on horseback again. If she was too sick to move, he could wave him over.

"Hey, don't do this." He shook her harder.

"Do-o-n't!" Her voice broke, on the verge of tears.

He coaxed her until she made an effort to stand. He reached both arms under her armpits, and she struggled to her feet. She cried out in pain when she tried to support her weight on her sore leg.

"Lean on me," he said.

She rested an arm over his shoulder, and they began their walk back home. They reached the street. She stopped, wobbled then lurched forward with a hard heave. The contents of her stomach splashed across the muddy gutter. He tried to avoid the warm yellowish liquid, but some splattered onto his shoes. She turned toward him, blinked with shock, then started to cry. A slimy chunk stretched and dripped from her chin. Broadie fought to suppress a violent urge to join her in the fun. She threatened to sit, and he started her walking again. The din from the park slowly diminished as they struggled down the street.

They reached the opening in the fence, he helped her through, and the last stretch down the trail seemed the most grueling. She cried out with every step and begged to sit down. They finally reached her back yard, and Mrs. Larson was still working in her garden.

"Mom!" January's voice was a small squeak.

"Janni, honey, where have you been?" Mrs. Larson dropped her hose and walked briskly across the yard, wiping her hands on her pants. "What's wrong?"

"I'm sick, and my knee hurts real bad."

"Honey, let's see." She knelt down and tugged at the dirty Band-Aid.

"Ow! Mom, don't!"

"Janni, it's infected! We're going to the doctor right now." She turned curtly to Broadie. "Friends have to go home!"

Broadie was embarrassed. He wanted to run, but in an act of defiance walked into her yard, over to the hose, and washed his shoes off. He waited for a rebuke from Mrs. Larson, but she had lost all interest in him as she led January to the car. He sneaked into his own back yard, hoping not to get caught by his grandparents, but too much time had passed, and he knew that he was in big trouble. He worked hard on his excuses as he slipped between the houses. He carried the purple monkey and Janni's cotton candy, knowing she would want them back when she felt better. He couldn't get caught with them, or they would know for sure that he had been to the park. In his own house, he could see that Mom was upstairs in the kitchen with Grandma. Tinkering sounds echoed from the garage where Grandpa was busy with one of his projects.

He was in too much pain to crawl into his bedroom window and had a powerful urge to urinate. He finally stashed the loot through his windowsill, then walked boldly through the back door. The creaky spring pulled and slammed it behind him with a loud crack.

Mom looked up and regarded him stoically. Grandma's voice warbled angrily again: "Where have you been?" Alisha tugged at Grandma's pant leg and held up an interesting component to one of Davie's toys.

"Hold on, be right back." Broadie ran for the bathroom. He heard the conversation in the kitchen. They were discussing whether he should be grounded or not when Grandma's voice was cut off by the flush. His shoulders itched from sunburn. He looked into the mirror at the bruises that had settled in like long-term guests. Old yellow from previous bruises rimmed the new purple around his swollen eye. His lips were still too sore to smile. The mirror told him cold truths that he didn't want to be reminded of. He moved slower this time. The wounds inside were just as raw as those on the surface—though he couldn't articulate it, he knew somewhere deep down that these were the kind that wouldn't heal as quickly. Diversion was only a temporary painkiller, but a good one. He felt no guilt for going to the park.

"We've been looking for you all afternoon," Grandma said. She wiped her hands with a clean dishtowel, then folded her arms in her I–mean–business pose.

"I was out in my clubhouse."

"Your grandpa went looking for you back there," Mom said, resigned.

"I guess I didn't hear—" Broadie swallowed with an audible click.

"Did you go to the park?" Grandma drilled the question.

Broadie shook his head.

Grandma and Mom regarded him, silently suggesting strong maternal similarities in posture and features. Mom broke the silence. "Why did you go?" It was clearly hard for her to speak.

"I didn't. I was—"

"We needed you to help watch your brother and sister—not to mention that its possible you could've run into those boys again. You were told to stay here. I'll tell your grandfather you're back." Grandma walked to the back door with a slight limp. Her knee was bothering her again.

Shame trickled into his stomach. It was bad enough to know it himself, but it was worse to have to face Grandpa. He turned to leave.

"You stay here! I'm not done yet!" Mom spoke angrily through clenched teeth. Small drops of spit sprayed in his direction.

"I didn't do anything!" He tried to assert himself, but sounded weak and whiny.

"You left without permission. You didn't tell anyone where you were going. You had me worried sick. How did I know you weren't hurt somewhere?"

Grandpa walked through the door. Grandma wasn't far behind him. He moved briskly to where Broadie stood, smoothly pulled the cigarettes Broadie had stashed behind the shed out of his pocket, and flicked them onto the table. Broadie's stomach churned a frozen slush while his face burned hot. The silence was charged and dangerous. Davie peeked quietly around the corner.

Mom looked equally ashamed.

Grandpa gestured defeatedly into the air with his hands, made an attempt to speak, then paused. His face twisted and rumbled with emotion. As sudden as a change of thought, he turned and walked back out the door letting it slam behind him. The air in the room was suffocating.

"Davie, go on!" Broadie commanded.

Davie ducked back into the living room.

"No, *you* go on!" Mom now seemed more like a petulant teenager passing the buck. The silent message about the cigarettes was directed toward her as much as Broadie. "You're grounded for a week. That means no fireworks tonight. You'll stay in your room!"

"But—"

"Now!"

Broadie waited until the yelling was over with before he retrieved his loot from the park. He didn't want to get it confiscated as part of the punishment. His body ached, telling him that he shouldn't have gone out. Though it was still early afternoon, he was exhausted and fell asleep as soon as he lay down.

He awoke fully to the shrill whistle of a firework. It was getting dark, and he heard the Larsons' car pull into their driveway. It seemed like forever until the light in January's room turned on. He wanted to talk to her and find out if everything was all right, but he was afraid of her parents. The way her mother had been acting toward him lately made him feel like he had to sneak around. Through dim, orange twilight, he occasionally looked to see if Mrs. Larson had left January's room yet. From his angle he could see her leave, then come back, puttering around to make her daughter comfortable. He could imagine her reaction if she came back to find him peering through her window.

Finally she was gone long enough that he dared to approach. He ignored his sore elbows and climbed carefully across to her side and knocked quietly. She threw aside her covers and limped to her window, She glanced back cautiously at the door, then quietly lifted the glass. Her eyes were dark and puffy and blinked against her waxy face in surprise.

"You're going to get in trouble," she whispered.

"So?" he said defiantly. "I can't get in any more trouble than I'm already in." He looked warily at her door, causing her to glance back in reaction.

"You're going to get *me* in trouble."

"Why?" He challenged. He was feeling even more defiant.

"I'm supposed to be in bed."

"What if you want to be up?"

She sighed in a way that told him that she didn't feel like arguing. He suddenly felt stupid for pushing harder than he had meant to, but he still thought that he had a point.

"So what happened at the doctor's?"

She sat down tiredly on a shiny cedar chest. "I have a bad infection, and I'm supposed to be in bed."

"Sorry," he said disappointedly. He pulled himself out of her window and started to reach out for his own.

"Where are you going?"

"You sound like you don't want me to be here."

"Well, now that you're here. . . ."

He paused. The sunset was gone, and mosquitoes whirred around him in the darkness. He slapped at them uncomfortably, trying to avoid pain in his elbow. Some bites on his neck and arms began to itch.

"I saved your things," he said, climbing back into his window to retrieve them. When he brought them back over, her eyes sparkled, and her face brightened. The circles around her eyes seemed to fade.

"I was so sick I forgot," she said, dangling the monkey by its ropy arms. She then pulled the plastic off the cotton candy and took a small bite. "I can't eat this." She savored it as if it were the first time tasting it.

"Why can't you?"

"It has to do with the antibiotics. Look, they gave me an I.V." She pointed to a bruise on her arm. "They were going to keep me overnight, then they changed their minds. And look here." She lifted up her pant leg. A new gauze patch covered her swollen knee where the Band-Aics had been earlier. "It still hurts. I can't bend it very well even though they gave me painkillers. They said I have to go back tomorrow."

A low boom echoed from far away, then another. A red image of her window shone then faded against her far wall.

"Look. Fireworks." She pointed out between the houses.

He turned sideways and sat at an angle where he could watch. She pulled herself closer and leaned against him so she could see. Instantly he wanted to stroke her hair or rest his arm over her shoulder.

"Oh, that was a pretty one!" She looked up at him, her face reflecting purple, pink, then white. A soft boom followed.

He could kiss her right then. He remembered the warmth from her breath and wondered what she would do if he leaned down right then and touched his lips against hers. His heart beat faster, but he sat motionless. The small shift of her head against his leg was all he sensed. Bright green sparks burst into an umbrella and slowly descended, winking out one by one behind the silhouettes of trees across the street. Though part of the show was hidden behind the corner of the house, he felt like he wasn't missing anything. Neighbor's voices and the smell of barbecues carried on the warm air.

January got up and switched off her lamp. "It's prettier this way."

The world was yellow, then blue, and then purple. Heavy booms followed by bright photoflashes were felt more than heard.

"I like the louder ones," Broadie whispered.

He stretched out . . . reached behind her in the flickering finale . . . brought his hand closer . . . then closer to her shoulder. . . . He wanted to touch her. A few of her hairs tickled his fingers. He stroked their fine tips but was loath to be discovered.

The last glitter fell. They waited in anticipation for more until the bluish glow of the park lights came on and illuminated the ghostly smoke tendrils that slowly drifted in the sky.

"That was neat," she said weakly. "I need to lay down." She rocked forward to stand up. He let his hand dangle innocently. She shuffled over to her bed.

"Good night," she said, curling up to her pillow.

12

The soles of his feet tingled when he landed on the ground below his window. He backed up and pushed himself as flat as he could against the bricks. His door clicked. He froze, not wanting to give himself away.

"Broadie? Broadie?" Grandpa called into an empty room.

"He was just here." Grandma's voice joined Grandpa's. "Did he have his church clothes on?"

"He was supposed to. Well, I'm not waiting for him," Grandpa said in a there-he-goes-again tone of voice.

"Broadie?" Grandma's voice was more distant.

He wasn't wearing his church clothes. He had left them in his closet. Instead, he wore his faded Levis with the hole in the butt and a hand-me-down T-shirt that probably came from Jared.

"Michelle, is Broadie down there?" Grandpa's voice was disappearing.

"No, he isn't." Mom was coming up the stairs. Her voice became clearer the closer she got.

"I'll check outside." Grandpa said.

That's when he ran. He loped like an animal fleeing a hunter's bullets. Thin, morning spider webs broke across his face. Dew soaked his shoes and pant legs as he ran past the shed, through the fence, and down the trail to the place where he didn't have to face persecution. Solitude invited him with open arms.

Part II

1

Grandma gave Grandpa a playful slap on the arm; as they sang "Happy Birthday" to Great-Grandma Grace, he tried to harmonize and sounded silly. Grandma Grace sat hunched in her wheelchair and didn't give much indication that she knew or cared about what was going on. Another old lady, her roommate, stared blankly at the visitors. The room was cheerily furnished, but underneath it all it was still stoically hospital. The disinfectant smell that permeated the building didn't mask the sickness and old age.

"Here you go, Mamma Grace," Uncle Will said, setting a piece of cake down in front of her and placing a fork in her hand. She nibbled vacantly.

Uncle Will dutifully cut the cake (yellow cake with chocolate frosting, Broadie's favorite) and passed pieces first to the kids, then to the adults. Kassicy was restlessly bored and frequently looked at her cell-phone. Davie and Tommy had already run out of the room with their pieces of cake. Richard, the oldest grandchild, had just arrived and, like an ambassador, sent greetings from Uncle Ned and Aunt Grace (named after Momma Grace) Odell—the very richest side of the family, indeed, and somewhat of a mystery.

Momma Grace's roommate didn't get a piece of cake. She sat in her wheelchair at a small distance from the party. Broadie watched her eyes. They seemed blank at first, but he found that the more he tried to look away from her, the more his lazy gaze was drawn back. Normally he would have dismissed her as something that belonged in the realm of the adults and gone on about his own business. But he saw something in the way she watched the crowd. There was a shimmer of awareness and emotion that she knew what was going on around her, and, inadvertently or not, she was excluded.

A nurse walked in. "Is it Gracie's birthday?" She turned to Grace: "Gracie, is it your birthday today?" Her voice was cherry syrup. It rose ten decibels even though everyone knew Grace could hear just fine. Mamma Grace slowly raised her head to speak. The nurse patted her on the shoulder, then turned away, leaving Grace talking in her quiet mumble. She picked up some folders and quickly left the room.

Broadie sprung from his seat without thinking and caught her at the door. "Ma'am!"

"Yes?" she said hurriedly, but smiled.

"Uh . . ."

The nurse turned to leave.

"Can that old lady over there have cake?"

"No."

"Why?"

"Not unless you want to feed her," the nurse said impatiently.

"I think she wants some."

"Well, why don't you leave one for her, and when someone gets to her they could feed her."

"What's her name?"

"Fanny." The nurse left.

"Thank you," he said to her back.

He went back to the table, and Mom handed him his piece of cake. He sat down, lifted his fork, then looked at Fanny. Their eyes met, and he saw her understanding. Her eyes drifted to the cake, then to the others. She wanted to participate. He didn't want to look at her. Helplessness was ugly. His mouth watered for his cake, and he was anxious to leave. He licked his fork and let it sink into the moist sweetness. Aunt Cheryl had made the cake from scratch, using one of Momma Gracie's old recipes. He lifted the bite, and his eyes raised with his hand. Fanny closed her eyes. He knew with certainty that she had closed her eyes to something she couldn't have. In her posture was sadness. He carried his plate over and set it down in front of her. Her eyes opened. He went back to get another. The table was still crowded and he waited for an opening. He looked back, and Fanny stared fixedly at her plate. The muscles in her right arm flexed weakly. Her hand rose an inch then fell. She breathed quickly, gumming her lips in frustration.

Uncle Will and Grandpa still blocked the way. Uncle Will's kids were going back for seconds—except for Kassidy, who said she was on a diet. Grandpa stepped back to make room for Jared. Broadie moved out of the way. He would just be patient until he got an opening.

Fanny had lifted her hand to the edge of the table. Her eyes watered with determination. Trembling fingers reached, slid back, then reached again for the plate.

Uncle Will bragged loudly about Jared's joining the junior football league and their summer camp, then complained about Kassidy's new boyfriend. Kassidy gave Uncle Will a snotty look and popped her gum. Broadie noticed her tanned shoulders under her spaghetti-thin tank top straps. He wondered if Aunt Cheryl really approved of her dressing like that. She crossed one smooth, tanned leg over the other, then folded her arms childishly. He suddenly wished she wasn't his cousin.

Fanny's fingers touched her plate. She couldn't quite reach the edge to pull it closer. She only bumped it further away.

Uncle Will laughed, then Grandpa erupted into a belly laugh.

With one last thrust of her disobedient shoulder, Fanny's hand rested on the end of the plate. It tipped up and started to slide to the edge. The fork bounced to the floor. Broadie missed the fork but he rescued the plate before it fell.

"Here, let me help," Broadie said.

She tried to raise her head to look at him. He picked up the fork (it looked clean) brushed it off on his shirt, then started to feed her. She was slow to respond, but, once she was able to open her mouth, she relished the cake. As he fed her bites, he talked to her. He knew she listened. He didn't want to sound condescending like some people did when they talked to the old and infirm. She chewed each bite and listened. When she finished the last bite, she tried to speak. Her eyes were bright. Broadie smiled and rested a hand on her shoulder. The table was clear, so he went back for a piece. Aunt Cheryl had closed the cake box and was gathering the remaining plates and napkins.

"Don't take it away yet," Broadie said.

"You're too late for seconds. It's all gone," Cheryl said busily.

He felt disappointed but looked back at Fanny. Her head was up and there was life in her eyes.

2

Late August sun roasted the black interior of Grandpa's Chevy Impala. It was heavy and merciless. Broadie rolled down his window and put out his hand, letting it surf the wind. A Wal-Mart bag with new school clothes crinkled between his feet. Davie watched him intently, and soon his window was down also.

"Put your hand in!" Mom spoke automatically. Her jaw was still wired, but that didn't stop her.

He ignored her, letting his hand drift up then down. He thought it looked like a snake.

"Do what your mother tells you!" Grandpa said firmly. He didn't turn around, but there was enough authority in his voice that the hand came in and stayed that way. He rolled his window up a couple of inches, and so did Davie.

"That's better," Mom said. She looked back just to make sure, then turned her head forward again, her new hairdo shifting lightly over her shoulders. She had dyed it a light shade of blond. It was still hard, getting used to her new look. She had lost weight while her jaw was healing and had started wearing make-up every day. Today she had bought a new outfit, and Grandpa observed that the skirt was too short. She promptly reminded him that she was almost twenty-eight years old and could make her own decisions. The atmosphere had been uncomfortably quiet around them ever since.

A radio talk-show host lectured a caller about the hypocrisy of some politicians in Congress. The caller argued back stubbornly.

"Blasted Democrats!" Grandpa fiercely switched off the radio.

"I'm a Democrat." Mom turned to Grandpa with the look she always gave him before they got into an argument.

"Well, that's your whole problem there," Grandpa said with a smirk.

"Oh, don't *even* get me started."

"I don't have to. It's self-evident."

Broadie tensed in the back seat, ready for a volley of screaming, but the banter had the opposite effect of calming the atmosphere. Soon Mom went off on the environment and gay rights, but stayed carefully away from anti-Christianity. Grandpa silently shook his head, then spoke, interrupting Mom's argument: "So, Davie, you excited about the second grade?"

"Yes!" Davie said enthusiastically.

Mom socked Grandpa in the arm playfully for changing the subject. Grandpa dramatized, "Oh, ouch, get me an ambulance, quick!"

Davie laughed. Broadie sat silently in the wind from the window.

"How about you, Broadie Bear?"

He closed his eyes and didn't answer.

They pulled into the driveway, and everyone went into the house, except for Broadie. There was activity in January's yard; it looked interesting. Shapes moved to and fro behind the bushes and the pear trees that lined the property. Sweet barbecue smoke drifted past his nose and down the neighborhood. Happy voices mingled, peppered with laughs; bursts of moans and cheers from a volley-ball game.

He sat in the house-shadow that covered the back porch. The porch was rough under his hands. Raw history showed through the concrete mask that crumbled away from the edges, exposing large, red sandstone blocks. It had never been painted like the rest of the house, and he often wondered what he would see if he could look back through time from the perspective of the old porch: the family gatherings; barbecues; cousins chasing around the yard; hide-and-go-seek; uncles and aunts as young teenagers, as young kids; the nineteen-seventies with Uncle Will's Star Wars action figures; the sixties, when Grandma and Grandpa were a young couple; the fifties: new additions to the neighborhood; the forties: blue stars and gold stars hanging in the windows; the thirties, where the old houses stood alone surrounded by farms and orchards; the twenties, then the tens with unpaved roads and an outhouse by the old shed; the bigger farms before the house was built in the eighteen nineties, then sagebrush and Indians.

His daydream puffed away with the barbecue smoke as January emerged through the hole in the back fence with three other kids. They had come from the direction of the clubhouse. His chest constricted, feeling like it was being squeezed by vicegrips. Had she broken their secret?

"Hi, Broadie! These are my cousins," January said happily

The two boys wore rich clothes like in Jared's family. The girl was slightly older and model-pretty. They all had that look in their eyes, the one that says: *I'm better than you are*, the cruel shimmer behind the face that could strike out with *Broadie Grodie, he's contagious*.

"You took them back there?" Broadie said briskly.

"Yeah . . . ?" She drew the word out long, with her what's-the-big-deal look. "They're my cousins."

Broadie sat quietly hurt.

"They don't live around here. Amber lives in Provo, and Scotty and Calvin live in Idaho. They're just—"

"You promised!" Broadie said reproachfully.

"I promised not to tell anyone around here. I don't want people finding out, just like you don't."

Her three cousins were uncomfortably quiet throughout the exchange.

"I looked for you earlier, because I wanted you to come back there with us, but you were gone, so we all went back before they had to go home." She waited quietly for his reply.

Broadie looked from one person to the other, embarrassment in his face. He felt himself plunging forward in a direction that he shouldn't go. Words were rising into his mouth that he knew he would regret. Why couldn't he simply believe that the circle of camaraderie that she held open for him was real? He stared at her silently, sticking hard to his notion of sole ownership of the clubhouse. He had allowed her in on his good graces. That was enough. "You ruined it. It's not special anymore."

She looked as if she had been slapped.

"Oh–my–gosh!" Amber the cousin intoned sardonically and rolled her eyes.

January's mouth worked for a moment, then settled flatly.

"Let's go," one of the boys spoke. He shifted uncomfortably.

"He doesn't seem like such a good friend to me," Amber mumbled.

Broadie stood ruefully obstinate, then turned to Amber: "Who asked *you* anyway?"

"Get a life!" Amber said. She walked away, Scotty and Calvin following close behind.

January watched them go then turned back to Broadie: "You didn't have to insult them! They didn't do anything!" Her face lit up in a way he had never expected.

The words continued to pour out like dirty water from a broken pipe.

"*She* insulted me, and *you* didn't have to break our secret!"

"I've got to go." She turned away.

"Fine! Go then! You can just *be* that way for all I care!"

She followed her cousins into the barbecue smoke next door. They blended into something that he didn't understand, but wanted.

"Janni! Wait!"

She glanced back, hurt blazing in her eyes, then left him alone on the porch like the insect that he was.

3

The warm morning air was sweet with newly cut grass. While clean sunshine bathed Kennedy Elementary School, the grounds were a deep summer green that whispered: *it's too soon to come back.* Davie skipped excitedly along next to Broadie. Mom followed a few paces back with Alisha in her arms.

"I hope Allen Peterson is in my same class," Davie said.

"I'm sure he will be." Broadie was trying hard not to sound annoyed. It wasn't Davie's fault that they didn't share the same excitement. He was trying to be a better big brother lately by working harder to pay attention to him.

"I think my class is on that side." Davie pointed to some windows on the far end. "That's where all the second graders go." He turned around. "Mom, is mine room nine?"

"Yes, it is," Mom said, slightly out of breath.

"What's my teacher's name again?" Davie's Pokémon backpack bounced eagerly.

"It's Mrs. Pulsifer, honey."

"Miss. Pulthifer." Davie spoke with a slight lisp

"Do you know where yours is, Broadie?" Mom asked.

"Room eighteen," Broadie said with little emotion.

"Allen!" Davie yelled as they entered the front doors. He ran into the milling crowd of parents and kids.

"Davie honey, wait!" Mom called out.

Davie and Allen jumped around each other in a circle.

"I'll show you our class," Allen said.

"Hold on!" Mom grabbed Davie by the backpack and playfully turned him around. "We have to go to the office first." They joined a line of people along the wall.

Broadie stopped under a large glass case that held a painting of a knight with a long jousting pole. Above it a sign read: "Kennedy Crusaders" in bright blue. He had always liked the picture since he started school there, but this time the fierce warrior on horseback looked down at him as if to say: *We'll crush you.* He suddenly wanted to run back out the doors and keep going until he fell down in exhaustion. January walked through the door with her mother. He hoped she would look his direction. He waved, but it was too late, she had already passed by. He wanted to go to her and apologize for the way he acted Saturday. He couldn't do that in front of her mom. He would have to wait until he got her alone. They disappeared around the corner in the direction of her classroom.

Mom and Davie were still in line; Broadie wandered freely. He could go to his classroom whenever he wanted, but he didn't. He knew what awaited him there. Instead, he slowly paced the green tile along the edge of the wall until he found the door to the library. It was locked. He looked through glass criss-crossed with wires and saw new computers that contrasted the old, dusty books along the walls. Mrs. Beeman, the librarian, sat in her office wearing glasses that she had probably worn since the seventies.

The halls were thinning; he knew it was almost time for class. January's mother walked out the door into the happy sunlight. He could follow her out and keep going until he was safely alone in his clubhouse. He wouldn't have to go to class at all. No one would force him to stay at this point. Grandpa and Grandma were back at the genealogical library downtown, doing whatever they did there. They wouldn't know. He could make some sandwiches and steal some pop out of the fridge; could live back there all day long, and no one would find him.

Mom left the office with Davie to take him to his class. She looked so young compared to all of the other moms. She was slim in her summer clothes—like a teenager. The only difference was, when she turned around and you saw her face, you knew she was a grownup. She had that butterfly tattoo just over her right shoulder blade. It would hide and peek behind her tank top as she walked. You could also tell by her face that she smoked. Most of the other moms were fatter, with soft, plump little doll faces: non-smoker faces.

The bell rang and the first announcements echoed from the intercom speakers. Broadie slowly walked to room number eighteen, Mr. Burt's sixth grade class.

The door was still open. Mr. Burt was busy calling out names and pointing to desks. Each desk had a number. Broadie stood quietly by the coat rack hoping not to be noticed. He waited and watched as each name was called in alphabetical order. He knew that his name had been called before he arrived, so he quietly slipped into a desk that was open in the far corner and hoped it would remain vacant. It was the perfect place to be. He didn't know any of the kids close around him. It was the most inconspicuous place in the room, where he would be out of sight and out of mind of everyone. The number on the desk said twenty-one. He saw January on the front row and wished he could be by her.

"Twenty: Pierce." Mr. Burt said. "Twenty-one: Williams."

A large girl walked over counting desks then stopped and stood expectantly over Broadie. He didn't want to move.

"That's my seat," she said.

By her looks he could tell that she would be quick to make a fuss, so he stood up and stepped away to lean against the back wall. The girl fell heavily into her seat. He now stood alone.

"Take your seat, young man." Mr. Burt said indifferently.

All heads in the room turned in his direction. His face immediately flushed. There was an empty seat in the middle by John and Tim, and another toward the front. Broadie moved for the one toward the front. January was two desks down. She watched him approach.

"What's your name?" Mr. Burt asked him.

"Broadie."

"Grodie Broadie," someone growled.

Snickers.

"Your last name . . . ?"

"Bennett." Broadie's face was a red furnace.

Mr. Burt slid his finger down his paper. "You're in number thirteen over there." He pointed to the one by John.

Broadie's heart sank. He walked and all eyes followed him.

"Duh!" Joey boomed.

Laughs.

"Knock that off, Wolff!" Mr. Burt commanded.

"Eww! Watch out, he's contagious!" Vanessa squawked. Some of the kids, including her, scooted their desks away from desk number thirteen.

More laughs.

January solemnly looked on.

Nine more months to go until June, and this was only the first day, he thought, fighting hard to hold back stinging tears. He could run. Oh, he could run.

The recess bell was heartily welcomed. Broadie waited until he was the last to leave the room; that way no one would be behind him to make trouble. He followed Mr. Burt quietly, temporarily safe from anyone ahead. January had left with Monica Prina and Amanda Berkley and gathered with other girls by the swings. On her way out, he thought that she had looked at him. When he met her eyes, she looked away; she seemed a little sad. Maybe he could talk to her, but it would be hard with her friends around. He stepped into the early day's heat watching John, Tim and Joey run out onto the field with a soccer ball. He was contently alone.

A fence running along the west side of the grounds held the neighborhood back. Next to it, just far enough away from the building to be out of anyone else's interest, stood an old utility shed. Its cinder blocks were thick with old paint. Rust streaked its metal doors. It was a quiet place that faced the playground. He could climb to the top and never be disturbed as long as he stayed out of sight of the recess monitor. Before he climbed the shed, he surveyed the playground. The monitors were all on the other side. He picked up a graying Popsicle stick that was on the ground and scraped it along the wall. Bits of old mortar crumbled from between some blocks. He climbed up the fence then crawled onto the grainy cement roof. The sun was hot, but pleasant. Propped on one elbow, he watched recess flow.

He scraped the Popsicle stick slowly, dreamily until one end was sharpened. He blew away the sawdust watching it float slowly to the ground. Children ran past in fuzzy blurs as he began to scrape again. Hollow *boinks* from bouncing basketballs echoed off of the building. His fingers began to get sore. He lifted the stick, admiring its smoothness, and ran his fingers over the small gouge that he had worn into the cement. He aimed it up into the sky like a gun and shot at popcorn clouds. He brought it down, aimed at John, following his movements back and forth across the field.

—*I've got a bone to pick with you, punk!*

—*Dude, do it!*

The smell of nacho cheese . . .

The kids all ran together: brotherhood in complete acceptance; back and forth chasing the ball, laughing and shouting, nothing to be sad about. They were complete. They had power. They drew it off of each other, charging each other. They were full at that moment. Broadie had no place with them. Their language was foreign. *He* was the alien that needed to be pushed away, destroyed.

He rolled over on his back and ran the sharp point up his arm slowly, watching a red welt appear. He did it again, fascinated by the design. He pushed harder on one of the strokes, gritting his teeth against the pain. Little beads of blood appeared. He closed his eyes, feeling the new burn in his arm. Small puffs of cigarette smoke drifted past his nose. He thought about his dad and wondered what he must be thinking about behind bars. He wondered if he knew that Mom had filed for a divorce. He had overheard her mention something about it to Grandma.

Who was smoking?

He became aware of a rustling in the thick vines behind the shed. He crawled to the edge and looked down. A boy that looked too old to be there moved out of the vines but stayed in the shadows. His head was shaved like the Latinos he had seen in the low rider, but he was white. He had earrings in both ears, and his pants were large and baggy and sagged deeply until his underwear showed around his waist. He had a black shirt with a picture of a vicious Doberman salivating (or was it blood?) that read: "Dawgs." He looked around unaware of Broadie. As he walked away, Broadie watched him, frozen and fascinated. There was someone right there who was meaner, by far, than John and all his friends put together. Though he had left the shadow of the shed, he carried one with him. As Broadie watched him go, he became aware of a subtle and disturbing feeling inside—almost like the one you get when you bite aluminum foil. His eyes watered at the thought.

The bell rang and he jumped.

The mysterious dark-boy had joined the crowd. Games ended. Recess monitors shouted, herding kids off the field. He waited quietly until John-and-friends were out of sight, then he dropped down into the shadow side. A smoldering butt lay on the other side of the fence in someone's garden. He left the safety of his hideout. The crunch of his feet against loose gravel mixed with other footsteps around him. They surrounded him, yet he was completely alone. They carried him back to the place of voodoo dolls and hot pokers. There wouldn't be relief today.

"Hurry up! Let's move it!" Mr. Burt hollered.

Some of the kids timidly picked up their pace. Broadie continued at his own speed. He absent-mindedly stuffed his sharpened Popsicle stick into his back pocket.

Amanda Berkley was the most eager to volunteer from her row. She was mousy in a green jumpsuit and ponytail. She passed out pencils, faithfully returning the remainder to a box on Mr. Burt's desk. Ebony and ivory, by Paul McCartney, played on an oldie's station that whispered from a large stereo in the front of the room. A sign hung on it, written in bold letters: MY STATION ONLY. TOUCH THIS AND YE SHALL WITHER TO DUST!

"I want everyone, row by row as I call them, to go sharpen your pencils. They're the only ones you'll get, so don't lose them. You'll keep them in your desks." Mr. Burt pointed to the first row. "Go ahead, the sharpener is over there above the garbage can."

Broadie lay with his head down and traced his finger along the edge of his desk. In his mind he was safely far away in his tree house feeling the September breeze beat its chest against the coming fall. It cleansed him like a desert wind hissing through the massive branches above him.

The grumbling burr of the pencil sharpener.

The wood of the tree house beneath him creaked and shifted assuaging him in its undulating cradle.

"Row three," Mr. Burt said.

Broadie arose trance-like and gazed into the back of Tim's closely cropped head. Large ears supported heavy glasses. He felt an urge to reach up and flick them with his fingers.

The pencil sharpener continued to rumble. One kid finished, and another took his place. Tim was next up to bat. Broadie pulled out his Popsicle stick and wondered what would happen if he stuck it into the pencil sharpener. He rubbed the new yellow pencil against the old graying wood. He was aware of the itch and burn from the scrapes on his arm.

A tussle behind him in the line: roughhousing.

"Give it up, punk " John laughed somewhere behind.

"WWF!" Someone hollered.

A sudden lurch, and Broadie was shoved forward into Tim His Popsicle stick jammed hard into Tim's back. Tim screamed and spun, his eyes bright with surprise and pain. He cupped his hands against the small of his back and waddled like a pregnant woman, yelling "Ow! Ow! Broadie stabbed me!"

Mr. Burt was already across the room, lifting up the back of Tim's shirt, assessing the damage. Tim swatted at his hands and wailed like a banshee. There was a tear in his shirt and a smear of blood on his back.

Broadie held the stick stupidly in shock. His stomach lurched as Mr. Burt turned on him in fury.

"Give me that!" He growled through clenched teeth snatching the Popsicle stick away.

"But I—"

Mr. Burt grabbed him hard by the upper arm and propelled him to the door. "We're going to the office!"

The class was frozen in shocked silence.

"But I didn't—"

"Oh, oh!" Tim wailed louder. His face was red, wet with tears. Snot oozed from his nose.

Mr. Burt turned to Tim: "Let's get you some first aid." Then to Broadie: "Get! Now!"

At the end of the hall, the door reflected the sun outside. His heart beat so heavily that it was hard to breathe. He felt as if he were helplessly caught up in some crazy mountain slide. He could run for the door, but somewhere deep down, Broadie still believed that the institutions around him would ultimately serve justice. His feet didn't carry him with a will to run, but toward hope that someone would see that it was all just an accident. He trusted.

Tim carried on like an injured dog all the way to the office.

"Stay right there!" Mr. Burt pointed at a row of chairs along the wall. Turning to the secretaries, he said: "Don't let him leave." He led Tim through another door. One of the secretaries followed them back, and Tim's pathetic voice muffled as the door closed. The remaining secretary regarded Broadie suspiciously, then shook her head, returning her attention to a computer screen.

The howls died down, and it wasn't long until Principal Barker leaned out from behind his door and motioned for Broadie to come in. He was a cheerfully slender man, younger than Mr. Burt with constantly appraising eyes. He casually leaned against the corner of his desk, folding his arms over a long, abstractly decorated tie. Broadie stared silently at the smooth grain of the thickly lacquered oak desk. Barker pulled the Popsicle stick out of his front pocket and set it down on his desk in Broadie's view.

"What happened with Tim Burton?" Barker paused waiting for an answer.

Broadie didn't speak. The silence was thick.

"You know, he's back there in the sick room with a mean looking scratch on his back. Now they're telling me that you stabbed him. I need for you to understand how serious this situation is, and I need you to tell me everything. Something this serious could end you up with an expulsion or the police could even get involved."

Another long pause. Barker lightly scooted the Popsicle stick back and forth with his finger.

"Have you ever heard of 'Safe School?'" In other words, we have what's called a 'zero tolerance policy' toward anything that could be conceived of as a weapon. If something were serious enough, a student could get expelled for good."

Broadie wanted to speak, but the whole situation was so strange that he didn't know where to begin. He was surprised at his own emotions. Where he expected to cry, he only felt disconnected and floaty. There was a vague sense of urgency at the idea of the police getting involved, but any way that he could imagine to explain what happened only ended in futility in his mind; he was completely doomed. How could they believe him? Instead of weeping, he wanted to laugh. This was the worst first day of school in his life, yet he hadn't meant any trouble at all. He let out a quick breath, a small laugh at the irony of his own urge to laugh, and shook his head slowly from side to side.

Barker must have interpreted his mannerisms wrong, because his eyes dropped and his lips thinned. He let out a tired sounding puff, picked up the Popsicle stick, and put it back into his pocket. He nodded his head in understanding and walked out. The door closed and the office was a small, silent box pressing against his ears.

A clock above the bookcase ticked.

Voices came and went behind the door.

He floated dreamily, no desire to move. He wanted to sleep and wake up again to a bright, white morning window and the smell of wet grass. He settled into his padded chair and let himself drift, eyes closed, into his own peaceful world.

The door clicked.

"Are you asleep?" Barker asked, slightly puzzled. Broadie rubbed his eyes and stretched as much as his jellyfish muscles would allow. He still didn't speak.

"I'm going to send you down to Mrs. Berling's class where you'll wait until we can contact your parents." He motioned with his hand for Broadie to follow him. Broadie stood and walked out into the scrutiny of the secretaries. The door to the sick room was open ,and Mrs. Burton, having already arrived, burned him with her eyes. He remembered her robot grip on his arm.

—You don't hit people in church!

He wanted to make a face at her but didn't bother. It would have taken effort.

"Sandra," the principal spoke, "will you take him to Berling's class while I deal with—" Barker nodded his head cryptically toward the sick room.

Sandra, the suspicious secretary, nodded and smiled, and soon they were together in the hall. She led him like a prison guard. He thought of his dad and wanted to sleep again.

Little third-grade marionette heads turned as on one string to watch the intruders. Mrs. Berling pointed at a desk that was pushed up against hers. She and the secretary spoke in quick whispers. Berling nodded knowingly and then continued on with her reading to the class. Sandra sat him down then left him alone.

He wasn't allowed to put his head on the desk and was given some worksheets on which he defiantly doodled in slow lazy scribbles. He couldn't see the clock, and every time he turned to look he was commanded to keep his eyes forward and not to interrupt her class. He began turning around anyway, becoming quite the comic hit (the kids laughed every time that he did it) until, to Berling's relief, he was summoned back to the office.

Grandpa and Mom sat, stone faces, on chairs outside Barker's office. Tim Burton was still in the sickroom with his parents. Ned also had just arrived. Fluorescent light reflected off of his balding head and glasses. Broadie was called in again, this time along with Grandpa and Mom. He faced the polished desk again like a repeating nightmare and sat stubbornly quiet. It didn't take much for Grandpa to get him to talk, and soon he recanted the story in matter-of-fact detail. The principal listened patiently, nodding his head from time to time. A lot of questions were asked until Barker left to talk to the Burtons.

"That still seems far fetched to me!" Mrs. Burton's voice drifted through the cracked door. "You don't stab a kid and call it an accident!"

Barker spoke. "His story coincides with the eye witnesses."

"I'd like to hear it from these 'eye witnesses.'"

"We have a statement from a young lady that clarifies things well enough. I don't think any harm was meant to Tim."

"No harm? That kid has hurt people before. I've seen him strike out violently with my own eyes. Now, who is this young lady?"

"I don't think it will be necessary for—"

"Now, if I have to get a lawyer to find out her name, I'll—"

"Beth," Ned broke in. "Let's not—"

"No, I think I have a right to find out who this girl is and hear her story."

"She's in class, and I've spoken to her as well as the other eyewitnesses, and they all say the same thing. I can't legally give you their names, but I have written statements I can give you a copy of." Barker's voice was smooth and controlled.

"I will find out who they are and get to the truth myself. If I have to go—"

"I'm ready to take necessary action to remedy any problems. The disciplinary action will be up to me and I will suspend him for—"

"Oh, you'll suspend him all right, but after that, what then?"

Ned spoke, "Beth, enough said now, I think we should—"

Grandpa closed the door with a brisk swat of his hand. 'That good-for-nothing old bag . . . !"

"Are you ok, honey?" Mom pulled Broadie close to her.

"I want to go home." He leaned closer to her, wanting to sleep.

4

A hornet landed lightly on a plum. It tasted and tested its way around the sticky skin until it found bare, sugary fruit. Its wings relaxed as it feasted on the sticky nectar. Its abdomen writhed up and down, flexing and unflexing. Its legs shifted for a better hold.

Broadie brought the stick close, moving slowly, steadily.

The hornet sensed the movement and froze. Its thorax tightened, bringing its wings up, ready to fly away. He waited until it relaxed, then continued his approach. It froze again, and he carefully stroked the tips of its wings with the stick. Its abdomen pulsed angrily, and it attempted to fly away. He held it prisoner with the soft strokes of his stick. He studied it carefully, unafraid of its nervous stinger.

Funny that something so small and inherently innocent could cause anyone to dance and swat frantically, that the buzz could inspire the worst of dread. So vulnerable and exposed under the constant caress of the stick, its wings sputtered but couldn't catch the air. It should leap away to freedom.

He let it go, watching it zigzag into the late evening shadows.

January appeared from under the rose bushes. She carefully pushed aside a thorny runner holding the other hand daintily. She stepped away from the stickers and approached shyly. Broadie stood, forgetting the stick as he let it go, and brushed off his pants.

"Hi!" His surprise was open and pleasant.

"I thought you'd be here." She tried to hide a grin but reacted instinctively to his mirth.

"I'm sorry," he spoke quickly.

"For what?"

"For what I said Saturday."

She looked down at a clump of grass and brushed it with her foot. "Oh, yeah, I guess I should have said sorry to you. I just thought—"

"Oh, no, please, I was being a jerk. I still think you're . . . I mean, this place is still special."

She looked away bashfully and was silent for a moment. "So, what have you done lately?"

"Not much, except today I painted a sign for the—our—clubhouse. It's over there drying until I can get some nails to hang it up over the door."

They walked to it together.

"Magnum opus," January read. "What does that mean?"

"It's Latin. My grandpa taught me some words. It means 'great work.'"

"It reminds me of a gun and an octopus."

"This is our great work, our *magnum opus*. It's strong enough to stand until we're long gone, and then some other kids will discover it and make it their special secret."

She nodded in approval.

Soon they were above the rooftops side by side, feet dangling freely, watching the dusky sky through black leaves. The air was still, but full of warm evening. They watched an old woman through her kitchen window as she puttered over the sink. In another house a silhouette hovered behind the frosty glass of a bathroom.

"Mrs. Burton came over today." January's voice was almost a whisper.

Broadie sank visibly.

"I'm sorry. I shouldn't have brought it up."

"No, it's okay. What did she say?"

"I don't know how she found out who I was, but she asked me what happened in class. I told her like everyone else for the fifth time that it was John Hamel messing with Joey Wolff and some other kids. John jumped on one of their backs, and they fell into the line, bumping into you, and Tim started screaming."

Broadie's face grew a grin that looked impish in the shadowy afterglow. "So, what's she saying?"

She stuttered then caught herself. "Just old-people gossip. I answered her questions then left. She probably stayed to play the ain't-it-awful game with my mom."

"Hum." He worked his mouth until he had a good wad of spit, then let it go slowly over the edge until it dripped gracefully away from his mouth into the grass below.

Both He and January raised their heads at a sudden, nonreverent noise of movement through the grass and bushes by the trail.

January gasped.

"Ssh!" He extended his hand to cover her mouth but she swiped it away. "Speak of the devils." He whispered and grinned again.

Her eyes widened and she froze at the sound of his words. Her face slackened as she recognized who was passing along the trail from the road.

"They can't see us, can they?"

"Ssh." He hushed her softer this time.

They passed several meters away and none the wiser, just more ignorant traffic on the old trail to the next block down. John, Joey, Tim, and Steve migrating home after a long after-school gallivant, whipping grass and bushes with long sticks, walking briskly to beat the final curtain of darkness. Their voices carried jovially up through the cooling air, floating above the buzz and clicks of the insects.

"I didn't know they came back here this often." She pulled her legs up quietly and wrapped her arms around her knees.

"Everyone does. That's why this is such a special secret. They only see the big rose bushes and nothing beyond them. They don't have a reason to look."

"You could hit them with something and they'd never know where it came from, like a BB Gun." She paused as if unsure, then added, "Or a good sling shot with marbles."

"Or my grandpa's thirty-eight revolver." His grin was back. "Yeah, they need to have their butts stung real good. . . ." Her words came out weaker, and she watched his face for a long time. "Hey, Tim sure didn't look very hurt," she said, changing the subject a little.

"He's not."

"The way his mom talked, you'd think you punctured his kidney or something."

"I'm sure."

"*Janni?*" Her mom's voice was distant but clear.

"Oh, crap!"

"Your mommy's calling."

"Shut up!" She slapped him playfully. "I can't go. They'll see me."

"Just stay here and wait then."

"I can't though. She grounds me if I'm out of her calling distance."

"You're almost twelve years old. You're almost a teenager."

"Yeah, and I'm almost dead right now." Her words caused him chills. He rubbed his arms.

"I'll vouch for you."

"That's the other problem."

"What do you mean by that?"

"I'm not allowed to play with you."

Those words hit him in the chest like a sucker punch. He could barely see her face as she looked away shamefully. They were quiet.

Janni?

"I better go."

He watched her lower herself down. She stopped to look back at him. He remained quiet on his perch. She waved. He waved back.

5

Broadie, alone in his room, admired the new addition to his coin collection: a Standing Liberty, pure silver, 1942 half-dollar. Grandpa had put him to work pulling weeds and cleaning the garage during the time that he had spent suspended from school. He was supposed to have been grounded. He couldn't wander the streets, but working with Grandpa had been sweaty heaven. Grandpa sang songs, told stories, talked about Jesus and the scriptures, and when Jesus would come again. Lady Liberty stood gloriously enhanced by tarnish. He rubbed the coin against his pantleg to bring out a shine and studied it along side his wheat penny, buffalo nickels, and the Indianhead penny that he had gotten for shoveling snow.

Far away in the kitchen, Mom's machine gun voice crackled against Grandpa's low, distant artillery.

"You were just agreeing that I needed a job. Now you criticize me for getting one," Mom complained.

"You could have used some discrimination at least, you're a mother of three kids and—"

"That's all *you* do, is discriminate. You're so damn high-and-mighty that—"

"—and, *and* you have the responsibility of being a good example. What kind of environment should a young mother—"

"What do you think I'll do, take my kids with me to work? My hell! My job doesn't affect them!"

"That's just it! You'll bring it home with you whether you like it or not: the smells, the influence, new friends, old friends, the wrong kinds of friends. . . . It's just the same old pattern again!"

"It's a job!"

"It's a bar!"

"It's a *private* club!"

"Oh yeah? What will you say when they invite you to start stripping?"

"Dancing! And I do have some pride."

"My daughter's not going to be a barmaid!"

"I'm a waitress!"

"And you're going to be out all night again."

"Well, they sure as hell don't do much business in the morning. It's a perfect schedule. I can sleep when the kids are in school. I'll be up when they get home."

"What about Alisha?"

"Mom said she would watch her while I worked."

"She said she would watch her so you could get a respectable job or finish your night classes so you could go to college."

"She can speak for herself, and this gets me more money than your *'respectable'* job. For once stop treating me like a kid. I need a life. I need money. Everything's gone to shit for me, if you haven't noticed."

"Can't you rely some on Brian's child support when he gets out? Maybe you could work part-time somewhere else, like—"

"Ha! He'll never pay. He won't have a job when he gets out of jail, anyway. He'll just go bum at his mother's."

A horn honk echoed between the two houses into Broadie's window.

"I have to go now," Mom said.

"Who's out there picking you up, anyway?"

The battle rolled from the kitchen to the living room. Broadie had to go to his door to hear what was being said.

"That's none of your business!" Mom yelled.

"You won't talk to me that way, I've been nothing but good to you!" A pause. "Is that who I think it is?"

"It's Porshia, and she's taking me to work."

"Don't tell me *she* got you the job?"

"So *what* if she did?"

"The prostitute herself."

Grandma broke in, "Little ears."

"She's my friend, and at least *she's* helping me get a new start in life."

"You're just going back to your old ways."

"I'm getting a new life!"

The horn sounded again.

"Bye!"

The door slammed.

"After everything we've done for her!" Grandpa's heavy feet thumped the carpet along the hallway. The sound that they made was cut off behind the whack of the screen door.

* * *

Grandpa usually spent time in his workshop after his arguments with Mom, and lately it was becoming more frequent; this time he had been out a lot longer before he came back in. The sounds of his tools had long since fallen silent, but Broadie remained awake, his bare feet swimming in the cool, dark air below his window. His newest coin reflected mild streetlight from January's hand. She held it up, squinting to discern any detail.

"It's pretty," she said. She reached out to hand it back. Their fingers touched briefly over the darkness.

"My grandpa said that he always thought the sun on the coin was rising on Lady Liberty, but now he wonders if it was really setting, with the wimps and traitors in Congress and all."

She lifted a pajama leg to scratch her shin. "I hate it when I don't feel sleepy."

"I can't sleep either." He shifted into a more comfortable position. "Hey! Have you wondered what the clubhouse is like at night?"

"Not really."

"Seriously, have you ever thought about it?"

"Well . . . now I'm thinking about it."

"Would you ever go back there in the dark?"

"Why?"

"Just for the fun of it."

She looked out into the crystal-white, moonlit yard. "Wouldn't that be scary?"

"Yeah, but wouldn't it be cool?"

"I guess, if you're crazy enough."

"I guess I'm crazy because I want to do it."

"Well go ahead."

"Come with me."

"No way! I would be grounded for life!"

"No one would ever know."

"Oh yeah? My parents check on me sometimes, especially since I've gotten sick a lot, and if they found me gone they would freak."

"We wouldn't be gone long. This would be the last awesome adventure before summer weather gets over with. We could just go and come right back."

Her eyes glistened, and a grin crept onto her face.

"We could build a campfire," Broadie coaxed.

Her grin grew into a toothy smile. "Okay, but not too long. We have to come back quick in case my parents wake up."

"I'll get a flashlight." He hunched himself back into his window. "Wait!"

"What?" He said, uncomfortably bent and anxious to go.

"Let's go from our windows so no one will hear the doors shut. My mom has perfect hearing."

He nodded, slid back into his room, and tiptoed out into the hall to the closet where Grandpa kept his tools. He remembered a flashlight that he kept there for emergencies, along with matches and candles.

He was the first to drop into the darkness, losing his balance and clobbering the back of his head against the bricks. He rubbed it madly, holding back a desire to swear loudly.

"Are you okay?" she asked, lowering herself to where he could catch her foot to help her down.

"I'm fine. I just hit my head." He laced his fingers together and cupped her foot. She dropped slowly until she was safe on the ground.

The trail snaked before them, colorless, washed clean by the moon. Trees gossiped in whispers. Dancing shadows brought the ground to kaleidoscope life. Dew-covered grass soaked their shoes and pant legs. When they were far enough away from their houses, he clicked on his flashlight disturbing the lunar symphony with its bright, yellow cone.

"Turn it off," she whispered.

"I can't see where we're going without it."

"Turn it off, it's beautiful. Let's see how far we can go in the dark."

He reluctantly flicked the switch, feeling uneasy as his eyes adjusted. Moving hadows filled the void with their cricket rhythm ballet. Before they were half way to the clubhouse, he began to repent of his hunger for adventure. He slowed, and January took the lead, her pajamas gray in the no-tone light and her hair a ghostly diamond white. She dropped into the ditch, disappearing into the blackness of the rosebushes. He paused cautiously, more aware of every tick and peep around him. He wanted to turn the flashlight back on, but at the same time the mystery and danger also enchanted him.

"You coming or not?" She emerged suddenly from the tunnel, almost colliding into him. Her face looked skeletal, eyes hollow and black, cheekbones deep, her hair hanging white and limp. The picture was wrong, and his mind's interpretation was irrational, and he jumped back in a bolt of unexpected terror and almost screamed. She covered her mouth with both hands to keep from laughing out loud.

"You scared me!" Broadie half-hollered.

"Ssh! You'll wake up the neighbors."

Someone's dog started barking from a back yard. He laughed nervously, adding to her giggles, and soon they were sitting in the dew-soaked grass holding their guts, trying to breathe and keep from crying at the same time.

They climbed carefully. Neither one had since turned on their flashlights. Up above, the breeze was constant and gentle. Two dark silhouettes sat side by side in the ebb and flow. Light patterns crisscrossed over them like magical symbols. Boards creaked soothingly underneath them. They were close, silent, and her warmth radiated next to his.

"I don't want to go back in," she whispered, barely audible.

"What?"

"I said I don't want to go back in." Her warm breath tickled his ear as he leaned closer to hear her. She lingered, her cheek brushing the side of his head as she slowly leaned forward against the two-by-four railing.

He closed his eyes, heart beating fast, savoring the sensation. He wanted to kiss her on the lips, to know what it felt like. He wanted her to love him and to feel her arms around him. He was paralyzed by the power of his feelings and fought to take in air with each breath. He was drowning in her nearness, trembling with each new wave of feeling. He gripped the board in front of him to stretch; he had to move, do something. Feeling faint, he lay back to stare into the twinkling movement above. She lay back next to him, her hair tickling the side of his face. "This is how Idaho used to be."

"It must—" he swallowed—"be pretty."

"It is." She turned and looked at him, her eyes wide and beautiful in the darkness. "My dad calls it God's country," she said. "I used to sleep outside with my friend Candice and her sisters. You could see the Milky Way even in town. We would get our sleeping bags out and look up and watch for falling stars."

"I saw a falling star once." He turned toward her, resting on his elbow. "I was coming back with my dad from Wyoming. We were driving through the Uintas, and it flashed across the sky. We both saw it at the same time."

"Did you make a wish?"

"No, I didn't really think about it."

"You know, that means your wish is still good. You could close your eyes right now and make it right now."

"Should I?"

"I would."

He closed his eyes, feeling a slight burn of sleepiness, and wished that he could be like this again with her, soon, side by side and full of joy, and that she would love him. The wish was so strong that it felt more like a prayer. He thought of God and wondered if he heard it. He opened his eyes and met hers, still wide, her smile sweet and guileless. She really was his friend. She was with him to *be* with him.

"So, what did you wish?" she asked.

"I can't tell you."

She smiled. "I guess I couldn't get you on that one."

"Do you think wishes are the same as prayers?"

"I don't know. Maybe God hears both."

He looked back up at the outlines of the branches waving back and forth and wondered if they were waving hello or good-bye. "How does God hear our voices or our thoughts so far away? I mean, where is heaven, if we can't see him? Is it out in the universe or around here?"

"I think he'll tell us when he wants to. Sometimes I think he shows us little bits of heaven along with hell so we'll know the difference when the time comes."

"What time is that?"

"I don't know. I used to think it was when we die, but now I think that our spirit leaves to a world close by, and we wait for the resurrection. Then we go to heaven after that."

"Could it be another planet or something?"

"I thought of it as another dimension right here."

"That sounds like science fiction."

"Well, then, why do they say our loved ones watch over us? Like, when my grandma died. My mom said she felt her close during that time."

"O-o-oh." He whooped softly like a ghost.

"Knock it off." She nudged him amicably. "After my grandpa died, Grandma said she saw him and spoke to him."

The back of his neck prickled. He felt something drift by beyond the shadows. "Let's build a fire." He was uneasy again.

The darkness swallowed her as she climbed down under the tree house. He felt watched. The shadows were suddenly sinister. He could hear her shoes scrape against the tree bark and boards and pictured in silent horror one breaking, and her, falling onto the clubhouse below. Her voice cried out in his mind, causing him to shudder. He followed her, and soon they were together in the pitch dark of the clubhouse. He struck a match and saw her looking out the window, concerned and rubbing the goosebumps on her arms.

"What's wrong?" The match flame flickered and extinguished in the breeze.

"I'm just getting goose bumps, that's all."

"Are you going to chicken out?" He knew she couldn't see his grin, but he could picture her proudly determined face.

"I don't know."

That caught him off-guard. He had secretly relied on her stubbornness, but now he wasn't so sure.

"I guess," she continued, "that all this talk about spirits has spooked me a little."

She moved closer to him and the glow he had been feeling lit him up inside like a sunrise. She was depending on *him* to be brave.

"You know, there's no such thing as ghosts." He felt stupid before the words finished coming out.

"I'm not talking about ghosts. I'm talking about real people: souls that bring a feeling of sweetness when they come around. It just suddenly doesn't feel sweet at the moment."

A new wave of chills crawled from his neck to his toes. "But it's a nice, beautiful night, remember?" His voice was weak.

"I'm sure it's nothing, anyway. Why don't you start a fire?"

He opened his mouth to speak, then closed it, surprised that she would send him out so casually into danger, even if it was an imagined danger.

"Why don't you come with me?"

"It's too scary."

Again he was surprised. She was openly honest and sounded on the verge of tears. "Do you want to go back?"

"I don't want to move." She put her hands over her face and turned to him until she was right against him. His arms hung awkwardly limp until he raised a hand and patted her tentatively on the back. He wanted to hug her but was painfully shy. She pushed closer, and he thought he heard a squeak or a sob. He raised his other hand, timidly resting it against her back. A wave of emotion flooded away even the hardest terror of the dark. He was holding her, and she accepted him. Blood pounded through his head. He breathed deeply the smell of her hair and was aware of every breath she took, every movement, every detail: the texture of her pajama top, the way it moved against her skin, her shoulders and bony ribs, her warm breath against his chest. Soon she took her hands from her face and hugged him back, resting her head on his shoulder. She slowly relaxed. Her breath was a gentle tickle on his neck. She rested her chin on his shoulder, and without thinking he kissed her softly on the head: a natural gesture. She raised her head and their lips brushed briefly in the darkness, both too shy to move together, both unable to move apart. He finally gave in, pushing his lips against hers, feeling their rose-petal softness. She kissed him back briefly, then let go and backed away.

They were silent.

He floated strangely in a culmination of feelings so sweet and terrible that he felt the urge to cry. He wanted more than anything to kiss her again; it wasn't enough. He wanted to tell her how he felt and to know if she felt the same. Her silence lingered. He began to wonder if he had done something wrong. Hadn't she brushed her lips over his? Or was it an accident that she might think he had taken advantage of? Was this her first kiss? He was sure that she had invited him. Hadn't she kissed him back? He tried to speak: "I—"

She was still silent.

"Uh . . . I could build that campfire now." He could have happily thrown himself over the edge of the tree house at that moment if she wanted him to. He lit another match.

She blinked her glistening, distant eyes. "I better get back before they find out I'm gone." She folded her arms, rubbing at them nervously, and walked out into the moonlight. He followed her, flipping on his flashlight.

The magic was gone.

He took the lead. They quietly walked the trail back to his yard. He helped her up into her window, then found a bucket to use as a stool to climb into his own window. As he crawled over his ledge, her window slid shut behind him and clicked. She pulled her curtains closed. He watched her darkened window until he couldn't hold his eyes open any longer, hoping that she would come back and speak to him, tell him her feelings.

She didn't.

6

After a few small "incidents," Mr. Burt was quick to separate Broadie from the rest of the class. His new seat was in the "retard spot" (as John had dubbed it), next to the teacher's desk, his back turned to the others. Now he was marked authoritatively as the "outcast," singled out and alienated. He wouldn't have a chance. Joey's newest game of burping, "Grodie Broadie," was slowly spreading among the others. Two newcomers to the game, Darren Petty and Benji Jones, had the ability to save up air and burp the loudest each time the teacher left the room, winning thunderous laughter that poured over him like acid rain. But the torment wasn't just saved up for when the teacher was absent; it came softly, like wisps of sewer gas: a snicker, a face, an accidental spill at lunch, missing papers, a wet, sloppy booger on his seat; nothing obvious enough to catch the teacher's attention, but to Broadie it was like a sliver of fiberglass constantly being rubbed.

Today was the day for the physical education teacher to come and run them around while Mr. Burt got a break. They gathered out in the ball field to play kick ball. The teacher (whom they called "coach") organized the teams by calling out names until both sides had equal numbers.

"Cory Anderson!" Coach hollered and handed him a red vest. "Broadie Bennett!" He pointed to the opposite team, where the teachers aide was handing out blue vests.

There were scoffs from among the reds.

"Eww, now they're contagious," Vanessa yelled, but still not chosen herself.

"Don't get the grodie team," Joey warned.

A rush of laughs.

The teacher's aide, a young college girl named Miss Beagly, handed Broadie a blue vest and winked sympathetically at him. He took it bashfully and tied it on, waiting for the rest of his team.

"Amanda Berkley!" Coach called.

January waved to her friend, looked at Broadie, smiled, then looked away. They hadn't talked since the night in the clubhouse. He had wondered if she was mad at him.

The game began, and, though no team captains had been called, John assumed the role naturally for Broadie's team. Joey took command of the other. Broadie was assigned outfield, of course. He took his place, watching the dark late-summer grass ripple lightly in the breeze. Heavy cumulus clouds drifted overhead, passing shadows across the school grounds. His attention turned to January. She moved up in line as each person ahead of her took a turn to kick the ball. There was something different about her, though he couldn't identify just what it was. She was withdrawn and grayly unenthusiastic. Usually she would be chattering like a bird.

Benji kicked the ball. It went high into outfield, but Broadie wasn't watching. It bounced harmlessly past him as he moved too late.

"Get the ball!" John screamed.

Benji ran hard.

"Get the ball!" others joined in. The opposing team cheered. He ran for it, but another outfielder grabbed it first and threw it back to the ball diamond.

"Stupid, lazy moron!" John yelled.

Broadie was frantically embarrassed and yelled back, "Shut up, dinkus!"

"Oh yeah, come on!" John charged at him from first base.

"Kick his butt!" someone yelled from the other team.

"All right! That's enough!" Coach yelled.

John ignored him and stopped within a few inches of Broadie. "You want to go right now, punk?" He thrust his chest out and held his hands out from his sides like a gunfighter.

Coach ran over and grabbed John by the shoulder. "I said that's enough!"

John glared back at Broadie, and stepped away reluctantly. The pink scar on his finger where Broadie had bitten him was noticeable. Broadie rubbed his scarred elbow. He said something low and quiet and insulting.

John broke free from Coach and shoved Broadie hard. He fell back but jumped quickly back to his feet. John pushed again and Broadie deflected the attack, catching John's shirtsleeve. It tore with a loud rip.

Coach grabbed John again, this time in a strong bear hug.

"Knock it off!"

"You're dead!" John yelled, struggling. His shirtsleeve flapped loosely.

"Go to the office now!" Coach yelled, shoving him toward the building.

"Bite me!" John yelled at Coach petulantly, then flipped Broadie his scarred middle finger.

Coach briskly escorted John to the office.

Broadie watched them leave, with a gloating satisfaction. For once someone had identified the real bully and acted accordingly.

"Let's finish the game, guys," Miss Beagly said, organizing the kids back into teams.

The boys in the class soon forgot about John and Broadie. The game continued, and they watched Miss Beagly intently, dreamy eyed. The girls gossiped.

January hung back, looking droopy. She didn't seem fazed by the fight like the other girls. She sat down while the others played. Miss Beagly approached her.

"Don't you want to play?"

January shook her head.

"Why not? We need you. Come on out."

January rubbed her face: a sickly gesture.

"I don't feel good."

The game went on, but Broadie also stood back unnoticed by his teammates.

"I can walk her in," he offered quietly.

"No, that's okay," January said weakly. "I'll go myself."

"Go with her anyway, then come right back," Miss Beagly said to Broadie, trying to move things along quicker.

January rolled her eyes, annoyed, unnoticed except by Broadie. They walked together. Her footsteps were even and sluggish.

"What's wrong?" he asked.

She didn't answer.

"Are you mad at me?"

"No!" She whined, her face strained, eyes tearing.

"Then why won't you talk to me?"

She sniffed. "You won't understand."

"Yes, I will."

She was quiet.

"Are you mad about the other night?"

"I said 'no,' didn't I?" She muffled a sob. "Just don't tell anyone about that, okay?"

"I won't."

Broadie was red-faced and escorted her silently until they reached the doors. She stopped, gripped the door handle, then staggered back limply. He caught her shoulder, and she put a hand to her head.

"Are you okay?"

She shook her head.

He opened the door for her and stayed by her side until they reached the office. John and the Coach were still waiting outside of the principal's office. John occupied the same seat Broadie had the first day of school. Broadie stopped, then backed away from the shutter-stripped window. "I better go back."

"Thank you."

She smiled and left him.

He watched her approach the secretary's desk, then walked back out onto the field hoping that P.E. would be over.

* * *

Broadie knew that John would be waiting for him after school. He watched from the restroom window as John joined up with Joey. They lingered out on the street corner where they could get the best view of the schoolyard. They seemed to give up and disappeared behind some bushes. John, not the master of stealth, soon peeked around impatiently. They had caught Broadie once that way unaware, but this time he had a new plan that would get him away easily without being seen, except Davie posed a new problem: usually on days like this Davie could just go home with Allen's parents, but they were on vacation. He couldn't let Davie walk home alone, because if he did he would get grounded for abandoning his younger brother. Davie didn't understand how serious things were; he didn't know how to run, hide, or look out for trouble. If they were chased, he would hold them back. They would just have to make the best of it.

When he picked up Davie, they left by way of the kindergarten hall. They stopped in the doorway. They would go back by the custodian's shed and climb the fence. He hadn't seen any dogs there, and the old lady he had seen in the garden from time to time probably wouldn't notice them. It would be a longer walk, but he would be free to go without looking over his shoulder.

"Stay right there," Broadie said.

"What are you doing?" Davie asked.

"Just stay there!" Broadie said more sharply than he had meant to. He went to the corner of the building for one more look up front. They were still there, now joined by other kids wanting to see a fight. He ducked back, sure that they hadn't been noticed.

"Are the mean kids over there?" Davie asked, his eyes wide.

"Yes, they are." Once again Broadie considered all the possible directions they could go. "Davie, I want you to do exactly what I tell you. Will you do it?"

Davie nodded his head: "Yes."

"Good. We're going to climb that fence as fast as we can, and then go around the long way back home, but you've got to do everything I say. Okay?"

Davie nodded his head, following Broadie down to the shed. The fence was partly concealed by grapevines. Broadie sent Davie up first. He struggled to find handholds, and, as he got to the top, he froze and whimpered.

"Come on, go!" Broadie hissed.

Davie didn't move.

Broadie climbed up behind him. The fence bowed and swayed under their weight. "Go!" he yelled.

"I'm scared!" Davie cried.

"Just climb back down the other side." Broadie looked over to the still-vacant corner of the building. In the front, the buses were now filled. Airbrakes hissed. Doors shut, and tailpipes farted heavy black clouds of exhaust as they began to pull away from the curb.

Kids trailed away down the street. The school grounds thinned. Perhaps John had given up. He gave Davie a small push.

"No, don't!" Davie screamed.

"Ssh!" Broadie spat.

"No! I'm going to fall!"

Broadie moved to the side, eased himself over behind Davie, then grabbed his backpack pulling on him. He screamed again.

"Come on!" Broadie said now angry.

"I can't move!"

The kindergarten doors creaked open. Benji stepped out into the sunlight. He looked around as if lost. Darren joined him from behind.

Blood drained away from Broadie's face.

"There he is! There he is!" Darren yelled, pointing.

Their faces shone with stupid elation.

Benji ran to the corner of the building. "He's here!" He waved his hands as if signaling an airplane.

Darren ran over to the fence. "Oh, John's going to kick your ass royally, dick-weed," he said with glee.

Davie sobbed in terror. Broadie grabbed him firmly, and they dropped hard into the old lady's tomato garden. He noticed scattered cigarette butts but didn't take time to contemplate them. Darren started to climb the fence. Broadie leapt to his feet, pulled a wooden garden stake from the ground, taking a tomato plant with it, and jabbed hard at Darren's fingers. Darren dropped back with surprised pain in his eyes.

"You dink!" Darren screamed.

"Davie, come on!" Broadie grabbed him up by the back of his neck.

"Ouch! My knee!" Davie cried out.

"Come on, Davie, run!" Broadie yelled in panic.

Darren jumped back onto the fence, emboldened as John and Joey appeared from around the corner.

"There he is!" Benji pointed excitedly.

"Oh, *man!* This is gonna be good!" John said.

Broadie batted at Darren's hands, causing him to drop again. "Davie, go to the street and run that way!" Broadie pointed towards the main road.

Davie stood frozen in terror.

"Go now!"

Crying, Davie limp-ran with his backpack pogoing up and down, out of the yard, and out of sight.

The fence rattled violently as John jumped against it and started climbing. The scar on his middle finger glowed red with strain. Broadie swung the stick hard, smacking it against John's knuckles. He hollered and swore. Benji was almost to the top. Broadie charged him like a jousting knight, ramming the stick into his chest. John's eyes bulged. He fell to the ground, breathless, with a heavy whump! Darren stood back, nursing sore fingers. Broadie charged at John, tomato plant sailing behind him, and John jumped back to avoid the blow.

"Oh! You're dead, punk! You're dead!" John said, sincerely.

Seeing that Davie had gained a good distance, Broadie threw the stick aside and ran hard. The fence rattled harshly behind him as they climbed. He cleared the yard at a full sprint. Instead of trying to beat them in a foot race, he doubled back and hid in the neighbor's yard.

"He went that way!" Joey yelled.

Head pounding with adrenaline, Broadie scrambled over a wooden gate and rolled behind a garbage can. He saw through a space between fence posts that they had taken the bait and continued into the street. John held the garden stake with the tomato plant still dangling from it. They looked around bewildered.

"I think he went that way," John said, pointing the opposite of where Davie had run.

Not smart enough to split up, they ran as a group to the next house down.

Broadie wanted to wait and rest but they would be wise to him within a minute; so he jumped back over the gate, into the old lady's yard, climbed back over the fence, trying not to make any noise, and ran back to the school. Some spectators were still standing around.

"There he goes!" yelled Chance Ellsworth, a kid too cowardly to try to stop him, but brave enough to rat him out.

"Here! Here!" The old lady cried from her back porch. "Get out of my garden! My plants! Oh, my plants! I'm calling the sheriff!"

Darren and Benji fled. Joey hesitated indecisively, but John wasn't deterred. He grabbed Joey by the shirt, propelling him to the fence.

"Oh my, get out!" The old lady hobbled, throwing her arms furiously as if she were shooing stray dogs.

Broadie stopped by the office and looked back at the kindergarten doors. They were waiting, pushing their faces up against the glass, unsure if he would go into the office or not. Chance hopped back and forth behind them like a sidekick puppy in a cartoon. He was safe at the moment, but no one in the office could do much. They only treat the symptoms, not the disease. John would be chased away, but he would always be around a corner somewhere; if not today, then tomorrow.

He sat down on the cold tile of the doorway to the office, trembling. He was sure that they hadn't gone after Davie; he was probably halfway home by now. His trembling turned into heavy sobs. He couldn't remember the last time that he had walked home from school not being terrified that the bullies would pop out of nowhere. Plenty of kids had witnessed what happened but no one spoke up or stepped in to stop it. No one took his side. They all wanted to see "Grodie Broadie" get beat up. Especially Chance Ellsworth: the thought of *him* set off hot sparks of fury. That little creep had nothing to do with John, yet there he was. . . .

There he goes! There he goes!

. . . giving him away—good-for-nothing coward. It was people like him who egged the bullies on, letting them get away with everything.

The wheels of the janitor's cart clacked down the sixth-grade hall. He thought of calling home. He didn't dare move; they could still be there waiting for him just outside the doorway. A classroom door shut. Keys jingled. Swift clicks from a woman's shoes echoed until they were gone. Another door closed, then another. He stared blankly at the crusader on the wall. He hated it. He wanted to pick up the chair underneath it and smash the glass. His eyes stung with a red-hot haze of rage. He could not only smash the crusader, but the bulletin board, office windows, classroom windows—it was the school: the place he was forced to go by law, and it didn't matter how they tortured him, he still *had* to go. He stood slowly, staring at the glass on the wall. If he took a step, he would never stop. He would destroy his torture chamber, then destroy the torturers. His throat tightened. New tears swam heavily in his eyes. He felt an enormous pressure inside like a nuclear bomb. Every manner of violent revenge flashed through his head. He could do it if he moved just an inch more, let the bulls out of the gate. Just a centimeter more and the pin would be pulled. Just a—

"Well, hello." A woman spoke.

He spun, almost falling.

It was the suspicious secretary. She had a tote bag in her hand. She reached back and turned out the light in the office. "Are you waiting for someone to—My, what in the world . . . ?"

She swam before him in broken prisms of afternoon light. She looked around, quickly assessing the situation, then reached out instinctively for the crying boy. He felt her arm close around him. He gave into her affection and let himself go. The pressure inside him burst harmlessly in her arms. She stroked his sweaty hair and whispered consoling words. Finally he pulled back, his face wet with tears and snot.

"Come in here for a minute," she said, turning the light back on. She led him to a chair by her desk, then sat next to him. Several minutes passed before he could talk coherently. The janitor's cart clacked past the doorway.

"They were after me," he finally spoke.

"Who was?" she looked mildly frightened. She gave him a cup of water, and he told his story from start to finish. She took out her note pad, took down some names, then had him call home. She waited with him until Grandpa arrived.

* * *

"Where's Davie?" Grandpa asked.

"He ran away when John and those guys were trying to get over the fence. I told him to go up the road and go straight home."

"Well, he hasn't come home yet, and your grandmother's worried sick for the both of you."

They walked together under the bright afternoon sky. Grandpa looked worried and thoughtful. "You sure they didn't take after him, those boys?"

"No, they didn't. They were after me the whole time."

The black seats soaked up a lot of heat; he rolled down his window quickly.

"Where did they chase you?"

"Over there."

He pointed at the neighborhood behind the building. His stomach was full of wires. Had something terrible happened to Davie? The possibility was a sharp icicle in his chest. Underneath the growing worry was the understanding that if something did happen to him it would be Broadie's fault. The burden was too heavy in his mind. He shoved it away with a physical shudder.

They drove slowly through the neighborhood until they reached the old woman's house. He saw the neighbor's yard and the fences he had jumped trying to get away. It all seemed strange now from the front seat of Grandpa's car.

"There," Broadie pointed.

Grandpa slowed to a crawl. "You jumped over the fence there?"

Broadie nodded.

"Then which way did Davie go?"

Broadie pointed back up the direction of the main road.

They circled the adjoining neighborhood until the evening began to draw down. Grandpa remained tensely quiet. Broadie's stomach growled. They pulled back onto the main road and stopped at a red light. On the corner was Beto's Taquería. The smell of cooking food caused his stomach to buzz harder. He wanted to find Davie, but he still needed to eat. Guilt glowed madly.

* * *

"Did you find Davie?" Grandma was waiting eagerly at the door. Alisha was in her high chair making a mess of mashed potatoes and gravy.

Grandpa shook his head and remained quiet. He stepped heavily into the kitchen. Grandma gave Broadie a quick inspection to make sure he wasn't harmed. He reached the top step and saw that Grandpa was already at the phone.

"Do you think he went over to play with the Peterson boy?" Grandma spoke sharply.

Broadie shook his head.

"Well, which way did he run?"

"I told him to go back up the road and walk home from there."

"Well, why in the world did you let him go alone?"

"The mean kids were—"

"Not now, Mamma." Grandpa interrupted. "I've been over it with him already."

He turned his attention quickly to the phone.

"Ah, yes, ma'am, I need to report a missing child. . . ." He walked down the hall into the next room and closed the door behind him.

Broadie couldn't eat. He picked slowly at his food and watched the sun drive sideways through the livingroom windows. It turned Grandma's curtains red and her knick-knacks into black silhouettes. Mom had been called home from work. Grandpa left twice to search the neighborhoods again. He had called the Hamels again, and it got ugly. He threatened to get a restraining order against John, and, of course, the Hamels insisted he was innocent: Broadie had somehow provoked the whole thing.

Broadie finally left the table and wandered outside. January was sitting on her front porch petting a cat. He approached stealthily along the lilac bushes in case her parents were around, then waved at her. She looked back at her doorway. When she thought it was safe, she walked quietly over to where Broadie stood.

"Hi," she said.

"Hi." Broadie looked her up and down. She was still droopily pale, with heavy dark circles under her eyes.

"I went to the doctor's again today," she said.

"Are you sick?"

"I might have the flu again," she said dourly. "But the doctor's not sure because, something's wrong with my blood, so she's having me take iron pills."

A gloomy pause.

"I'm surprised your mom let you outside."

"I'm not supposed to be, but I'm tired of being cooped up. I don't have to go to school tomorrow, though, and I have an appointment in a few days to go see a blood specialist at Primary Children's Hospital, too."

"I wish *I* didn't have to go to school."

He looked up at the bruised, dusky sky.

She sat down tiredly on the grass and picked at a dandelion green that was trying to recover from a previous mowing.

"So, what's going on at your house?" she asked

"Davie's missing."

She looked at him for a while, unable to comment.

He spoke again: "John-and-friends chased me again. This time Davie was there, and we got split up. He never came home."

"Oh-my-gosh! Did he get kidnapped?"

She looked more frail in the deepening shadows.

Broadie wanted to cry, but held it in in front of her.

"I'm not sure. I'm afraid some of the kids chasing me might have gone after him." They were quiet again. The street light came on adding deeper shadows. Mosquitoes whined. There was a chill in the air announcing the approach of fall.

"Ow!" January said, breaking the quiet. She had been touching her head impulsively.

"What's wrong?"

"I'm getting these weird sore bumps on my head. See, feel this."

She took Broadie's hand and guided his fingers along her scalp. Her hand was small and cold, but he savored her touch.

"That's weird. Did you bump your head?"

"No, they started coming a few days ago. That one hurts the worst."

"Broadie?"

Grandma stood bathed in porch light.

"I guess I better go."

"I hope you find Davie."

She stood slowly, her bony, not-quite-teenager knees bent smoothly, but there was fatigue in her face.

* * *

Mom was pacing the hall crying in her skimpy work clothes. Broadie didn't want to see her like that, so he passed her quickly into his room. January's light came on, and he smiled. He saw movement beyond the crack in her curtain. He wanted to talk to her more, but she had looked too tired. He left his window open just in case. On his bed lay the new book Uncle Will had given him: *Ender's Game*, by Orson Scott Card. He had never been a reader before, but this book he knew he would read a second, maybe a third time. Ender was a character he identified with deeply. The odds were always against him, but somehow he did everything right and always foiled the bullies. Broadie wanted to be Ender.

He flipped it open where he had doubled the corner of a page. He was three quarters of the way through, but he couldn't concentrate enough to read. Mom's crying jags and panicked voice cut into him like a drill. He set the book down and pulled his pillow over his head.

* * *

The doorbell rang. He groggily swatted the pillow away.

The living room door opened. Voices. The mood in the house had changed. Something was happening. He sat up dizzy and blinked his eyes against the sleep-sting. It was completely dark outside, as was January's window. He had fallen asleep. He staggered out of bed, and before he reached his bedroom door he heard Mom's frantic footsteps, then the piercing warbles and babbles of her voice.

His stomach dropped to his feet, and he wanted to throw up; he wanted to scream. His legs started to buckle. A policeman was at the door. He heard that much. He couldn't hear the man's words over Mom's excited voice. Perhaps he was there to tell them that Davie had been found dead, or something worse. He was a statue of ice. It was *his* fault. He had killed his little brother. A scream began in his stomach and trapped itself behind his contorting face. He let loose an explosion of spit, then forced a breath through a clenched throat.

Grandpa laughed

Why would Grandpa laugh if Davie were dead? Before he knew it, he was down the hall, and there in the living room *was* a police officer. Mom was on her knees hugging Davie's little tear-stained face. Relief wouldn't describe the indescribable. He could only support his weak knees against the sofa and watch.

"We found him at a supermarket where a call about a lost boy fit the description we were given," the officer said, his whole face a smile.

It must not be very often that things turn out well for the police, Broadie thought.

Grandpa leaned against the wall looking like a cowboy silhouette that he had seen cut out of iron and standing in a neighbor's yard. He was discussing Broadie's troubles with the officer. He wished that the police could make all of the troubles go away, but he knew that police were just like teachers: they always showed up after the fight, and the fight was only the head of the boil.

His throat was still painfully clenched. Sobs came on like hiccups. He shuffled back to his room completely blinded by tears. He had to feel his way to bed. In his anguish he thought a lot about his dad and the way his long, greasy hair fell over his eyes whenever he lost his temper. He wondered if he would look that way when he finally had John by the throat. It was hopeless, though. Joey and others would always be there. He pictured smashing Joey's feminine features with a rock. It didn't make the pain go away. It only grew in overwhelming waves.

In the grotto blackness of the early hours, an idea of how to stop this once and for all sliced its way through nightmares and sleeplessness. It came up like a sour geyser, and, unlike most midnight notions, this one didn't wash away in the morning light.

7

Grandma and Grandpa left early to the genealogical library, Davie was in the kitchen eating Cheerios, and Broadie sat on a box in Grandpa's closet. In his hands was the small Thirty-eight Special revolver that his grandpa kept hidden in case of an intruder; it was unloaded, but it didn't take long for him to find some ammunition and put the two together. He felt the mute weight of the gunmetal in his hands. He fiddled with it until he was able to click loose the cylinder. It hung open: six empty holes like small mouths open in agony. He lifted the cardboard lid to the box of bullets and took them out one by one. Each was a shiny cartridge with a hollow tip point that Grandpa said would leave an exit wound the size of a baseball in any sleaze that tried to invade his home. He slipped the last bullet into place, clicked the cylinder back in, and aimed the gun at a calendar Grandma had on her wall. With a cold stomach he folded the lid to the ammunition box and tucked it back into its dusty corner. He shut the gun case, shoved it back on to the top shelf, then tiptoed out of the bedroom dropping the revolver into his backpack. Almost as an afterthought he reached in and disengaged the safety switch.

He trembled, the weight of the gun increasing with each minute. A movie of scenarios featuring Broadie the gunslinger played out in his mind, but his real plan was just to show them that he had it. That would be enough to put the terror into them. He could fire a shot at their feet or into the ceiling. As bad as he hated the kids that terrorized him, he still hadn't found it in his heart to murder someone. He just wanted to be left in peace. He was tired inside. He was like a trapped animal biting its own leg off to get away.

Grandpa had arranged for the Peterson's to take them to school and afterwards he would be there to take them home. Davie was elated to ride with Allen, but Broadie now wished that he could walk alone to meet John-and-friends on an empty street corner. Perhaps he could forfeit the ride after school and just say that he forgot. Of course, that wouldn't be very believable after all that had happened. Still, it was his best excuse.

Allen rang the doorbell and Davie completely forgot about his cereal. Broadie didn't feel like trying to make him eat the rest or throw it away. It would sit where Grandma would find it and perhaps castigate him later for not watching his little brother. He picked up his backpack feeling the heavy lump against his right kidney, locked the front door, and climbed into the space that Mrs. Peterson had made for him by throwing a pile of newspapers into the back of her red Honda.

"So how are you doing, Broadie?" Mrs. Peterson asked.

Hearing his name spoken played his nerves like piano strings. "Fine," he said, working hard to sound normal.

She turned the corner driving maddeningly slowly. Their neighborhood slinked away behind them like a beast that had just decided not to attack. A group of girls (January's friends) skipped together in unison. Amanda Berkley and Monica Prina wore matching jumpers. His gaze shifted from them to the graying sky. Heavy thunderheads were gathering to the southwest already shadowing the valley behind them. The sky to the east was a diminishing blue. He looked back at the distancing girls skipping happily without jackets. *Looks like rain,* he thought. The lump in his backpack slid over his groin as the car shifted gears. He pushed it back, feeling cold.

They arrived at the drop-off area behind the school buses. Army-ant parents herded their kids into the school, then came out alone. John, Joey, and Tim were just ahead, walking slowly and jabbering amongst themselves. Davie ran off with Allen without looking twice—of course, he had nothing to worry about. He turned his attention back to John-and-friends. He watched them intently, noticing their every move: the way Tim turned his head and blinked; the way his pants were getting too short; the way John's proud eyes moved against his freckled face and swaggered—ironically, like a gunslinger; the way Joey's blond hair and chiseled face made him too pretty to be mean.

He stepped carefully onto the sidewalk trying not to let his bag swing. Inside, he felt like pillow stuffing that would blow away in the wind. Normally, seeing John like that with his friends would be enough for him to run to the other end of the building and hide, but now he felt he could walk right up to them and *show* them that they wouldn't ever mess with him again.

The trip through the doors and down the hall was a dream in slow motion. He was sure that everyone around him knew that he had something to hide, yet no one looked his way or spoke to him. The weight in his backpack swung, subtly ticking away to its own time, undulating with each step.

"Grodie Broadie," someone said. There were titters among some girls, maybe Vanessa Davis and her friends. He didn't turn to look. He kept moving forward, watching the door to his classroom. It hung open, vibrant with morning pre-bell life. White light and movement reflected off of the glass window in the door.

He slowed down.

Muffled, animated voices mingled with the hallway din. He looked around the edge of the door, and saw his classmates gathered in their respective groups of friends. John, Joey, and Tim were face to face with Darren and Benji. They were happy and laughing. Someone was talking about the wrestlers on TV. Mr. Burt's desk was empty. He took a couple of more steps and looked around.

No teacher.

No one had noticed him standing there. He slowly backed away until he was in the hall again. He leaned his back against the wall and listened to his heartbeat: he was a hot ague of nerves. He knew better than to try to go in there. Without the teacher, things always happened.

He had an opportunity right now to make his point. Almost everyone that had made fun of him was in that room. There wasn't a teacher around and he could do what it took to scare them into leaving him alone. He could fire a shot into someplace noticeable like the TV that they watched those stupid math shows on. He could make them all cower and remember what they had done to him.

He felt the zipper with his fingers. They were almost too weak to pull.

"Watch out. Contagious," Vanessa said to her friends, making an extra big show of avoiding the area where Broadie stood. They followed her like chicks to a hen.

A hot, white fury flashed through his head like a gasoline fire that brought instant tears. "Witch!" he choked.

"Witch!" she cawed back, then cackled theatrically. Her friends all laughed. They grouped around her desk gossiping, never missing a beat.

He pulled the zipper slowly, feeling it click down each tooth; he could almost count each one in his head.

Someone from John's group laughed. They were teasing amongst themselves but *that* teasing was good-natured and quickly forgotten: the boys-will-be-boys banter that represented fraternal acceptance. They wouldn't tease with Broadie that way. If he were to approach them right then, the mood would change. What they would say to him would be cruel and meant to hurt. They would quickly affirm his status as the freak, the mutant, the unacceptable.

The zipper clicked.

His elbow connected with the cold tile on the wall. Someone was writing on the chalkboard and was soon joined by another. The hiss and tick from their writing echoed off the bare walls.

Someone else laughed.

He reached in slowly, feeling past his homework that he hadn't done, pushing one book aside, then another.

Vanessa's haughty voice yapped on and on, gossiping about a girl, probably the female equivalent of Broadie, that they tortured somewhere else. It was important enough to spend five minutes on the girl's childish butterfly hair clips and how fat she looked in her baby-blue overalls.

The bell rang.

His fingers probed deeper, then touched cold metal. They wrapped around the raised grip; it fit solidly into the palm of his hand. His forefinger slipped sweatily close to the trigger.

"Broadie, what are you doing out here?" Mr. Burt appeared out of nowhere.

Broadie yanked his hand from his bag like pulling it out of a burning coal stove. He spun guiltily and faced his teacher, heart hammering, eyes pulsing in and out. His throat squeezed until he couldn't take a breath. "I—" He felt an insane need to explain but couldn't speak.

"Well, get in there, class is starting." With a friendly pat on Broadie's shoulder, Mr. Burt escorted him into the classroom.

As he walked to his "retard spot," somebody "raspberried" a farting noise in unison with his footsteps. This won a collective bray of laughter. With trembling fingers, he zipped his backpack closed and sat down. It rested deftly against his chair. He wanted to throw up. His body thrummed continuously. He kept pulling the backpack nervously closer to him, but it was already as close as it would get. Mr.Burt spoke. His words were far away. Because his back was turned to the class, no one saw him crying. He would stop, calm himself a little, try and go along with the lesson, then lose it again.

Amanda Berkley faithfully passed out worksheets as usual. He hardly noticed the one that slipped onto his desk. He just kept staring at a picture on the wall of a stork with a frog in its mouth. The frog had the stork by the throat. Under it was the caption: "Never give up." There were other small posters with trite sayings and cliches. He wanted to tear them to pieces in maniacal frenzy. He kept looking over at January's empty desk and wishing she were here. Just seeing her would make things better. His head fell forward, then slowly down onto his desk. He listened to the tips of his hair make cracking noises against the paper. He bumped his head softly, over and over, against the phony, woodprint desktop.

The room was quiet except for the shuffling of papers, and the scribble of pencils. On the teacher's desk was a metal in-basket meant for turning in assignments. Out of the corner of his eye, he saw a hand toss in a work sheet. A minute went by and there was another, then another. Students began lining up by the desk. The large girl who had kicked him out of her seat the first day of school stood close enough to touch the backpack. She moved, and Monica Prina took her place. He reached down and shifted the backpack to the other side of his chair. The line moved again. Tim was next to him now. He looked up. Tim waved amicably, then moved further up the line. He was caught with such a surprise that he hardly noticed the tiny sprinkle on the back of his neck. He absentmindedly wiped it away, watching as Tim looked back at the other boys with a scowl.

Another drop of wetness.

A snicker.

He wiped the back of his neck looking for the source of the wetness. Joey was hidden behind another kid pretending his attention was elsewhere. On the teacher's desk was a shiny brass clock with a smooth back. He could make out in the reflection the distorted shapes of those behind him. He saw Joey lean forward and lightly spit.

More little drops.

More snickers.

He pretended to ignore them. Benji joined the line, then Darren. John was still back at his desk, but well aware of Joey. Broadie looked down at his backpack, then back to the clock. Mr. Burt was in the back of the room in his big chair under a reading lamp. It reminded him of Grandpa: they peered through their glasses in the same manner when they read. Looking annoyed, Tim paused and said something to Joey. Joey shoved him away playfully, but Tim stayed serious as he walked back to his desk shaking his head.

Another tiny sprinkle.

This time it was Benji. All three of them held their hands over beet-red faces trying to conceal their laughter. Darren kept looking back at Mr. Burt, hoping he wouldn't notice what was happening.

Broadie boiled inside. He gripped his desktop with white knuckles.

Joey now took the place in line next to Broadie.

A low, distant peal of thunder. Raindrops began to pelt the windows outside.

"Gee, I think the rain is getting in," Joey said, his face straight as a ruler.

More tiny droplets.

This time a girl had joined the muffled laughter.

As unexpectedly as the first drop of saliva, Joey dropped his paper, backed up, aimed his butt right into Broadie's face, and farted. Broadie jumped out of his seat trying to evade the assault on his nose and shoved Joey to the ground. The line broke apart in howls of laughter. Joey was laughing too hard to get back up.

"What's going on over there?" Mr. Burt said, putting down his book.

No one could answer. The laughter spread like nerve gas. The only one not laughing was Tim. He walked over to Mr. Burt as he was putting away his book.

Broadie backed away, his eyes firmly on his backpack.

"Oh-my-Gawd!" Darren hooted. He also fell to the floor and rolled with tears in his eyes.

Mr. Burt was now up the second aisle. Joey pounded his fists on the floor like a temper tantrum, tears peeking from the corners of his eyes. The laughter finally hit critical mass as the entire class stood to get a view of the commotion. People started to leave their seats.

Broadie backed up between the wall and the teacher's desk. The filing cabinet prevented him from moving any further. Benji rolled on the floor holding his stomach and making a strange wheezing noise like an exotic animal.

"That's enough!" Mr. Burt yelled, trying to take control of the class, his own face cracking a bewildered smile.

Broadie watched their lollipop faces, all looking at *him*. Everyone was there, together, facing him and . . . laughing. This moment changed the direction of his life. He thought of his dad behind bars, thought of his mother and her so-called "new life." Davie was just down the hall and completely unaware of the circus of guffaws that surrounded his older brother. "Grandpa," he squeaked.

"Why can't you guys knock it off?" Tim yelled. Strangely, in contrast, was now crying.

The laughter died down. Some turned around in shock to hear even a hint of profanity squeeze from between *Tim's* lips.

"I said, no more!" Mr. Burt roared, grabbing Benji by the arm and lifting him firmly to his feet. "Go sit down!" He pointed to the rest of the class. They turned back to their desks.

"What in chimney cricket's hat is going on here?"

Broadie couldn't speak. He just stared blankly at his backpack.

Joey was finally on his hands and knees trying like a drunk to stand.

"Judas priest!" Mr. Burt grabbed Joey up in indignation.

There were still bursts of snickers and sniffles among those who laughed the hardest.

"Get to your seat!" Mr. Burt gave Darren a swift coaxing, and he nearly stumbled.

Broadie slowly walked back to his desk, his eyes frozen wide like he'd just seen the devil. He barked his shin against the teacher's desk, but continued unfazed. He rested a shaky hand on his desk as Mr. Burt hollered more orders to the class. He bent down slowly, reaching for his backpack, the toggle to the zipper glinting in metallic, fluorescent light.

Outside: a flash and a clap of thunder.

A girl squealed.

"That was close." Someone else said.

He gripped the toggle with his fingers and pulled.

"What? I didn't do anything." Joey said innocently.

Tim said something and the attention of the class turned to him. Vanessa rolled her snotty eyes.

"Now that was the stupidest thing I've ever heard!" Mr. Burt yelled at Joey.

The backpack was now open.

"When will you kids ever grow up?" Mr. Burt continued. His back was turned to Broadie.

Joey walked back, slowly strutting, to his seat for more laughs.

Broadie closed his hand on the wooden grip and clicked the safety switch inadvertently back to the "safe" position; the feeling of it traveled up his arm, bursting inside his head like a slap. The trigger wouldn't move. He tried it again, forgetting what he had done earlier in grandpa's bedroom. His knees gave out and he fell against his desk. He raised himself slowly, his small hand burdened under the weight. He sobbed heavily.

John and Joey high-fived each other. Darren and Benji joined in with congratulations. Chance Ellsworth panted over, his face rapturous. "That was so-o cool!" He said. Darren shoved him away like a pesky bug.

Broadie flexed his finger on the unmoving trigger once more, and just as his hand was about to clear the backpack. . . .

* * *

. . . he let go, the revolver falling harmlessly behind his books. He yanked the zipper closed and, behind a curtain of tears, grabbed up the backpack and ran past Mr. Burt. Heads turned. Conversations stopped.

"Hey!" Mr. Burt yelled.

Broadie cleared the door, sliding into the hallway, almost falling. He caught himself against the opposite wall, then ran as hard as he could. Green and white tile flew past him. Lights drifted over his head.

"Broadie wait! Come back!" Mr. Burt's voice echoed behind him.

He didn't stop. He turned the corner, throwing himself out the glass entrance into the icy rain. The blowing rain fell in sheets, and he was soaked before he reached the other end of the parking lot. He ran to the street corner where John had waited for him every other day since the fourth grade. He ran, crying out loud, gasping for precious air, taking in rain, coughing and pumping his legs as hard as they would go. A dangling rosebush caught his cheek, but he kept going. His side ached, but he kept going. He kept going.

8

The wood in the tree house was still damp from yesterday's rain. The air was cool now, and would stay that way, gradually increasing from a mild nip to a bite as the world moved on its way to winter. Yellow leaves appeared in the green canopy above and began to break free drifting away in the breeze. One fell in a slow, spinning, swaying dance landing softly against Broadie's cheek. He wept in shifting patterns of morning light. He had been crying off and on since yesterday. At the moment he was crying in relief. He had decided to stay home from school forever, regardless of the consequences. He didn't have to be there. It was as simple as that: no one could stop him. He was free. No matter what he did, it was his choice, and he had more power over his life than he had ever thought. That his grandpa's gun was safely back in its place was an even greater relief.

He had found an unexpected escape that mercifully anesthetized most of his waking days: he bunched up his jacket, making a crude pillow, and pulled some books out of his backpack. Blinking the tears out of his eyes, he would finish *Ender's Game*, then start on *Lord of the Flies*, by William Golding. He also brought along a dusty, worn-out paperback of *The Stand*, by Stephen King, that he had found in his mom's bookshelf. He marveled at the number of pages that it held. The only other book that thick that he knew of was the Bible. He loved the picture on the cover of a man dueling with a demon. He had read the synopsis on the back and was intrigued with the idea of a worldwide plague. Grandpa had once told him about the thousands of sheep that had died south of Tooele, Utah (which had one of the biggest stockpiles of nerve gas in the country), and wondered if there was any inspiration from that in Stephen King's story. He flipped the pages with his thumb, setting a goal to have it read by Valentine's Day. He took some food out, then decided he wasn't hungry. The thing he wanted to do the most before reading, though, was to sleep. He lay back, sensing the shifting light under closed eyelids, smiled, and thought about January.

Part III

1

There was something different about Dad. He wore a suit and his hair was cut short like the other men's at church. He was clean, shaved. But it wasn't just that. His whole countenance had changed.

"Come here, Broadie Bear," he said. He held his arms open, and Broadie saw that his eyes were bright like clear water on a summer day.

Broadie ran to him, feeling his arms draw him firmly close. His strength was sweet comfort that brought a rush of tears. His breath was clean. He missed him, the special things that only they did . . . the rides in the canyon; helping him work on the car. His real dad: the one that had been buried under a mountain of bitterness and alcohol. There he was exposed, like a gem shattered from its matrix of dull rock.

"I missed you," Broadie said.

Dad looked him in the eyes. He gripped him firmly by the shoulders, squatting like he did when Broadie was six.

"It's gonna be good from here on."

His smile was sweet truth; teeth white and free of the cigarette-yellow.

Broadie's dream blew away like dust from an old shelf. When he opened his eyes, a sense of loss fell heavy in his chest, and his pillow was damp from tears in his sleep. He curled up, looking out at the yellow that was left on Grandpa's pear trees. Today was Halloween, and also the day that his dad would come home from jail.

The house was busy, and he was too nervous to eat breakfast. Davie was all ready for school, but Broadie had no intention of going. He was still wearing the sweats he'd gone to bed in, and he had "chicken-feather hair." Grandpa huffed up the stairs with more boxes of Dad's stuff that Mom had packed and set them out on the porch. Since they were getting a divorce, Mom had decided that it was better that he move in with Grandma Bennett in Riverton.

"Get in there and get ready," Grandma said, preoccupied with finding her keys.

"You can take my car if you want," Mom said from the stairwell. She put Alisha down by her side. She was getting too big to hold.

"That's all right. I think I had my keys in the other coat." Grandma passed Broadie again. "Go get dressed. You're going to make us late."

"Do what your grandma tells you!" Grandpa hollered from the porch.

Broadie reluctantly left the table and walked back into his room. It wasn't fair that they weren't going to let him stay home to see his dad. It was stupid. They let him stay home when they knew he was playing sick. What was the big deal about having to go today?

"We know it's best this way for right now," Grandpa had said when he explained the restraining order.

"Let's go," Grandma called from the hall.

He decided that it would be easier to comply now, then run back home after Grandma dropped them off. He was determined to see his dad, whether they liked it or not.

They were late, and Grandma was mad. She was silent throughout the drive. The schoolyard was empty, and the crossing guard was reaching up to turn off the flashing school zone-lights. There was supposed to be a Halloween party in class today, but he didn't want any part of it. January wouldn't be there, anyway. She had been sick again. He walked Davie up to the doors and watched in the reflection as Grandma drove away. Davie put on his Poké-mon mask and ran in enthusiastically. Broadie zipped his jacket up to his chin and pulled his collar tight around his neck. The car was finally out of sight. He turned away from the school. Leaves crunched under his feet as he walked on, confidant that he would get grounded for skipping school again, but seeing his dad was more important. He felt a leap of excitement in his chest and walked faster.

He hunched through the opening in the fence that led to the ditch, trying not to catch his backpack on a loose chainlink. He would go the back way and hide behind the shed in case Grandpa was close. The weeds had turned brown, and the fall colors were pretty in the glistening morning light. Fuzzy frost still covered everything in the shadows. The big box elder was quickly losing its leaves. He was surprised how easily he could see the tree house now. He began to worry that someone might see it and try to find a way through the rose bushes. Though it was still hard to see the secret passage, they were also thinning. If he looked hard enough, he could see the small trail that he and January had made. The best solution would be to cut off some branches and block off that side of the ditch completely. That would force people to stay on the trail. He could probably do that later in the afternoon, if he remembered.

Dad was already there with his brother, Uncle Justin, loading boxes into his truck. Broadie hunched in the weeds, watching Justin go back and forth from the porch to the truck. He hadn't seen Dad yet and became impatient. When Justin turned his back, he scrambled to the shed. Flakes of white paint broke off onto his jacket. He inched his way to the edge to peek around the corner. From this angle he could see through the Larsons' window. January was at the table eating breakfast. He envied her that she didn't have to go to school.

There was a buzzing sound above his head, and he looked up surprised to see yellow jackets this late in the season. Animated by the morning sunlight, they crawled lethargically over their nest in the eaves. They had built it perilously close to where he kept his secret stash—not so secret since Grandpa found the cigarettes. He felt an urge to find a stick and smash one, but another conflicting feeling told him to let it be. They were innocent, and now helpless. There was something special about life, no matter how repulsed he was by it. Mercy won. He concentrated on his dad. He inched out further until he was on his hands and knees in the dewy lawn grass. His fingers ached in the cold, but he didn't want to move too quickly and be discovered before he had a chance to see Dad.

Grandpa and Dad appeared from the garage carrying the camping gear. He felt a pinprick in his chest. Dad had kept promising to go camping. He wondered if there was still a chance. He waited until they passed out of view, then ran hunched like a soldier to the back porch. He was about to inch around the corner of the house when he heard voices carry through the open back door.

"Stay in here if you know what's good for you," Grandma said.

"I don't care what happens. He's not taking my stereo." Mom was agitated.

"Please don't make things any worse."

"He wasn't supposed to come into the house! That was the deal!"

"You weren't supposed to be here either. *That* was also part of the deal."

"What? Do you expect me to just go away and let him take everything?"

"Is a stereo worth causing another incident?"

Alisha started to fuss, masking their voices. Instead of trying to go by way of the driveway, he ran back between the houses. Broadie slowed down when he was sure he was out of sight and walked by January's window. It was open. He hoped to talk to her soon. He edged along the wall until he could see the front yard. Grandpa and Dad were talking. Then Dad picked up his big red toolbox, muscling it over to the truck. He set it down, stretched his back, and took a big drag of his cigarette. Grandpa walked around back. Now was his chance. He dropped his backpack and ran hard to the truck. Dad spun around in surprise. His hair was longer. He looked a lot like the country singer Keith Urban, that Mom always listened to.

"Dad!" Broadie said.

"Broadie Bud!" Dad's eyes were clear and sharp. Broadie stopped, feeling a swimming hit of déjà vu.

"I miss you, Dad," he said, a little too loud.

"I miss you, too." He looked worriedly over at the front door. "Come here." He led him out of view of the house past the naked lilac bushes. "You've got to go, ok?"

"But why?" Broadie was hurt.

"Please, I'll talk to you soon. Now aren't you supposed to be in school?"

"When will I see you next?"

Dad took another drag of his cigarette and let it out slowly, scratching his whiskers and glancing back over at the house. Uncle Justin heaved another box into the truck and walked away, not noticing them. Dad turned back to Broadie.

"When this restraining order that your mom sicked on me is lifted."

"I don't care about that stupid restraining order."

"Do you want to send me back to jail?" Dad said quickly.

"No, but—"

"Then go back to school."

Broadie started to cry.

Dad squatted down like he used to, reached out and took Broadie firmly by the shoulders. His cigarette hung crookedly from the side of his mouth, like a movie star's. He glanced back, then said: "Things are different now. They're going to be better. You can call me at Grandma Bennett's. I don't think *she'd* stop you."

"Ok," Broadie sniffed.

"Come here." Dad pulled him close and they hugged. They hadn't hugged in a long time. Broadie didn't want to let go.

"Get your hands off him!" Mom spoke with foul words and a surprising petulance, shattering their moment.

Dad spun around, horrified.

She came out of nowhere, wearing a black dress that Broadie had never seen before. He'd seen her wearing strange things, but nothing as garish as this backless dress with slits up both sides that revealed a hint of lace on her hip when the wind blew. She didn't seem to mind the cold. A sludgy embarrassment masked his horror at being caught, and for the first time he could see that his mother wasn't such an innocent victim.

"I ought to call the cops right now and send you right back to jail!" Mom said with stupid triumph.

Dad's face darkened. "He came to *me*."

Grandpa came running with Uncle Justin from behind the house. Grandma limped down the porch steps.

"Mom. Please. Don't. It was me. I just—"

Mom turned on Broadie: "You get out of here! You're grounded again!"

"Go on, Broadie," Dad coaxed, then looked at Mom, his eyes burning.

Grandpa arrived out of breath. "Just let it go, Michelle." Grandpa spoke with warning in his voice.

Mom didn't move. Dad tried to pass her to go to the truck, and she jumped in his way.

"Get in the house!" Grandpa grabbed Mom firmly by the arm.

She yanked it away fiercely. "He violated the restraining order!"

"I said, leave it alone!" Grandpa shouted. It wasn't very often that Broadie had ever seen Grandpa this angry.

"Broadie came up to *me*, you stupid woman!" Dad had violence in his eyes.

"See! See! That's verbal abuse! Do you see why I'm divorcing him?"

Dad shook his head in bewilderment and defeat. Uncle Justin calmly stepped in front of Michelle and rested a firm arm on Dad's shoulder. Mom tried to shove Uncle Justin, and Grandpa gave her a hefty yank. She fought him. Grandma joined the struggle. Alisha was alone on the porch, crying.

"I'm taking my stereo back!" Mom screamed.

Dad looked back at Broadie as he walked to the truck with Uncle Justin.

"Go get your sister!" Grandma yelled at Broadie.

"See how you are?" Mom carried on with more foul words.

As Broadie ran to attend his sister, he glanced over in time to see January's mom spying from her front door. The fight must have looked like a scene from a tawdry television talk show. He looked away in shame.

The fallout around the house was poisonous. He was grounded to his room for the rest of the week. Mom left for work, and Davie left with Aunt Cheryl to go trick-or-treating.

Seeing Mom as she was earlier exposed her in a new light. He now wondered how much Dad had been provoked the night that he had put her in the hospital.

He lost concentration on his book and sat up to adjust his pillow. Being alone in his room for long periods of time wasn't much of a punishment at all. In fact, the time seemed to move quicker as he read. He found solace in his books. They gave him enough fantasy to be able to take reality in smaller doses. He was becoming a better reader every day and had lost interest in television. That he didn't spend so many hours in front of the tube had become another worry with his grandparents. For a while, Grandpa would often check on him until he was satisfied that it was the books and not something serious that kept him alone and quiet for so many hours. One day he came in to find that Grandpa had tossed a book of scripture onto his bed. He took it and put it alongside the other books he intended to read.

His reading had also temporarily buffered his problem with un-excused absences from school. His reasoning was that he was too far behind anyway. He was willing to do homework and study, but he couldn't do it around the kids that picked on him. He feigned sickness until the school demanded a doctor's notice, then Grandpa demanded that he go back. If he was taken physically to class, he eventually found an escape. Principal Barker finally told him that one more unexcused absence and he would go to juvenile court. Barker had also promised that they would change his class, but they were dragging their feet, and again today he hadn't shown up at school.

The doorbell rang, the front door opened and pipey voices tuned: "Trick-or-treat." He looked up surprised at how dark it was outside. January's light was on. He closed his book, got up, and opened his window. Her parents had moved a television into her room, but it was dark and silent. This made him smile. She was sitting on her bed with a blanket bunched up on her lap like a table and was writing in a small book that was probably her journal. He picked up his "knocking stick," as they called it (January had one, too), and lightly tapped on her window. She looked up surprised, put her book on the night stand, threw her covers aside, and slipped her feet into some oversized "puppy" slippers. She looked soft, very girlish, but also didn't look well. She was losing more weight. Her eye sockets were dark and heavy, cheekbones more prominent. The tanktop that had fit her well in the summer now hung loosely on her shoulders. She opened her window.

"Hi." She smiled, then quickly glanced back at her door.

"What's new?"

"Nothing much. Was that your dad today?"

"Yeah, that was him."

"He looks scary."

Broadie didn't quite know what to say to that. He looked out and watched some witches and bloody soldiers walking past.

"I didn't mean anything by that," she whispered.

"No, it's okay. I know. He can be a nice guy, though. He looked like he's doing better."

She nodded.

Another different chorus of "trick-or-treat."

"Hey, I got an idea. Hold on." He left her at the window and peeked out into the hallway. Grandma was handing out candy at the door. Alisha was content with some toys on the floor, and Grandpa was watching something on TV about World War II. Grandma had her back turned, so he quickly tiptoed into the kitchen where she kept the extra bowl of candy. He returned to his room cautiously, looking back with every step, carefully closed the door, and breathed a big sigh of relief as he arrived back at his window. January was still there.

"Trick-or-treat," he said, handing her some pixy sticks and a box of lemon heads.

"Thank you," she beamed. She was more touched than he thought she would be.

"Wait here," she said. She mechanically shuffled to her door, trying not to lose her over-sized slippers. She left her room a lot more confident than Broadie had his.

While she was gone, he looked around, feeling the chill from outside and hoping she'd be back soon. There was a small pile of get-well cards and a bouquet of balloons tied to a post on her bed. There were medicine bottles and a lot of evidence that she hadn't left her room much lately. As she came back, he instinctively ducked in case it was her mom or dad.

"It's just me," she giggled. "Here—trick-or-treat."

"Wow, you got the good stuff." He admired his new handful of Hershey bars.

"I know. My mom's a chocolate freak." Her breath came out in small puffs of steam, and she rubbed her arms. "I'm cold," she said. She grabbed the cover off of her bed and wrapped it around herself. She sat down on a small chest (probably an old toy box) and started working on a pixy stick. "What book are you reading now?" she asked, her tongue purple.

"*The Stand*," Broadie said, retrieving his own blanket.

"Who's it by?"

"Stephen King."

"Eww, yuck!" She puckered her face, tearing at another stick.

"What do you mean: 'Eww, yuck'?"

"My dad says Stephen King writes devil stuff."

"This isn't devil stuff. This is the coolest stuff I've ever read." It was only the third book he had ever read. He walked over to his bed and picked it up. "See," he said, holding it up.

"That's huge. How can you read something so big?"

"I just do, I guess. I thought it would take me until Valentine's Day, but tomorrow is November first, and I'm halfway done. I bet I can finish it by Christmas."

"Cool," she said, tilting her head back to let the lime-flavored powder empty smoothly into the back of her mouth. She tapped the small paper tube, then threw it aside.

"What are *you* reading?" He motioned to the paperback by her pill bottles.

"*Anne of Green Gables*, by L.M. Montgomery," she said braggingly, as if it were better than *The Stand*.

"Eww, yuck!" he said back.

"It's not yucky."

"Yes it is. It's a girl book."

"How would *you* know?"

"I saw it on TV. It was too girly for me to watch."

"Shut up!" She bantered good-naturedly, but there was still a hint of annoyance.

They quietly worked at their candy as the Ghost Rider and the X-men passed by on the sidewalk.

"I know a real cool book you ought to read," Broadie said more seriously.

"What's that?"

"*Ender's Game*, by Orson Scott Card. It's awesome. I'll lend it to you if you want."

"Are you sure?"

"I wouldn't let you take it if I wasn't sure." He went back to his growing book collection and picked it out. Grandpa sometimes took him to secondhand stores where he found old paperbacks for less than a dollar.

She leaned forward to take it from him, looked it over, and nodded knowingly: a very adult-like gesture. "I'll start on it as soon as I finish *Anne of Green Gables*." She emphasized the title. Broadie ignored her. "I have to go back to Primary Children's Hospital tomorrow," she said glumly.

He blinked away his thoughts. "Why is that?"

"I guess they're worried something might be really wrong with me. They say my blood's all wrong and I keep getting real sick."

"What are they going to do?"

"They're going to take a bone sample from my hip."

"How do they do that?"

She shrugged her shoulders, and watched an ape-man lead a group of Draculas and other nameless things to the house across the street. He tried to picture how a doctor would take a bone sample. Would they cut her open? He imagined the TV version of an operating room.

"I'm cold," she said.

Broadie expected her to close her window or something, but she seemed to want to stay even though they didn't have much more to say. They watched Halloween continue on beyond their rooms.

2

When Broadie was called to Barker's office, he thought: *This is it. Finally.* He was also asked to take all of his things with him. He figured Grandpa or someone would be there waiting, and he would go to juvenile court. He heard that when kids go to juvenile court, they go to detention for young criminals. He was surprisingly happy. Now he wouldn't have to go to class this time because *they* said so. His feet felt lighter and he double-checked his backpack to make sure *The Stand* was in there.

"Have a seat, Broadie." The secretary spoke his name with routine familiarity. "Doctor Barker will be out in a minute."

He nodded and sat in his favorite chair. The secretary smiled, resuming her work. Amanda Berkley appeared from a back room holding a stack of papers. He knew that she had noticed him. She went about her business, ignoring him and stuffing envelopes with adult-like airs—only the very good kids got the privilege of spending a couple of hours a week doing slave work in the office, and the bad kids got to sit and watch them. He lost interest in her executive toil, brought out his book, and started to read.

"Young Mister Bennett."

Barker opened the small gate by the counter and motioned for Broadie to come in. He rubbed his temples as if he had a headache.

Broadie tucked his book under his arm, retrieved his backpack, and stood, making another quick glance at Amanda. She was one of the few who never joined in with the teasing, but she made great efforts to ignore him. He wanted to bump her table just to see if she would look up; instead, he followed Barker.

"Don't tell me you're reading *that!*" Barker said, walking past his office door. Broadie was surprised they hadn't stopped there.

"Yes," Broadie said proudly.

"What is it?"

When he told him, Barker gave him a look as if he'd just smelled something bad and stopped. "Let me see that." He took it from Broadie's hands, and flipped through its worn pages. He looked at it over his nose, then handed it back with a small nod.

A thoughtful pause.

"And you're *really* reading that?" Barker continued.

"Yes, I am."

"Now wait a minute. You haven't done any schoolwork for . . . a month and a half, maybe? Five, six weeks . . . since school started, anyway."

Broadie looked silently at the floor.

"Here, look at me." He softened his tone of voice and smiled.

Broadie looked up.

"You mean to tell me you can't read your text books, but you can read a book with what, over a thousand pages? And do you really understand what you're reading?"

Broadie nodded.

"How far have you read?"

"Halfway."

"No kidding."

Broadie looked back at the floor, and they were silent again.

"You must really like to read."

"A-huh," Broadie said affirmatively.

"Let's make a deal here." He folded his arms and leaned against the wall. "Do you know where we're going?"

"No." A nervous bubble swelled in Broadie's stomach.

"I'm taking you out to Mrs. Smith's class. She teaches a mix of fifth and sixth graders, mostly students with special needs. Now, hold on before you misunderstand me. She can help you. We have two teachers there, and they can dedicate more time to you, and you won't have to deal with the kids you had problems with any longer. Your mother gave the go-ahead. Now, about our deal: I'll talk to Mrs. Smith and have her set up more special reading time for you than what she usually has, but you have to pay attention in class and do all your schoolwork first. Do we have a deal?"

"Okay." Broadie smiled. He was relieved that he wasn't going to juvenile court and elated to be away from Burt's class. His eyes were moist, and his throat was tight. This was more of a relief than he expected.

They walked out through the kindergarten doors to the direction of the "Relocatables," portable separate buildings used as classrooms. The other kids usually called them the "retard rooms." Broadie glanced back at the utility shed and hoped to take his recess on top in the warm sunlight reading his book. Barker led him up the graying wooden stairs. They opened the door and drew the attention of the class.

"Dr. Barker, come on in out of the cold," a kindly woman said, approaching from her desk. "We've been waiting for you." She turned to Broadie. "Now, you must be Broadie Bennett."

Hearing his name spoken out loud in front of strangers was a momentary jab at his nerves. Everyone was staring at him, and, as a natural reaction, he backed away with the urge to turn and run. Barker must have sensed it because he put a hand on his shoulder, gripping it firmly, but not noticeably to the others. He stood relaxed, looking down at Broadie in a way that let him know he didn't want a problem.

"Everyone," the teacher continued. "I'd like to introduce you to Broadie. I'm Sarah Smith, and over there in the reading circle is Mrs. Kistler. She likes you to call her Joslyn."

A dark-haired, stern-looking woman waved with one hand holding a book and trying not to spill her coffee in the other. She looked back down and resumed reading.

"Remember, that's *Joslyn*, not *Jaws*," the boy nearest to Broadie, spoke.

Sparse laughter.

"Yeah, and his name is *Craig*, not *Lurpy*." Leroy, a kid a few desks down spoke.

Greater laughter.

"Shut up!" Craig said back with a nasty insult.

"Kick your butt, punk," Leroy said promisingly.

"That's enough!" Joslyn snapped. "Sarah, will you drop these two down a level."

"Sure," Sarah said happily. She approached a bulletin board on the wall that had five colored strips from top to bottom. On different strips were nametags. Purple, on the top, must have been the best, and red must have been the worst. She took Craig's name and dropped it from blue to green, and Leroy's from yellow to red.

Craig put his head down on his desk with a sigh of disappointment. Leroy brooded.

Barker spoke quietly with Sarah.

Leroy continued to glare at Craig. His head was shaved except for a ponytail in the back. His pants were so baggy that they almost looked like a dress. Craig tried to ignore him.

"You're dead," Leroy said quietly.

"Leroy, I can send you out with Mr. Barker right now," Sarah said over Barker's shoulder. The principal turned around. Leroy shrank back in his seat.

"Whatever," Leroy mumbled.

"What's that?" Joslyn put her book down and walked over to his desk. "Do you want to make a show for the principal?"

"No," Leroy said derisively.

"What? I couldn't hear."

"I said *no*, you stupid, deaf—"

"Let's go, Leroy." Barker's voice meant business. He motioned for Leroy to get up.

"Fine!" Leroy stood. As he passed Broadie, he stopped and spoke menacingly in his face. "What are *you* looking at?" He sized Broadie from head to foot.

Broadie backed away, intimidated.

"Come on," Barker said, placing a firm hand on the back of Leroy's neck.

"Go ahead and take a seat by Craig," Sarah said, assisting the principal to the door.

Barker guided Leroy out the door. Leroy tried a threatening look back, but the muscles in Barker's arm tightened, and suddenly Leroy was looking forward and walking faster. The door closed.

Sarah turned around, letting out a long breath. "Okay, everyone quiet down." The class was agitated. "Well, Broadie, I'm sure that was the most pleasant of introductions."

Broadie smiled shyly.

Craig leaned over to whisper: "That was the second meanest kid in the school."

You haven't met John, Broadie thought.

"The meanest," Craig continued, "is sitting tight over there behind Jaws."

Broadie looked over, not seeing to whom Craig was pointing at. Joslyn was in the way.

"Okay . . . Broadie Bennett, will you come over here for a minute?" Sarah motioned him over to her desk.

"Hey, that's the kid they call 'Grodie Broadie!'" Gayle, a girl with short, dirty blond hair, spoke.

Shocked, Broadie stopped and looked at her, trying to decide if he'd seen her before.

"Gayle, if you want to drop another level, just keep on talking," Sarah said.

Gayle looked down at her desk, exchanging a sideways glance with the girl next to her, and they both giggled.

As he walked to Sarah's desk, he got a good look at the kid Craig had pointed at. It was the dark-boy he had seen behind the utility shed the first day of school. The kid looked up slowly, meeting Broadie's glance. A strange current moved through Broadie's head, and, for some reason, he thought of an empty well. He looked away quickly. Sarah motioned to a chair next to her desk. He sat down, feeling uncomfortable that his back was turned.

"Now, I'm sure they've explained to you why they've moved you into this class," Sarah said, looking at a file with Broadie's name on it.

"It's because the kids kept picking on me in the other class."

She nodded slightly. "Well, now, you also have had a serious truancy problem that nearly landed you in juvenile court." Pause. "That's pretty serious. You also haven't done any schoolwork for over a month. You don't want to fail the sixth grade, do you?"

Broadie sensed that she was waiting for an answer, but he stared quietly into a sticky garbage can that left a dark ring of coffee on the floor.

She spoke again: "Here, we're not going to let you fail." She lowered her head to look him in the eyes. "I hear that you like to read."

Broadie looked up.

She smiled. "That's good. I'm a reader too. I *want* you to read. In fact, I want to give you time to read, but you've got to do something for me."

Broadie nodded.

"You'll do all the work I assign you first, and we'll get you caught up. See that board over there?"

"Yes," Broadie said.

"Everyone starts on blue level, and every level represents certain privilege. Blue means you can have recess, and every day you spend on blue level you get a ticket. When you get five tickets, you can buy something from the class store. You can get treats, gifts, something fun or useful. Now, purple level gets you a lunch or breakfast every Friday at the place you pick plus, you get to go to all the assemblies and activities. Sounds good, doesn't it?"

Broadie smiled, nodded, glanced back at the dark-boy, then at Gayle. She had the same look of proud meanness that Vanessa Davis had, but there was an underlying sophistication, a sadness that added a punch like angry nitrous oxide to a hot engine.

"Broadie!" Sarah snapped her fingers in front of his eyes. "Please pay attention."

"Sorry," he said, not meeting her eyes, but looking at his file.

"Now, green level, you don't get any tickets. Yellow level, you get to go out for recess, but you have to stay by me and you can't play with the rest of the kids. Red level, you don't get any recess, and you have to stay here with Joslyn during lunch."

Gayle squealed and the girl next to her laughed. They had been playing some sort of game. "Sorry," Gayle said, still laughing.

"Quiet, girls," Sarah said.

"I said 'sorry!'" Gayle said belligerently. She reached back with both hands to adjust her ponytail, and her shirt slid loosely over two small swells on her chest.

Broadie felt a momentary curiosity, then remembered January. His emotions changed to worry. She had gone to the hospital again for that awful . . . what was it? Core sample? Bone sample?

" . . . fighting, stealing, truancy will drop you automatically to the red level. Swearing, name-calling, talking back to a teacher, and noncompliance or disobedience will drop you one level. Now, your goal is to work your way to purple level and maintain that. Each one hundred percent that you get on assignments automatically raises you a level, and each week of good behavior raises you a level. If your grades drop below a C, you drop a level. Does that make sense?"

Broadie nodded.

"We're doing this math worksheet," she said, handing him a paper. "Go back, sit in the seat by Craig, which will be your assigned seat, and start on it. If you don't understand it, that's okay, because I just want to see where your level is."

Broadie sat down and worked quietly through the easy problems, then read a little, waiting for what came next.

The room was quiet, except for an occasional giggle from Gayle's direction. He learned that her friend was named Raelynn, and over in the reading circle with Joslyn were Mike and Jeff, and the dark-boy whose name he hadn't learned yet.

The recess bell rang. Joslyn put down her book. The kids all rushed for the door.

"Hey! Hey! Jeff!" Joslyn yelled. Jeff, a dirty scratchy-voiced kid, turned around, feigning disappointment with a sly smile. "*You* stay by me."

Broadie looked over and saw Jeff's name on yellow level.

The dark-boy stepped outside, to Broadie's relief. Broadie turned to talk to Craig when the dark-boy came back in, walking quietly to his desk. A cold breeze followed him. He snatched up his jacket. There was something in the way that he moved, a sort of shadow: a glimmering potential of violence. He glanced over to the teachers, then looked at Broadie with a vacant unnaturalness that revived the sparking current that he had felt the first time that he had seen him. He walked innocently enough until he nudged Broadie's back with his shoulder. He looked around satisfied that the teachers hadn't noticed, then walked out the door.

"That was Jim Blackstone," Craig said. "I call him Mr. Brownstone when he's not around."

What grade's he in?"

"He's in sixth, but he does seem older. Maybe he'd been held back. I don't know."

"Who are the fifth graders?"

"That's Mike and Jeff."

"Talkin' about me?" Jeff perked up. He stood by the door, waiting for Joslyn.

Craig spun around surprised and a little scared, but Broadie looked at Jeff, knowing that he wasn't that tough. Something clicked right then. Jeff didn't know him. There was no history. A crazy revelation flashed in his mind that he could make his own history. Fighting back the butterflies in his stomach, he met Jeff's eyes without showing fear. He tried to copy the dark-boy look. Jeff was the first to break eye contact, changing the direction of his strut more toward Craig. He was probably just showing off, but something entirely new had happened: a message had been sent that Jeff believed. Jeff was a bully and not too smart, at that. He might need some reminding, but it was a first impression that would last. Jeff kept a wary eye toward the teachers who were conferring over Sarah's desk. Craig cowered back, looking pitifully the same direction. Broadie recognized that look as the one that had been seen so many times in himself: the pathetic hopelessness of a beaten person. With a crazy glee, he vowed never to let it happen again. It was so terribly sweet and fragile, but it moved inside like a bull let out of its gate. He didn't want to overdo it. He really had to go somewhere and think about this one.

"Puss," Jeff whispered.

"Jeff!" Joslyn yelled. "Do you want red level? Because I can drop you, and you won't get any recess."

Jeff slinked away, keeping his distance from the teachers. "Puss," he whispered again.

"Well, *do* you want red level?"

"No." He sat down into a desk.

"What was that?" Joslyn put her things down and leaned her slight frame over him. She lowered her voice almost to a whisper: "Answer me good."

"No, Mrs. Kistler." Jeff said penitently this time.

"That's better. Let's go out, now." She turned to Craig: "You know, you don't have to stand there and wait for me."

"I know," Craig said, looking at the floor.

"Have you taken your Ritalin yet?"

"I haven't eaten yet." He looked warily at the door.

"Why don't you take Broadie out with you?" Mrs. Smith spoke from her desk.

"*He* can go. I don't want to."

Joslyn escorted Jeff out the door. Broadie watched quietly as Mrs. Smith talked to Craig.

"Let's give it a try." She put a hand affectionately on his shoulder.

"No!" He yanked his shoulder away sharply.

Mrs. Smith turned to Broadie. "Go ahead and go."

Broadie walked out, hearing Mrs. Smith's soothing voice disappear into the background.

Kids played as usual. His former classmates grouped in their various cliques. John, Joey, Benji, Darren, and Tim all played soccer in the cold sunshine. A group of girls followed Vanessa, and others grouped with Amanda Berkley. He wandered down by the shed, hoping to climb up to the roof. The fence bowed a little where he had crossed it fleeing John and friends. The old lady's tomatoes were drying up. She had picked most of them, and only a few green ones hung ruined by frost. When he started to climb, he caught a whiff of cigarette smoke. There was slight movement behind a mass of dry, fall-reddened leaves. He leaned over to get a better look and saw the edge of Jim's jacket.

"What are *you* looking at, dickface?" Jim's voice hissed low and dangerous from the shadows. He sounded big, like a junior high student.

This was his chance again: "Someone afraid to get caught smoking." Horrified, the blood draining from his face, Broadie couldn't believe his own answer. The moment with Jeff was over, and this wasn't Jeff. He must have been crazy. He wanted to run away, but knew he couldn't back down now. Doing so would mean a hell of a lot worse than John. He had to put him self immediately on Jim's level or it would be too late.

"Get out of here, or I'll kick your ass," Jim said.

Broadie climbed back down and pushed himself into the vines. Leaves broke off, falling clumsily around him. Jim's eye stared out at him, promisingly deadly. His hand lifted, and the coal glowed. Tobacco smoke blew through the remaining shriveled leaves into Broadie's face.

"I'll only warn you once," Jim said, his voice as cloudy as the smoke.

Trying to conceal the tremor in his voice, Broadie said: "I need a smoke." It was the only thing he could think of to say. He had

probably just signed his death warrant, but he'd been through it before. Now he had nothing to lose. He didn't budge. Jim continued
to stare at him, and he stared back unblinking. "I'd do it for you if
you needed one," he said, now sure he was talking too much.

Jim shook his head and let out a smoky sigh. The leaves next
to Broadie crackled. A dry hand with a deep healing cut on the
thumb pushed gradually through, holding an unlit cigarette and
the lighter between two fingers. Broadie was so surprised that he
stood statue-like until the hand started to drop. He quickly took
them. Jim looked out, watching for the recess monitor and probably Joslyn. Broadie lit up and pulled the smoke into his mouth as
he had practiced. He was afraid to cough and make a fool of himself. Jim took another drag off of his cigarette, blowing the smoke
expertly out of his nose. His hand appeared again to retrieve the
lighter. Broadie slipped it back between the chapped fingers.

They quietly puffed into the autumn air until the bell rang. Jim
smoothly flicked his butt, still smoking, into the old lady's yard.
Broadie watched it fall among the dry tomato plants, then looked
back up. Jim was gone. He looked down at his own smoldering
half-smoked cigarette and wondered what to do with it. He had a
silly notion to keep it for fear of insulting Jim, but what would he
care? He smashed it against the cinderblock wall and slid out into
the exodus of kids.

3

Broadie was too entranced with his book to pay much attention to Mom's argument with Grandma. Instead, he walked in a world where he sympathized with a remnant people divinely guided: heroes of a postepidemic landscape gathering to stand against an ominous evil as it gathered its own forces far away in the west desert. People with bigger problems than his own; people whom he identified with symbolically. Somewhere unconscious to himself, he knew he would have to make his own stand. When, how, or where didn't matter. He just felt it.

"I deserve a break!" Mom yelled.

Broadie lost concentration on his book and listened, automatically looking up at January's darkened window.

"All I said was that you should spend tonight with your kids. You didn't have to go off on me like that. I've been taking care of them day and night. You know what? I think it's *me* that deserves a break. I'm getting your dad as soon as he gets back and *we're* going out!" Grandma said, losing her temper.

"You don't have to be that way. What's wrong with me having a little sanity now and then, huh?"

"Oh, now let's talk about sanity. . . ."

"Yeah, *let's* talk about sanity. I *deserve* a little sanity."

"Sanity is not going out on the town when you're still married!"

"I'm as good as divorced!"

"You're *not* divorced!"

"Sorry, Mom, but I don't come from your little Leave-it-to-Beaver world, and I'm an adult now, if you haven't noticed. I'm free to make my own decisions!"

"Oh? And what do you think you're teaching your children?"

"I'm teaching them to be more openminded. At least—"

"You're teaching them that you can neglect your kids and go chasing after other men when you have a husband."

"I don't have a husband, and I'm not chasing other men. I'm just going dancing with some friends for—"

"Dancing with other men!"

"Well, what do you want me to do, dance with other women? Oh, hey, that's an idea! There's one thing I haven't done in my sinful life."

"You're selfish and ungrateful. You have no gratitude or respect toward us and none toward God."

"I'm going. Goodbye!"

"You don't have to parade around like a common slut!"

The door slammed.

Grandma moved deftly, angrily through the kitchen as she made dinner. A pan fell to the floor, taking some dishes with it. She murmured under her breath. Davie watched a video in the other room.

Mom dancing with other men.

The thought had a strange taste. It made Broadie feel floaty, as if the things he understood to be true and constant like light and gravity weren't really true: man and woman together. Husband and wife bound together by covenant and commitment; family; something more precious than gold . . . all second to Mom's sanity; her fun; her work; her dancing.

The back door opened then shut. He heard footsteps. Maybe Mom was back. No. It wasn't the sound of her shoes, but Grandpa's heavy feet, then Grandma's angry murmurs. Grandpa sighed loudly and was probably shaking his head.

"Broadie, come on and eat." Grandma tried to sound pleasant. "Davie? Broadie? Come on."

He put his book down and left his room, stretching. Grandpa came out of the bathroom adjusting his belt. He was wearing his shirt and tie. He ruffled Broadie's hair as he passed him into the kitchen.

"Well, where are you going now?" Grandma asked Grandpa. She leaned her oven-mitted hand on the counter, trying to keep her weight off her sore knee.

Grandpa motioned her out of the room. "Wait here," he said to the kids. "I have to talk to your grandma for a minute."

"Broadie, help your little sister into the high chair, and get the pan out of the oven when the buzzer rings," Grandma said.

Broadie nodded and watched them walk into the living room.

Grandpa talked low, but his words could still be overheard. "I'm going to the hospital with the bishop to give the Larson girl a blessing. From what I hear she—"

Davie made a burring noise with a toy truck scraping it across the table.

"Ssh!" Broadie spat fiercely.

Davie continued and Broadie grabbed the truck out of his hands.

"Hey!" Davie hollered.

"Ssh!" Broadie said again.

"Oh, the poor little thing. Oh dear, that's just not fair! She's so young!" Grandma sounded close to tears.

"They say this kind comes on when they're young but it can be treated, but she's—"

The buzzer sounded. Broadie ran, nearly tripping, and flipped it off. He put on the oven mitts and pulled out a cheesy-looking casserole that made his stomach growl.

"I'll stay for a bite, but I have to meet them there at eight," Grandpa said, walking back into the kitchen. Grandma shook her head sadly.

"What's wrong with January?" Broadie asked immediately.

Grandpa and Grandma exchanged looks.

"She's very sick, hon," Grandma said.

"But what does she have?" He was getting annoyed that she wouldn't answer him directly.

"We're not completely sure. We don't want to start any rumors just yet. She's still getting tests done," Grandpa said.

"I won't say anything," Broadie pleaded. He was losing his appetite.

"I'm going to find out tonight, and I'll let you know as soon as I can. Things are a little touchy with their family right now, and I don't want to cause a problem." Grandpa dished himself a serving and ate standing up.

"Just tell me what you told Grandma," Broadie insisted.

"It was pretty much the same thing I told you. Now, will you help them out and let it go for now? And, as soon as we can, we'll talk about it." Grandpa spoke between bites.

"I'm not a little kid anymore! I'm old enough to know things!"

Grandpa swiped a napkin from a cow shaped holder on the counter and wiped his mouth. "I've gotta go." He gave Grandma a kiss on the cheek then left quickly out the door.

"Grandma?" Broadie looked at her pleadingly.

"Look, the wait is just as bad for us. Now, don't keep insisting or I'm gonna get mad." Grandma dished him a plate.

Broadie stood up from his chair and left the room in a huff. Grandma shook her head with that suit-yourself look that she so often gave his mother.

4

Craig stared blankly at the wall. Sometimes he didn't blink for a long time. Broadie wondered what he thought about when he did that. Gayle and Raelynn, in their own little world, gossiped quietly. Leroy and Jeff were kept on an invisible leash next to Joslyn. Sarah had stepped out for a few minutes to get her some lunch.

The biggest difference between Broadie's old class and his new one was that the students were *never* left alone. If you were on red level, you even got escorted to the restroom. He thought about his dad and how he must have felt in jail, for this class was really a jail for misfit kids that no one else would take.

Writing the solution to the last problem, he finished his workbook pages and opened his novel. He was three quarters of the way through now.

"Are you finished?" Joslyn asked Broadie.

He looked up and nodded: "yes."

"Let's see." She had a way of speaking that automatically made a person feel guilty even when they weren't. She approached his desk, picked up the workbook, and silently read the answers while holding her red felt-tip pen ready for the slightest mistake.

Gayle looked up and met his eyes with a sensual arrogance that was as garish and out of place as a large weed in a flower patch.

"You got a one hundred percent!" Joslyn said excitedly.

Gayle rolled her eyes and sneered. Any other achievement besides her own was a personal insult. There were gasps and sighs from among the other students, but Jim sat back, quietly doodling in the corner.

"Hey, I'm done, too." Leroy said.

Joslyn went to his desk and checked his work. "Leroy has a one hundred percent, too!" She went to the board and raised Broadie's from blue to purple and Leroy's from red to yellow.

"*Yes!*" Leroy threw a fist into the air and ostentatiously stole the moment, singing to a familiar tune, "I'm so good, I'm so good, Baby, I'm so good."

Gayle laughed approvingly. Craig put his head down on the desk in disgust. Jim still sat alone, thinking his own mysterious thoughts.

The recess bell rang.

Gayle and Raelynn were the first to leave. Mike walked out the door, putting his headphones on. He had his very own iPod. Jeff and Leroy waited for Joslyn, making reverent space for Jim to go past. Jim didn't look at Broadie at all this time, but looked straight ahead, ignoring him. It was probably an improvement from last time.

The day threatened snow, but that didn't deter the faithful sports players. Basketballs pounded the blacktop. Footballs were thrown back and forth, and soccer dominated most of the field. Girls hopscotched, swung on the swings, and gossiped. Leroy and Jeff started a game of horse. Broadie wandered with his hands in his pockets and regretted leaving his book behind.

"Look! Broadie's in the retard class now!" Vanessa yelled pointing at him. Her friends obediently looked his way, then went back to whatever they were doing. Some gave a token laugh along with her. She gloated, satisfied enough with herself to go onto something else.

Broadie felt like showing her his middle finger. He noticed that some heavy chunks of asphalt had broken away from the curb and imagined throwing them at her. His anger was a quick and violent storm. He turned away, hard, seething, and feeling blood rush to his face. He was a razor's edge away from charging at her in a rage.

Jeff ran to the hoop to do a layup, missed his footing, and fell hard, grinding his elbow against the pavement. It took him a moment to realize his situation, and soon he was crying out in exaggerated agony.

"Come on, let's go clean you up," Joslyn said, brushing him off. She turned to Leroy, who stood close, admiring the small drops of blood. "Can I trust you to stay out of trouble until Sarah gets back, or do I have to take you to the office with me?"

"I can be good." Leroy's face was angelic.

"I'll trust you, and if you're good I'll put you up another level, but I'd better not hear of any problems."

"Okay," he said, bouncing his ball to the next hoop over.

Broadie watched Joslyn and Jeff walk into the building. Sarah hadn't returned, and he eyed Leroy distrustfully. He continued to walk along the ditch. He kicked a heavy piece of asphalt and felt a sting in his toe. Leroy's basketball bounced rhythmically, broken only by a throw at the hoop.

Craig stood in the doorway.

Broadie watched him. Craig looked around with wary eyes. They flickered in the direction of Leroy. Then, satisfied that Leroy was well occupied, took a step, then another.

Jim walked casually from behind the shed. Craig saw him and paused. He waited until he was sure that Jim's attention was elsewhere, then with a determined look, finished his descent. He looked like an astronaut floating away from his space capsule without a tether line. He moved one step at a time until he reached the grass. He quietly watched the soccer game. Leroy looked in Craig's direction and with stupid glee maneuvered himself between Craig and the relocatable. Craig took a deep breath and smiled in triumph. He looked at the sky, then back at the playground. A group of girls walked past, and he pulled into himself like a scared turtle, but didn't go back in. He put his hands into his pockets, walking carefully along the curb.

"Look, everyone! Lurpy's outside!" Leroy yelled.

Craig's face was a bloom of horror. He tried to move for the relocatable, but Leroy shifted into his way and shoved him. He staggered and shrank back like a defenseless mouse.

Broadie saw Leroy through a bright tunnel of fury. He moved with wolf-like speed, the world disappearing around him. In Leroy's face he saw John Hamel, Joey Wolfley, Steve Bartlett: everything that was bad in his world.

Leroy moved at Craig again. He flinched back, but, before Leroy could move any further, Broadie seized him by the collar of his jacket. Leroy's eyes popped wide with surprise. There was a loud tear, and Broadie stumbled back. Leroy gained his footing and spun on Broadie.

"Oh! You mother—"

Broadie didn't give him a chance. He fired a volley of fists, feeling the concussions all the way into his shoulders. Leroy's nose sprayed droplets of blood into Broadie's face, but he didn't stop. Leroy threw out his hands, begging for mercy. He caught his little finger in the cuff of Broadie's jacket. There was a loud pop, and he screamed. Broadie still didn't stop. They fell together onto the asphalt, and he began to pound Leroy's head against the ground with both hands. Someone with a strong grip lifted Broadie into the air. He fought until he exhausted himself against the solid, hairy arm of a recess monitor. Leroy curled up into a little ball, his nose spouting blood. Another teacher, a woman, attended to him. There was no exhibition or exaggeration like Jeff's, his trauma was real. Someone joined the helpful teacher, lifting Leroy to his feet. The hair on the back of his head was a bloody, matted swirl. He sobbed and coughed. The woman looked at Broadie with shocked accusation.

As Broadie was being dragged away, he saw Jim nodding his head and smiling in approval.

5

Broadie spent his twelfth birthday grounded after he was expelled from school. His family still gave him cake and presents, but he couldn't invite any friends—the irony didn't escape him that he didn't have any friends to invite. January was home from the hospital, but the devil would have to wear an Eskimo coat before her mother would let her come over. Broadie slept. His book was a lump behind his pillow. He didn't mind. Grandpa had taken away all other books, except the one Broadie had tucked under the car seat when Grandpa wasn't looking. When everything had died down, he had sneaked out through his window and retrieved it. He rolled over, kicking his blankets aside as a light snow gave the world a thin, white blanket that told of more to come.

The morning air was heavy and gray. Grandpa and Grandma left to do their thanksgiving shopping, Mom was asleep downstairs, and Davie was in school. Broadie did the dishes, cleaned the fridge as he was told to, then went into his room. He lay back, folding his hands behind his head, and listened to the furnace die out into silence.

Mom's light laughter and a man's voice.

Dad must be here!

He moved quickly to the air vent and listened. Their voices were faint. They were making a great effort to be quiet. He heard the creak of his mother's bed and more laughter. His chest was cold, and he forced a swallow, hearing a little click in his ears. Maybe Mom had decided to let Dad come back. Their voices became more distant, masked by the shower. He left his room and waited by the stairs. He didn't dare go down for fear of shattering something that to him was as fragile as a snowflake. His hope swelled with each minute's passage. He waited and listened, waited and listened. The voices were still too distant to discern. His stomach churned with excitement to the point that he nearly threw up. He kept his ear close to the heater vent.

Finally, footsteps on the stairs.

He ran into the living room, legs shaking, peered into the stair-well, and met the face of a stranger. He was older and harder look-ing than his dad: taller, shaved head and goatee, earrings, heavy bar-bouncing arms covered with tattoos, and eyes just as surprised as Broadie's. Mom stopped behind the man smiling up at him un-comfortably. He quickly adjusted the perplexity on his face to a friendly, diplomatic grin.

"Who's this little dude?" His smoky voice rumbled in the stair-well.

Mom looked up at Broadie in horror, then in anger.

"That's my son," she choked with a smile.

"I didn't know you had kids." He turned his brawn in her direc-tion, smile fading from diplomatic to pasted poker.

"Oh, yes, I—" Mom smiled widely, but her eyes turned hard to Broadie.

An uncomfortable pause.

"She has three," Broadie said cheerily.

The man looked back up at him, expression unchanging. Mom mouthed silently: "Shut! Up!"

"Me, my brother, and a baby sister almost two," Broadie contin-ued, with an ice pick of anger in his chest. Weak, he wanted to run.

"Broadie! Get back to your room. You're still grounded!" Mom said.

The man glanced back at her now, looking more interested in leaving.

"And she—"

"Broadie! Shut up!"

"—and she's not even divorced yet!"

Mom swallowed hard.

The man raised his eyebrows, openly uncomfortable to be there. "Well, hey! Great!" He said sarcastically. "That was a great night and, uh . . . I'll see ya." He gave her a loose salute, a ring on his own finger, and ascended to the door.

Broadie moved out of the way. Mom followed the man outside, and they walked to a large truck. He gave her an uncommitted hug then jumped in. Mom walked away, rubbing her arms in the cold. The large engine cranked loudly, and "Dirty Deeds Done Dirt Cheap" by AC/DC blasted deeply from hidden speakers.

When she came back in, he already had his coat on and was heading to the back door.

"You had no right to butt into something that was none of your business!" She went after him, and he felt a slap coming.

He ignored her as he zipped up his coat, moving as fast as he could shy of running. He had such a sensation of unreality that he couldn't speak. He understood too much about what had just happened. All he wanted to do was go someplace where he didn't have to think about it. He couldn't face her. He was embarrassed in a way that scared him. The cold air was uncomfortable already, before he even jumped off the porch. The door slammed behind him, a temporary but effective barrier. He started to run. He was already to the shed when Mom screamed for him to get right back there that instant. He didn't care.

He kept his fire small so the neighbors wouldn't notice. The sun was going down, and he was warm. Mom had gone to work long ago, but he didn't want to go back to the house. He knew Grandma and Grandpa were probably upset that he had gone. He lay on the railroad tie, listening to the sounds of the fire. Smoke rose peacefully through the hole in the ceiling, displacing the air, giving the tree house a shimmery texture.

There was movement in the trees close by. He thought that someone might have been passing on the trail: soft crunches though the freezing grass.

He sat up, slightly dizzy, and blinked; he'd been close to sleep.

To his dismay, Grandpa was coming up the trail. Broadie waited in defeat, not bothering to think up an excuse. He would probably be grounded for another week.

"Broadie?" Grandpa said through the door. He didn't look angry, only concerned.

Broadie stared with easy tears into the fire. He sniffed hard. Grandpa's image floated and divided as he blinked. A cold tear dropped down his cheek. Grandpa leaned against the doorway, not speaking for a while, probably waiting for Broadie to say some-thing. When he didn't, Grandpa hunched in, filling the doorway and darkening the room. He sat next to Broadie. Together they watched the breeze enliven the white-orange coals.

"What happened today?" Grandpa finally asked.

"My—" Broadie couldn't speak, only sobbed.

Grandpa pulled him close holding him until the fire died down to a few flickering flames. "You're not in trouble; I just wanted you to know that."

"Ok," Broadie whispered.

"Grandma's got some dinner for you if you'll come."

Broadie wiped his eyes with a cold sleeve.

"Come on," Grandpa said, urging him up with a one-arm hug.

They kicked dirt over the smoldering coals and together walked through the shadows to the house.

"Your mother went to work early," Grandpa said. His breath came out in puffs.

Broadie shrugged.

"Well, I have an idea about what might've happened." Grandpa lowered himself carefully into the ditch, then waited for Broadie. They cleared the thorn bushes. Grandpa zipped his coat to the neck and turned up the collar. "The neighbors saw and heard some things this morning—nosy woman, that Mrs. Larson." Grandpa looked at Broadie again but didn't wait for him to speak. "Did you see a truck parked in front of the neighbor's?"

Broadie finally spoke freely, angrily. Grandpa listened as they ducked through the opening in the fence. Leaves from the pear trees crunched under their feet.

"Well, you're not grounded anymore as far as I'm concerned. They say that Leroy kid's mother wants to press charges, and I know you know that, but don't you worry, we're going to handle it. I think you've been through too damn much lately. You just hang in there, okay?" Grandpa gave him another quick hug, and they went up the back porch together.

Grandma was waiting at the door. "Where have you—"

"Momma!" Grandpa said with a smile, hushing her with a look.

"There's chicken and rice on the stove," she said, putting her hands on her hips. Davie and Alisha were already eating. "Go get cleaned up, the both of you. You smell like a forest fire."

Early the next morning, Broadie was startled awake by tapping on his window. He pushed his blankets aside sleepily and had difficulty opening his eyes.

More tapping.

He sat up, rubbing his face. There was movement in the window, and it reflected strangely onto the wall. For an instant, all the vampire movies he'd seen came to life, and a cold sobering cup of fear splashed over him. He forced himself to walk to the window. January was there, wrapped in a blanket. He blinked and squinted in her mild lamplight.

"It took you long enough. I was about to give up and go back to bed."

"Sorry," Broadie said groggily.

"I can't sleep." She pulled her blanket tighter.

Broadie shivered, though he wore sweats for pajamas.

"I'm reading your book."

"Huh?"

"*Ender's Game.*"

Broadie blinked vacantly, then caught on.

"Oh . . . oh, yeah. How do you like it?"

"I love it. I'm almost done."

"Cool." He wrapped his arms tight around himself.

"I didn't have anything else to do in the hospital but read, and this book helped me to keep my mind off of things."

"Why were you in the hospital for so long this time?"

January looked down into the darkness. "I've got A.L.L." She paused. "Have you ever heard of it?"

Broadie shook his head.

"Acute lymphoblastic leukemia."

He felt a cold nausea. In his sleepy state, this news was almost too much to take in. He knew enough about leukemia to know that people died of it.

"They've started me on treatments." Her voice was a small whisper over the black divide between them.

The cold air made his teeth chatter. He didn't want to hear anymore. He wanted to shut the window and hide. "What time is it?" was all he could say.

She looked back at her clock. "Six-thirty-nine. It's morning."

"What was it like in the hospital?"

"Terrible. I hate it. I have to go back in a few days." Her voice wavered. A tear trickled down her cheek and disappeared below them.

He was ashamed of not wanting to talk to her. He was glad he hadn't gone, but could see that she wanted to talk, and he had missed her.

"I have to get IVs, drips, shots. . . . The worst thing is the spinal tap."

"What's that?"

"They make me curl up into a ball so there's a space in the vertebrae. Then they stick a needle in to take out spinal fluid, then they put new fluid back."

"Does it hurt?"

"Yes."

"What does it feel like?"

"I don't know. I guess there's the weird needle feeling that goes deep, then the terrible pain. It's more than I ever felt before. The big nurse guy holds me down because I can't straighten out, or get away from it. If I did, it would do damage inside, or break off."

Broadie felt a cold flip in his stomach trying to imagine a needle going into his own spine. He rubbed his back in empathy.

"I'm also getting chemotherapy."

"Is that like radiation?" Broadie grabbed his blanket from his bed and wrapped it around him. His room was icy.

"No, the chemo is the drips. It's a chemical that kills the leukemia cells." She leaned on the sill, looking tired.

"I guess it's cool that you get to stay home from school."

"No, it's not." She started to cry again.

Broadie felt uncomfortable and wished he hadn't said anything.

"I'm so lonely." She couldn't speak for a moment. "I can't have any friends over because my mom thinks they'll get me sick. I'm on home hospital, so I have to do school work anyway."

"I'm sorry."

"No, don't be." She gathered herself. "So why were you home?"

"I got expelled again. So I'll be here for you." He felt corny saying that.

January smiled bashfully behind watery eyes. She looked like she was going to cry again. They were quiet for a moment.

"Why did you get expelled?"

"I got in a fight."

"John Hamel?"

"No, some kid name Leroy."

"Who won?"

Broadie smiled smugly.

"Oh, did you get your butt kicked again?" She smiled innocently.

His face drooped under the weight of his pride, but he held back an angry retort. She might have been joking, but there wasn't any guile in her eyes. "I hurt him," he said unenthusiastically.

January's mouth slackened; she looked away, surprised at his words.

I hurt him, Broadie thought.

I *hurt* him. His own words were high ringing chisel blows in his conscience. All through the day he had wanted to blame his mother for his misery, but it was his own guilt for beating on Leroy. Leroy hadn't done anything directly to Broadie, but as he bullied Craig he became the apotheosis of all bullies. At that moment, emotion and circumstance had become a wildly dangerous combination. He could easily have said that it was impossible to control, but that wasn't true, and he knew it. He had done to Leroy what he had wanted to do to John. Above all, he had liked it.

"I'm freezing," Broadie said.

"Me, too." January was visibly shaking.

"I'm going to bed now," Broadie said. He reached up to pull down the window. His heart ached. He didn't want to face her anymore. She probably thought he was a terrible person.

"Wait," January said.

Broadie paused, anxious to get warm.

"Did he deserve it?" She asked, her eyes dark and intense behind her shadow.

"Yes."

January smiled, then nodded thoughtfully: "Good night." She made a move to pull down her window, then stopped again. "Wait. . . ."

She looked east between the two houses. Small puffs of breath disappeared into the morning. "Have you ever seen the sun come up in the morning?"

"Yes," he said, with teeth chattering, and wishing that he hadn't sounded so impatient.

"Like, really watched it come up from behind the mountains?"

Sleep had now frozen away, but he wanted his warm blankets. The sky was now gray and sharply brighter at the edges of the mountain peaks. He looked through her window to her clock and saw that it was now past seven.

"Will you watch the sunrise with me?" she persisted.

He was thinking only about the cold until her request hit home. Instead of being annoyed, he started to feel adventurous. The frost-covered grass was now visible, and the still, freezing air was other-worldly in a strange way. It was true that he hadn't ever thought of watching the sun come up, and for the first time in a long time he felt like he was about to discover something new.

"Let me get my blanket," She said.

She smiled as he left the window to stand over his heater vent in relief. When he returned, she was bundled up and had pulled her window down a little. She rested her head on the sill, staring out at the brightening pinks that were appearing.

"Can you believe that at this moment the sun is going down somewhere far away?" she whispered.

He pulled his blanket just over his head, and rested his cheek on the cold, peeling paint. His eyes still burned a little for sleep.

"I wish we were in the tree house watching this," he said.

"Me, too."

6

Broadie and Davie were cleaning the living room while Grandpa peeled potatoes and yams. Grandma was trying to be everywhere and do everything at once. Her limp was getting worse as the morning progressed.

"Broadie?" Grandma called from the kitchen.

He turned off the vacuum to hear her better. "What, Grandma?"

"Will you please go with Grandpa to help bring in the folding table?"

"I guess," he murmured. The old table was dirty and covered with spider webs. She had made him wash it off last year; it was a miserable experience. "It's Davie's turn to wash it," he said, passing her in the kitchen. Maybe he stood a chance this time.

"You *know* he's too little. What if he gets bit by a black widow?"

There went that chance. "What if *I* get bit?"

"You're big enough to watch out for them. Now, go on!"

He let the screen door slap shut on its own—which always annoyed her. Grandpa was rolling some old tires cut into the driveway. His rakes and shovels had been piled into the wheelbarrow and moved aside. It was different to see so much room in the back of the garage.

"Here, move these boards around back," Grandpa said, lifting one end of a small stack. Broadie lifted his own end. As he moved backwards he saw how the thick, dusty webs pulled away from the other junk. There weren't any spiders. It struck him as silly, all the talk about spiders at the end of November. Grandma had known that all along. Still, he watched carefully, occasionally raising the boards higher to look underneath for anything crawling his way.

"Now, go get a bucket and wipe off all the dirt," Grandpa said, walking a bicycle out of the way.

"I knew you were going to say that."

"Don't get smart with me," Grandpa warned. He sounded more brisk than usual, giving Broadie a chill of embarrassment in his stomach. He ran for the bucket.

Though the water in the bucket was steaming warm, it quickly turned ice cold on the rag. He flipped away some spider egg cases stuck to dried leaves and resumed wiping. He stood to stretch his back and warm his hands and saw January on her back porch. She waved. He waved back and resumed wiping, but watched, as she looked carefully into her back door, then tiptoed out of sight. Soon she appeared from around the back of the garage.

"Hey," she whispered.

Broadie smiled back at her.

"What are you doing?" she asked, still whispering. She glanced warily toward her porch.

"I have to clean this stupid table because company's coming." He kept working.

"I only have two more chapters to go in your book. I'm going to finish it today at my grandma's, if my head doesn't start hurting again, that is."

"Cool! That's the best part." He put down his rag.

"My dad saw me reading it and got excited. He's read every one of Orson Scott Card's books."

"Did you tell him it was mine?"

"No, I just said that a friend from school lent it to me."

"Oh." He looked down at his bucket, sighed, and started cleaning again.

"I don't want to sound weird or anything, but I think it's neat we're reading the same book. I mean . . . well . . . it's kind of like having a special experience together, you know, something we've both had. Kind of like. . . ." She paused.

Broadie's face flushed, and he thought about that strange night they had shared together in the tree house. He was suddenly embarrassed and wanted to run back into the house. He had thought about it many times and wondered if she did, too, but neither of them ever brought it up. He was sure she would bring it up now.

"Have you ever thought about growing up?"

He must have given her a funny look, because she quickly looked away and started rubbing the toe of her shoe against the concrete the way she did when she was shy or nervous.

"Yeah, I guess," he whispered.

"Like really thought about it?"

He shrugged.

"I saw my oldest cousin get married in the temple. I mean, I was too young to go in, but we waited for her to come out. When she did, we all took pictures and followed her around the temple grounds. Her husband is a real cool, tall guy from Logan, and they met in college."

He wanted to stop listening and go back to work. He felt funny, like when she had confessed her leukemia. It was like he wanted to plug his ears and not hear what she had to say. He didn't want to know the fear of not being able to grow up.

"She was so pretty in her big white dress. Chad (that's her husband) lifted her and carried her up the steps to the big wooden doors. She was so happy, and now they have a little baby. I'm going to see them today. I hope they let me hold the baby." Her voice weakened.

He continued to scrub silently, forcing a mental thumb into a breaking dam of thoughts.

"I better go," she said, turning to leave. A thin fog puffed from between her lips.

He watched her walk away. Before she cleared the garage he spoke: "Janni!"

She turned around, her eyes so tired, yet full of . . . *her*. He couldn't imagine her not being around. He opened his mouth again to speak. "I. . . .' *I love you*, he wanted to say. Such big words, but he felt a fire of emotion in his chest that made him want to cry. "I . . . hope you . . . do get to hold the baby."

She gave him an intense look, as if she had read his mind, and he shrank inside with sudden horror, believing this was so. Then she smiled.

"Thanks," she said, then was gone around the corner and back into her yard.

Will and Cheryl's family came in, pushing Grandma Grace in her wheelchair. The house was alive with their company. Kelsi and Kassidy sat on the sofa, looking through Grandma's photo album. Kristen played with Alisha. Tommy was gone somewhere with Davie, and Jared sat with Will and Grandpa in the kitchen. Grandpa's star grandson was getting the warm welcome, while Broadie sat in the living room ignored.

"Humph!" Kassidy said, pushing the photo album into Kelsi's hands. "I can't believe she kept that picture. He's *totally* out of my life. That's *totally* ancient history."

"That was just this summer," Cheryl said.

"That was *forever* ago. Besides, I look like a dork." She folded her arms over her breasts.

"No, you don't, you look cute. You both looked cute together."

"Oh-my-gosh, Mom!" she said, rolling her eyes.

"Where's your mom?" Cheryl asked, turning to Broadie and changing the subject.

"She's downstairs baking rolls."

"Oh?" Cheryl nodded. She looked surprised. "So she didn't have to work today?"

Both girls looked up with sudden interest.

Broadie flushed, feeling the attention. "No, she didn't," he said softly.

"Good." Cheryl nodded. "Is she gone a lot these days?"

He didn't know how to answer her. He felt that it was more like a prying question than just casual curiosity.

"Yeah," he said, feeling all along that he was adding to something. He quickly fell quiet.

Mom's footsteps in the stairwell.

Cheryl looked back at her girls. They glanced quickly down at the photo album.

"Hi, everybody," Mom said, as she cleared the banister, holding two hot trays of rolls.

"Michelle! You look good today," Cheryl said.

Mom wore nice pants and a shirt that covered more than usual, but it was still low-cut in front. Every time she leaned forward she exposed a new tattoo above her right breast.

"Thank you." Mom paused long enough to make eye contact with Cheryl. Her smile thinned. Cheryl's grin widened. The two girls sat statue-like over the photo album.

"Oh, good, the rolls," Grandma said, walking into the room. She took the pans and quickly returned to the kitchen. "Broadie, please help set the tables," she said, leaning back into the living room.

He sighed. Grandma Grace sat quietly, hands folded, and looking dreamy-eyed toward the kitchen. Broadie smiled at her, but she didn't seem to notice.

"I'll be back," Mom said. She walked quickly to the stairs. "I'm working on the vegetable dip. It's *low fat*." She emphasized the last two words looking at Cheryl.

"Take your time," Cheryl said. Her pleasant face was a cardboard cut-out.

Broadie noticed what was coming and let out a breath as he entered the kitchen. Grandpa sat at the table with Will and Jared.

"Broadie Bear!" Will said. "Come on over, my man."

"Did you hear Jared's the class president for the eighth grade?" Grandpa said proudly.

Broadie smiled politely. "Cool." He grabbed a handful of silverware from Grandma's "special occasion" box.

"Let's go see some football," Will said excitedly. The three of them got up and left the room. No one noticed whether Broadie went with them or not.

" . . . Dad and Michelle aren't talking." Grandma's low tones drifted in.

Cheryl spoke: "I just don't see how you could permit *that* to go on any longer."

"Who would take care of the kids? We might push to take custody of the baby if we have to."

"If I were *you*—" Cheryl cleared her throat as she came through the door with Grandma. Red faced, Broadie worked around the table, pretending that he didn't hear anything.

The doorbell rang again. Aunt Gracie and Uncle Ned walked in with five of their six kids. They were by far the richest of the family: Ned was a chemist for an international oil company, and a big stockholder. He flew around the world regularly. It wasn't a surprise for Grandma and Grandpa to get a gift or a letter from some exotic place. Gracie did real estate, and their kids were magazine quality, sterile and pressed. The two oldest boys were Brigham Young University students; the one just younger was on a church mission to Japan. The younger three were girls, all close to Cheryl's kids in age.

Grandma and Grandpa both greeted them at the door—unlike any of their other guests. Gracie hung her coat (probably bought in England) on the clothes tree by the door and visibly sniffed the stairwell. She probably smelled Mom's cigarette smoke. Grandma quickly took her by the arm and led her into the living room.

"Oh, come in, come in from the cold," Grandma said nervously.

"Oh, Mom, you don't need to fuss," Gracie said, smiling through expensive makeup. Her hair-do had changed every year with Princess Diana's and had stayed the same since her death.

All the girls hugged and greeted each other enthusiastically. Then Kelsi and Kassidy yielded their seats naturally, as if to royalty.

"Nana!" Gracie said, giving Grandma Grace a hug. There was a hint of a smile on the old woman's lips.

The men all shook Grandpa's hand, then Will's, each calling each other by name, then commented on the game.

"Now, how's young Jared?" Ned said, shaking Jared's hand. "I hear you're following in your dad's footsteps."

Will smiled proudly.

"Oh . . . uh, Mom?" Grace said. "You don't mind if I take my coat into your bedroom do you?"

"Oh, not at all." Grandma walked with her. "I'm sorry. Michelle's been living down there for a while and, you know. . . ."

Her voice faded behind the others.

"Now, you must be Davie, Michelle's son?" Richard, his oldest cousin, spoke. He was a tall man with thick, dark hair and a clear, commanding voice like his father, Ned's. He was almost finished at the university and was destined to be a big business man like Ned. He held out his hand. Surprised that Richard was talking to *him,* he took it and they shook. "Oh, that's . . . uh . . . I'm uh . . . Broadie."

"Oh, yes, Broadie. I remember." He smiled, and his attention went back to Will.

"Dad," Ned spoke to Grandpa. "Would it be a bother if I were to park my car in your garage?"

"Certainly not! Go right ahead."

Ned turned to leave. Grandpa watched him go, then followed after him. "Oh, I better move mine out of the way."

Grandma and Cheryl started to bring out the food.

Broadie went to the window and watched as Ned pulled his shiny, silver car into the driveway. Cars like that were out of place even in this nice old neighborhood. So were people like Ned and Grace. They lived in a big house up by the Bountiful temple. He had heard Grandma say once that it was worth a million dollars. She liked to point it out when they went for rides up that way. It had five fireplaces and real metal statues in the front yard. The driveway was cobblestone. He had never been in this house, but he remembered vaguely visiting them when they had lived in Cottonwood. That house had only three chimneys, but they had made him take his shoes off when he went inside.

"Oh, just smell that gravy," Gracie said, as Cheryl set a china bowl with a matching ladle.

There was a burst of excitement from the men as someone made a touchdown on TV.

Broadie left the room and wandered down the hall. The smell of food made his stomach growl, but he was tired and wanted to lie down. He felt a headache coming on. He opened his door, surprised to see Kassidy lying on his bed and talking on her cell phone. She placed her thumb over the mouthpiece. "I'm sorry, I just needed some privacy. I'll go if you want me to."

"No, don't worry about it,"

"Ok," she said quickly. She lay flat and crossed one knee over the other, resuming her conversation. She slowly twisted a lock of her hair between her fingers.

He closed the door, then walked outside.

When the family was finally together, they voiced their approval as Grandpa carried in the steaming turkey.

"Where's Michelle?" Will asked.

"I'll go get her," Grandma said. "Last time I saw her she was going to make the dip."

"Mamma, don't bother, I'll do it."

"Please, not right now. It would be best if I—"

Grandpa walked to the stairwell. "Shelly?"

No answer.

"Shelly, we're gonna eat," he called again.

"Was she going anywhere?" Cheryl asked.

Gossip among the girls continued unabated. Cheryl gave Alisha a small plate of mashed potatoes. Davie stole an olive.

"I'll be right back." Grandpa started down the stairs.

Mom called from below: "Don't worry about me. Just go ahead and start."

Grandpa shrugged his shoulders and walked slowly back to the table. Everyone watched him. The machine of tradition turned smoothly as he assumed his patriarchal position. The table quieted.

"Andrew," Grandpa said, speaking to Gracie's second oldest boy. "Will you offer us a prayer before we eat?"

There was a surprised hush.

"Grandpa, I—"

"Go ahead, I insist. You're the newest returned missionary, and we're excited that you're here with us this year. Anyone who argues with me won't get any pie."

"I guess I can't argue with that," Andrew said.

Ned smiled proudly.

Everyone bowed heads. The prayer was humble, to the point, but also eloquent. He finished, and everyone began passing the food.

"I hear there's a special young lady in Richard's busy schedule," Grandpa said.

Richard smiled bashfully.

"Woo-hoo!" Kassidy voiced her approval.

"What's her name?" Cheryl asked, looking at him coyly.

"Amanda," he said, letting a little pride show through.

"So, is there a ring somewhere in this?" Kelsi asked, looking like she was wishing that they weren't cousins.

"We'll see." He smiled.

"She's the granddaughter of one of the church's General Authorities," Gracie added with importance.

"Well, well!" Will said with a crooked smile.

"Sorry I'm late, everyone," Mom said. She walked quickly to the table.

"This is good." Grandpa said smiling. "We have three of our four children and their families here today. Jeff is in Germany, you all know. His wife, Becky, is going to have a baby, so that will be fourteen grandchildren . . . ? Momma?"

"That's seven granddaughters and six grandsons and one on the way," Grandma proudly said, passing the salad bowl.

"I didn't know this," Cheryl said to Grandma, and then locked at Will. "Why didn't you tell me?" She gave him a playful slap on the shoulder.

"I didn't know, either."

"Becky wanted us to announce it when the family was all together," Grandma said.

"Well, if you can keep a secret like that, I wonder what other secrets you've been keeping," Gracie said.

"Ssh, don't say anything about the gold in the safe, Mamma," Grandpa whispered.

"Or the bodies in the basement," Jared added.

"Jared!" Cheryl reached out and popped him on the head.

"I hear you're working, now, Michelle," Gracie said.

The table quieted down. Cheryl threw Gracie a look, but it was too late before she caught on. Mom didn't answer right off. She thoughtfully arranged her plate.

"Why, yes, we've been curious. So where *do* you work these days?" Ned asked. He really didn't know.

Broadie saw Gracie give him a nudge with her knee.

Grandma tried to change the subject: "Cheryl, I just *love* this stuffing. What did—"

"The Rock-n-Roll Bush," Michelle said, looking at everyone with a challenging smile.

All of the older boys looked up, losing interest in their cranberries and mashed potatoes.

"So what is it you do?" Sharee, Gracie's oldest daughter asked.

Will cleared his throat.

"I waitress," Mom said.

There was a visible relief in some parts of the table.

Sharee spoke again: "I mean, like, I've been looking for a job lately so I can pay for a car when I get my driver's license, and—"

"You have to be over twenty-one," Michelle said.

"Oh," Sharee said, then looked over at her mom with a puzzled look on her face.

"What's the Rock-n-Roll Bush?" Jared asked. He kept a look of innocence, but anyone who knew his personality would see that he was sardonically egging on the conversation. He hadn't missed a thing.

"We're not going to discuss that over the table," Cheryl said.

"I think I've seen that place," Richard said.

"Oh?" Ned raised his eyebrows.

Richard flushed. "It's not far from the office where I did some training last semester. It's across the street from Hooters."

"What's Hooters?" Kristen asked from over in the "kid" table.

"It's where they keep the owls," Andrew said.

Will's face turned red as he tried to choke back a laughing fit.

"Yeah, the ones with the great big eyes," Richard said, winking at Jared.

Kelsi gasped.

Will let loose. Some potato flew out of his mouth and stuck to his glass. Grandpa belly laughed, while Grandma tried hard to maintain her dignity.

"Richard!" Cheryl chided.

The laughing spread like a disease, even Grace struggled to hold a pinch in her face. Will pounded the table, making his silverware jump, and a tear trickled out of his eye. Ned vibrated like an old engine sputtering, holding his gut.

"Leave it to the men," Cheryl said, shaking her head. She grinned widely.

"Hu-hoo-hooge eyes," Jared said, holding his fingers in loops over his eyes.

Andrew almost fell out of his chair. Will turned to Jared, giving him a sloppy high five. He gasped for breath.

"I wanna go to Hooters!" Tommy said, and sent the entire table into the outer limits.

Several minutes passed before anyone was able to eat. Grandpa went into the kitchen to splash some water on his face. The humorous atmosphere carried its own momentum throughout the dinner. By the time the pies were cut, everyone was full and exhausted. Football was back on the TV, and Kassidy was back on the phone.

"Anyone want seconds?" Cheryl called from the kitchen.

"No, thanks," Will said.

Mom cleaned the remaining plates. "Everyone done?" She asked. Richard held out his plate, and she expertly balanced it along with others.

"Hey, you're pretty good," Cheryl said as she held the kitchen door open for her.

Mom looked worn out and wired at the same time.

"What are you up to these days?" Andrew asked Broadie.

"Not much, I guess." He worked at his last few bites of pumpkin pie.

"Any sports?"

"Basketball." He lied quickly. It wouldn't have hurt to sound a little normal.

"Hey, basketball, that's pretty cool. What is it, Junior Jazz? County rec?"

"Uh . . . yeah." He shoved another bite quickly into his mouth.

"Which one?"

"Huh?"

"Which one?"

"Oh . . . uh, Jazz."

"Hey cool, same as Jared, right?"

Jared looked up, hearing his name. Broadie flushed. He was digging himself into a pit faster than he expected.

"Well, I—"

There was a commotion in the kitchen. Heads turned in time to see Mom storm through the door. She crossed the room in a huff, opened the front door, and slammed it behind her.

Grandpa puffed his cheeks letting out a long heavy breath.

"I wonder what that's all about?" Ned said.

Grandpa and Will exchanged glances, then Will got up and walked into the kitchen. Grandpa shook his head.

"I need to go do something," Broadie said, but Andrew's attention was already elsewhere.

Broadie felt lucky to have the last piece of pumpkin pie, luckier not to have been called to help clean up. The day had passed. He had finished his book in peace, and in the early dark he lay ruminating in the afterglow of the story. Floating on a cloud of accomplishment, he slowly slid his fingers, flipping the soft pages, marveling at having read, cover to cover, the biggest book he had ever seen.

He heard January's window slide open, followed by a brisk knock on his glass. He got up and closed the door to his room. He couldn't wait to tell her that he had finished *The Stand*. He parted the curtains and lifted the window, letting in a gust of snowy air. The way things looked outside, tomorrow would definitely be a snow fort day. He already had the elaborate plans in mind: outside the clubhouse, he would build four heavy walls, a snow cave, slide, and turrets to hide behind in case of a snow ball fight with January—if she felt good enough. A big door that—

Ender's Game flapped at him loosely, like an out-of-control bird, pegging him squarely in the mouth. January's window slammed shut. The pain, delayed by shock, came sharp and burning. His upper lip was already beginning to swell. He staggered back and sat on his bed. The book he had lent her lay sprawled on the floor. Part of the cover had separated from the pages. Dry, brittle glue stared back at him like an old wound. Before he had time to think, he kicked the book away in a fit of anger and left his room.

Grandpa sat in his big chair under the lamp reading. Grandma was asleep on the couch. Davie and Alisha were in bed. A moist log hissed lazily in the fireplace. He walked up to the front window to watch the snow sift past the streetlight. It was beginning to drift over the bottom step on the porch. He licked the stinging lump on his upper lip. He couldn't think of any reason why she had acted like that.

He heard January tapping on his window. She tapped quietly, but he was surprised how well he could hear it out in the living room. He saw through the reflection in the window that Grandpa had noticed it too. He regarded Broadie, then went back to his reading. The tapping sounded again. He ignored it. He wasn't going to go back just to get something thrown at him again. He left the window and sat by the fire. The prickly heat made him feel sleepy.

The phone rang.

"Who's calling this time of night?" Grandpa grumbled. He set his book down and walked stiffly into the kitchen.

Broadie closed his eyes and listened to the fire.

"Broadie," Grandpa said from the kitchen.

He didn't move.

"Broadie!" Grandpa insisted.

He got up and reluctantly walked to the phone.

"Sounds like your little lady friend," Grandpa said in passing. He gave Broadie a wink that made his face flush.

"Hello?" Broadie said.

"I'm sorry." January started to cry.

Her pitiful voice was too much for him to maintain his grudge.

"It's like I feel crazy sometimes . . . and why did you make me read that awful book?"

"It's not awful; it's my favorite."

"It's so sad, and it made me cry. I sat and bawled in front of all my cousins. Everyone thought I was weird or something."

"What's so sad about it?"

"It was that end part. It's awful."

"That's the coolest part."

"You could have warned me, at least."

"Why'd you throw it at me?"

"I'm sorry." She started to cry again. Broadie was guiltily silent. "I'm at the window," she said, gaining some composure.

He walked to the door of his room and saw her waving. "I'm gonna hang up," he said, waving back.

She looked worse than ever when he raised his window. Her thinning face was hollow looking, except for her large eyes, swollen from crying. It made him feel uneasy.

"Hi," she said weepily.

"Time to go to bed soon," Grandpa said from the other room.

"Ok," Broadie called back, then looked at January: "So, what's the matter?"

"I got to the sad part just as everyone was sitting down to eat. I started to cry. Everyone thought it was because of my leukemia, but it was the book. I tried to tell them, but I ended up having to hide in my aunt's bedroom. I didn't feel so good, so I fell asleep and missed the whole dinner. I went back out to eat, and then I got sick. And on the way home I tried to finish the book, and my head hurt too bad. So I asked my mom to read me the rest, and she read a little, but she was tired and had to get up early tomorrow. I tried to read again, and I got so mad that I just gave up and wanted to give it back." She paused, then looked at him with her swollen eyes. "That's when I threw it. I'm sorry," she sobbed.

They both shivered. A breeze carried in some snowflakes that quickly melted on his warm rug. He picked up the broken book, trying to fit the separated sections back into place.

"I broke it," she cried.

"No, I kicked it when you threw it at me."

"Oh," she sniffed.

"Here." He leaned out to hand it to her. He remembered the last time she had reached for something from his window. She was getting weaker.

"Thanks," she said, holding it like an injured animal.

Broadie started to speak. "I better—"

"Will you read it to me?"

"Uh . . . it's freezing. Don't you think—"

"You could read it to me over the phone."

"My grandma would get mad at me for staying on the phone too long."

She looked down, defeated. It was too much for him to say no. "We could . . . You could come over, and I could turn out the light and pretend like I'm asleep. We could use a flashlight."

"I don't feel good enough to climb over, and if I went out, my parents would know."

"Would they know if I came over?"

She looked back at her closed door. "No, I don't think so."

Broadie turned out his light and closed his door. He eased himself into his windowsill, feeling the bite of snow on his bare feet. He turned around, slid his window down until there was a small crack just big enough to get his fingers into, and then slipped into January's room. The lamplight was soft. Her room was messy. She eased her window down softly, wrapped a blanket around her shivering frame, then smiled and locked her door.

He breathed a sigh of relief rubbing his numb toes into her carpet. She crawled into bed, snuggled herself comfortable. She looked at him expectantly. He felt funny sitting by a girl on her bed. She patted the space next to her and he scooted closer. He found where she had left off and started to read.

7

Grandpa made Broadie go back to adjust his tie for the fourth time. He went to his mirror and loosened it again. On the floor was the Deseret Industries charity box that Grandma would donate sometime this week. In it was his old outfit: pants that rode two inches too high, shoes that were too tight, and a shirt that was too short on the sleeves. Grandma had him put them on the day before and decided that that wouldn't do. She took him to ZCMI. The name had long since turned to Meier and Frank, but she still called it ZCMI.

"Let's see how ya look," Grandpa said from the doorway.

"I'm not done yet," Broadie said.

"We need to leave in just a few minutes."

"I know."

There was movement beyond January's curtains. He hoped she felt good enough to go to church. People always seemed nicer when she was around. Maybe that wasn't exactly so, but he always felt better knowing a friend was close by, especially today. He was to receive the priesthood, which would move him from Primary to the deacons quorum. He would pass the sacrament for the first time. He didn't like going to church because of John and Joey, but he did believe in God. He understood that what he would do wasn't just a rite of passage into young adulthood, but something sacred. He passed the interview questions with the bishop, promising to stay out of fights and try to be like Christ in his life. The one thing he didn't mention were the cigarettes he had tried. He figured that that was in the past. He wasn't addicted and didn't plan on smoking like his mom. So he set that one aside.

"Let's see it." Grandpa walked into the room and examined him. "Much better. Let's go."

The weight on Broadie's head increased as each man placed a hand on his head. He shifted in his chair, straightening his back to get more comfortable. The bishop smelled of musk cologne, and his tie had a food stain. He still maintained his football stature, except for the straining waistband on his pants. Grandpa cleared his throat and began to speak. Broadie concentrated on the words being said. He thought of his new responsibility. He was one of the big kids now. He was leaving John and Joey behind, and Steve hardly came to church anymore. He hoped the other kids, like Dave Burton, would accept him now that he was one of them.

"Amen," Grandpa said.

"Amen," the others repeated.

The men stepped back. Broadie stood and shook each hand. Grandpa smiled proudly.

As he left the room, he saw a picture of Jesus kneeling by an olive tree. He wanted spirituality. He knew the gospel was true. He wanted to have more God in his life and felt that things would be better if he followed that direction. He felt positive about his present and future. He would go to church more and stop swearing. He would be nicer to Davie and do what he was supposed to at home. He would try to be a peacemaker instead of fighting.

The hall was almost empty as everyone gathered in the chapel. Broadie had to use the restroom. He turned the corner, pushed through the door into a bright, tiled room and found a stall. He sat down relaxed, looking at the toilet paper dispenser. The door creaked open. Someone walked in. He watched his feet move, then stop at the urinal next door. There was a heavy pause, a rush, a tinkle, then a sigh. The tinkling man's shoes moved large and heavy to the sink. There was a splash of water, the crank and roll of the paper towel cabinet, the swish of hands wiping on a towel, then the man left.

Someone else walked in. His shoes were smaller and the walk quicker. He, too, stopped at the urinal.

Broadie finished his business, pulled up his pants, and adjusted his shirt.

The urinal flushed.

Broadie stepped out face to face into Joey.

"Grodie Broadie," Joey said, nudging Broadie with his shoulder on the way to the sink.

Broadie didn't respond. The chances of Joey's trying to pick a fight alone were small anyway. He stepped to the adjoining sink, and started washing his own hands. Joey flicked his wet fingers at the mirror spattering it with droplets, then wiped a wet hand against Broadie's neck. "Teach me to wipe," he said.

Broadie fiercely slapped his arm away and spun around to face him.

Joey was suddenly uncertain: "Ooh, retard class boy's getting tough. Ooh." He backed to the door, pulled it open moving quickly into the hall. "Retard class boy." His voice muffled as the door shut.

Broadie's legs shook weakly. He had come close to losing his temper at Joey the way he had at Leroy. His face felt cold, then hot as he steadied himself by resting a hand on the counter.

January sat with her parents in the second row back. She smiled and waved at Broadie, unafraid that her mother would notice. He made eye contact with her and smiled back. He shifted nervously in his seat, feeling like the whole congregation was staring right at him. David Burton handed him a small map showing which rows he would pass the sacrament to and quickly explained what he would do. At the table were two priests, both big high school guys, adjusting the trays of bread and water. He looked back at the paper, then to the congregation, and counted each row, memorizing the order that he would serve. His stomach fluttered, but he was confident he would do well and that people would see him up there doing well. He would be accepted. He counted down the order of the meeting. Opening hymn, then prayer, announcements, then the sacrament hymn. He found himself gripping the arms of his chair with sweaty palms.

The older boys gave a nod. All the deacons and teachers stood in a line. Broadie took his place, glancing past Dave Burton's shoulder to January. Her head was already inclined. He knew that for her that sacred moment was now especially between her and God He understood that there was a sincere depth of emotion behind those closed eyes that was far greater than the world around her would understand.

The congregation hushed, bowing their heads. The priest at the table said the sacrament prayer, and then the trays were handed out one by one. Broadie was up next, received his tray, and stepped nervously into the congregation. Grandma and Grandpa smiled proudly as he stopped at his first row. The tray passed to a large family, from one child to the next, each taking a morsel of bread. The next row had some old ladies who smiled up at him warmly. The Peterson family, Welburns, Andrews, and then . . . the Hamels. John sat at the end of the bench. As he reached out to take a piece of bread, Broadie noticed the scars on John's fingers and felt a memory of the sensation in his teeth when John had tried to force the cigarette into his mouth. He clenched his jaw, fighting to keep pious thoughts. Mrs. Hamel sat looking sternly forward. She took her piece, then handed the tray back Broadie's way without looking at him.

As he turned to rejoin the line of deacons, he lifted his foot, feeling it catch on something. He quickly caught his balance, glancing down in time to see John's foot dart back under the pew. For a sick, swimming moment, his nerves electrified, and he began to raise the tray to hit John deliciously over the head. Forcing himself to walk away was like rolling a boulder up a hill, but his strength to move was in knowing what the bread in that tray meant. He felt his stewardship and the responsibility carry him back to his place.

8

The gable overlooking the front of the house was his new quiet place since it had become too cold to spend much time out in the clubhouse. He sat with an old *National Geographic* magazine in his lap. It was the March 1957 issue, and the article was about Formosa. It was almost fifty years old. He was enthralled by the history that he was learning. In school he had only heard about Communist China. He didn't know that part of the old free China still existed on the island of Formosa (or Taiwan). Wouldn't it be more important to know about free China? Everything that he heard about on the news and in school made Communist China sound more important. Now, as he read this, he felt that Mainland China was being held hostage by something that most of the people really didn't want.

The air outside was misty, and the sweet, homey smell of burning wood drifted in the air. It was early evening. The mild winter sunset painted the west a dull pink. Barren trees were a sharp relief against the fuzzy background. Roofs, cleared of their snow, blindly faced the sky, waiting for a new blanket. He put the magazine aside, straightening his legs over the cold, dusty attic floor. His foot had fallen asleep and tingled uncomfortably. He kicked out his leg, bending and straightening it until it felt back to normal. He picked at the ancient windowpane. The paint was a curious faded green that spoke of other styles. Images of old photographs in grandma's photo album blinked in and out of his mind. He closed his eyes and tried to see the street as it would have looked fifty, sixty, or seventy years ago. Grumpy old trees were once saplings held straight by twine and a stake. The road was once muddy gravel as old rubber tires churned the cold slush.

He left the window, shaking his legs, and hunched out of the old gable into the murky shadows. He could have turned on the light that hung from the apex of the ceiling, but its yellow glare would have spoiled the mood. He moved slowly among the old boxes, contemplating their contents.

The attic was an island of time existing apart from the rest of the world: a reservoir of alien memories of generations before his own, a resonance in the back of his mind of emotions that had no names or explanations. A small jar of buttons, a coffee can of this and that. He lifted them one at a time, feeling their weight in his chest and hands. He moved some boxes away from a chest of drawers. He opened a drawer and found a cigar box full of old letters. He examined their stamps: cool, dry colors like candy that left a ghostly flavor that he couldn't taste nor smell.

They were addressed to his great-grandparents. One in particular was addressed to Grandma Gracie alone. The stamp was red and said: "*Par Avion*," the date slightly smeared, but he could read: Aug 2, 1944. He picked it up, feeling the ancient dustiness of the old envelope, and reverently slid the letter into the open air that it probably hadn't seen since it was first opened. The paper inside still felt clean, and strangely new. He read:

Dear sis,

Bon joir ma soeur. How do you like that? Cest francais—I hope I spelled it right. I've been here in France for over a month now. Can you believe it? We've been staying in an old hotel for the past few days waiting to replace a different company that gets to come back for a little R&R. I'm jealous. Things have been hard, but probably not as hard as at the front lines. It seems like the Germans are getting beaten back further and further every day. France isn't like I had pictured, of course what do you expect when all you see in the movies and in pictures are the glamorous Paris streets and Mediterranean vacation advertisements. I sure ain't seen Paris yet.

The most action we got today was herding an old man's cows out of a muddy road so we could get some supply trucks through. I wish I could tell you exactly where we're at but we have been ordered not to write anything that could tell the Germans where we're at in case they got hold of the mail. It wouldn't hurt to say that we've been scratching fleas in a village that you'd probably only hear about in storybooks. Most people still ride in horse and buggy around here. The only pavement is a cobble stone street next to a bombed out cathedral. I probably just described half of France.

By the way, congratulations. I never thought I would be an uncle so soon. I can't wait to come home and spoil the little guy. I'm sure he's gonna be a boy. We'll be playing baseball soon, and happy birthday. Tell my brother in law he owes me another game of poker. Watch out, I'm getting good, seeing all the sitting around we've been doing lately.

Love

Your brother Howard

Broadie felt a chill as he put the letter back and remembered the stories of how Uncle Howie was killed in World War II. How long was the letter written before it happened? Maybe his last words home were to congratulate her.

He flipped through the bundle that was tied by a piece of string and watched Lincoln, Washington, Grant, and Jefferson fly past in different colors. One stamp in particular impressed him: it was a purple-colored commemorative of the pioneers in covered wagons.

He replaced them and searched further into the drawer. He carefully put aside some lacy handkerchiefs, finding more letters, an old magnifying glass, some hat pins, a tiny calendar from 1965, some pens, and an old transistor radio. He put the drawer back together, hands moving dreamily. Another drawer down held an old, round sewing box, some dictionaries in other languages, a tiny book of hymns that looked older than everything else. In the very back was a small face-powder box. Curiosity rising, he reached in, carefully lifting it, and felt a thrill as he tightened his grip against its weight. It was heavy in the palm of his hand. Heart pounding, he opened it.

Holding his breath in the dusty light, he slowly tipped the contents into his hand. Gleaming silver felt cold on his skin. A large round dollar fell onto the floor with that telltale clunk, instead of clink, that Grandpa had taught him to recognize as real silver. Indian Head pennies peeked around edges of Liberty quarters and old nickels with big Vs on the back. He felt each one, looking it over and giving it its own special attention.

Below the last silver dollar was a different coin with a different Indian head. He lifted it to get a better look. His heart jumped; he was electrified from head to toe. With painful elation, he read the golden date: 1909. It was a 1909 five-dollar gold piece. Until then he had only seen them in pictures.

He swallowed, wondering if Grandpa knew it was there. Of course, he wouldn't. Grandpa kept his treasures in the bank. He knew that from having overheard a conversation with Uncle Will after they had moved in. Grandpa was afraid Mom would relapse into her drug addiction and start stealing valuable things for drug money. He seemed to insinuate that it had happened in the past. They probably hadn't checked through all of Grandma Gracie's things when she had had her stroke and gone into a rest home. Ned and Grace had seen to it that her house had been sold for a good price, but before they did the family had divided all of her good things. Grandpa and Grandma kept most of the things that pertained to the family genealogy, while Aunt Gracie and Uncle Will got the antique furniture. The only thing of Great Grandma's, besides boxes of old books and magazines, was this chest of drawers.

Underneath the thrill of having discovered real treasure was the sophisticated rationalization that he wanted a solid heirloom that was special, like what was given to other people in the family. Deep down he had always thought that Grandpa and Grandma favored the rest of the family because they were rich, but he was growing embarrassingly aware of his parents' irresponsibility. It would be a mistake to alert Grandpa to the coins. If he were to ask for them, he wouldn't be taken seriously, and they would quickly be taken out of his hands and spirited away to safety. He could keep them, and no one would know. Just holding them made him feel richer than he thought he ever would be.

At first, as he gathered them back into the face powder box, he had every intention of taking them down to his room and adding them to his collection. He even made it as far as the small stairwell before another nagging thought stopped him. He hesitated at the edge of the shaft of light from the doorway. As Grandpa was cautious of his daughter, so was Broadie mistrusting. The image of his coins disappearing with one of Mom's friends, like the guy with the tattoos, made a cold lump in his stomach; he knew that these coins would never be safe in his room. He even thought vaguely of burying them at the base of the old box elder, but that would be more foolish than keeping them hidden in his drawer. He went back to the chest of drawers, moved the contents of the drawer aside, then tucked the coins in the very back where, he hoped, no one would notice them.

He stepped into the fresh air closing, the attic door behind the linen closet. The house was quiet except for an occasional buffet of winter air outside. Excitement carried him buoyantly down the hall. Fantasies of what he could do with his new wealth grew like lavish balloons. He jumped around, unable to contain his emotion.

Clink. Clink.

What would everyone think if he brought a real gold coin to school? That would be crazy, because it would get stolen in a heartbeat, but would he be their envy? How fun would it be to make someone else suffer with jealousy?

Clink. Clink. Plink.

The sound of coins falling brought him out of his daydream. It was coming from his room. He arrived at the door and saw some of his things scattered on the floor. His drawers were open, their contents hanging out. Davie knelt over the heater vent, holding Broadie's coin box. He daintily dropped a silver coin through the grating—plink!—then bent over to see where it had gone.

Horrified, Broadie moved across the room, swiftly, tackling Davie. Davie curled into a little ball, too surprised to scream. Broadie proceeded to pummel him on his back and shoulders, feeling the violence feed on itself until his knuckles connected against Davie's cheek with a squishy clock! Davie stopped struggling and, blinking, looked up at him helplessly. Broadie was instantly ashamed. His shame triggered more fury and amazement that Davie would look so innocent when he knew he had done a terrible thing. Broadie continued to slap him until Davie started screaming for Grandma.

"Shut up!" Broadie yelled, pushing his hands over Davie's slobbering mouth, causing him to bite his lip.

Davie squirmed and fought for breath. "Grandma!" he screamed again.

"Shut up!" Broadie said, punching Davie harder on the shoulder. Davie screamed.

There was a rustle at the door, and, before Broadie could turn around, Grandma had him by the hair on the nap of his neck. He screamed, joining Davie's hearty cries.

"Grandma! Grandma!" Davie now cried, over and over again, theatrically.

"Let loose your brother!" Grandma yanked harder. Broadie stumbled back. "I . . . How . . . You bully! You big bully!" Grandma fumed.

Davie scrambled out of the way, found his footing, and ran out of the room crying.

"Ow! Ow!" Broadie screamed and slapped at Grandma's hands. She spun him around, pushing him against his bed. He yielded, throwing his hands up to ward off her coming slap.

Her face trembled indignantly. "Why were you hitting that little boy? How could you hit that little boy?" She grabbed his shoulders and gave him a shake.

Broadie sobbed at the unfairness knowing that he was in big trouble. "My coins!" He tried to roll away, but Grandma held him firmly.

"I won't have this behavior in my house!" Grandma said, giving him another shake. Davie's wails continued in the other room.

"He put my coins down the heater vent!"

She paused, considering what he had said.

"That's no excuse for hitting you little brother. You'll stay in your room until your grandfather gets back!" She let go of his shoulders, turned, favoring her bad knee, and limped out of the room. The door closed hard behind her.

He pulled himself quickly off of the bed and fell to his knees over the old heater vent. His face burned. He ached with both shame and horror. He bent down until his face was pressed against the iron grid. The old metal throat sank into the blackness below the house. He weaved his fingers into the grid, pulled, and then realized that it was fastened down with screws. He immediately disobeyed his grandmother and left his room to find a screwdriver.

"Get back in your room!" She hollered from the living room where she was consoling Davie.

Broadie didn't speak. He opened the tool cabinet, grabbed a screwdriver, and ran back to the heater vent. He had it off in seconds, then reached down into the dirty blackness. His fingers didn't reach. He tried a coat hanger, and then the knocking stick, and only managed to retrieve a penny. He lay on his floor and cried in defeat.

* * *

Grandpa's hollow grunts drifted on puffs of dust. With a grind and a metallic pop, the ancient duct came loose, revealing a circle of dim, work-lit basement. Grandpa's face filled the hole, meeting Broadie's desperate gaze, then he went to work shaking the loose elbow. The coins scattered on the floor like high, sonorous cheers. Grandpa set the section of duct aside and gathered them up.

"Your Grandma wanted me to take them away, but I told her to let you keep them." His voice was muffled as he bent down for each coin.

Broadie stayed quiet.

"Come and get them."

He moved quickly past the kitchen where Davie and Alisha sat eating ice cream. Grandma looked up from her Relief Society lesson that she was preparing and watched him go by. He nearly lost his footing on the way down the stairs. Grandpa emerged from the storage room, holding the coins with sooty hands. He didn't give them up right away, but looked at them thoughtfully, moving them around with his finger.

"I guess you might think that these are really special, that they are worth quite a bit."

Broadie nodded.

"There isn't a speck of matter in this world worth the way you treated your brother today." The tone of voice fanned the burn of Broadie's guilt into an inferno. "There was a man once that gave up his Savior for thirty pieces of silver." He held up the silver liberty half-dollar as if to get a better look at it. "Go make up with your brother." He poured the coins into Broadie's hands.

He didn't go directly to Davie. He felt that just going and saying sorry wouldn't be good enough. He still felt rumbles of anger every time he remembered seeing Davie's hand loose the coins over the heater vent, but he also knew that Davie didn't understand what he was doing. Davie needed more reassurance than just empty words.

Maybe there would also be a way to reinforce the value of the collection. He had other reasons for waiting: he hadn't forgotten about the gold coin. It was something so extraordinary that it couldn't be kept a secret. It had to be shared with someone, and the only person that he could trust was January.

* * *

Broadie admired the globular stalagmite of ice that formed under a huge icicle that hung from January's back porch. White morning light sparkled through icicles that hung from the eaves. He tightened his collar, then tucked his hands deeper into his pockets. Thin white puffs of breath drifted away into the frosty air. He hopped quietly from one leg to the other, fighting back the cold, checking his watch, and waiting patiently for her to come to the door. He had made arrangements last night through the window to meet her today. This was the bravest rendezvous that they had come up with yet. He wasn't supposed to knock; she would meet him there at nine on the dot. It was now ten after, and he was considering risking a phone call.

Finally, the door gave with a small pop as it was forced from its icy jam. As he turned to face the door, he suddenly wondered what he would do if he turned to face January's mom. He decided before he completed his turn that he wouldn't feel guilty for just wanting to talk to her. He took a deep, cold breath and was relieved that January was peeking through the crack. "Hold on just a minute more," she whispered. She then shut the door again.

He let out a long, frustrated breath, hopping a little more vigorously. He was tired of sneaking around for everything he wanted to do. It was Saturday morning, and he should feel free to move about as he pleased. He was tired of tiptoeing around her parents. He wanted to march in, yelling that she was his friend and there wasn't a damn thing they could do about it. He wanted to scream at her mother, tell her that she had judged him wrong. What did he have to do to prove to her that he was worthy to be her friend?

"Okay," January answered back to her parents from behind the door. She looked like an over-stuffed animal as she made an effort not to open the door too wide. He moved closer to the big icicle, hoping not to be seen through the door, and let her through.

"How did you—"

"Ssh!" She put her finger to her lips, then tugged on his coat sleeve. He followed her into his own yard. When they reached the shed, she spoke: "Sorry it took so long. I told them I was going on a walk, which was true, but I didn't want to risk a problem."

"How did you get away so easily? I thought you couldn't go outside at all."

She smiled deviously as she spoke: "I begged the doctor to tell them that I needed fresh air from time to time. They're afraid that I'll get pneumonia or something. Now are *you* sure that your Grandma won't say anything?"

"She went Christmas shopping with my mom, so it's just me and Davie. She wouldn't care anyway. She likes you."

"I just have to make sure that I'm back in time to help put up our Christmas tree."

"Wow! You guys wait a long time to put up yours."

"Not really, it's just been harder with me being sick."

"We hardly had Thanksgiving dinner done before Grandma decided to put up the decorations. She hangs up antique ornaments that were our great-grandmother's, then yells at us to stay away from them."

They stomped the snow off their feet in the kitchen doorway. The smooth warmth of the house was welcoming. January took one quick look back at her house before the door was closed completely, then took off her coat and hung it up by Broadie's. Jaunty cartoon voices drifted in from the living room.

"Good. He's still watching TV." He motioned for her to follow him, and they tiptoed into his room.

"I haven't seen your room from this angle for a while." She walked to his bookcase and looked at his new additions. "So, what are we going to do?" She sat down on his bed looking tired.

"Check this out." He smoothed out a large piece of paper on his bed.

"Cool," she said, moving closer.

He had used Grandpa's fountain pen, going to great lengths to draw an authentic-looking treasure map. With grandma's help, he baked it in the oven, as he had seen on TV, to make it look old.

"So, what's the treasure?"

He smiled as he rolled up the parchment, tied it with a string, and remained silent.

"Hey, I thought I was in on this whole thing."

"You are."

"Then why won't you tell me?"

He shook his head, tucking the roll into his shirt. Then together they walked into the living room. He pointed at Davie.

"Oh . . . uh, hi, Davie," January said, distracting him as Broadie went past.

Davie smiled and waved at her, then turned quickly back to his cartoon.

"I'm going to get the mail," Broadie said, slightly raising his voice to make sure that Davie heard. He stepped out of the front door, giving a quick glance back to see that Davie wasn't looking. He pulled the map out of his shirt. He was relieved that the mail had come. He grabbed the envelopes, shuffled them to see who they were from, then went in, smoothing down his shirt. "Hey, look, we got a Christmas card from Uncle Jeff and Aunt Becky in Germany. Wow! What's this?"

Davie looked up. Now Broadie had his attention.

"This says it's for Davie."

"Something for Davie?" January joined in.

Davie jumped up, completely forgetting the cartoon, and ran to Broadie. "Let me see! Let me see!"

"Hold on," Broadie said, holding it up above his head, out of habit, to make him work for it.

"Give it!" Davie whined and jumped up and down trying to retrieve it.

"Oh, just give it to him," January said.

Davie snatched it out of his hand. Broadie grinned at January. She gave him back a scowl. He shrugged. It was hard to stop a good thing when he got it going.

"What is it?" Davie said, pulling off the string.

"Here, I'll take it if you don't want it," Broadie said, reaching out his hand.

"No!" Davie said, pulling it away.

"Here, let me see. I'll tell you what it is," January said. Davie relinquished it trustingly into her hand. She stuck her tongue out at Broadie. "Look, it has your name on it."

"I know that already. What is it?" Davie stretched up onto his tiptoes to look at it as she unrolled it.

"What do you think it is?" she held it out and he examined it carefully.

"Is it a treasure map?" he said mysteriously.

"It's a treasure map," Broadie affirmed, copying Davie's tone of voice.

Davie's eyes widened; he took it from January's hands. "Where does it say to start?"

"Here, I'll do it," Broadie said, reaching out for the map again.

Davie yanked it away distrustfully.

"Here, *I'll* do it." January took the map. She leaned closer so Davie could see and pointed to the place that said START. "It looks like your house and it says to start in the kitchen."

"How did somebody know what was in our house?" Davie followed her. Broadie fell in behind them.

"There were old people that lived here long before Grandma and Grandpa bought this house. That was in the olden days," Broadie said.

Davies eyes got bigger. "If it's the olden days people, then how did they send us the map if they died?"

"Maybe their ghosts did it," Broadie said with a smirk.

Davie let out a scared whimper.

"If you scare him it won't work," January said, now mothering him outright. For a moment Broadie wanted to be angry but quickly accepted her rebuke, realizing that he was going too far with the teasing.

Their treasure hunt took them through the house, out into the garage, the shed, and back to the house. The closer they came to the treasure, the more excited Davie became. January started getting tired, so she relinquished the map to Broadie on the condition that he not tease Davie. He would have argued with her, but in a funny way he could tell that she wasn't just trying to be bossy. There was sincerity in the way she spoke that passed beyond his pride like a ghost.

Their last stop was at the bottom of the stairs to the attic. Davie had always been afraid to go up there by himself, but now he led them bravely through the linen closet.

"Hold on, I need to sit down." January trembled so slightly that anyone who didn't know her condition wouldn't have noticed. She sat down on the bottom step and took off her hat.

"We can't stop now, we're almost there!" Davie said dramatically.

"Just let her rest for a minute," Broadie said, trying not to show that he had suddenly noticed that she was going bald.

"It's okay. Go ahead. I just want to stay here for a few minutes," she said.

"Hey, what happened to your head?" Davie said, right on cue.

"Davie!" Broadie tried to shut him up.

"He's fine." She spoke to Broadie, then turned to Davie. "That's what my medicine does."

Broadie turned away embarrassed. Davie continued to stare at her until she finished scratching her head, then put her hat back on.

"Does it hurt?" Davie asked, now raptly interested.

"Sometimes," she said. She glanced up at Broadie with a smile, as if to say that she thought Davie was cute.

Broadie folded his arms, and leaned against the old, creaky wood on the wall that probably hadn't been painted for more than fifty years. It was a dull, dusty cream color that looked even more yellow in the dim attic light. The stairs were unpainted and were smooth with wear.

"You know, you guys can go ahead if you want," she said, watching Davie move slowly to the top of the stairs. He stopped at the door and looked around at the boxes.

"The surprise is for you, too," Broadie whispered.

"You could bring it down and show me here."

"I can't." He tipped his head toward Davie.

She paused, thought for a moment. "Okay," she said, with more enthusiasm than she probably felt.

"I found it!" Davie yelled from somewhere above.

She reached out her hand; he helped her to her feet. Her hand was small and cold. They came to the top of the stairs. Davie was in the gable kneeling over a box that had "TREASURE" written with bold, black magic marker.

"This has been here for a hundred years!" Davie said, opening the flaps and reaching in. January grinned again, and looked curiously over Davie's shoulder. He pawed through it, then looked up disappointedly. "It's just a bunch of old books!"

"You have to dig for treasure," Broadie said.

Davie grunted impatiently, pulling the books out one after the other.

"Wow!" January whispered. She walked up to some old dresses that were wrapped in plastic, lifted them from the bottom, and admired the old lace.

"I think that's my grandma's wedding dress." Broadie left Davie to join her. She lifted it off of the hanger and held it up to her neck. It dragged on the floor.

"I found it!" Davie yelled.

He lifted out an old jewelry box and opened it up. His face fell; he gave Broadie a strange look.

"What is it?" January said excitedly.

Davie didn't say anything. He held the box out so they could see. January took it and lifted out its sparse contents. Davie pulled her hand down to his eye level.

"They're your—"

Broadie lifted a quick finger to his lips to hush her.

"Hey, Davie," he said, "you have your own Indian head penny." He took it from her hand and placed it in Davie's. "And you . . ."–he placed the Walking Liberty half dollar in her hand—" . . . Get this."

She gasped. "I can't take this." She tried to hand it back, but he closed her fingers over it.

"I like to think that the sun is rising."

She smiled.

"Now, Davie, this is a special treasure that you have to take care of. There aren't any Indian head pennies around anymore. It's not supposed to be spent on candy in the store. You have to keep it a special secret. That's your special coin collection. Here, keep it in the little box so it doesn't get lost."

Davie took it and put it back into the box.

"Now, go hide it someplace that you won't forget." Broadie coaxed him back to the stairs. He quickly left Broadie alone with January.

"Come here," he whispered, waving her over to the chest of drawers. She watched with great interest as he opened one of the drawers and lifted out the box of coins that he had found yesterday. "I've got a secret that I want you to see, but don't say anything."

"I won't," she also whispered.

He took the lid off, and her eyes widened. "You're rich!"

"There's more." He bent down, dumping the coins slowly onto the dusty, wooden floor, then with reverence held up the gold coin.

"Can I see?" She held out her hand tentatively. "What is it?"

"It's real gold. I think it's my great-grandmother's. All of this is hers. I don't think my grandpa knows it's here."

"Maybe you should tell him."

"No, it's too good of a secret. He would just give it to one of my rich uncles and aunts. They have everything, so I think I should at least have something."

"Maybe he would give it to you, anyway."

"No, he wouldn't."

"How do you know?"

"Why do you care?"

January closed her mouth and looked hurt. He suddenly felt terrible for that comment, but he didn't know how to take it back. He slowly gathered the coins back into the box.

"I just hoped you would do the right thing," she said quietly.

She made him feel guilty. He wanted to justify himself, but she was right. He put the lid back on and placed it back into its spot in silence.

"I better get back before my mom and dad go looking for me."

"I'm sorry," he finally said.

She gave him a half smile and took herself to the door.

9

"Hi, Broadie," Gayle said. This time there wasn't any "Grodie Broadie." She admiringly watched him pass.

His desk had been moved to the far corner by Jim's. Leroy, who was sullenly quiet, was in the opposite corner of the room by Rae-lynn. His eyes were bruised; his finger was splinted and bandaged. They both pretended to ignore each other, and both were on red level.

"Take a seat," Joslyn said flatly—and completely unnecessarily. She probably wanted to establish that they weren't on friendly terms and to reaffirm her authority.

Broadie put his bag aside, sat down, and kicked the rest of the snow off his shoes. He didn't bother to take off his coat because he still felt cold. Jim nodded chummily, which was more than he had ever done for Jeff or Leroy. Jeff had noticed and looked down at his desk in envy. Sarah began a lesson. Everyone was to take notes. Jim leaned forward to write. Broadie looked over his shoulder, caught a glimpse of Gayle looking his way, then glancing away as quickly as their eyes met.

"Where is Pearl Harbor? Can anyone answer that question?" Sarah asked. She looked from person to person. No one spoke.

"How about Hawaii?" Joslyn said, turning her hands in small circles as if to say, *"Get with it, folks."*

Jim put his head down on his desk. The little glance-and-look-away with Gayle repeated itself.

"Come on guys," Sarah said. She rolled her eyes and threw her hands up theatrically. "December seventh, nineteen-forty-one, the Japanese attacked Pearl Harbor, and brought us into World War Two. Don't tell me none of you know this?"

"I knew," Craig said sheepishly.

* * *

Jim leaned back in his chair, closing his eyes. A buzz of heavy music seeped through his headphones. Leroy kicked and fidgeted in his corner, mocked by the excruciatingly slow hands of the clock. Broadie read his book delightedly unconcerned with time. The worksheets that they had just completed were of the same difficulty as the rest of the math that they had been working on since he had joined the class. He had completed it in only a few minutes and now awaited his grade as Sarah corrected his paper at her desk.

"Raelynn has a hundred percent!" Sarah said enthusiastically.

Leroy groaned.

"All right!" Joslyn said, moving her from blue to purple.

Raelynn beamed and whispered with Gayle. Jim seemed unaware that that the grades were being announced. He quietly tapped his pencil on the edge of his desk to the rhythm of his music. Jeff looked over at him annoyed but didn't say anything.

"Congratulations!" Joslyn said to Broadie as she walked to the color board. "You got a hundred percent, and I think you're the fastest one off red level this year." She moved his name to yellow.

"*No fair!*" Leroy cried, throwing his pencil. It bounced off the far wall and hit Craig.

"Leroy!" Sarah said.

"You can't do that!" Leroy's face was a bitter red. He held up his splinted hand. "He did *this* to me! He shouldn't be first off red, he don't deserve it!"

Sarah walked briskly to his desk. "Let's go calm down," She said. She reached for his good arm. He yanked it back.

"*Don't touch me, you bitch!*" Leroy screamed.

The class watched with intense silence. Jim acted as if he hadn't noticed, but the tapping of his pencil slightly intensified.

Joslyn moved to the other side of Leroy's desk.

"Let's you and me go to time out, and after you've calmed down you can come back to class," Sarah said, with a calm voice.

"Put *him* in time out!" Leroy was now sobbing with rage.

"Let's go somewhere we can talk about it," she said soothingly. She moved in closer, offering her hand.

Leroy fiercely slapped it away, spat the f-word, and told her what she could do with herself. Joslyn seized his bad arm. He swung a fist with the other. She smoothly dodged it and twisted it around his back, pinning him against his desk with her weight. He let out a shrill scream. Raelynn and Gayle moved away from the struggle.

"Everyone go outside and take a break," Sarah said to the class.

As people gathered their coats, Jim, eyes closed, still blissfully listened to his music. Broadie decided to let him enjoy himself. As he got to the door, Craig blocked his way, watching hypnotically as Leroy writhed, fought, strained, and screamed obscenities. Jim finally opened one eye. He looked from Leroy to Craig, and then to Broadie. A funny smile slightly turned on his lips. Broadie suddenly felt like he should get Craig out of that room as fast as he could. Jim was tapping his pencil harder on his desk now. Broadie put a hand on Craig's shoulder. He jumped as if he had been slapped.

"Come on," Broadie whispered.

Craig's eyes were wide. Jim was now standing, still smiling that crazy smile. Broadie moved Craig out the door and into the bright, cold morning air. They moved together away from the relocatable. The eastern sun enlivened the dull, tawny brick of the main building. He could see through the windows of the classrooms as the rest of the school went mutely about its peaceful business.

"Hey, what's up?" Raelynn asked Broadie.

"Hey," Broadie said. He saw that Jim had come outside and was moving toward the shed.

Raelynn looked back at Gayle, as she pretended to be preoccupied with a "No Parking" sign. It was odd that those two had separated even for a minute.

"I know someone who likes you," Raelynn started to speak.

"NO!" Gayle screamed, ran over, shoving her hand over Raelynn's mouth. They laughed and tousled in the silly way that all twelve-year-old girls seemed to do. They moved away, laughing.

He watched them go, then thought about January.

* * *

The warm afternoon didn't melt all of the snow. The parking lot was a sea of dirty slush and salt. He stepped carefully to avoid a black puddle. He began to feel hot in his coat, so he took it off and tied it around his waist. Davie and Allen ran ahead side by side.

No John or Joey today, he thought. A car backfired, and a huge mass of sparrows exploded from the trees above him.

A hand rested on his shoulder.

He spun, ready to fight. Jim stared at him, a half-grin under stoic, unblinking eyes.

"S' up dude?" Jim said. He took a long drag from his cigarette and fell into pace side by side with Broadie. A bee buzz of music seeped from the headphones that hung around his heck.

"You scared the shit out of me," Broadie said.

Jim reached deep into his jacket, pulled out his cigarettes, and offered one to Broadie. He took one with the lighter and cupped the end against the breeze. He sucked the smoke into his mouth, watching for any uptight adults.

"Have you ever heard of Cradle of Filth?" Jim asked.

"Who?"

"It's black metal."

"What?"

"Like death metal, only darker."

Broadie felt stupid, as all he could do was blankly shake his head.

Jim sighed impatiently: "It's hell-rock."

"You mean music?"

"Shit!" Jim shook his head in disgust, and looked away.

Broadie's face went red. He wondered if he meant the old heavy metal music that his dad listened to, like Black Sabbath.

"Here," Jim said, like a frustrated parent. He shoved the earphones over Broadie's head and cranked the volume. Broadie winced, pulling them away from his ears. Heavy guitars exploded against complex mechanical rhythms. Voices screeched, strained, and whispered like demons escaping from hell. It was terrifying and intriguing.

"They're tough, aren't they?" It was a statement demanding an affirmation more than a question. Jim talked in a way that seemed so old and mature. Broadie felt inadequate to try to converse. He just shrugged his shoulders, pretending that he was listening carefully.

"I have some new 'Ozzy,' and some 'Disturbed,'" He pulled a small stack of CDs out of his coat like a magician.

Now, Ozzy Osbourne was something that Broadie could relate to, because it was something that his dad listened to. "Cool. Ozzy," he said, hoping to save some respect.

"I stole them from one of my mom's boyfriends; it doesn't matter to him because he's in jail." Jim smugly took the headphones back.

Broadie absently rubbed his ears as if he secretly wanted to wipe away something dirty. Jim was once again alone behind his unreachable face and the privacy of his headphones. They walked together, not speaking. Broadie watched the destruction that his feet made on the slushy sidewalk. Every step that he took left a wide crater; the harder he stepped, the further it would splash. He began to angle his foot so that the splashes would go into the road. He was soon trying to hit the cars as they went past. Jim made smoke rings as he let out a breath. Broadie tried to copy him but still didn't dare to breathe the smoke. He didn't want to cough and embarrass himself. Jim flicked the ashes from his cigarette a certain way, then so did Broadie.

"Let's stop here," Jim said, pointing to a gas station. They crossed the street. Jim dared the traffic, forcing it to slow down. A woman yelled out her car window for them to get out of the road, and he held up his middle finger to her as she drove past, indignantly putting on speed.

Broadie hopped a large, oily puddle, then they walked into the greasy, coffee smell of the Quick-Mart.

"Hi, Mom!" Jim said.

"Steal any cigarettes, and I'll kick your little ass." A muffled, raspy woman's voice came from behind a door that had a big sign that said NO PUBLIC RESTROOM.

"I ain't stealing nothin'," he said cheerily, as he walked behind the counter. He reached up, popped out a couple of packs of Marlboros, then grabbed a can of Copenhagen; the whole time looking steely eyed at the back door. He moved swiftly, smoothly.

Broadie felt a sick fear of getting in trouble. He looked outside, wanting to escape, as a beat-up, gray, body-puttied mustang pulled up to the pumps. It ran over a rubber tube, and a chime rang from the back room. His attention turned to the women, who pushing the door open in front of her, lumbered out of a storage room carrying a large box of cups. By then, Jim had moved to the soda fountains. "Can we have a Coke?" he asked, sounding relaxed and natural.

The woman eyed him suspiciously: "Who's 'we'?" she said, dropping the box.

She was a young woman, like Broadie's mother. She was hard looking. With a leap in his stomach, Broadie realized that she was the biker woman with the yap-dog that he had flipped off the day that John and his friends had beat him up. She regarded him with angry eyes. Had she recognized him?

"Whatever," she said, then walked to the counter.

Jim filled his cup with Coke, drank part of it, then filled it up again. Broadie cautiously filled his, staying at a distance from the counter. He examined the nacho bin, wishing he had some money.

The man from the Mustang walked through the door. He nodded at Jim with recognition. He was skinny, with long hair and a black leather motorcycle jacket. "Hey, Lexi," he said, leaning onto the counter with familiarity.

"Hey, Russ." Jim's mom was suddenly friendly.

"Give me a couple packs of Marlboros," he said, opening his wallet. The cash register beeped.

"Oh, shit," Jim whispered. "Let's go." He moved Broadie quickly to the doors. "Bye, Mom," he said, trying to distract her.

"If you don't go straight home, you'll be in deep shit," she said.

They pushed through the doors into the frigid, smoggy air.

"As soon as we get out of sight, run like hell," Jim said.

They turned the corner just as the doors swung open.

"Jim!"

His mother yelled a string of obscenities. Heavy footsteps slapped the concrete with a metallic echo. They both knew it was Russ. Broadie froze, but Jim pushed him forward. Jim scrambled over a dumpster and onto a fence. Broadie reached the top just as Russ came around the corner. With ice in his stomach, Broadie found the momentum that he needed. He tossed his drink away, then threw himself over the chain link fence, gouging the palm of his hand. His feet stung as he hit the ground. Jim was already ahead and running onto the parking lot of a seedy apartment complex. Broadie followed him into the small maze of concrete stairs, porches, and uniform doors. They stopped around the corner of one of the buildings as Russ cleared the fence. Jim was laughing. Where he didn't seem to have expression before, his face was now antic; his eyes were wide and excited. Russ started in their direction.

"This way!" Jim tugged on Broadie's jacket.

Once again they were running. They turned and ran through a different building and back the direction they had come. Russ was now nowhere in sight.

"Up here!" Jim started up a dark and dirty flight of stairs.

Broadie hesitated. A woman, somewhere in the bowels of the building, was scolding loudly in Spanish. Behind her voice was the steady thunk of rap music. The sick smell of beer and rot emanated from a garbage bag that had been torn open by a stray dog and left in the space below them.

"Come on!" Jim now sounded urgent.

Broadie began to move. They reached a row of battered doors beyond the numbered apartments. They were boxed in. He now wondered what Jim had been thinking. He watched in the direction that they had come; his worry increased with every second. Jim stopped at one of the doors. He pulled out a pen and jammed it into the latch. He struggled, swore, then struggled again. The pen snapped, but there was also another click along with it. The door popped open.

"Yes! I thought they'd fixed it," Jim said, as they moved inside a dirty, empty storage space. It wasn't much bigger than a closet He turned on a grimy yellow light and locked the door behind them. He breathed a big sigh of relief and looked around.

"I used to live in the apartment next door, ya know."

Broadie kept silent. He had the terrible feeling that something was out of control. The best thing that he could do was to leave now, head straight home, but he was paralyzed with indecision. There really *was* something terribly wrong about Jim. He knew that whatever he did with Jim would turn into trouble.

Jim continued to speak: "We lived here until my mom's exboyfriend was thrown in jail, then we moved in with Russ, her ex's best friend. She says he'll kill us if he gets out and finds out, so we're probably going to move somewhere else. Check this out."

Jim started to pull on the paneling on the back wall. The nails were loose and came away easily. He maneuvered himself behind it in the cramped space. Broadie moved with him. The supports for the wall and the insulation were exposed. Down below was a heater vent. Jim bent down, working at it until it came free from the wall.

"Look in there." He said.

Broadie bent down and looked into the empty living room of an apartment. The carpet was dirty and torn in places. There was an old sagging couch against the far wall. A lot of junk was piled around the kitchen. He was hit with a suffocating smell that made him gag and cough; it was an ammonia-like smell mixed with other dirty smells—whatever it was, it wasn't right.

"They're cooking," Jim whispered.

"They're what?"

"It's a lab."

"A what?"

Broadie pulled his coat over his nose and mouth so he could breathe better.

"They make their shit here, then sell it at the gas station. If Russ knew we were here, he'd kill us; he's crazy enough to."

Jim smiled as he let the information sink into Broadie. He seemed to enjoy the fear that must have showed on Broadie's face. "They never knew I could do this. They never cared where I went when they did what they did, but I was here watching the whole time. They don't think I know, but I do. I saw it all."

Broadie moved from his hands and knees, sat against the wall, and stretched his back. Jim reached into his coat pocket, pulled out a pack of cigarettes, regarded it thoughtfully, then tossed it down to Broadie. He then sat down with the heater vent between them. Broadie held it, looking at it as if it was something rotten.

"What, no thanks?" Jim's eyes twinkled

"Maybe we should take them back."

"Maybe I should deck you."

Broadie's face flushed. He wished now, more than anything, that he was home. He would rather be reading to January; he looked forward to that every day.

"Ssh!" Jim froze.

There were footsteps in the hall outside. They were quick, almost desperate. Keys jingled. The doorknob to the apartment rattled. The door swung open, and Russ charged in feral and dangerous. He was flushed and breathed like he had run a marathon. Both boys sat dead silent as Russ searched from room to room. He came back into the living room. They could see his boots shift left, then right. He kicked an empty box, then walked back out the door. The doorknob rattled again, and keys jingled, as the locks were set.

Neither boy moved for a long time. Broadie was weak and nauseous. The ammonia-like, dirty smell made his eyes water.

"I knew they still used this place. I wonder what they'll do when the lease is up," Jim whispered

"I'm going to be grounded; it's way too late," was all Broadie could say.

Jim chuckled, then his face fell serious.

"I can't go home tonight. My mom will get over it, but it's Russ I have to worry about. He's crazier than her jailbird ex." He finally stood, brushed off, then proceeded to put things back into place.

They had taken a long route, well out of their way. Broadie's shoes were soaked, and his feet hurt from the cold, but now they were finally in familiar territory. They passed the 7-Eleven, and Jim lit up another cigarette.

"Keeps me warm," he would say each time.

Broadie picked at the unopened plastic of the stolen pack in his pocket. He felt terribly nervous each time a police car went past and wondered if Jim's mom had called the police. He couldn't wait to be home, even thought he knew that he would have to answer for being so late. They turned down Jim's street. Broadie recognized Jim's house right away. He pretended to be ignorant of that knowledge as they slowed down.

"Hold on," Jim said. He stopped cautiously in front of the driveway. "Get ready to run if we have to."

Broadie was tired of the games. He just wanted to rest his feet over the heater vent in his room.

"I need to get home," he said.

"Just wait a sec," Jim insisted.

Broadie lifted one foot, then the other. He began to ache all over in the cold. He looked ahead where he would turn onto his own street and contemplated just walking off and leaving Jim to his problems. Someone turned the corner riding a bike. Jim was now sneaking into the carport. No one seemed to be home.

The person on the bike passed them, slowed down, then turned around. He was well bundled against the air. He passed again, looking right at Broadie, then stopped a few feet away. Broadie didn't feel like a fight. Whoever it was hadn't said anything yet, but he was acting funny. He quickly looked up the street, back at Broadie, then pulled away his scarf. It was Tim Burton. Jim came back from the house, looking suspiciously at Tim.

No one spoke until the three were together on the wet street. Tim backed away a little as if his bike were a nervous horse.

"What are you looking at, geek?" Jim spoke dangerously.

Broadie was about introduce them, but Tim dismissed Jim's threatening question and spoke worriedly: "Don't go down to the ditch."

For a moment Broadie didn't know what Tim was talking about. He was still thinking about the day's excitement.

"Who's this?" Jim asked.

Broadie shook off his stupor. Tim backed up a little more, the urgent expression draining from his face as he now probably considered what he had just done.

"What about the ditch?" Broadie said coldly. He felt as if things were going more terribly wrong yet.

"Please, I didn't go with them," Tim pleaded. "I didn't know you'd be coming this way."

"Go with who?" The words caught in Broadie's throat.

Jim seemed to sense the importance of what was happening. He watched intently as Tim struggled with his predicament, and Broadie stepped forward, demanding to know what he meant.

Broadie suddenly ran.

Cold yellow sun slanted through the evening haze, flickering in the empty bushes and trees. His shadow, stretched against red brick houses, turned golden. His foot falls clapped and echoed. They were desperate, rapid, clipped. He swung himself around a signpost to turn the corner nearly loosing his footing. He crossed the street indifferent to traffic. Someone honked as they passed. The fence by the ditch was just ahead, but miles away. He cleared a pile of muddy snow left over from the plow. Each breath was burning metal, freezing and congealing in his stomach. He lost his backpack as he dived through the hole in the fence, slipped on cold mud, fell, and rolled into the ditch. Burrs and stickers clung to him scraping his skin. Not too far off he heard pounding and the cracking of heavy wood.

He reached the denuded rosebushes and saw Joey in the tree house kicking at a sadly tilting wall.

Laughs. Hoots.

It fell, cartwheeling in slow motion through bare branches.

Triumphant yells.

His panic was rapturous. Deep gurgles wheezed from his chest as he tried to scream through consumed lungs and throat.

John swung a two-by-four viciously, ravagingly against the tilting walls of the clubhouse. Joey and Steve kicked with ecstasy. An invasion into the deepest part of Broadie: a desecration, a rape, their joy at his worst anguish, and the murder of his private creation. He found the entrance and pushed through, insanely unaware of the jabs and pricks of the thorned runners. His hands found a board that had known his labor. He swung madly at the back of Steve's head. The board connected with a loud *boink!* Steve reeled staggering forward in horror. He spun, faced Broadie. His hand reached up to his ear. Broadie swung again, as Steve let out a girlish scream and began to wail.

"Oh, hell, yes!" Jim said, from somewhere back in the bushes. Tim wasn't far behind him.

John had stopped his assault on the tree house. His face dropped in shock. Broadie bypassed Steve, and charged at John. The scene was like a grainy film in fast motion. John was frozen in place. At the last possible moment, he ducked and staggered in fright. Broadie swung again clipping John's shoulder.

"Help! John screamed. He raised the board with which he was demolishing the clubhouse, but he was too late, as Broadie swung again, smashing John's hands. The board wobbled through the air.

"No! No!" Tim cried.

Joey skittered down the footholds, jumped, and tackled Broadie. They struggled viciously in the freezing mud. Steve got back up and backed away from the fight. He took his hand from the side of his head and sobbed, staring unbelievingly at the blood he had discovered. John jumped around, shaking a smarting hand.

"Stop it!" Tim screamed.

Instantly, Joey was knocked off Broadie. Jim grappled with him; a strange smile filled his face. They rolled over and over, cigarettes flipped out in different directions. Jim maneuvered until he straddled Joey, pummeling him deftly, happily. Joey threw his arms over his face until Jim finally stood and gave him a kick to the ribs. "That was for my cigarettes," Jim said contemptuously.

"My toof!" Joey sobbed.

As Broadie scrambled to his feet, John had picked up another board. Nails jutted dangerously out of the business end. He took a sadistic swing at Broadie, favoring his sore fingers. Broadie fell on the ground, rolled. John swung again, and the nails caught in Broadie's coat, ripping it at the shoulder and gouging his skin. Broadie screamed, grabbed the board, yanking it hard out of John's hands. It flipped harmlessly at Jim's feet. Broadie looked up at John and received a hard kick to his nose. He felt it smash; he was blinded for a moment.

Tim was helping Joey to his feet, then suddenly screamed again. Broadie blinked in time to see Jim bring the nailed board down onto John; brought it down again, then again. John struggled to crawl away under the blows, moaning in terror and pain. One swing smashed into his hand, leaving a finger unnaturally bent. Jim raised the board high for a devastating swing. Tim threw himself over John. "Please, no!" He yelled, his glasses reflecting the red sunset. He held out a hand to impede the attack. Broadie struggled to his feet and reached out for the board. Jim looked at him, then down at John.

"Puss," he said, tossing the board aside. He backed away.

Broadie looked over the destruction numbly, his vision clouded in puffs of white breath. Drops of blood collected on the small sign, the spatters turning the words MAGNUM OPUS red. He backed away, feeling the flow of warm blood over his mouth and down his chin.

"Let's go," Jim said urgently.

Broadie looked up. Steve was leading some adults from a couple of houses away.

"Come on!" Jim started backing away.

Joey saw them coming, and ran in their direction.

Tim knelt over John, who lay curled in a shivering ball. He looked up at Broadie pleadingly: "He's hurt bad."

Jim broke into a run. Broadie watched him go and wiped some blood away from his mouth with his sleeve.

"I need help," Tim said.

Broadie walked back and knelt beside Tim. He felt sick as John convulsed, and blood poured from the tears in his head and neck. Tim took off his coat and laid it over John. "He's going into shock," he sobbed.

"What do I do?" Broadie whispered.

"Put pressure on that bleeding there." Tim took Broadie's hand, and pressed it on the ugliest wound. "Just push as hard as you can."

Both Tim and Broadie wept from the trauma. John shook as Tim whispered in his ear, telling him everything was going to be all right. Broadie felt his ragged breathing and no longer hated him. Tim prayed vocally as the adults crashed through the bushes.

"Over there," Joey's voice echoed through the naked, darkening trees.

"Broadie?" Grandpa called.

He came up the trail followed by Mr. Larson, Steve, and Joey. Other neighbors had gathered further back.

"Call an ambulance!" Tim yelled.

"Call an ambulance!" Mr. Larson repeated back to the others. Someone ran.

"Broadie!" Grandpa's voice was more urgent.

The men approached, and immediately took charge. Broadie didn't let go but continued the pressure on the bleeding.

"What in the world happened here?" Mr. Larson asked as more people approached. He slowly rolled John onto his back to get a better look at his injuries. John came to semiconsciousness and moaned.

"It was him! He did it!" Joey yelled, and pointed at Broadie.

Tim lost his temper, and pushed Joey. "Do you have to keep it going, you liar! You sick liar! Can't you just leave things alone?" He sobbed.

Grandpa took Joey aside. "Where's the other kid?" he asked sternly. Joey didn't speak.

"He ran away!" Tim said.

Another neighbor handed his coat to shivering Tim and took Broadie's place at John's side. Grandpa quickly hugged him.

"It wasn't Broadie's fault!" Tim insisted.

"Is that true?" Mr. Larson drilled the two boys. Both Joey and Steve nodded their heads in shame. "You'd darn well better be honest with the police, then."

An ambulance made its way through the neighborhood, then stopped up at the road. More sirens could be heard approaching. The flashing red and blue lights could now be seen reflecting in the windows of the near by houses. The paramedics came down the ditch with a stretcher. A police officer led them. The gathering crowd parted to let them through. Broadie saw January among them. He could tell, even from a distance, that she was crying. Broadie left the group and began to gather the scattered pieces of his work. He lifted the doorframe and tried to prop it back into place. It balanced for a moment, then fell inward. He looked up, and, in a funny way, was relieved that the platform was still there. He closed his eyes. Everything was green again. He imagined the sweaty handle of his hammer and the shady, warm summer air.

"Are you Broadie?" An officer asked.

Broadie nodded his head slowly.

"Come with me please."

Broadie turned, and through a flood of tears, followed the officer down the trail. He felt the sustaining weight of grandpa's arm around his shoulder. January stared at the ground as they passed. Broadie was led up the ditch to the police car on the road, and January walked back to her house alone.

Part IV

1

Davie and Allen took off their jackets and raced each other in their roller blades on the sidewalk in front of the house. Their happy voices carried through the open front door. Mom carried another box up the stairs and set it down in the kitchen. She wiped her hands on her tight pants. Then she walked back to the stairs. Grandma sat at the table with her leg propped up on another chair and an ice pack on her knee. Broadie picked up the box, moved it to the front porch, and added it to the growing pile. He took a deep breath of spring air, he saw the daffodils that would soon bloom and craved a cigarette.

"Here comes the van," Davie yelled, and pointed down the street.

Broadie didn't look. Instead, he walked back in and grabbed another box. He didn't want to see the moving van. He would rather have gone with Grandpa when he had refused to help and went out for errands. He hoped to say goodbye before they left, but he didn't want to hear another screaming match with his mother

"Will you grab your sister?" Grandma said.

Alisha had opened the box with her toys and had already scattered them around the living room. He set the box down that he was carrying, picked her up, and set her back in the kitchen. She fussed, trying to run back to her toys.

"Here, we'll play. Do you want to play, Leeshie? Come play with grandma." She held out her hands.

"No!" Alisha whined—that was her new word lately.

Broadie started back to his box when Grandma spoke: "Your grandpa and I have been talking."

Broadie didn't say anything, but he stopped to listen in the doorway.

"You and Davie can stay. I know your mother didn't want me to say anything, but you have a home here. What she's doing isn't right. I just wanted you to know that we're doing everything we can to." She paused. "If things get bad, you call us and bring the other kids, if you can."

Broadie nodded.

"You don't let anyone hurt you or the others. You're the big brother. You promise me you'll do what you have to."

Broadie nodded again.

"Now you promise me!" Grandma said again with deep intensity. She waited for Broadie to answer.

"I promise," he whispered.

The van backed into the driveway, and the man who months ago Broadie had mistaken for his father downstairs with his mother pulled up in front of the house in his large truck. AC/DC once again blared from the cab.

Grandma grimaced.

Instead of picking up the box he had been carrying, he left it where it sat and walked out the back door.

"Hey, Davie dude!" Broadie heard Ty (that was the man's name: Ty) say, as he got out of his truck.

Broadie didn't like Ty. He was fake and carried his entire self as a man carries a chip on his shoulder. He worked hard to win the kids over, but he was selfish with their mother. He was the reason they didn't see their mother very much, and even less now that they had been partying a lot more lately. There was something else about him that stood out wrong, like a wolf's tail pokes out of a sheep's costume. Grandpa and Grandma sensed it, too, but were powerless against Mom's stubborn stupidity. This crazy whim to move up to Ogden with this man made Broadie sick. To Mom, it was a new and great adventure. Mom used Grandpa as her excuse for moving. The more she fought to justify her "lifestyle," the more Broadie hated her, and the more terrified he became. They were leaving the only security he had ever known.

"Broadie?" Mom called from the kitchen.

He ignored her and kept walking to the shed; the sun was warm behind it. The fresh smell of young, green grass soothed him. He sat on the moist ground, picking at a dry clump of last year's growth of weeds. He soaked himself in the peaceful breeze and noticed, maybe, for the first time, the sounds of insects and birds. A cat, its white fur luminous in the sun, appeared up the ditch in the weeds. It crept along until it stopped abruptly, intent on something hidden in the grass. It leapt, pounced quickly, then lost interest in whatever had caught its attention.

When the inquietude of his craving overrode his relaxation, he peeked around the corner of the shed to make sure no one was around. He stood, reached into the eave, pulled a loose board aside (one that his grandpa hadn't discovered yet), and found his cigarettes. He shook the pack until the loose, crisp cylinder slipped out between his fingers. With practiced smoothness, he had it lit, and in his mouth in what seemed all one motion. He took a small puff, then a deep breath, and let the rest of the smoke drift by in the clean sunlight. The sound of a screen door banging shut echoed his way. He knew without looking that it was January's. He knew every sound here and its quality without having to think about it; he knew the smells, the textures, and the place of every plant, tree, bush, and fence post; he could close his eyes and see a vivid picture of his world and know how it was supposed to be. Where would he go now? How would he call that strange place home? After another puff, he held his cigarette out of sight. He looked around into January's yard. She was coming, so he mashed it out and hid it in a crack in the boards.

She knew where he was. There was a rustle as she hunched through the old, rusty fence. He watched as she appeared from around the corner.

"Hi," she smiled.

Broadie smiled back, then glanced down to where he had hidden his cigarette, hoping that she wouldn't see it.

"Here, I brought these back. I really liked reading them with you," she said, holding out *The Stand* and *Ender's Game*.

"No, you keep them."

She looked down at the books thoughtfully for a moment. "Here, you keep *Ender's Game*."

"I have something for you, for your scrap book." He lifted a school picture out of his back pocket.

She took it with a smile. "Thank you."

The white cat that had come down the ditch appeared from the weeds with something in its mouth. It pranced proudly down the trail, head and tail high, until it saw them. It stopped, then warily turned back the way it had come. January watched it. Her hair was beginning to grow back a little, but the medicine had caused her to swell disproportionately in places. Her face was swollen, as was her stomach. Her arms were skinny. The doctors were beginning to hope that she was in remission, but for some strange reason she was still struggling, and it was getting terribly harder. She seemed strong today, but her strength came and went.

"She has kittens," she said, when they couldn't see the cat anymore.

"Where are they?"

"I think in someone's back yard. They come out sometimes and follow their mother."

"What do they look like?"

"Probably the daddy cat. I can't see them well from the house."

She looked back at him and seemed bashful about what she wanted to say next. They were both uncomfortably quiet. Broadie looked down at the crack in the boards again. She took a breath, then spoke: "Let's write each other like I do Candice. She doesn't write like she used to. I guess she has new best friends now. I brought a pen so we could write each other's addresses, but I don't have a piece of paper."

Broadie felt his pockets in vain for something for her to write on. He thought for a moment about the pack hidden above their heads, though he knew that it wouldn't do to bring it down.

"I don't know what mine will be. You could write yours on my hand. Wait. Hold on." He smiled. He took *Ender's Game* and flipped it to a blank page. "Here, write yours, and I'll send you a letter when we get to where we're going."

"Okay." She wrote with that open, happy handwriting that he had learned to recognize. To her surprise, he tore out the page, folded it up, and put it in his pocket.

She held the remaining book to her chest and crossed her arms. They were quiet again. Broadie scuffed the drying earth with his foot.

"I better go now," she whispered, then turned.

Broadie reached for her, but hesitated. She started to walk away. He felt like he was missing something. He took a step forward, hesitated again. She must have heard him move because she turned around. Before he could stop himself again, he reached for her again. She shifted the books to one arm, and they hugged. She held on tight even though he loosened to let her go. He renewed his embrace, and she began to shudder. She buried her face in his shoulder. He heard a soft sniff then another. He kissed her head like he had done ages ago, and it seemed right. He felt her strength seep away. She let go. He watched her walk back to her house. The cool breeze gusted around him, and the leafing trees swayed, and his heart broke.

* * *

Broadie hadn't moved the boxes from his room. He didn't care about what Mom would say, or whether she would make him leave without his things. He would prolong his time here as long as possible. Wherever they were going it wouldn't be home. Ogden was only less than hour away, but that was too far. There were places much farther away than Ogden. He had no way of knowing the future, but he did know when something wasn't right. He could stay, as Grandma had suggested, but how could he be somewhere that Mom wasn't? He also couldn't shake away the imperative that he should be there for Davie and Alisha, that they should all be together.

The night air was cold. The window would stay open; he would leave it open as someone—not him—loaded his things into the van. He hoped that Grandma would forget about it, perhaps not realize at all that it had been left open, and let it stay that way forever; it would be left that way for January, to remind her not to forget about him.

He didn't sleep that night. It was the first time that he had ever watched the sun go down, to let the night flow around him until it brought the sunrise again. In the deepest hours, when the occasional breeze lifted his curtains, he saw the movement of January's curtains along with his. Her window was also open. He wondered if the air was too cold and was afraid that she would get sick. There was always the danger that she would catch something that would be worse than the slow cancer, or the faster poison that was supposed to kill it, somehow, without killing her.

Under a small reading lamp he recorded himself reading *Ender's Game* on some dusty tapes that had old church talks on them. He read with a steady beat, sometimes choking back tears of his own. Twice he had to stop the tape, rewind it a little, and start over. He cringed at the sound of his own voice, but he didn't give up. A few times he was almost overcome with the sensation that he had entered into a world of perpetual night, to be lost forever, drifting in this strange place where the only island of light on earth was this tiny reading lamp. It broke when he had to get up to use the bathroom, but it didn't quite disappear all together. Even as he heard Grandpa's early feet moving down the hall and saw the first gray hints of change on the bricks outside his window, it still hadn't gone away.

When the sun was high enough to dazzle through the new green on the pear trees, Broadie wasn't there to see it. The birds were loud enough to awaken January and for her to stretch and pull a pillow over her head. The dewy breeze pulled her curtains in a little, then out a little at a time. Between them stood a stack of tapes over a small note. Across the chasm, Broadie's window remained open, empty and still.

2

Under a different sky, the night air was heavy and charged. Clouds of dust moved, illuminated by city glow, over the sleeping neighborhood. A transient was urinating under a shabby apartment window. The splashes of his urine mixed with the sparse, dirty raindrops that splashed over an old piece of paper that blew in from somewhere unknown. Yellow light revealed his dark shape as he moved away from the building to seek shelter from the storm.

In the room behind the window above him, two brothers slept on old mattresses on the floor. The older of the two dreamed. He was in a vividly green field that stretched freely beyond a rustic barbed wire fence. The sky was bright blue, and the air was filled with clear moisture. A perfect morning sun exploded over the eastern Wasatch Mountains. He lay in clean, cool, dew-covered grass that was tall and rich. The sky turned above him, and he was happy.

Cool air softly blew through nearby trees, slowly warming in the celestial glow. There was a hush, a whisper, a majestic rush, then another whisper. He turned to face the Oquirrh Mountains in the west. Their curving peaks were broad and present in the clean light. They were pristine, untouched by neither man nor drought. They were his. They spoke to him with an ancient voice that could be heard only in his heart. He wanted to climb them so he could look down upon the beautiful organization of God, then reach up and take him by the hand. He would be complete then, filled with fulfillment and peace.

He walked west through the vast, clean fields. Small white butterflies danced before him. Heavy alfalfa and sunflowers brushed against his naked legs, but instead of scratches they left behind comforting caresses. They didn't impede him but encouraged him, and every step was joy. He held out his fingers and let them slowly comb through the plants, letting the dew moisten them. He raised his hands to his mouth to let the water touch his tongue. The sun warmed him as it followed him in his journey. He looked up to the highest peak, knowing that when he reached it he would be complete, he would have fulfillment. There was a faraway rumble of thunder. It came from the wasteland behind the mountains that he wanted to climb. A terrible thought pierced him, that if he didn't hurry whatever was behind them would beat him there. A voice from that warmth and glory around him said: "Swallow the storm!"

* * *

He was jolted awake by a powerful flash of lightening and blast of thunder outside his window. Heavy summer rain pounded the dirty carport across from his building. Rain struck the window ledge, sending a spray through the torn screen, making him wet. Orange light from the street lights spattered crazy, wet designs across the bedroom wall. He got up and groggily shut the window as far as it would go. He covered it the rest of the way with a dirty T-shirt that was the only thing he could find quickly.

Davie was still asleep at his feet. He was curled up so that the only thing exposed from under the blanket was his shaven head and the glint of an earring—Mom had had his ears pierced, thinking that he looked cute. Broadie left the room, walked down the dirty hallway, and into the living room. Alisha was asleep on the couch with the television still on. The blue glow fell over her ratted blond hair. He would have picked her up and carried her into Mom's room, but she looked too peaceful. He went over to the tiny kitchen to look for something to eat. The leftovers were gone. He felt a growl of anger that harmonized with a rumble of thunder.

Mom had been gone two days now, and with her the rent—the apartment manager had been by to look for her. He had lied and told the manager that Mom was at work. She would probably show up tomorrow, asking to borrow some of his newspaper money that he had been saving until she could get another job. At least she won't be moving another loser into her bedroom soon—hopefully. Since Ty had left, life had been somewhat peaceful, but he still had been wondering if he should hide their last pawnable possessions in the empty storage next door.

He sat down at the sticky table, stared at the dark wall, and thought about leaving. He could go anywhere in the world, leave it all behind. His mother could take care of herself, but who would take care of Davie and Alisha? She still lay peacefully in the in the dim glow. If it weren't for them, he would leave right now. The shadows trapped him there as they always did. They kept him a lonely prisoner. He wouldn't sleep anymore tonight. The paper truck would be by soon, anyway. He walked over to the couch, careful not to wake up Alisha when he sat down, and surfed through the cable channels that should have been turned off months ago— at least some things in life did come free.

3

The sidewalk was dusty, and, where the taco vendors worked their stands, a little greasy. A clean breeze ticked through dripping trees as a skinny, stray dog sniffed around graffiti-covered dumpsters. A yellow street light came on, momentarily cutting off the rest of the world. It sputtered and dimmed; it was broken. Corona beer bottles glistened in sparsely shattered piles as Broadie took each tired, routine step along the wet concrete street. He knew that he shouldn't be cutting through this area, but it was the quickest way back to the apartment. His arm quietly ached where the nylon ropes of the newspapers that he had emptied from a van had pinched him. He drew his good arm thoughtfully across his forehead, wiping away the day's first grime. As the last puff of his lingering cigarette died away, he flicked the glowing butt against a fading mural of "Che" Guevara. It fell, sparks winking out, into a dried pool of vomit that he didn't notice.

He looked up at the yellow moon that was setting over a windowless cinderblock building. The storm had passed, but it was a bland sky. There were no stars as he remembered seeing every night at Grandpa's, though he wasn't conscious of this thought. He was only aware of the thin, paper paycheck that represented the last two weeks of sore feet, scraped arms, smelly clothes, and humiliation from an over-zealous new paper-route manager. Broadie was way too young to drive, so he was given the job of paper separator and folder. A paper route in his neighborhood wasn't something someone could do with just a bicycle. It was dangerous. Grandpa would say that times had changed. He had to be there earlier than everyone else—which wasn't fair. He was also paid the least. Supposedly he would receive a raise and his own route when he turned fourteen. Why fourteen? Hadn't he stayed on longer than everyone else there? Wasn't he the most responsible and quietly dedicated of the many losers that had come and gone over the past year? He knew the business better than that damn, braid-headed Jamal—at least that's what he calls himself—his real name was probably Eugene. He was old enough, for hell's sake. He never met his share of the order and always left more for Broadie to haul off the truck to fold and put in plastic bags because it was raining. But if Broadie were to quit, where would he go? No one hires just one young kid to mow lawns anymore. You had to have a lawn-mowing business full of Spanish-speaking employees to get past the front gate. He didn't own a lawnmower, anyway.

He put the thought of work out of his mind as he approached the dingy low-income apartments where his family had finally settled down. There were a few bad characters hanging around the parking lot left over from last night. They were the diehards, he guessed. Most came out at night, sitting on their expensively modified cars, drinking, and getting high. They usually filtered away by two or three in the morning. There were never enough drive-by shootings to get rid of them all, he thought cynically. He made himself small by staying in the shadows until he reached the orange light of the stairwell, then ran up as fast as his aching legs would take him. Though nobody ever gave him trouble, he wasn't going to take any unnecessary risks. He was still white and stood out no matter how he camouflaged himself by dressing like the environment: never too flashy to catch attention; never too clean cut; most probably figured that he was too poor to bother with.

The heavy latches on his door had already been unlocked. He hoped Mom was back. The apartment looked about as cluttered as he had left it. Where had she been this time?

"Mom?" He quickly tucked his check away so she wouldn't see it. He would eventually have to cash it with her present, but at least for now he could enjoy a little wealth.

Davie was still asleep. Mom wasn't anywhere to be seen. Alisha wasn't on the couch were he had left her. He went to the bathroom. She wasn't in there, nor in Mom's room. He shook Davie awake.

"Where's Alisha?"

Davie blinked and curled a small fist over an itchy eye. "In her bed." He closed his eyes and snuggled himself better into his blankets.

He could tell that Davie didn't know. Broadie was suddenly aware that things had become serious. Alisha had recently learned to open the latches to the door and frequently went out looking for Mommy. He shouldn't have left them, even if it was just for a couple of hours. Yesterday he had Davie watch a cartoon with her. He worked fast so he could come back quickly, but this time he had thought that he could simply let them sleep through it.

He ran back to the door. Outside it was quiet as ever, but that was changing. The pink sunrise made the courtyard look gray. The swimming pool, normally filled with trash, was filled with wet trash: a sort of wet trash soup. He ran down the terrace hoping to see her around the stairs somewhere. Snoop Doggie was already behind the door of a nearby apartment preaching to the dogs behind the wall. She wasn't there. He ran the other direction. Down from that angle, most of the lights were out and had never been fixed as long as they had lived there. A small group of Polynesians were still loitering around the dilapidated playground. Directly below, a drunk was sleeping in the bushes.

He ran again, making no effort to suppress his panic. He thought of all the child abductions lately. It was bad to catch people's attention around here. Attention or not, he started to yell her name. It echoed out between the buildings. Someone on the way to work looked up in time to pass out of sight and into the parking lot. He would have to call the police. He didn't see any other choice. They would all be quickly taken away from Mom and separated. Did it matter, if it meant getting Alisha back safely? He ran back in the direction of his door and remembered that they hadn't had a phone for months. Mom never paid the bill. His breath was coming out in small, meaningless hoots that would soon turn to sobs. He didn't want to be a puss, but who was around to see? He yelled her name again.

Just then a door opened just a crack. It was held back by a heavy chain. The strong smell of cooking tamales brought him into focus. It was Mrs. DeAvila. "Hey!" she said.

Broadie didn't hesitate: "Help me! I can't find my little sister. She got out and—"

"Calm down. She's right here."

He could see Alisha peeking out from behind Mrs. DeAvila before he even stopped speaking.

"Where's her mommy?"

The smell of the tamales hit him in the stomach, this time reminding him that there wasn't anything to eat in the apartment. Mrs. DeAvila had a small, portable tamale business that seemed to keep them afloat. She had given Alisha and Davie some from time to time. He figured that she suspected that they weren't getting regular meals.

"*¿Quién es?*" "Who is it?" An old man's voice came from behind the door.

"*Está bien, papá.*" "It's okay, dad." Mrs. DeAvila's voice traded places with the old man's. The chain swung loose, and the door came open freely this time. Her sympathetic and matronly face regarded him closely.

He reached out to take Alisha. Instead, Mrs. DeAvila motioned for him to come in. He felt a rush of shame and fear in his chest. He knew exactly what she wanted to talk to him about. Alisha's pull-up diaper was sagging heavily. She hadn't been changed since sometime last night; they were almost out of diapers, anyway.

"Don't just stand there, come in."

He hesitated. She motioned again with her hand. He had the impression that she was about to pull him in physically. She stepped aside as he shyly moved over the threshold.

Most of her family was already awake and gathered at the table, helping prepare the cornhusks for the tamales. They all turned to look at him. Several large pots were cooking on the stove. Mrs. DeAvila quickly secured the door. There were toys on the floor by the table. Someone had stacked phone books on a chair to make a place for Alisha. Above it, on the table, was a plate with a half-eaten tamale.

"Would you like something to eat?"

His pride told him to say no, but he was very hungry. She was about to bring up something that he knew he had to lie about. He didn't want to make things worse by offending her hospitality. "Yes ma'am." He followed her into the kitchen. She made him a place at the table next to Mariela, her youngest daughter. They were almost the same age, and she was beautiful. They had talked a few times but had never built a friendship beyond that.

He felt silly just sitting there being served as if he deserved it. He had to do something or say something. He looked around at all their busy faces. The boys ignored him. They didn't seem too keen to have him at their table.

"Can I help?" Broadie said.

"Sure." Mariela handed him her pile of corn husks. She gathered a new pile out of a large plastic bag under the table. She showed him how to straighten them out, then passed them to her grandfather, who put in the *masa* and rolled them up. Her brothers moved quickly in their enterprises.

"I knocked on your door and no one answered. How did this little baby get out? You need to watch her better," Mrs. DeAvila said, as she set before him a steaming plate.

He suddenly felt sick and trapped. He looked up at the picture of the Virgin of Guadeloupe that was illuminated by burning candles. There were fresh flowers in a vase next to it, and some black and white photos of family members. He wanted to lie and say that he was asleep and not away. It seemed that whatever excuse he tried would ultimately lead her to ask about his mother. He was too tired to make up a story. He simply chose the truth after all. "It's my fault. I went to take care of my newspaper job while the kids were asleep. I thought I could be back before they woke up."

She cut to the chase: "Where is your mother?"

"She's at work." It didn't occur to him until that moment that Alisha had probably told them that she's missing.

"She's working a lot lately." Her words didn't quite sound like a question.

Their grandpa mumbled something in Spanish.

"*¡Ay Papi!*" Mariela spoke sharply. The boys laughed.

Broadie worked assiduously with his tired hands to show the best appreciation he could for their kindness. He took bites in between handfuls of cornhusks.

"Do you like them?" Mrs. DeAvila asked.

Broadie tried a little Spanish. "*Muy ricas.*" Very tasty.

"*Ricos.*" She corrected him. "*Son muy ricos.*"

They all conversed in Spanish, and he listened intently, though it was hard to understand everything. Grandpa didn't speak any English, didn't want to. Mariela finished her last pile and went to the sink to wash her hands. Broadie glanced over her appearance, trying hard not to stare. She was one of the few girls he had ever known that were absolutely beautiful. Her brown eyes and dark skin were perfect. She was modest and harshly intelligent. Even though she was in middle school, she acted like a college girl—at least that's what he thought of when he watched her.

"I'm going to go read, *Mamá.*" She wiped her hands on a towel that was draped over a chair, and turned to leave the room. He tried to make eye contact with her, if only to see if she acknowledged his presence. She hadn't said anything to him and wasn't eager to hang around.

"What are you reading?" he asked her, for at least one attempt at conversation. He loved to read and was confident that they could establish some mutual interest.

She turned around, looking slightly annoyed. "Borges."

"Who?"

"Jorge Luis Borges." Without another word she disappeared around the corner.

She was a reader like January. It had been months since he had received any letters. He had tried to record the whole novel of *The Stand* for her but had run out of his dad's old tapes. He had made it half way through. The last he had heard, she was reading again. He thought it was one of the Harry Potter books. She was feeling a lot better. They were supposed to set up a time to call, but the phone had been turned off before they could make plans. The boys glanced in his direction, still not saying anything. He felt slightly embarrassed and insecure; he had the impression that his welcome had ended for the day.

"Is there anything else I can do?" he asked.

Mrs. DeAvila shook her head and smiled. He saw himself out the door.

* * *

The wall felt humid under his touch. The paint was old, nicked a thousand times. His forehead pressed against a cleaner spot that had an ancient shadow from someone else's sofa. The carpet was rank, and he would wash his hands as soon as he had finished. He unscrewed the tiny screws that fastened the cracked, plastic cover to the electrical outlet, then lifted it away in two pieces. He pulled out the plug sockets that were live, functional, and still attached to their wires, and slipped his hand deep into the wall. He didn't try to ponder what that space had been used for in the past, except for once when he had secretly explored it with a flashlight and a mirror hoping to find something valuable. On a small, dusty shelf he had found a dead cockroach.

In the hazy, quiet morning light, he scraped the inside of his elbow against the crumbling wallboard and grasped the only real treasure that he'd ever had. He felt the weight if it in his fingers, then transferred it to the palm of his hand. He listened for a few cold seconds to some footsteps outside his door. It could have been Mom. If she found out about the hiding place, it would be ruined, and there wouldn't be any more—at least inside the apartment. When the footsteps had passed by, he relaxed and carefully lifted the box the rest of the way out. It was the small face powder box that he had found in his great grandmother's chest of drawers. He lifted the lid and probed the pure metal that represented true wealth. It was hard and cold and happy. The words "God" and "Liberty" shone out in a yellow reflection of light, as if from another time. Sadness drifted through him like smoke from a distant fire, and his hand trembled. They were on the verge of going hungry. He had been desperate before, but never as much as lately. Something told him deep down inside that things were only going to get worse. He pushed his head against the wall in despair, and his hand tightened into a fist of grief.

He put the plug socket back together, then stood to stretch his legs. "Are you ready, Leeshie?" he asked Alisha, who was in the bathtub. He had cleaned an outfit for her, using dish soap in the sink, and had let it dry over night.

"Dolly's hair." She said, then walked out into the hall naked, dripping, shivering, and holding her doll. He had left her for only a minute.

Broadie pulled back a frustrated rebuke before it could escape. He walked her briskly back to the bathtub. It was dirty and draining slowly. He didn't have time to worry about that right now. He threw the toilet seat into place, sat down to be more on her level, and quickly turned her around to slip one of the last pull-up diapers onto her red bottom. He didn't know much about raising children, but he wondered if her potty training wasn't overdue. After putting on her clothes, he made an attempt to run a comb through her hair. Each time it pulled, she screamed and struggled The slow burn of anger that he felt at Mom for not being there flared. He had to let go all at once for fear of tearing out her hair. None of this was her fault. It would only hurt her more to blame her.

On the way to the bus stop, they moved quickly, though it was morning, and anyone who was likely to cause them problems was probably still sleeping off the night before. He pushed Alisha's stroller with one hand and held the other over his jingling pocket. Davie hopped over to a small tree in a planter to tug on a dry branch hanging over and iron bar. The humid, smoggy air was heavy, and the monotone sky promised a hot, miserable day. The street was a smoky, sweaty drone.

He tried to cash his check at the bank. As he had predicted, they required his mother to be present. With some of the change that he did have in his pocket, he bought Davie and Alisha some candy from the quarter machines. He noticed how happy Davie looked and wondered when was the last time that he had gotten to go somewhere other than the neighbor's or the grocery store. This was a fun adventure for him; the longer they were out, the lighter Davie walked over the pavement. Broadie looked down at Davie's crappy shoes, then at his pants that were too small. The first day of school wasn't far away. He felt a shudder. Who would take them to school if Mom never came back? Where *was* the school? He placed his hand again over the pocket with the small amount of savings and his coin collection.

Davie was quiet at the beginning, but as they moved along the storefronts in the shopping center he talked more and more.

"I know what *abuelo* means in Spanish," Dave said.

"Oh, what does it mean?"

"It means *grandpa*."

"Oh, yeah? Who taught you that?"

"Lupe."

"That's nice," Broadie answered him, but he was more interested in the window-shopping and the cute, rich-looking girls that
moved past them as if they weren't there. He slowed down as they
approached a music store.

"I miss grandpa and grandma," Davie said.

That stopped him cold. He had thought a lot about them lately.
He was silent, but there was something to Davie's statement that
inspired a flood of positive feelings. As a habit he tried to shut them
away, but they escaped like invisible sweet vapors that tempted
him to breathe deeply. He suddenly didn't feel so alone. They had
family. He could call Grandpa to come get them. He was suddenly
sure that Grandpa would, but what about Mom? What if Grandpa
came and they left without her? He couldn't just leave without her.

"I do, too," he finally said.

"Can we go to Grandma's?"

He couldn't bring himself to answer anymore of his questions.

* * *

Broadie waited nervously as the young man with the clean hair,
clean shirt, and tie looked at the gold piece under a magnifying
glass. He turned it over and let the bright light from a lamp re-
flect over Broadie's eyes. Davie stood on tiptoes to look, too. Alisha
reached out from the stroller to wipe her hand slowly along the
glass counters and marveled at the treasures. The man switched
off his lamp, leaned forward over a display case scrutinizing the
coin with an exaggerated intensity, then set it down on the glass
between them and stretched and yawned. "One hundred," he said
with another quick breath and turned away as if he had better
things to do.

"That's not even what the lowest price was in the price guide. I
know this is worth more than two-fifty."

"Sorry to tell ya, but that's a piece of junk and wouldn't even
price this high anywhere else."

"I know what I'm talking about. I researched it."

"I'm sure you did." The man smirked and went about his business.

"And what about the silver?"

"I can give you what the silver's worth. I'd say nine or ten bucks. We'd have to count it."

An older man, fat with gray hair and gigantic suspenders, walked out of an office and up next to the younger man. He had a pistol on his hip, and there was a shotgun on the wall behind them. "What we got here?" He spoke like an old cowboy.

"It's a 1909 five-dollar gold piece, San Francisco mint, and I'm looking to sell it," Broadie said past the younger man.

The young man smiled and walked away.

The older man, looking friendlier, picked up the coin, examined it quickly, then put it back down. "Oh, I'd say one-thirty, maybe. What do ya say, Frankie?" He winked at Broadie.

"That's more than I offered him, but suit yourself," the younger man said without turning around.

Broadie was tense. Inside, his stomach worked in small circles, and he felt that he was being taken. He swallowed and found himself shaking with desperation. One hundred and thirty dollars could bring in a lot of groceries.

"Well, you think about it for a while. That's a real good deal. You wouldn't get it anywhere else."

The older man began to walk away.

Broadie gave in with a terrible sense of guilt. "Sir, I—"

"*Don't do it,*" A man whispered in his ear from behind.

He felt the man's breath in his ear. He turned around. Grandfather DeAvila was in line directly behind him. Surprised, he wanted to say: *so you do speak English!* He held his breath, not wanting to be rude.

"Come with me. We go together." DeAvila pocketed something. His shoulders were hunched. His eyes moved slightly above Broadie's head to the men behind the counter. "We go now, no?"

Broadie looked back at the man with the moustache. The spell of quick money broke. He gathered the coins and put them back into his pockets. He took the gold piece, putting it into a side pocket so the others wouldn't scratch it. The man shrugged and walked over to another customer.

"I no buy gold from that man, no more." DeAvila shuffled in the direction of the door. He walked with a cane.

Broadie nudged Davie forward. He picked up Alisha, and they all left together.

The bus ride was hot. The smell of exhaust gave Broadie a headache. He struggled inside. The idea that he was making a mistake and that they would need that money haunted him. He fought the feeling away with the thought that cash was as good as the paper it was printed on. It would burn away in an instant, and he wouldn't have anything left. The gold coin was solid, real, and restored a hidden hope that the future would be better.

Alisha kicked her legs contentedly. Davie was up off of his seat looking out the window, so she had to do it, too. Broadie lifted her out of the stroller and set her next to Davie. She slipped down, pushing herself next to Davie. Annoyed, he pushed her against the seat with his hip. She whined, pushing him back. He braced himself against the seat in front and shoved his butt into her chest. He kept thrusting backwards, slowly moving her away from the window. Her whine turned to a squeal. She slapped his back and started to cry.

"Knock it off!" Broadie pulled Alisha away and kicked Davie in the butt.

"I didn't do anything!" Now Davie was crying and rubbing his backside. He always made it look worse than it really was. That made Broadie angrier, and he wanted to show him what a good hard kick would really feel like.

Alisha was struggling on Broadie's lap. He could tell that she had messed her pants. He moved her back to the place where she had been sitting when it all started. She slipped off the seat again and went right back at it. This time Davie didn't push her away. He leaned against the seat in front and pouted.

"Where you get gold?" DeAvila had leaned forward to speak quietly into Broadie's ear again.

Broadie turned around. "It was my great-grandmother's."

"Why do you sell it?"

Broadie looked down. "I need money." He was quiet for a while and watched the neighborhoods go by. The bus stopped to let off a large black woman with kids that looked about Davie and Alisha's age. The little girl's hair had been woven into tiny braids. She stood on the last step. The woman waited for her, motioning with her hand. She had said something, but it had been lost behind the idle of the engine.

"I can do it myself, Grammy!" The little girl jumped off and took the woman's hand. Broadie watched as the bus left them behind.

"You like coins?" DeAvila asked. He leaned onto his cane.

"I collect them. You collect them, too?"

"I like Mexican money. It's beautiful."

"Can I see some?"

DeAvila glanced around cautiously. There weren't many people on the bus. No one looked like trouble. He worked a small bag out of his pocket. In it was a small plastic container like the ones in the display cases in the coin shop. He handed it to Broadie. It was a gold coin almost the size of his of his own. On it was printed: *Diez Pesos*, 1910. He flipped it over. The sun reflected on the plastic. On the other side it read: "Estados Unidos Mexicanos."

"Who's the man on the front? Is that a president?" He handed it back to DeAvila.

"He's Miguel Hidalgo; he's father of the first revolution." He worked the coin back into his pocket. "Do you know what the coins are?"

Broadie shook his head.

"It's heritage. I think you know that. Don't carry that no more. People steal it. You put it in the bank. When you grow up, you get a family, give it to your boy when he's old enough to know better." He nodded his head and sat back looking satisfied.

Broadie nodded back. He was now anxious to put the coins back into their hiding place.

4

Mom was home when they came up the stairs. "Where the hell have you been?"

"Mommy!" Alisha held her hands up in the stroller.

"Where the hell have *you* been?" His answer was quick. He might repent for his tone of voice in a moment, but didn't care. It was a small relief. At least some his worries, like food and school starting, might be lifted off his shoulders.

"I've been working my ass off for you ungrateful little shits. Where do you think I've been?"

Broadie walked past her without saying a word.

"Don't walk away on me!"

"Mommy, I'm hungry," Davie said, tugging on her arm.

She yanked her arm away and followed Broadie through the door. "Haven't you fed the kids? Why the hell is this place such a mess? I leave you to tend the kids, and I come back to a disaster."

"You didn't say anything about tending. You just left. What am I supposed to do when you don't come back and I don't know—"

She slapped him. "That's for being a smart ass. When I'm gone, you watch the kids!"

His face burned. "I *did* watch them!"

There was a man on the couch. He hadn't noticed him until he turned around. Broadie felt a little jump in his chest. It was someone he had never seen before. The man acknowledged him with a little toss of his head. He looked like so many of the men out in the parking lot and in the streets. He had a knit hat on his head, pulled down just above his eyes. His arms were covered in tattoos that disappeared under a white tank top.

"Meet my ungrateful kids." Mom gave Broadie another pop up the side of his head and walked into the kitchen.

Broadie didn't say anything. He left in search of someplace quiet.

5

Davie hurried to finish his bites of chicken. He still had fries at the bottom of the bag that his meal had come in. He was supposed to eat all of his food before he could play on the slides in the back of the Macdonald's restaurant. It was taking him forever to eat. If he didn't hurry, Mom would get impatient, not let him go play, probably briskly take him outside, and slap him on the side of his head in the parking lot where everyone could see. Alisha was already over there watching the older kids climb to the upper sections and slide down. The kids were supposed to take off their shoes in that area; Alisha still had hers on. Mom wasn't paying attention or didn't want to bother with it. Either way, it was making Broadie feel antsy.

Davie took another bite of chicken, brushing off his hands. He hopped off the bench. Mom caught him before he could go any further. "You done? You can't go play if you ain't done yet."

"Yeah, he's done," Broadie said quickly.

"Then get over there. We don't have time to wait all day." Mom gave him a little shove and turned her attention back to whatever she was doing.

Broadie quickly transferred the rest of Davie's food into his own bag. He would give it to Davie when he got hungry in the afternoon.

"Aint you gonna go play?" Mark asked.

Mark was Mom's new man. His eyes were hidden behind those stupid dark glasses. A knit beanie was pulled down low over his head, even though it was hot outside. He had been coming around for the past week, mostly staying the night and leaving in the morning.

"No." Broadie tried to see his eyes through the glasses. It suddenly occurred to him that he had never seen Mark's eyes. He imagined Jim's strange eyes and felt chills.

"That's right. babies play on little kid's slides. You're not a babies, are ya? Huh."

Broadie looked over at Davie. He was already at the top waiting for an Asian-looking boy to slide down. Alisha had made it to the first platform.

"Huh." Mark hadn't let it go. What was he after?

"What?"

"*What?* Can't you hear? I said, babies can't hear."

"Whatever," Broadie said quietly.

"You bad? You bad, ain't ya?" Mark's dark glasses were steady. His whole head was steady; it was glued in Broadie's direction.

Broadie felt a weight in his stomach. He no longer had an appetite. Not saying anything, he picked up his bag of food and left the table. Mark made a gesture in the air with his fist about level with Broadie's ribs. Broadie flinched; he moved aside fiercely, heart beating coldly. He was sure that Mark would have hit him had he not moved quickly. An arrogant grin grew over Mark's face. He turned and looked at Mom for approval. The room began to swim around Broadie's head as he watched a similar grin spread across Mom's teeth. Why had she not defended him? She had sometimes, when Dad had become violent. He didn't want to believe it, but he was discerning something undeniably clear: Mom wasn't Mom anymore. He had begun to notice it when they first left Grandpa's after some better life where people were more "tolerant." That was the word that Mom had used: "*tolerant.*" She had wanted her kids to see the "real world"—whatever that had meant.

Emotion pushed into his face like a wellspring. He turned around as fast as he could, knowing that, if Mark saw him, things would get exponentially worse. He made it to the door as the first sob hiccuped its way out.

The parking lot was a dusty spread of concrete. The street, out in the busy afternoon, disappeared into the place where the mountains should be. Smoke from nearby fires clogged the valley. Everything was hazy. The sun was a dirty, yellow ball. There was no horizon. He knew that they were somewhere in North Ogden, but that didn't mean anything. There was no home in North Ogden.

* * *

At the bank, the teller counted out one hundred and twenty dollars. She was a pretty girl. Broadie liked the way she talked. Her hair was cut short in the back and long in the front, which was strange, but all the same, she had bright eyes, and he couldn't take his eyes off of the way that the buttons stretched on the front of her blouse. In contrast, Mom looked old and haggard. There were sores on her face that looked like pimples that wouldn't heal.

"Let's go." Mom abruptly turned as soon as the money was in her hands. The girl looked surprised as Mom quickly shoved the cash into her purse.

As they moved to the door, Broadie felt a sickening feeling that she didn't intend to give him his money. "Mom." He slowed down to try and stall her at the door. She didn't slow down. "Mom!"

"What?" she said when they were outside beyond earshot of anyone in the bank.

They were getting perilously close to Mark's car. He was standing outside of the open driver's door, smoking. The kids were jammed in the back, sweltering in the heat. Broadie knew he had to say something before they reached Mark. "Can I have my money?"

"I'm paying the rent with it. I'll owe it to you next time we get paid."

There was no "next time." She didn't have a job. What did Mark do for a job? Why couldn't he help? He was hanging around at all hours. "Mom, I need my money."

"I told you it's going to the rent! Now, get in the car!"

"That's not enough to pay the rent."

She slapped him. He flinched away, stunned. She suddenly grabbed him by the hair and yanked him in the direction of the car, spitting sharp profanity and turning heads all the way across the parking lot.

"It was my newspaper money!" he yelled, trying to pull away. He could feel his hair tearing out of his scalp.

She shoved him into the back with Alisha and Davie. His head stung terribly where his hair had been pulled. She slipped into the car, and so did Mark; when he was behind the wheel, he slipped off his beanie, revealing a crude bluish tattoo on his head of a marijuana leaf with some fancy lettering surrounding it. Broadie watched the tattoo in painful silence as it swam around in teardrop dances.

* * *

As Broadie had guessed, both Davie and Alisha were hungry enough for the leftovers from Macdonald's. His own stomach was growling. He wished for more tamales from the DeAvilas. Outside it was getting dark. They had been grounded to that back room since they had gotten back from the bank. Every time one of them tried to come out, Mark would threaten to kick their asses. Alisha was roasting in her pull-up, and Davie had simply peed in the corner of the room. He kept crying that he was thirsty.

Loud rap music incessantly punched its way down the hall and into Broadie's head. As he sat on the bed with nothing to do but stare at the wall and smell Alisha's diaper, he decided that he would never listen to rap again in his lifetime.

* * *

The noise still filled the apartment. Mom and Mark were busy. They kept moving into the night. Davie and Alisha had fallen asleep out of simple exhaustion. He felt himself drifting to sleep, and then he would snap awake again. The yappity-yap of the rapping made him want to scream. Why didn't someone call the police or something? His own bladder was about to explode. He was terrified of Mark. He had been hit by his Dad and by Ty, but he had never been hit by Mark. There was just something about him that flowed through Broadie like a dangerous electrical current.

Broadie finally got up and relieved himself into the same corner that Davie had used. He looked out through the torn screen. Orange light reflected off the dirty window. He ran his fingers along the aluminum of the window sill. It was flimsy, cheap, like everything around him. There was dirt in the grooves where the window slid back and forth. Something in that dirt reflected back at him. He tried to scoop it out with his finger, but the space was too small. He looked around the room for something, kicking aside dirty clothes and looking between the mattresses and the wall. He pulled the door of the closet away. It had once hung there, a clean, working, sliding door, until Ty had yanked it off its runners. It now leaned against the opening of the closet: a perfect lean-to to hide in when things got bad. Just like at grandma's house.

Who was he kidding? There was no place to hide in there. It was just a skinny place full of Davie's broken toys. Davie had turned it into a kind of a clubhouse all his own. The funny thing was that it was clean in there. He looked at the shiny brown carpet in the corners. It was the only place in the apartment that wasn't filthy.

Broadie pulled down a hanger: there were no clothes hanging up, only hangers. It was so empty and lonely up above. He took the hanger and bent the hook out a little. It would serve perfectly as something to dig out whatever treasures might lie in the groove of the window sill.

He found the shiny thing in the dirt. He carefully dug at it until it came free. Soon he was sliding it up and over the aluminum runner. It landed on the dirty white paint on the window sill. It was a tiny, bright purple, shiny, reflective, plastic heart that changed colors slightly as it moved. It was something that a girl would have had. Could it have been stuck to the window once? There was a rainbow-shaped sticky spot on the aluminum. This had been a girl's room once. He could suddenly imagine a window covered in hearts and rainbows. It must have been pleasant to look at. Maybe she had been his age. What if she were cute? The room must have been clean, and smelled nice, like January's room.

He looked out over the parking area. There was plenty of carport. That was the view: carport. Corrugated, rectangular, gleaming orange and black in the nighttime parking lot. There were thick, bushy pine trees beyond it in the blackness.

He opened the window. The cool air was so fresh and free. It was mountain air from the canyons above town, cool, moist, like mountain water. He had a vision of mountain water sparkling in the sun. It was clear like the spinning water that he had dreamed of. He pushed the screen the rest of the way out and watched it disappear into the black bushes below. Above him, to his right, within reach, was the corner of an upstairs balcony. All he would have to do to leave would be to stand in the window sill, jump a little, and grab the railing. He slid the window all the way open and leaned out. He could do it if he wanted to.

But there was Davie on the mattress with the metal stud reflecting in his ear. He slept so soundly in the noise that continued down the hall. There was Alisha, stinky little Alisha, curled up with her swollen pull-up diaper poking out behind her, poop smears caked around the elastic edges. He couldn't leave them.

After some time standing in the open window, he became aware that the busyness out in the apartment had ceased. It had ceased a while ago. The only thing out there was the droning of the music. If he were to leave. . . . He simply couldn't go without his treasure. It was out there in the living room, and there was no way to get it with Mark and Mom in the way. He couldn't bear the thought of her taking it as she had taken his paycheck. She didn't deserve what was in the wall.

He went to the door and put his ear against it: nothing but rap. He put his hand on the doorknob feeling his chest freeze. Mark had said that he would "kick his ass" if he were to come out. There was something terrible about him, something truly dangerous that held Broadie prisoner in his own room. He had been held prisoner before, but not like this. He turned the doorknob ever so slightly, thinking how absurd it was, given the noise. It continued to turn under his hand until it wouldn't turn anymore. He tried to push it open, but it wouldn't quite give. He knew that he would have to shove it, and the friction would probably give him away. He pulled on the door until all the pressure was on the hinges. He gave it a small push. It opened with a little, sticky pop.

The crack in the door was so thin. He tried to look out. He pushed his eye against the opening, but there was nothing but hall shadow. He allowed it just a few more centimeters: still hall shadow. He let the doorknob slowly turn back to its neutral position. With another careful push, the door opened an inch. In his mind, terrible visions of Mark violently yanking the door open caused the awful iciness to spread further through his chest. It was now painful to breath. His heart thrummed like an idling engine. It pounded so hard that he couldn't swallow.

He suddenly became aware of a smell that called up a strange familiarity. He had smelled it before at a similar time when his heart had pounded and he had held his body still to keep from being discovered.

They're cooking.

It was something like burning plastic at first. As he tested the smell again, it came to him like hot, old urine. It was foul, hard, chemical. He pushed the door enough to finally see into the hall. The smell made him want to shut the door again. He slid against the wall slowly, step by step. He thought he heard voices coming form the living room, but it was too hard to tell over the hateful noise that jabbered from the stereo. It was a constant chant about owning the neighborhood, pigeons, shooting cops, bad bitches, bad money; his head pounded with the incessant repetition: beat against beat against beat. He was sick. The smell hurt his head. When he got to the end of the hall, he stopped to listen again. There were voices. It might have been that the door was open and they were outside. Would it be worth it to chance just one glance?

Someone laughed. It was clear that there was no going into the living room. He tried to steal a glance into the kitchen, but it was too hard to see without exposing himself. He slowly took a step back, then another. He started to pick up momentum when he hit Davie. Davie had followed him out. Broadie tried to brace himself, but it was impossible to stop. They fell together. His elbow flew up and connected with Davie's ear. Davie let out a loud whine. The more Broadie tried to put a hand over his mouth, the more he cried. Broadie desperately hushed at him.

It was too late. Mark's feet approached heavily over the dirty carpet. A large foot swiped hard over Broadie's thigh. It must have missed its mark as he scrambled in panic over Davie. There was another hard swipe. This one hit hard, square in the seat of his pants. He stumbled forward onto his knees. Mark kicked again, this time catching Davie in the stomach as he tried to stand up. His breath came out as a sharp *huh!* He curled up. Mark kicked him again. The foot landed against the forearm that held his stomach. Broadie saw the stress on his face as he tried to take another breath. Mark pulled back and kicked again viciously. The shock went through Davie, his eyes wide, rolling him and pinning him against the wall.

Broadie stopped scrambling. Only one thought broke through his terror: he had to get Mark off of Davie. He reversed himself and, like a football player, he threw himself over Davie and into Mark. Hitting a wall wouldn't have been any different. He felt Mark's adult strength; his arms pistoned Broadie to the floor. Broadie curled up just like Davie, taking blow after blow.

"Mom!" Broadie screamed. "Mom! Mom! Mom!"

Davie finally took a breath and wailed.

Mark's heavy hands yanked Broadie to his feet and shoved him over Davie. He reached down and picked up Davie by his shirt, tearing it around the neck, and threw him into Broadie. Davie fell again. Mark Shoved Broadie hard through the doorway. He stumbled backwards, tripping over one of the mattresses. For a moment he was sure that he would throw himself through the window. It was his only way to get away. Would the bushes break his fall? Suddenly Davie flew into the room.

Broadie was still screaming, "Mom! Mom!"

"What did I tell you?" Mark said, stepping over Davie, who was curled up and crying loudly. Every other word he used was the f-word.

Alisha was now awake from the commotion and crying.

"What did I tell you?" His tattooed gangster arms spread out wide. "Look what you did!"

"Mom!" Broadie screamed again. He screamed, hoping that someone outside would hear.

"She's not here! She's out working, so shut up! SHUT UP!" He slapped Davie on the side of his head. Davie fell over on the mattress screaming louder.

"Okay! All right!" Broadie cried out. "Okay! Okay!"

"When I tell you to stay in your room, you stay in your room! You ain't comin' out 'til she gets back!"

"Okay! Okay!"

Mark backed out, his eyes hard on Broadie. He slammed the door shut, cracking the wood along the edge by the doorknob.

* * *

Outside the window, the sky was a deep liquid blue over dark pine trees. They were the pine trees that surrounded the apartments. There was supposed to be some illusion about living in a mountain resort. There was nothing of a resort about it; no cool mountain air, no deer grazing in meadows, no crystalline lakes full of fish, only a precipitous drop and covered parking to enjoy.

Enough of a breeze came through the window to make the smell bearable, but it was a hot breeze. No air conditioning came into this room. Davie had finally stopped crying, but Alisha stood at the door emanating a constant moan, punctuated by sobs. She was terribly thirsty; they were all terribly thirsty and hungry.

Broadie couldn't stand it anymore. He rolled off of the mattress, feeling pain all over his body. Mark had hit him hard. When he was finally on his feet, the smell and the heat made him dizzy. He went to Alisha, took her by the arm, led her over by the window, and pulled off her diaper. It slid away, smearing her legs to her ankles. He threw it out the window. He chose among the dirty clothes on the floor until he was satisfied with an old T-shirt. He used it to wipe her off the best he could. Most of the poop had dried except for the places where urine had moistened it again. She was terribly raw; everything down below was a dark excruciating red. As he wiped, she screamed in pain. She needed a bath. He threw that shirt out the window too. When he was done, she walked back to the door and recommenced her moaning with a bare, red bottom. At least she could get air on it.

Davie lay curled on the mattress. He hadn't cried in hours. Every once in a while he would turn over and let out a high whine and rub his ribs. Sometimes he would sniffle.

The rap music hadn't stopped. It kept going on and on: niggas and gangstas and dope and hos and killas and mutha this and mutha that and on and on and on . . . the heat kept coming in. The sun was now turning the parking area below into Death Valley. People came and went, and the crack on the door stayed stamped on his eyes and in his ears like a final promise.

Cars came and went below. For a while there were a couple of kids with skateboards, but they moved on. A girl screamed. It was a fun kind of scream. There was no distress. There were squeals and laughs and another scream. It was out beyond the pine trees and the wood fence. He could see bits and pieces of movement in someone's back yard. Kids were jumping on a trampoline. Their happy voices mixed with the awful dark rhythms from the kitchen, but they didn't mix. They weren't mixable. They fought each other.

It was a clash. Those voices were so free. He started to cry again. There was something inside of him that reached out for those voices. He had seen a picture once of a plant growing at the bottom of a sink hole. It stretched desperately for every moment of light it could get.

The glare and the heat reflected off of the parking lot and slapped him in the face, but he couldn't pull himself away from that wonderful place through the trees and past the fence. His thirst became ravenous as the kids sprayed each other with a garden hose as they jumped on the trampoline. Each time a girl was sprayed she would scream.

"I want mamma." Davie started to cry again.

Alisha still stood at the door, moaning and sobbing.

Broadie turned to look at Davie, but as he did he caught a passing glimpse of someone walking into the parking lot. It was like a jolt of electricity. He yanked his head back into the direction of a man with baggy pants, a tank top, a beanie irrationally on his head, and a long chain that looped from his belt.

That was Mark.

Broadie's heart raced so hard that his legs collapsed. Both knees hit the wall under the window. The shock kept him from passing out. He grabbed the aluminum windowsill.

Was Mark leaving?

He couldn't tell where he had gone. He had lost sight of him when he had started to fall. He couldn't see from this angle whether he had gotten in his car to leave, or whether he had simply gone out for something. He leaned out as far as he could, but there was no way to see through the covered parking.

He suddenly turned away from the window and ran over piles of filthy clothes and broken toys. He lifted Alisha out of the way; she stood over Davie and cried. He gripped the doorknob to pull open the door. It turned, but the door wouldn't budge. He gave it a yank, then another. He was cold and shaky. His legs wanted to collapse again. They were hungry and thirsty and trapped. He had to get some water. All he wanted was water. Where was Mom?

He kicked the door as hard as he could, then yanked the doorknob again. He realized that he was crying out loud. He hit the door with his shoulder, and all the places where Mark had hit him bloomed in pain. He was out of breath. He ran back to the window to look out again. He couldn't tell whether Mark was still out there or not. It was just a blazing, bright parking lot.

He ran back to the door. Davie was crying again. He sat up, startled by Broadie's panic. Broadie yanked the door knob again and again. Nothing happened. He got down on his hands and knees to look under the door. There was a small space that allowed him to see a blurry sliver of the opening to the kitchen and living room. It looked empty; it felt empty. He could see the dark opening of the bathroom, and wanted so badly to get to the sink.

He tried the doorknob again.

He fell against the door, pushing his ear against the thin wood. That rap music kept going "da dawgs, da dawgs, da dawgs." Oh God! Da Dawgs! He screamed in frustration. He stood and kicked the door again and again. He was weak. He pulled on the doorknob, now sobbing frantically.

"I want Gramma," Davie cried.

Broadie started to pray. All he could do was to pray. He fell on his knees, leaning against the door, and begged for God to help them. He weakly turned the door knob over and over, praying and sobbing. He could feel that something inside the doorknob had broken when Mark had slammed the door shut. The latch was frozen in the strike plate. He tried to stick his finger in the crack to feel something, anything about the latch. He knew that his finger wouldn't fit all along.

The hanger.

He ran over to the window and kicked through the mess until he found the hanger that he had bent to scrape the little heart out of the windowsill. He brought it back to the door and shoved it into the crack where the latch was. He could feel the metal against metal. It scraped as he pried it against the latch. It was cheap brass-looking metal that scraped and peeled bits at a time. The latch moved a little. His heart leapt. He pried at it again more carefully. It would move a little, then when he reached as far as his leverage would go, the latch would slip back. He needed something to hold the latch in place as he pried further. It was like an absurd puzzle. He could pry it a little, then he would have to pry it again to get it to go further, but he had to let go of it to pry again. He ran back to the closet and grabbed another hanger. He bent the hook straight like the other one. With his right hand he pried the latch into its assembly; with his left, he held it in place when his right hand couldn't take it any further.

Behind him was the sound of liquid hitting the carpet.

"Alisha's peeing," Davie said.

Broadie didn't take his eyes off of the tiny glimmer of latch in the crack. He pried again and again. With every tiny move, the latch retreated further and further into the assembly.

There was a click. He almost had it. Suddenly, his left hand weakened and the latch let go, slipping back into place. Broadie screamed. All that work for nothing. He beat his head against the door.

Outside, the afternoon heat arose from the parking lot in one constant blast. Hot air blew into the room. Davie and Alisha were both crying again from thirst.

Broadie had to concentrate. He struggled to focus his eyes. Once again, he went after the latch. His fingers ached with every slow pry of his hanger. One after the other, he would pry, then hold; pry, then hold. The metal was raw and gleaming where he had scraped at it. His head pounded. He held the latch and squeezed his eyes shut. He opened them, blinked, and sweat dripped into them, causing him to blink again. He couldn't let go to rub his eyes. He held them shut again, but the stinging wouldn't go away. He pried again and again. Suddenly the hanger that he was using to hold the latch in place slipped inward. His eyes opened in hard shock. God! Did he have to do all that over again?

Not daring to move, he analyzed the latch through blurry eyes and a pounding head. It was open. But could he let go to pull the door open?

"Davie," he said in a shaky voice. "Davie, please come open the door."

Davie shook his head. He was terrified of Mark.

"Davie, open the door!"

Davie stayed where he was and cried.

"Come on, Davie! Mark is gone. Do you want Grandma? Come on Davie, let's go get you a drink."

Davie got up off of the mattress and came over.

"Just grab the doorknob and pull. Please, Davie, just grab the doorknob and pull."

Davie reached up and took the doorknob. Broadie's heart raced again. He was losing his grip on the hangers. His arms couldn't stay in that position forever. It was excruciating. His hands trembled.

"Pull, Davie, pull! *Now!*"

Davie pulled.

The door came smoothly open, and a tiny cool breeze whispered over Broadie's face. His arms fell and the hangers went loose on the carpet. He sat there for a crazy moment, unable to move. Finally, he lifted himself to his feet. Davie was still too scared to go out into the hall. He just stayed where he was.

"Come on." He took Alisha by the hand and grabbed Davie by the shirt. He led them cautiously to the kitchen. The smell in there was overwhelming, like ammonia. Alisha coughed.

There were no clean dishes. Davie went to the sink anyway and tried to lift himself up. Broadie searched around through the garbage. He opened cabinets. There was no food. Finally he found a dusty sauce pan in the drawer under the stove. He rinsed it out and took a long heavy drink. Alisha grabbed onto his pants. He refilled the pan and held it out to her. Davie had found a cup of his own; he didn't care whether it was dirty or not. Broadie yanked the power chord to the stereo out of the wall. The sudden silence was a relief. He wanted to smash the stereo onto the floor.

The kitchen table was covered by garbage. There was more in the living room. There was antifreeze, fuel cans, and weird, oily-looking liquid in glass jars. Dirty, stained coffee filters were all over the place. The whole apartment had turned into a shed. The smell was making Alisha rub her eyes.

Broadie went to the window. The curtains were drawn. He looked out into the courtyard. No one was around. He checked the door; it was locked. They had to leave now. He felt it so strongly that he had to catch himself to keep from running out the door. He went to the wall socket and loosened it up. As soon as he had his coins, he went to look for Davie's Pokemon backpack. It was tucked in a broken laundry basket in the closet. He grabbed Alisha's and Davie's shoes. There were no clean socks. There also weren't any pull-up diapers around. He moved quickly into mom's bedroom. It was filthy. There were things in there he didn't want to look at. They made him feel embarrassed. He looked for money and the diaper bag. The only thing in the diaper bag was junk. No money.

Davie had turned the television on and was watching cartoons. Broadie found a pair of pants for Alisha. He ran back into the kitchen to look for a bottle that he could put water in. Alisha was standing in front of the open refrigerator. She had a stale pizza crust in her hand. He thought about taking it away from her but it probably hadn't gone bad yet.

He went to the table to look through the mess. He moved a large bottle of rubbing alcohol. Behind it was drain cleaner. He pulled aside a towel and found a large brown envelope. It was the type that you could seal shut with a string. He undid the string. It yawned open. Broadie almost dropped it. He froze. It was money, a whole stack of it. There were twenty dollar bills, like the ones that his mom had taken from him. He took the whole stack and shoved it into the backpack.

They couldn't wait any longer. He ran back to the window. Still, no one was out there, only high, hot afternoon. He went over and slapped the television off. Davie didn't react. He only looked listlessly up at Broadie. Alisha was still in the kitchen with the fridge open. Her bottom was still bare, red, and dirty. Should he risk the time to clean her off? He could just throw her in the tub for a minute and wash her with the water running. There was no time. He pulled her pants out of the backpack, dragged her into the living room. He kneeled down. She held onto his shoulders as she slipped one leg in and then another. He then helped her and Davie both with their shoes.

He had them out the door when he remembered one last thing: his books.

"Wait here," he said to Davie. "Don't move a muscle. Don't let Alisha get away!"

He ran back down that stifling hall and into the room where they had been held prisoner. In the back corner, not the one where he had relieved himself, but the other, was a small stack of paperbacks. In a hole under the mattress that he had slept on were the cigarettes that he had stolen from his mother. He grabbed those, too.

He reached the door. Davie and Alisha were still there. He slipped the backpack over his shoulders and took Davie by one hand and Alisha by the other. It was then that he looked out into the courtyard. He looked down and face to face with Mark. He was coming up the walk, and fast. His first reaction was to run back into the apartment and bolt the door. That wouldn't stop Mark. He lifted Alisha, grabbed Davie, and ran to the DeAvila's. He reached the door and pounded frantically. There was no answer. Mark's feet made quick hollow noises up the stairs. Broadie beat his fists against the door, over and over. There was movement in the curtains, then a soft click of the locks. Broadie could smell Alisha and thought irrationally of how embarrassing it would be for them to smell her. The door opened a crack. It was Mariela.

"Yes?" She looked at him like he was interrupting something.

Mark was at the top of the stairs and coming at a brisk walk that turned into a jog. Broadie didn't say anything. He shoved Davie into the door, pushing Mariela back. Mariela let out a surprised gasp as he forced himself through and tossed Alisha onto the floor.

"¡Hay Papi!" Mariela tried to shove the door into Broadie's face. Instead, he pushed her back as hard as he could. He made it through the door. Just as he slammed it shut, there was aloud strike against it. He threw the deadbolt into place. Mariela slapped him repeatedly in the face and on the head. There was another strike against the door. It shuddered hard. Mark had kicked it. Alisha was crying. He must have thrown her in pretty hard.

"¡Papi! Mariela screamed again. Then into Broadie's face: "Get out of my house!"

Suddenly Mark was at the window peering in. He pounded on it, making it shudder. He put his face up to the glass, backed away, and pounded on it again.

"Mari!" Grandfather DeAvila appeared in the doorway to the kitchen. He motioned for her to get out of the room. He also motioned to Broadie and pointed at Alisha. "Get la nena!" He held his hand out to Davie. In his other hand he held a pistol. "¡Vamos!"

Broadie picked up Alisha and carried her into the kitchen. Mariela looked terrified and let out a small scream as Mark beat the glass with his fist. Grandfather DeAvila walked to the window and held up his pistol. Mark quickly backed away. He went to the door, gave it a hard kick, and then there was silence.

DeAvila stood shaking, still holding the pistol in the direction of the door. "*¡Llame la policía!*" Call the police.

"No!" Broadie said. "Please, no."

Mariela was already at the phone. She had been there since she had run into the kitchen. Her eyes were wide as she described what had just happened.

DeAvila sat for a long time in the living room, keeping guard, and holding the pistol on his lap. Mark had gone, but everyone was still terrified. Broadie sat in the kitchen, listening to the ticking clock and holding Alisha. Davie sat in his own chair, crying in terror and exhaustion. What were they going to do now? He used to think that if only Mom were home everything would be okay, but it was Mom all along; all this was her. He had to call Grandpa. It was time to go home. Grandpa's house was home. He wanted his tree again. It would be a full canopy of green shade, all his. It was there in his mind. He drifted and swayed with its grand branches.

"Can I use your phone?" Broadie asked Mariela. It seemed like everything he did or said was a bother to her, but he didn't care.

She handed him the phone.

He remembered the number. It was long distance, but he felt his heart swell as it rang. It kept on ringing. Soon the computer voice was telling him that he could leave a message. He did. Tears came out with every word: "Please, come get us, Grandpa." He was about to hang up. Grandpa didn't know where they were. Mom had wanted it that way. He didn't even know his own address. He paused. "Where are we?" he said to Mariela. She gave him the address. He repeated it carefully, then hung up.

Finally, there was a decent knock at the door. DeAvila discreetly tucked the pistol into the lamp stand and walked over to the window; he then went to the door and unlatched the deadbolt. The door opened slowly. DeAvila greeted two men in uniform and invited them in. Davie ran down the hall to hide in the bathroom. Broadie continued to hold Alisha. She watched the men curiously as DeAvila and Mariela explained what had happened. One of the officers said something into his radio and went quickly out the door. The other officer glanced up at Broadie several times. He also said something into his radio. He took a step back to look out the door in the direction of the apartment. He came back in. DeAvila pointed in Broadie's direction. The officer looked at Broadie and smiled. He came across the living room, each step making him larger. Broadie's stomach sank. He gripped Alisha tighter. He came through the door of the kitchen, filling the doorway. He stopped over Broadie and introduced himself. Broadie just stared into his massive face; a huge G.I. Joe; a movie general tough enough to drive a tank. His gun rested heavily on his belt. "What's your name?" he asked.

Broadie whispered his name. Alisha sucked her thumb and also looked into the large man's face.

"So, what happened here, Broadie?"

It was then that Mrs. DeAvila came in. "¡Hay, mi hijita!" She threw her arms around her daughter, rattling away in fast Spanish, kissed her father on the head, then hugged her daughter again. Mariela said something to her mother. She pointed at Broadie.

The officer glanced around as Mrs. DeAvila stopped in the doorway, hands on her hips; she clucked her tongue and shook her head. More officers moved outside the apartment behind her. A woman, also in uniform, came in and stood behind the officer.

The officer turned back to Broadie. "It's okay. You're safe now."

Broadie looked past him at the lady behind him. She had rubber gloves on her hands and a first aid kit. He started to speak. It came out as a whisper. He cleared his throat. What he really wanted was a good meal and to go to sleep in his old bed, in his old room, under his old open window. He told them everything he could about Mark. He didn't know where his mother was, but when he described her frequent absences and that he didn't know what she did for work, the officer exchanged a knowing glance with the woman behind him.

Mrs. DeAvila coaxed Davie out of the restroom with a glass of milk and a cookie. She gave a cookie to Alisha. Broadie was nauseous with hunger. He looked at the cookie with a wild urge to snatch it from Alisha. That was when the officer backed away so Mrs. DeAvila could give Broadie one, too. He took it gratefully.

The female officer kneeled down by Davie and began to look him over. She ran her hand through his hair and checked a swollen spot on the side of his head. She suggested that paramedics come and look the kids over.

It seemed as if the whole apartment complex had filled with police. It was fine. He had done all he could do. He only wanted to make sure that his backpack stayed safely by his side. He had to guard his treasures that no one else could know about. He asked for the phone again. Mrs. DeAvila handed it to him. It rang This time Grandma answered. Broadie began to sob.

6

Broadie lay in the grass, looking up into the green that never seemed to end—except for the few leaves that were changing color. The evening air was autumn's. He wished he hadn't left his jacket back at the house. He was sleepy. A mosquito whined by his ear. He swiped it away, waking himself up a little more. The breeze slowly rocked the massive branches above him. He swayed and drifted with them, loving them. He could almost feel the earth turn. He wouldn't have cared if the soil beneath him had suddenly opened to swallow him. To him it would have been an embrace. He picked a piece of grass and put it into his mouth. It was a warm summer's-end taste. It was real. Everything around him was real. He would never leave it again.

Grandpa and Uncle Will had come to get them at the McKay-Dee Hospital. Davie talked a lot about his ambulance ride. He had suffered a mild concussion and some internal bruising from when Mark had kicked him. Now, when Broadie thought about it, he wished Mr. DeAvila had shot him through the window. He had to push the thoughts away, because Mark's face inspired rage, a lot like John-and-friend's used to.

Mom was nowhere to be found, neither was Mark. In the end he had fled like a coward. Uncle Will said that the apartment had been nothing but a meth lab. That meant that Broadie, Davie, and Alisha would be going back to the doctor's office a lot to get check-ups because they had been exposed to poisons. He thought that he felt just fine except for bad headaches that Grandma said were because of the chemicals. Maybe that was true. Alisha was on antibiotics because of an infection caused by her diapers never getting changed. Davie didn't seem to talk much. That worried Grandma. When they came back that next morning, she immediately took the earrings out of his ears, and Cheryl took them to buy new outfits. It felt strange to have new clothes.

Grandma said that Dad had heard that they were back and wanted to see them. She didn't like that idea, but it excited Broadie. He wondered if his dad looked the same. Uncle Will said that it seemed like he had sobered up. He was holding a job. Dad would be coming to visit them tomorrow. There was something going on with lawyers, but that was complicated. All Broadie knew was that he was home. He could feel it as real as he could feel the occasional sun on his face.

He was tired of resting. He had things to do. His hands wanted to move and build. He sat up and stretched. It was a sweet, grassy stretch. The day was heading into evening. The shadows were longer and the sunshine was thicker though the trees in the west; it made the bugs and the dust in the air glow like something magical.

His feet moved over the cool, shady earth. He picked up a hammer that lay over a pile of boards. From them he chose a piece of two-by-four that would work well as a foothold. He nailed it to the tree. It took three nails to make it solid. He tested it by stepping up on it. He embraced the massive trunk as he did it. He picked up another one. The sound of his hammering rang out through the trees and into the slanting sun. Each swing of the hammer was sweet. Soon another foot hold was solidly against the trunk, then another.

He wasn't aware of the footsteps through the grass behind him. He was deep in his work, measuring, cutting, pounding, until his head and shoulders ached. When he turned to search out a new piece of wood, he was startled to see someone there, a shadow in the sunset. He blinked and wiped the sweat out of his eyes. It was January. She smiled and waved. He waved back. She made her way through the mess of boards until she was next to him. She looked up into the branches.

"I know where there's some new wood. It would make a better floor." She pulled herself up onto the first foot hold.

"We can make it twice as big this time," Broadie said.

She smiled. She looked well, strong, like when they had first met. Only there was something different in her eyes. She had faced something that had made her different. She was the same January, but . . . deep. Her eyes were deep. He felt as if she was bigger than she looked. She talked about big things, things that other kids didn't care about. She talked about God and nature and who we are as people. She always discovered the details that no one else saw. There were other things that she didn't have words for.

As Broadie examined another piece of wood, January made her way carefully up into the tree. The branch that paused on to look higher into the tree was like a strong man's arm. It made her look small. She stopped for a moment to let her feet hang over the side. Her girlish shoes and socks appeared and disappeared as she freely kicked her legs in the open air.

Broadie watched her. In time he would learn the things that she couldn't say; he would learn that when he had left that spring, he had left behind a gift that was more special than any other friend could have given her. Her books had been her way to escape the pain of chemotherapy until it became too hard to read. He had left her tapes of his voice reading one of her favorite books. She had kept a tape player and headphones by her bed and listened to them every lonely night when it was too hard to sleep because the drugs had made her sleepy during the day. Then more tapes came in the mail. Each one was something more to look forward to. Each one would take her to a soothing world in her imagination where she didn't have to focus on her sickness. Then one day the tapes stopped coming, but she was getting stronger by then. She still looked for the mail every day. Eventually it became clear that the tapes would never come again, but she was in remission. She was gaining weight. She was seeing friends. She had the support of the young women in her church. She was even able to go to a camp with them for a few days. Her parents and doctor said a few days would be fine, but the whole week might be too much. When her dad came up to get her, she begged for him to let her stay. She cried when he made her come home with him. She was strong.

Then one day she had looked out her back door and saw Broadie standing out behind the shed. She knew that her friend was back. She wanted to hug him, but maybe he might have thought she was weird. What if he was only visiting, and would have to go back to that mysterious place where he had disappeared to? But he was there to stay. He was home.

"We should make a rope that you can climb up and swing back down on." She climbed further up the tree and found the branch that she had sat on so long ago.

"We should make it a huge swing," Broadie said, looking up at her.

"*Janni?*" Her mom's voice echoed down the ditch.

January leaned her head back and groaned.

"Your mommy's calling."

"Shut up!" She threw a nail at him that she had been holding. He dodged it, laughing.

It was getting late. The sun had set behind the western mountains, and the air was cool. It was time to go back. She climbed down. She helped him gather his tools—or his grandpa's tools, anyway. They walked together down the trail that ran along the ditch, and back up to the houses. They laughed about some joke that she had heard in school, something about fat butts and stinky farts. When they arrived at the shed, she waved to him and went on into her yard. He watched her go. When he thought she was gone, he reached up and pulled back a board. Behind it were the few cigarettes that he had left. He pulled one carefully from a baggie and lit it. The first rush into his lungs made him cough. The smell of the smoke brought to life recent memories that he didn't like. It brought back all the things that he hated, and especially the images of people that he didn't want to be like.

He held the glowing cigarette in the dusk, looking at the way the smoke curled into the fresh air. He suddenly hated that smell. It wasn't a comfort. He wanted to flee from it. It was an ugly, staining thing. It was the basic symbol of what he had desperately escaped when he had knelt before that door with trembling hands and a couple of bent hangers. He dropped the cigarette into the dirt and ground it in with his heel. He then pulled back the piece of wood that hid the others, found them, emptied them onto the soil and ground them in too. Tears came to his eyes. They did so quite often now.

He took in a deep breath of fresh dusk air and was glad for the smell of the ditch and the grass and the trees. When he turned back around he was startled to see January standing there. He instinctively ground his heel in harder, hoping to hide what he was trying to destroy. She looked down at his feet. Her eyes brightened. She walked to him and they both looked at the mess on the ground. He searched for something to say, some way to explain himself. Was she angry? What did that look mean? It wasn't disappointment. He had seen her disappointment before. He held up the palms of his hands. "I . . . uh . . ."

She didn't let him say anything. Suddenly she was giving him a hug. It was a quick one. Before he had a chance to really hug her back, she let go and turned around, embarrassed. She ran back to her house, aglow in the remnants of what had been a fantastic sunset.

Epilogue

Morning light left shadows on freshly bulldozed earth. A cool breeze made its way in through a grove of trees and lifted a ribbon tied to a surveyor's stake. A few feet away, a patch of grass rustled in the same breeze. The sound of a pounding hammer disturbed the early morning peace.

"Can we tie a rope to it and make a swing?" A boy's voice rang out over the pounding hammer.

A man's voice answered back: "Well, I don't see why not."

"Don't you think that would be a little dangerous?" A woman holding a baby stood watch over her husband as he showed their boy how to build a tree house. "I mean who's going to climb up there to tie it on?"

The man turned to look at her. He had the same ironic smile that he had had in the sixth grade when he had first tried to build a tree house in the same tree. "Has it ever occurred to you that you sound just like your mother?"

"No! Don't *even* start that. My mother was—"

"Janni?" he called out, in a high trembling voice.

"Oh, shut up!"

"Janni?" He called out again.

The boy looked from his mother to his father and back and laughed. They often teased each other. Two little girls came running up through the trees holding roses that they had picked down by the ditch. "Look, mom. Look at what we found!" One of them had a scrape on her knee. She ran up the trail as if nothing had happened. The smaller girl held up her roses first.

Her mother drew in a deep breath of pleasure and took the roses to smell them.

"Janni?" the man said, almost as a whisper in her ear.

She playfully swiped at him.

He dodged her swipe and walked out from under the shade of the big tree. His feet left the softness of the grass and found hard earth. He followed one surveyor's stake to a cement foundation that had been freshly poured. He looked it over, satisfied that the construction workers hadn't damaged the fruit trees on the north side. He reached into his pocket and pulled out a heavy coin. It reflected a bright golden yellow in the sunlight. Soon the woman joined him at his side. He slipped the coin back into his pocket and put his arm around her. The hammer rang out again behind them as their boy nailed in another foothold so he could get up into the tree.

"I like how the kitchen faces the tree," she said. She laid her head on his shoulder.

"See how the driveway follows the ditch out to the road on the north side. This is going to be so private that it won't even be like living in the city." He looked up and over the rooftops.

"It's almost a shame," she said.

"You think so?"

She looked back at the grove by the rose bushes. "Well, no, not at all, really."